COGEWEA
The Half-Blood

COGEWEA
The Half-Blood

A Depiction of the Great Montana Cattle Range

by
HUM-ISHU-MA
"Mourning Dove"

Given through Sho-pow-tan

With notes and biographical sketch
by
LUCULLUS VIRGIL MCWHORTER

Introduction by Dexter Fisher

UNIVERSITY OF NEBRASKA PRESS
Lincoln and London

Introduction to the Bison Book edition copyright ©
1981, by the University of Nebraska Press

Manufactured in the United States of America

First Bison Book printing: 1981

Library of Congress Cataloging in Publication Data

Mourning Dove, Okinagan Indian, 1888–1936.
  Cogewea, the half-blood.

  Reprint of the 1927 ed. published by Four Seas Co., Boston.
  1. Okinagan Indians—Fiction. I. Sho-pow-tan. II. McWhorter,
Lucullus Virgil, 1860–1944. III. Title.
PS3525.0872C6 1981   813'.52   80–29687
ISBN 0–8032–3069–9
ISBN 0–8032–8110–2 (pbk.)

☯

INTRODUCTION

by Dexter Fisher

The Collaboration of Mourning Dove and McWhorter

To study the work of Mourning Dove, an Okanogan and perhaps the first American Indian woman to write a novel, is to observe a fascinating collaboration. The person who would become Mourning Dove's literary mentor and coauthor, as well as personal friend and confidant for twenty years, was Lucullus V. McWhorter. A pioneer of encyclopedic interests and founder of the *American Archaeologist,* McWhorter left his native West Virginia to homestead in the state of Washington in 1903.[1] It was there in 1914 at a Frontier Days Celebration in Walla Walla that Mourning Dove and McWhorter first met. After their meeting, a mutual friend, J. W. Langdon, wrote to Mourning Dove, encouraging her to seek McWhorter's help with her manuscripts:

> While you were here . . . you mentioned in the presence of . . . Mr. McWhorter that you had been collecting for some time past, reliable data on certain Indian history. . . . As I understand the matter, you were having some difficulty in arranging your manuscript and putting the data you have secured in proper form for publication, and the thought has occurred to me that while you are at North Yakima, you ought to take that matter up with Mr. McWhorter, who is perhaps the best versed individual in that section of the country on Indian tradition, and has a large experience along this very line of work. [September 30, 1914][2]

Mr. Langdon could not have been more astute in his assessment of McWhorter. He was a man of the utmost

v

integrity whose genuine interest in Indian history and culture became the center of his work and publications. He had, for example, defended the Yakimas in their struggle to protect their irrigation rights and had in 1913 published a pamphlet entitled *The Crime against the Yakimas,* which exposed the pattern of abuses against Indians by the Bureau of Indian Affairs. Adopted into the Yakima tribe, he was given the honorary name of He-mene Ka-wan, or "Old Wolf," which he used repeatedly in his correspondence with Indian friends. He was also known as the "Big Foot" of the Yakimas because of his size; that name stuck with him throughout his life and was used by Mourning Dove in her letters to him.

McWhorter also met and became fascinated by a Nez Perce named Yellow Wolf, who had fought with Chief Joseph in the Nez Perce War of 1876. In 1940, McWhorter published *Yellow Wolf: His Own Story,* the first book to describe a major military battle between the U.S. Cavalry and the Indians from the Indian point of view. Although McWhorter died in 1944, he had completed enough notes on the Nez Perces and their history for Ruth Bordin to edit and publish *Hear Me, My Chiefs!* in 1952.[3]

In contrast to McWhorter, Mourning Dove had few of the advantages of education, having barely achieved more than three years of formal schooling in the Sacred Heart Convent at Ward, Washington. She briefly attended government Indian schools, and in 1912, when she was twenty-four, she enrolled in a business school to learn typing and improve her English.[4]

The daughter of Joseph Quintasket (born in the Upper Okanogan community in British Columbia but identified with the Lower Okanogans of the United States) and Lucy Stukin (a full-blood Scho-yel-pi, or Colville, as the tribe was to be called after the establishment of Fort Colville in 1825), Mourning Dove was born near Bonner's Ferry, Idaho, in 1888. Given the English name of Christal Quintasket and the Indian name of Hum-ishu-ma, or Mourning Dove, she was reared for a time by her grandmother and imbued with respect for the traditions of her tribe that would later inform her writings. Her paternal grandfather had been an Irishman who worked for the Hudson's Bay Company and who apparently had married her Indian grandmother under false pretenses in a tribal ceremony. His name was Haynes (or Haines), but his son took the name of his stepfather, Quintasket. (It is not surprising that the betrayal of Indian women by white men is central to the plot of Mourning Dove's romantic novel, *Cogewea*.)

Mourning Dove's first husband was Hector McLeod, a Flathead Indian. In 1919, she married Fred Galler, a Wenatchee, and was addressed most often thereafter as either Mrs. Fred Galler or Mourning Dove. She had no children by either marriage. She and Galler worked as migrant laborers, traveling with the seasons, picking hops and thinning apples, pitching tents and camping out under every imaginable condition. And everywhere they traveled, Mourning Dove took her battered old typewriter and tried to work after long hours in the field or orchards. In one letter to McWhorter, she describes the difficulties under which she labored: "I have had too much to do outside of my writing. We got work apple thinning at Brewster, Wash.; . . . and after working for ten hours in the blazing sun, and cooking my meals, I know I shall not have the time to look over very much mss . . . between sand, grease, campfire, and real apple dirt I hope I can do the work." (June 8, 1930). And in another letter, she says, "We move around so much that I am disgusted getting a frame for my tent and making a comfortable place to live . . . I am trying to write, but lordy with all these mountain pests, I get frantic" (July 1919).

Even more than the physical hardship, Mourning

Dove's greatest obstacle to gathering the material that she continually referred to as the "folklores," which would later be incorporated into *Cogewea* and *Coyote Stories,* were the Indians themselves. In her letters to McWhorter, she repeatedly complains that the Indians are suspicious of her and will not share any legends if they think they are to be published. From Fairview, British Columbia, she writes in 1918:

> They are such hard people to get anything out from. . . . There are some that are getting suspicious of my wanting folklores and if the Indians find out that their stories will reach print I am sure it will be hard for me to get any more legends without paying the hard cash for them. A whiteman has spoiled my field of work. . . . This Mr. James Teit has collected folklores among the Indians and has been paying five dollars a piece for good Indian legends and naturally that has spoiled the natives and of course they wish the same price from me whether the story is worth a nickle to me.

What was particularly frustrating for Mourning Dove was that it had never been her idea to write "folklores" exclusively. Rather, she aspired to write novels, like *Cogewea,* based on the material of her tribe; she would have proceeded in that direction had McWhorter not passionately encouraged her to record the tales of her tribe before they were hopelessly corrupted by inter-marriage and the influence of white civilization. Only a year after he met her, he wrote a feverish plea to her in the form of a romantic vision:

> Why should this young woman hesitate . . . I see in her vast possibilities. I see a future of a renown; a name that will live through the ages, if only she will decide to take the right-hand trail. Helping hands are held out to her, and the trail will not prove so rough as it appears. Her race-blood will be of actual benefit to her in this work. It is a duty she owes to her poor people, whose only history has been written by the destroyers of their race. Let the Mourning Dove of the

Okanogans take cheer and step out from the gloom of ghastly fears, into the golden light of opportunity, exulting in her own strength and show to the world her nobility of purpose to perpetuate the story of her people in their primitive simplicity. Nothing is in the way of your success. [November 29, 1915]

Such a plea would have been hard for anyone to resist, but for an Indian woman with little education and no expectation that her deep desire to write should be recognized, let alone appreciated and so enthusiastically encouraged, McWhorter's urging became a command, and so began a lifelong friendship between Mourning Dove of the Okanogans and "Big Foot" of the Yakimas.

With McWhorter's aid, Mourning Dove published *Cogewea* in 1927 and *Coyote Stories* in 1933. She tirelessly collected and recorded tale after tale of the Okanogans and became dedicated to preserving their traditions. Always encouraged by McWhorter to share her knowledge with a wider audience, she began to give public lectures on the traditions of her tribe and was invited back east to speak, but her appearances were infrequent because she was uncomfortable before strange audiences and could not afford the money to cover her travel expenses. The one accolade she did eventually achieve, and the one that meant the most to her, was her election as an honorary member of the Eastern Washington State Historical Society.

Of her death, Donald Hines, author of *Tales of the Okanogans* (based on Mourning Dove's *Coyote Stories*), writes, "She was plagued over the years with pneumonia, flu, black measles and, particularly, inflammatory rheumatism. In 1936, she was stricken with severe headaches and 'flu' in the back of the neck and on 30 July she was admitted to Eastern State Hospital at Medical Lake, Washington. She died there within a fortnight on 8 August 1936; she was 49 years of age."[5]

The Okanogans

The Okanogans belong to the Salishan language family of north-central Washington and British Columbia and speak a dialect of interior Salish that is identical with that of the Sanspoil, Nespelem, Colville, and Lake Indians; their language differs only slightly from that of the Wenatchi, Chelan, Kalispel, Pend d'Oreille, Spokan, Coeur d'Alene, Flathead, Thompson, Lillonet, and Shuswap tribes. All of these tribes inhabiting the highlands and river valleys in central and northeastern Washington are referred to as Plateau Indians. Historically, the Okanogans have been divided into two groups, the northern Okanogans of British Columbia, and the Southern Okanogans, or Sinkaietk, of Washington. The latter is their name for themselves and means "People of the water that does not freeze."[6]

By an edict of President Grant in 1872, the Colville Reservation was created in the county bounded by the Columbia and Okanogan rivers and the Canadian border, and to it were assigned the Colville, Methow, Okanogan, Sanspoil, Lake, Kalispel, Spokan, and Coeur d'Alene tribes.[7] The present-day reservation is somewhat smaller than the original one, but it still occupies part of the Columbia River Basin. The Okanogans live on the western part of the Colville Reservation and as of 1930, during the period when Mourning Dove was writing, they numbered only 250–300.

The Okanogans' account of their origin occurs in the naming myth, in which the Spirit Chief, qolunco'tn, names all of the animals. In this story, Coyote (the culture hero of the Okanogans and often regarded as their ancestor) is given the special responsibility of killing the people-devouring monsters, thus preparing the way for the coming of the "new people," the Indians. Both a trickster and a hero, Coyote is endowed with the power to change himself into any object to protect him-

self from danger and to kill his enemies. He can also be
recalled to life, if but a hair of his being remains, by Fox,
who also has certain powers.[8]

The concept of power is central to the Okanogan
world-view. Power may be thought of as a guardian
spirit and refers to the special relationship between an
individual and an object, usually an animal. One's
power was most often obtained in a dream or vision
during a "power quest" which took place before puberty.
Both boys and girls were urged, sometimes forcefully,
by their parents to fast and then go to a remote and
isolated spot where they would spend the night preparing themselves to receive a vision of their power. Such
an ordeal was designed to develop within the child a
proper mental attitude, as well as qualities of courage,
honesty, concentration, and perseverance. Having
reached power through a dream, the voices of an animal,
or a sign of some sort, the initiates could then write their
own power song. Adults with power were entitled to
wear an emblem of their power, such as a bear claw or an
eagle feather. Power was deemed essential to the success of all endeavors, to protection from danger and
illness, and to luck in games of chance.

Besides the possession of power, the sweat house was
also central to Okanogan culture. In the naming myth,
the Chief Spirit names his wife Sweat House and gives
her as a deity to the animal people and the people to
come to purify them physically and spiritually. Walter
Cline decribes the sweat house ritual thus: "As one
dashed water on the hot rocks, he chanted prayers to
Sweat House for health or for success in hunting, gambling, love, or any other enterprise of the moment"(p.
167).

Just as Coyote, power, and Sweat House are essential
to Okanogan culture, so they are to Mourning Dove's
work. Indeed, the inspiration behind *Cogewea* is an
Okanogan folk tale that has been variously titled "Lit-

tle Chipmunk and the Owl Woman" and "Coyote Kills Owl Woman." In each version, "Little Chipmunk (Kots-se-we-ah) is a gay, mischievous girl who frisks about without a care until trouble appears, then runs for shelter to her patient, hardworking grandmother."[9] One day while she is picking berries for her grandmother, she is spotted by Owl Woman, who eats the hearts of children. She runs to hide, but Owl Woman captures her and tears out her heart. Meadow Lark brings her back to life, and Coyote plots to kill Owl Woman. Though Mourning Dove ultimately transforms these traditions into fiction in *Cogewea,* yielding inadvertently at times to pressure from McWhorter to change some of the "facts" of the legends and traditions in the interests of taste and decorum, the impulse reverberating through *Cogewea* is Okanogan, and the final result is a curious and intriguing blend of oral and written forms.

Cogewea, That "Little Squaw"

When Mourning Dove first met McWhorter in 1914, she had already drafted a version of the novel that would be published thirteen years later under the title *Co-ge-we-a, the Half-Blood: A Depiction of the Great Montana Cattle Range.* Encouraged by McWhorter's interest in her, she apparently sent him her manuscript for his comments. There is no record of that initial correspondence, nor is there an extant copy of Mourning Dove's original manuscript, but subsequent correspondence indicates that she agreed to let McWhorter "fix up" the story of that "little squaw" and to handle all the negotiations for its publication. Of her collaboration with McWhorter, she wrote the following to their mutual friend and mentor, J. P. MacLean, in 1916: "We both worked hard on it and we sometimes almost went on the warpath, but we always patched up a peace and continued friends. He helped me with Cogeawea, but the next time I am going to let him make the plot and I will help him."[11]

And in 1933, long after the publication of *Cogewea,* Mourning Dove wrote to McWhorter, "My book of Cogeawea would never have been anything but the cheap foolscap paper that it was written on if you had not helped me get it in shape. I can never repay you back."

Both MacLean and McWhorter were extremely optimistic that *Cogewea* would be successful. They were convinced that Mourning Dove was the first Indian woman to write a novel of any sort—which alone should arouse the curiosity of the reading public—and certainly the first to incorporate the oral traditions of her tribe into a literary work. But because there was no precedent for an Indian woman writing romance, McWhorter felt compelled to "strengthen the statements" of Mourning Dove, as he put it, by providing ethnographic notes on the stories and traditions that she had woven into the narrative line. At the same time, he had agreed to be the Sho-pow-tan of the title page and allow the story to be "told through him." As both editor and annotator, McWhorter unquestionably had a tremendous amount of control over Mourning Dove's manuscript, leading to what Charles Larson has described as the "confusing voice" in *Cogewea.*[10]

Mourning Dove's intention from the beginning had been to write a romance about the half-blood Cogewea that was based on her own experience and would preserve in novel form some of the unrecorded stories of her tribe. Despite the inclusion of the Okanogan elements, Mourning Dove regarded *Cogewea* as fiction, refusing at one point, for example, to allow McWhorter to use a picture of her on the title page because that was appropriate only for historical works. (Eventually she relented and allowed her picture to be used.) Despite her reluctance to view *Cogewea* as historical, Mourning

Dove did agree with McWhorter that the value of the novel lay in its expression of the Indian point of view. Unfortunately, McWhorter felt compelled to reaffirm that point of view by constantly inserting into the narrative innumerable didactic passages about the injustices suffered by Indians at the hands of government agencies, as well as historical facts about other tribes that are hardly relevant to the story. The result is that the narrative, which is very much within the tradition of the western romance, with its stock characters and melodrama, sags at times under the weight of vituperation.

Though Mourning Dove and McWhorter had finished their collaboration on *Cogewea* by 1916, it was not published for another eleven years. This delay created a particularly difficult situation for Mourning Dove, who had been interviewed in the spring of 1916 by the *Spokesman Review* of Spokane and hailed as the first American Indian novelist. Given such fanfare, it was embarrassing to continually have to explain why the book was not yet published, as she does in one letter to the editor dated January 13, 1918: "This work has been delayed in its publication because of the war, but will now soon be placed before the public."

Despite the war and the mood of the reading public, the biggest obstacle that Mourning Dove and McWhorter faced was finding a publisher for *Cogewea.* Apparently, they had to guarantee sales and arrange partial financing for the book before some publishers would even agree to look at the manuscript. In his letters, McWhorter tried to persuade publishers that advance publicity would ensure sales, or that they should publish the book for moral reasons because, "coming from the pen of an Indian," it would serve to bring about much needed reforms in the Bureau of Indian Affairs.

Eventually, McWhorter did find a publisher in Boston, the Four Seas, to agree to publish *Cogewea,* but only on the condition that Mourning Dove and McWhorter finance part of the publication. To raise her part of the money, Mourning Dove worked longer hours thinning apples and even opened a lunch stand for a brief time. Finally, the money was raised and the manuscript turned over to the publishers. But publication was delayed for another two years, causing McWhorter to irately accuse the "Four Puddles" (his favorite name for the Four Seas) of being "carelessly negligent," while Mourning Dove accepted with stoicism her disappointment in that "little squaw" who seemed to be a "quitter."

But if she had been disappointed by all the setbacks encountered in getting *Cogewea* published, Mourning Dove was completely overwhelmed by the final product in which she suddenly realized the full extent of McWhorter's influence. On June 4th, 1928, she wrote:

Dear Big Foot,

I have just got through going over the book *Cogeawea,* and am surprised at the changes that you made. I think they are fine, and you made a tasty dressing like a cook would do with a fine meal. I sure was interested in the book, and hubby read it over and also all the rest of the family neglected their housework till they read it cover to cover. I felt like it was some one elses book and not mine at all. In fact the finishing touches are put there by you, and I have never seen it.

The "finishing touches" consisted of poetic epigraphs at chapter openings taken from western writers such as Badger Clarke, as well as from *Hiawatha*; sixteen pages of detailed footnotes explaining Okanogan words and customs and corroborating various stories and incidents in the novel; and explanations within the text of such things as the custom of exchanging gifts among the Pend d'Oreille and Nez Perce tribes. Besides inserting his own research into the novel—for example, he includes historical notes about Chief Joseph and the Nez Perces—McWhorter also apparently plagiarized the section on Indian music in chapter 8 from Anna Hurst, a scholar of Indian music. On June 23, 1928, she wrote to McWhorter that she has just read *Cogewea* "with great pleasure," but she also noted that Mourning Dove had "used almost the same words and phrases" that she had used in her "little talk on the stage."

It is in the language of the novel that McWhorter's impact is most obvious because some of the passages are totally unlike Mourning Dove's own direct and simple style as reflected in her original drafts of *Coyote Stories*. Language was for her a constant challenge as she struggled to translate into English what she knew in Okanogan. Even as late as 1930 she wrote to McWhorter, "I am still studying hard nearly every day, so I can learn to place my words for my writing and recasting of my new novel of the Okanogans."

Deeply offended by the accusation of the local Indian agent that McWhorter had written all of *Cogewea,* and perhaps sensitive to the element of truth in that charge, Mourning Dove determined to prove to the world that she could write a novel by herself. (Unfortunately, whatever she did write has not been discovered.) Despite the overwhelming evidence of their collaboration in the correspondence, McWhorter wrote a letter to the agent publicly proclaiming Mourning Dove the sole author of *Cogewea,* and the agent recanted his statements. Yet it is hard to imagine that Mourning Dove would have written such passages as Cogewea's description of the Bureau of Indian Affairs: "A nasty smear on the Government escutcheon . . . a stagnant cesspool swarming with political hatched vermin! stenchful with the fumes of avarice and greed; selfishly indifferent to the Macedonian cry of its victims writhing under the leash wielded by the hand of Mammon! Pitch is a fastidious cosmetic, compared with the Bureau slime."[12] Or Cogewea's response to Densmore when he asks if she is in a "scalping mood": "If I were, the subject material immediately available would hardly suffice for the appeasement of my warlike proclivities" (p. 147).

During her reveries on her favorite rock on the butte overlooking the vast plains below, Cogewea becomes the mouthpiece for set pieces ranging from exhortations against the "blighting curse" of the Indian Bureau—an "octopus with life extracting tentacles reaching into every Indian reservation of the Union. A Vampire! whose wing cools with the breeze of never-to-be filled promises" (p. 140)—to elegies on the demise of the Blackfeet—"Heroes, patriots! Victims of plutocratic chicanery and broken faith on the part of the 'powers that be' " (p. 141).

Throughout the novel there are many such passages in which the language is stiff, formal, and highly rhetorical. McWhorter himself apparently had some doubt about whether such language was appropriate for an Indian writer, because he sought the advice of his close friend, Martha McKelvie, who indignantly asked, "Why shouldn't a high class Indian use decent language?" But "decent" language need not be stilted and unnatural; such passages are particularly obtrusive in contrast to the Okanogan tales told by Cogewea's grandmother, which seem to reflect Mourning Dove's own unadorned style.

In contrast to the obviously inflated style of parts of the book is an equally self-conscious use of slang, which is reflected in passages about riding the range. Slang is the medium of the range, a kind of lawless expression full of "infelicities," reflecting the open freedom of the West that men such as the cowboys in *Cogewea*—Rodeo Jack, Silent Bob, Celluloid Bill, Jake, and Frenchy— have sought. It is their bond of mutual understanding and acceptance, a regional code that can be both humorous and frustrating if the listener doesn't fully comprehend all the short cuts taken. Despite a friend's warning not to overdo the use of slang, Mourning Dove and McWhorter liberally sprinkle *Cogewea* with words and phrases like "savey," "tumble, " "hittin the trail," "busted tenderfoot," "hater," "callin of the blood," "hit the hay," and so forth.

Even Cogewea's speech reflects the wide swings between rhetorical formality and colorful colloquialisms employed throughout the novel. Perplexed by her inconsistent language, Cogewea's faithful friend and admirer, Jim, comments to her: "Sometimes you talk nice and fine, then next time maybe you go ramblin' just like some preacher-woman or schoolmarm. Can't always savey you" (p. 33).

Cogewea cannot always comprehend her situation either, and her language reveals the conflict she feels in being caught between two worlds. From the opening paragraph of the novel, Cogewea wonders if there is any place for the " 'breed'!—the socially ostracized of two races." She declines at first to marry Densmore because white men have notoriously taken advantage of Indian women. Yet, when she enters the horse race for "Squaws" at a Fourth of July celebration, she is as spurned by the Indian women as she has been by the whites in the "Ladies' " race. Of her dilemma, she exclaims, "We are between two fires, the Red and the White. . . . We are maligned and traduced as no one but we of the despised breeds can know" (p. 41).

In Cogewea's world, the tension of opposites exists between the Indian and white worlds, tradition and change. Assimilation is, in part, inevitable, and the old way is passing. Cogewea reflects, for example, on the plight of her grandmother, who "knew many interesting tales of the past . . . but who was lingering pathetically in the sunset of a closing era." In contrast are the young people, who "are interested in their tribal legends only to the extent of 'cramming' some ardent writer with palpable absurdities. They have progressed beyond the pristine days. The airy tepee has given place to the stuffy houses of their conquerors." The primitive has yielded to the modern and the natural world has receded behind the material advances of technology.

As a half-blood, Cogewea has the apparent option of choosing either the white world or the Indian world. She stands between her two sisters, who represent both. Mary has remained with their grandmother, the Stemteemä, and observes a traditional way of life, while Julia has married a white man and has been assimilated into white culture. The difficulty that Cogewea faces is how to find the middle road that will afford her the amenities of civilization without compromising her traditional beliefs. If there is a confusing voice in the novel, it is in part due to this ambivalent attitude toward assimilation. Except for the villain, Densmore, who is variously described as a coyote, arch conspirator, and rattlesnake, all of the white characters in the novel are sympathetically drawn. John Carter, Julia's husband, is a model of warm respectability, tolerant of the mischievous pranks of Cogewea and the boys, and yet firm and fair-minded in running the ranch. Silent Bob, the quiet southerner, reveals his deep capacity for brotherly love in his friendship with Dixie Canary and his concern over Cogewea's fate with Densmore. And Frenchy is completely charming as the foreign tenderfoot who perseveres in spite of himself to become a cowboy and loyal friend to the other riders.

On the other hand, the recurring motif of Densmore's insistence upon an Indian marriage ceremony is a reminder of the ignominious way white men have deceived Indian women by devaluing their rituals as much as they devalue the women themselves. The half-blood offspring become visual images of the powerlessness of Indians whose only weapon for counteracting the evils of a prejudiced white world is to rely on the age-old traditions of their Indian heritage that have thus far ensured their survival.

And it is to those teachings that Cogewea ultimately must turn. Despite her decision to elope with Densmore, Cogewea has not been deaf to her grandmother's teachings or to the voice of her own "Indian Spirit" that has warned her she is "stepping wrong" and embarking on a "questionable course." Indeed, the real struggle in Cogewea's soul centers on the truth of the beliefs she has inherited from her Indian half. Though she is quick to defend the Indian customs and ceremonies against Densmore's disdainful cynicism, she suffers her own doubts at times about the place of those traditions in the modern world.

But the Stemteemä does not doubt, and it is primarily through her character that Mourning Dove incorporates elements from the Okanogan oral tradition into the novel. Stemteemä is the embodiment of the oral tradition, appearing in the narrative at key points to instruct Cogewea in right action. Stemteemä and Densmore counterbalance each other, representing the various tensions in the novel—Indian versus white, truth versus falsehood, tradition versus "civilization." Stemteemä is tradition itself. More than a hundred years old, she is the link to the past, the one who has learned the stories of her tribe and been charged by her father to pass them on. As the oral historian of the Okanogans, she adheres to as many of the "old-time customs" as her age permits. She arrives in her "semi-civilized garb," wearing "wampum and ear ornaments . . . and beaded mocassins." She prefers her tepee to the ranch house, "after the ancient manner of her fading race," and pursues basket weaving in the morning hours. Before every major decision and before telling a story, she ritualizes the occasion by smoking a pipe. And although times have changed, she continues to instruct her grandchildren in the customs of another era, recounting stories about the coming of the first white people and tragedies that have befallen her tribe. Most

important, perhaps, the Stemteemä consults the Sweat
House and evokes her spirit power when she is troubled
and seeks the solace of a spiritual force greater than
herself.
Whether Stemteemä recounts the history of her tribe
or admonishes Cogewea to beware of Densmore, the
language is direct, simple, and slightly stylized to em-
phasize the wisdom of the aged storyteller.[13] Her position in the narrative is almost that of a Greek chorus
commenting on the action. By delineating the landscape
of another time, she creates the context of history to
which Cogewea must ultimately respond. In the preface
to her first story, Stemteemä emphasizes the importance of storytelling in perpetuating cultural traditions:

> This story I am telling you is true. It was given me by my
> father. . . . He told me the tales that were sacred to his tribe;
> honored me with them, trusted me. Treasured by my
> forefathers, I value them, I know that they would want
> them kept only to their own people, if they were here. But
> they are gone and for me the sunset of the last evening is
> approaching and I must not carry with me this history. [p.
> 122]

As the Stemteemä must pass her stories on orally to
those beyond the tribal circle, so has Mourning Dove
assumed the responsibility for preserving those traditions in literary form for a wider audience.
What is most interesting is the way in which Mourning Dove has synthesized various elements from
Okanogan culture to fit the dramatic demands of the
narrative. An example of this synthesis occurs in the
first story Stemteemä tells, "The Dead Man's Vision," in
which a medicine man of the Okanogan had long ago
prophesied the coming of the first white men, the "Black
Robes," or missionaries. The time of year is winter, and
the people are celebrating the "Spirit's Days" to continue "His favors to the tribe; that the trees, the grass

and herbs be perpetual; that the deer and all game be plentiful the coming season and that the red salmon again swim up the Swanitkqah" (p. 123). In this description, Mourning Dove combines the two traditions of the Winter Dance and the First Fruit Ceremonies celebrated by the Okanogans. The Winter Dance was a time to pay homage to the spirits, but not to the Great Spirit as much as to one's own individual spirit power. At the Winter Dance, new initiates sang their power songs, thus communicating to other members of the tribe that they had successfully completed a power quest and obtained the power of a guardian spirit. The First Fruit Ceremonies, on the other hand, would have been performed in the spring to celebrate the rebirth of the land and the regeneration of plants and animals after the long winter.[14]

The Sweat House sequence is another example of Mourning Dove's successful integration of Okanogan traditions into the narrative. Having exhausted her storytelling resources for turning Cogewea away from Densmore, Stemteemä turns to the Sweat House. In Okanogan culture, the Sweat House was consulted in matters ranging from love and war to success in hunting and gambling. The supplicant would cover a small pit with a cone-shaped structure of tightly bound poles, bark, and earth. Hot rocks were placed inside, over which the individual would sprinkle water to create steam. Bathing to purify and prepare the body to receive the full benefit of the Sweat House preceded and followed the ritual. Upon entering the sweat house, the petitioner sang a ritual song to invoke the aid of the deity and then chanted requests for aid. To these details of the tradition, Mourning Dove is faithful, but she introduces the belief that the explosion of a hot rock is "a precursor of misfortune," while a wish made on a stone that is placed without breaking inside the sweat house will come true.

Although there is little ethnographic evidence about
the exploding rock theory, rocks did constitute a very
important part of Okanogan culture, particularly for
girls, who, according to James Teit, would make circles
of stones in which each represented a wish or prayer.[15]
Carrying the stones from some distance, the girl would
pray for strength and endurance to carry her burdens in
later life and then would specify what wish each stone
represented as she placed it in the circle. By shifting the
emphasis slightly, Mourning Dove has remained faithful to the tradition of wishing upon rocks and, at the
same time, has created a tight dramatic device that
works very effectively. Upon hearing her grandmother's invocation of the Sweat House spirit, Cogewea
goes to place one of the stones inside the house and make
her wish, but at the last moment the rock explodes into a
million fragments, leaving her in anguish over the
meaning of the event and effectively serving as an omen
of the disaster that will befall her when she elopes with
Densmore. But Jim and Mary have also participated in
the ritual and their rocks do not explode, thus preparing
the reader for the eventual happy outcome.

It is in the recurring motif of spirit power that Mourning Dove is most faithful to her Okanogan heritage. Jim
knows that Cogewea will win the horse race because his
spirit power has told him so. Stemteemä bases her
judgment of Densmore upon the signs her "guiding
spirits" have given her in her dreams. When Cogewea
goes to her favorite haunt, she "makes medicine" over
the buffalo skull. As Green-Blanket Feet escapes from
the Blackfeet who have enslaved her, she calls on her
secret powers for aid and is not abandoned by her spirit
protector. Jim and Mary construct the sweat house for
Stemteemä according to the "guidance of the spirits,"
and Cogewea senses from her "Indian Spirit" that she is
"stepping wrong." When Jim informs Stemteemä that
Cogewea has eloped with Densmore, the ancient

grandmother already knows the truth revealed in her dream by the spirits and is singing the "spirit-song." And, finally, Cogewea realizes her deep love for Jim when her beloved buffalo skull "speaks" to her.

All of these examples are variations upon the Okanogan concept of power, which Mourning Dove describes as the "spirits' communication through an animal to a person either in a dream or vision. This . . . is not favored to all but to persons who have found that 'medicine' in their fasting time of life." What is most striking about power is its auditory nature in that it usually comes to the person through a voice or song. This relationship could not be more accurately depicted than in the last chapter of *Cogewea*, "A Voice from the Buffalo Skull":

> The fall of an unshod hoof on the stony ground and the jungle of spurs broke upon Cogewea's ears. She did not look up, but intuitively knew who the horseman was. Her eyes dropped to the old skull. She started visibly. Could she be deceived? A voice seemed to issue from its cavernous depths in the Indian tongue; a laudation of—
> "The Man! The Man! The Man!"
> . . . The voice ceased as suddenly and as mysteriously as it came. [Pp. 381–82]

Here, Mourning Dove has effectively fulfilled her wish to weave folklore into novel form, and the most fundamental belief of the Okanogans has been transformed into an organic element of the plot.

This, it seems, is the singular achievement of *Cogewea*, the attempt to translate the concepts of one culture to another through literary form. In a sense, Mourning Dove is herself the "half-blood," standing between an Indian world that seems to be rapidly disappearing and a white world that is either indifferent or bent on government control of Indians. She wants not only to save the heritage that is slipping away, but also to present her way of life in a manner that is intelligible and acceptable. Given her insecurities about her education and her fear of being ridiculed, it is not surprising that she would turn to McWhorter with gratitude for his help in "fixing up" *Cogewea*. But it is the complexity and extent of their collaboration that makes it so difficult to render a final evaluation of the novel.

Even friends and critics of McWhorter and Mourning Dove had a difficult time assessing the novel. On the one hand, there is the view of Martha McKelvie, who wrote to McWhorter, "There is no chance that anything bad would come of the world knowing that you practically wrote *Cogewea*. . . . In the field of all arts, interpreters are necessary. . . . I do think it would be safe to say on an inside page, 'Translated by Shopowtan.' " On the other hand, Granville Lowther wrote to McWhorter criticizing the use of unnatural language in parts of the novel and praising other sections:

> The highlight of her story is the description of the races. *There* Mourning Dove is entirely at home. She knows her subject perfectly. Also the stories told by the Old Indian Stemteemä are excellent. She knows that woman and the woman knows her so much better than either of them knows the Easterner. If Mourning Dove would confine her writings to the life she knows and the people she knows and understands, she would have a brilliant future as a writer. [June 16, 1928]

And from William Brown, a lawyer from Okanogan, Washington, who subsequently helped Mourning Dove in the translation and spelling of Okanogan words for *Coyote Stories,* comes this evaluation:

> I was much impressed with the final suggestion of her *taumannouwis,* the buffalo skull, which spoke to her, advising as to the man she should marry. That idea is very Indian indeed, for I have heard Indians talk so much about the *taumannouwis* that the individual looked upon it as his special guardian angel, good fairy, or whatever you might call it. The buffalo was apparently hers. [June 7, 1928]

In the final analysis perhaps the most that can be said is that neither Mourning Dove nor McWhorter could have written the book without the other. Their collaboration was unique and all the more special because they were breaking new ground in bringing together two disparate traditions: the oral culture of the Okanogans with the literary form of the western romance. Without question, the book is uneven, wrenched in parts, replete with clichés and unnatural language. Nevertheless, it stands as the first effort of an American Indian woman to write a novel based upon the legacy of her Indian heritage, and for that alone, as well as for the preservation of those beliefs and stories of Okanogan culture that might have disappeared, we must be grateful for Mourning Dove's aspirations and McWhorter's assistance.

Notes

1. For more biographical information on McWhorter, see Nelson A. Ault, *The Papers of Lucullus V. McWhorter* (Pullman: Friends of the Library, State College of Washington, 1959).

2. This letter appears in folder #395 of the Papers of Lucullus V. McWhorter, Washington State University Archives, Pullman, Washington. Unless otherwise specified, the correspondence cited is from the McWhorter collection. The date of the correspondence will subsequently be included in the text.

3. These works represent only a part of McWhorter's published canon and the merest fraction of his unpublished manuscripts and correspondence. For the study of Mourning Dove, the McWhorter collection is essential because he saved virtually all of her correspondence, as well as various drafts of her manuscript for *Coyote Stories* (Caldwell, Idaho: Caxton Printers, 1933), all of which offer a rare opportunity for understanding better the creative process of this singular woman.

4. There is little biographical information available on Mourning Dove's early life. The facts that are included here have been taken from McWhorter's preface to *Cogewea* and from her own introduction to *Coyote Stories*. In her later correspondence with McWhorter, she

does confirm her lineage but rarely speaks of her education except to lament her lack of knowledge, particularly of English.

It should also be noted that there is some discrepancy concerning Mourning Dove's birth in the records of the Bureau of Indian Affairs. In a letter dated February 8, 1979, Mitchell Bush of the Tribal Enrollment Services states that she is listed on the Colville tribal rolls as Christine Quintasket, born in 1887. I assume that this was an error made by a local BIA official, because Mourning Dove always signed her name as Christal in her early letters. Bush confirms her marriages to Hector McLeod and Fred Galler.

There is one other interesting fact to note about her name. Before 1921, she signed herself as Morning Dove. Then, on December 27, 1921, she wrote to McWhorter from Spokane, Washington: "By the way, I have made a sad mistake. I have misspelt my name, I found out at the museum. Looking over the birds, I found that I was wrong." And so "Morning" became "Mourning."

On February 23, 1926, she wrote again about her name: "You asked me about Humishuma. As far as I can translate it, it really has no meaning at all besides the name of the bird Mourning Dove. And it does not mean Mourning Dove at all, and as far as I can judge it, the whiteman must have invented the name for it as Mourning Dove because the translation to Indian is not word for word at all."

It is entirely possible that whites did "invent" the translation for Humishuma, because, according to Leslie Spier, Okanogan women were never named after animals or birds, but rather were most often given names that referred in some way to water, emphasizing the importance of rivers and fishing to their culture. See Leslie Spier, ed. *The Sinkaietk or Southern Okanogan of Washington,* General Series in Anthropology, no. 6 (Menasha, Wis.: George Banta Publishing Co., 1938), pp. 1–262.

5. See introduction, *Tales of the Okanogans,* ed. Donald M. Hines (Fairfield, Wash.: Ye Galleon Press, 1976).

6. Leslie Spier's study (see note 4, above) gives a good introduction to the history and ethnography of the Okanogans. Of special value in Spier's volume is the essay "Religion and World View," by Walter Cline, in which he discusses in great detail the concept of power and the sweat house ritual. Other works on the Okanogans include: C. Hill-Tout, "The Far West—the Home of the Salish and Dené," *British North America,* vol. 1 (London: Archibald Constable & Co., 1907); Leslie Spier, *Tribal Distribution in Washington,* General Series in Anthropology, no. 3 (Menasha, Wis., 1936); and James Teit, "The

Salishan Tribes of the Western Plateaus," *Forty-fifth Annual Report of the Bureau of American Ethnology* (Washington, D. C.: Government Printing Office, 1930), pp. 198–294.

7. Edward S. Curtis, *The North American Indian,* vol. 7 (Seattle: E. S. Curtis, 1911), pp. 43–114.

8. For a fuller discussion of Coyote, see Cline, "Religion and World View"; Eileen Yanan, *Coyote and the Colville* (Omak, Wash.: St. Mary's Mission, 1971).

9. "Okanagan Folk Play—an Animal Tale from the Inkameep Indian Reserve in British Columbia," *Carolina Play-Book* 12, no. 4 (December 1939): 154. This is the preface to the play that follows, entitled "Little Chipmunk and the Owl Woman," which was recorded by Elizabeth Renyi (pp. 155–58).

10. Charles Larson, *American Indian Fiction* (Albuquerque: University of New Mexico Press, 1978), p. 179. Larson discusses *Cogewea* in an appendix rather than in the main text of his book because of his "suspicion" that Mourning Dove worked with a collaborator rather than writing the entire book herself. However, he offers no evidence to support his supposition or to identify Sho-pow-tan.

11. I have been unable to discover the reason for the different spellings of Cogewea. Throughout her correspondence with McWhorter, Mourning Dove spelled the name "Cogeawea," but when the book was published, the spelling was standardized to "Cogewea" throughout except on the title page, where it was hyphenated (Co-ge-we-a). I have used the published spelling in my comments, retaining McWhorter's and Mourning Dove's spelling in direct quotations from their correspondence.

12. *Co-ge-we-a, the Half-Blood: A Depiction of the Great Montana Cattle Range* (Boston: Four Seas, 1927), p. 145. Page numbers for all subsequent direct quotations will be cited in the text.

13. For a discussion of storytelling among the Okanogans, see Rachel S. Commons, "Diversions," in *The Sinkaietk or Southern Okanogan of Washington,* ed. Spier. According to Commons, Okanogans generally told stories only during the winter evenings because of a taboo against telling stories in the summer or during the day. Anyone who broke the taboo would suffer from baldness. Old men and women were exempt from this taboo, however, because they were already bald, so Mourning Dove is well within Okanogan tradition in having Stemteemä tell stories during summer days.

14. For a full discussion of the Winter Dance Ceremony, see Cline, "Religion and World View." Cline also discusses the First Fruit Cere-

monies, as does C. Hill-Tout in "The Far West."

15. James Teit, "The Salishan Tribes of the Western Plateaus," ed. Franz Boas, *Fortieth Annual Report of the Bureau of American Ethnology, 1927–28* (Washington, D.C.: Government Printing Office, 1930), pp. 198–294.

ERRATA

Page   15. 4th line—For "Brand" read "Bend"
Page 132. 37th line—For "thrills" read "thralls"
Page 141. 32nd line—For "wept" read "weeping"
Page 145. 6th line—Read—"A nasty smear on the"
Page 145. 26th line—For "claimed" read "claiming"
Page 180. 30th line—For "caps" read "chaps"
Page 182. 5th line—For "Boy" read "boys"
Page 187. 12th line—For "canoe" read "cone"
Page 206. 25th line—For "go" read "yo"
Page 208. 16th line—For "But know" read "But I know"
Page 218. 17th line—Omit "we"
Page 228. 1st line—For "returned" read "turned"
Page 229. 20th line—For "train" read "trail"
Page 248. 34th line—For "he" read "she"
Page 267. 10th line—For "corral" read "rock"
Page 282. 21st line—For "he" read "her"

Numbers in the text refer to the Notes, pages 287–302.

COGEWEA
The Half-Blood

HUM - ISHU - MA —— MOURNING DOVE

CO=GE=WE=A
The Half - Blood

A Depiction of the Great Montana Cattle Range

By

HUM-ISHU-MA
"Mourning Dove"

Author of "The Okanogan Sweat House"
Honorary Member, Eastern Washington State Historical Society
Life Member, Washington State Historical Society.

Given through SHO-POW-TAN

With Notes and Biographical Sketch
By LUCULLUS VIRGIL McWHORTER
Author of "The Crime Against the Yakimas",
"Border Settlers of Northwestern Virginia",
"The Discards", etc.

BOSTON
THE FOUR SEAS COMPANY
PUBLISHERS

The Four Seas Press
Boston, Mass., U. S. A.

TO THE MEMORY OF

MY GREAT GRAND FATHER, SEE-WHELH-KEN,
VENERATED CHIEF OF THE SCHU-AYLP^K; THE
SONG OF WHOSE GOOD DEEDS WILL FOREVER
MINGLE WITH THE MIGHTY ROAR OF THE
FALLS OF SWA-NET^K-QAH, AND THE MOURN-
FUL SOUGHING OF THE MOUNTAIN PINE:
EARTH'S PRIMITIVE NOBLEMAN WHO, IN
PEACE WELCOMED THE COMING OF THE PALE
FACE, ONLY TO WITNESS THE SEEDS OF DES-
TRUCTION SCATTERED WIDE AMONG HIS OWN
ONCE STRONG AND CONTENTED PEOPLE. TO
HIM AND TO THE CROWDED DEATH HUTS AND
BURIAL CAIRNS OF A NATION IS THIS VOLUME
MOST ENDEARINGLY DEDICATED BY ONE
WHO EVER YEARNS FOR THE UPLIFTING OF
HER MOST UNHAPPY RACE.

CONTENTS

To the Reader

THE author of *Cogewea* occupies an unique sphere in the literary field. So far as the writer of this sketch is aware, she is the first Indian woman to enter the realms of fiction. Believing that the reader would be interested in a brief portrayal of her life and ancestry, she was at last prevailed upon to let the same here be entered. This was not attained without difficulty. Her racial sensitiveness shrank from what she termed "unwarranted presumption."

Hum-is′hu-mā: "mourning dove," was born while her mother and maternal grandmother were crossing the Kootenai River in a canoe near Bonner's Ferry, Idaho, about 1888. Her people at the time were on their way from Fort Steel, British Columbia, traveling by pack-horses to the States. She bears a remote strain of good *Celtic* blood, dating back to the earlier advent of the Hudson Bay Company into the Northwest. This, in a measure, accounts for her deep sympathy so manifest throughout her book for the mixed-blood, the socially ostracized of two races.

Mourning Dove is a maternal great granddaughter of *See-whelh-ken*, head Chief of the *Schu-ayl-p^k*, or *Schwelpi; Schoyelpi*—spelled in various ways—now embodied with the Colvilles, including the Okanogans proper. She is identified with the latter tribe, whose language she speaks.

See-whelh-ken's tribe resided at the *Swa-netk-qha*: "big river falls," known in history as Les Chaudière, or Kettle Falls, of the Columbia River. The Okanogan appellation, however, applied to the stream in its entirety, so famed in legendary lore. These Falls have ever been renowned for their great fishery, and the Schu-ayl-p^k were generally blessed with an abundance of salmon. The Chief was noted for his generous distribution of fish to the less fortunate bands and tribes remotely situated. Regarding the fishery as a direct provision of a benign *Spirit-ruler*, he deigned not, at any time, to accept compensation for the food. The beautiful sentiment of ceremonial gift-exchange so universal among all the tribes, should not be confounded with sordid commercial barter. To this day the older Indians —even to the distant surrounding tribesmen—speak of the great See-whelh-ken, of the "big heart," so strong is the memory of he who, in other snows drove famine from the door.   Tall, well proportioned with strong, pleasing features, he ruled with a firm, though just hand.   Stressed on communistic ideals, his every action was governed by magnanimous wisdom.

Descended from an ancient line of warrior-chieftains, See-whelh-ken saw the advent of the white man into his domain, and was ever that alien's most steadfast friend. It was owing greatly, if not wholly to his influence that his own, and neighboring tribes maintained friendly relations with the strange intruders. The rapid decimation in the ranks of See-whelh-ken's once virile follow· ing, is ghastly testimony of the recompense that was meted to him.

Of happy childhood, Mourning Dove recalls none. At the age of seven she was placed in the *Sacred Heart Convent*, at Ward, Washington, but the following year was brought home to aid in the care of her small brothers and sisters, all younger than herself. When thirteen she was returned to the convent, but her mother dying within the twelve months, was recalled to take charge of the bereaved home. For the next three years she was a mother to the four little ones.

At last there came a period of exhilarating life with her maternal grandmother, *Soma-how-atqu*. Under the tutelage of this venerable parent, the girl's impressionable mind became innoculated with the principles of ancestral philosophy. In the fishing village by the streams; in the hill and mountain camps where the women digged and cured the various edible roots; where they harvested and dried the wild berries; gathering basket-weaving materials within the deep forests; did she acquire a lasting knowledge of the customs of her tribe. She learned the magic, invigorating virtue of the native foods, and the religious significance of the *Song of the Mountain Herb*. She was made to understand, and to believe in the mysterious, and sacred power of the *sweat-house*, as a cleanser for both body and mind.

Mourning Dove took long horseback rides into remote sections of the neighboring mountains, bivouacing alone and wherever overtaken by night. Fond of hunting—but not in the sense of sport—a good shot and wholly self-reliant, these excursions through wilderness mazes grew with the years. This wild girl was endowed with a primitive sense of security not born to her civilized-reared sister. A daring and graceful rider, she often figured in the dashing relay, and "squaw" races, and other equestrian sports peculiar to the Western range.

In 1908, Mourning Dove became more closely connected with the cattle range. She witnessed the last grand roundup of buffaloes on the Flathead Indian Reservation, Montana; when the famous *Pablo* herd was disposed of to the Canadian Government. She saw the scattering of this remnant of the plains monarch, and the reservation thrown open to settlement. Her sympathies were with the buffaloes—the one remaining link with an era forever past. The animals fought desperately before at last driven from their native haunts. Some burst from the railway cars in the process of loading; one being dashed to the ground with a broken neck. This scene brought tears to the eyes of some of the aged Indian bystanders, a race renowned for unemotional stocism.

A sensate longing by Mourning Dove for an education was never realized. Her people, as an integral, contended that her convent schooling, where she reached the third grade, would suffice for all practical purposes. But from seventeen to twenty-one, through her own efforts, she attended Government Indian schools. During this time she was acting matron for sixty to seventy girls. Although this service occupied half of her time, barring her from study, it carried with it no salary—no compensation whatever—apparently a feature of Departmental economy. While strict with her charges, the young matron was markedly kind. Loved by them all, they confided to her their many little troubles and childish grievances. Zealous of duty and responsibility, she had no hesitancy in crossing swords with her superiors for what she deemed to be justly right.

The winter of 1912-13 found Mourning Dove enrolled in a Calgary, British Columbia, business college. English, and typing were her principal studies. The humiliation from wanton contumely because of her Indian blood, were multitudinous, but, using her own phraseology, she "stuck" through the term, not missing a class.

Mourning Dove is endeared to her people. A warm personality, and sound judgment has enabled her—despite her tinge of Caucasian blood—to render signal and telling service to the dependent tribesmen. The grafting land-grabber, arbitrary and unjust Departmental rulings, and the unnecessary harshness of U. S. guardians of the Canadian border line, have all felt her corrective influences. Seldom, if ever, has she failed in commanding the admiration, if not respect, of those opposed. A single instance:

An aged Indian couple unacquainted with English, were arrested near the Canadian boundary for some infringement of intricate international law. Infirm with years they were being driven afoot along the hot, dusty road by the two arresting officers in a buggy. Observing this from her own camp the intrepid girl mounted her horse and overtaking the procession, shamed the younger man into alighting, and permitting the woman to ride. Not satisfied with this she secured the release of the old prisoners, in defiance of usual red-tape procedure.

It was amid such scenes that the idea of writing *Cogewea* was conceived. Years of tutelage in the tepee of the primitive minded Soma-how-atqu on the wild Kootenai, with a later village residence by the scenic Flathead Lake under entirely different environment, tended to qualify the author most admirably for her task. How well she has succeeded, the impartial reader must determine. Her characters are all from actual life, and throughout the narrative, she has endeavored to picture the period as she actually saw it—an Indian— in the closing days of the great cattle range, and the decadence of its King, the *cow-puncher*.

Yakima, Washington LUCULLUS V. McWHORTER

COGEWEA
The Half-Blood

CHAPTER I.

COGEWEA THE HALF-BLOOD

Grew up like the prairie lilies,
Grew a tall and slender maiden,
With the beauty of the moonlight,
With the beauty of the starlight.
—*Hiawatha*

IT was sunset on the river Pend d'Oreille. The last rays of the day-God, glinting through the tangled vines screening the great porch of the homestead of the Horseshoe Brand Ranch, fell upon a face of rare type. The features were rather prominent and well defined. The rich olive complexion, the grave, pensive countenance, proclaimed a proud descent from the only true American—the Indian. Of mixed blood, was Cogewea; a "breed"!—the socially ostracized of two races. Her eyes of the deepest jet, sparkled, when under excitement, like the ruby's fire. Hair of the same hue was as lustrous as the raven's wing, falling when loose, in great billowy folds, enveloping her entire form. Her voice was low and musical, with a laugh to madden the gods.

Cogewea's mother had died when she was but a small child, and her father, Bertram McDonnald, had followed the gold rush to Alaska, leaving her and two sisters to be cared for by the old Indian grandmother. Through the aid of friends—an inherent principle in Indian life—the wolf was kept from the tepee door. During all the long years no word had come from the silent North, and it was supposed that this father had succumbed to death in the realms of storms and ghastly whiteness.

Ofttimes the *camas* and *salmon* were not plentiful in the smoky lodge, and the little orphans were no strangers to hunger. But despite this, the children were endowed with good health and vigorous constitutions, due

15

to the devoted care of the primitive-minded grandmother. Life in the open, the sweat house and cold river baths, had stamped their every fiber with bounding vitality.

Cogewea, more than her two sisters, was own-headed and at times wilful. She could ride well and made long strolls into the bordering mountains. These runaway-trips were not unattended with danger and consequently were a source of considerable solicitude on the part of the old grandparent. Unlike other children, the repeated warnings that *Sne-nah* (1) would catch her, had no effect. Contrary to all precedent, the little "breed" defied this dreaded devourer of children by extending her rambles farther and still farther into the luring wilderness. Like some creature born of the wild, neither fancied nor actual dangers deterred her from her set course.

At last, notwithstanding her antipathy to the culture of the pale face, the aged squaw was constrained to listen to the pleadings of the good Sisters, and at the age of twelve the little "woods-savage" and her two sisters were placed in the convent school. This measure was resorted to only after Cogewea returned one evening, her horse bearing an ugly cut on its hip, received from the claws of a cougar. The fierce animal had leaped from a tree and the child escaped only through the agility of her mount. With a mighty bound the horse had thwarted the hungry cat of its prey, with no other injury than the knife-like wound, neither deep nor serious.

The weaning process from the old life was slow, but in time Cogewea adapted herself to the new conditions and was an apt student. She seemed to imbibe knowledge, and not content with the scant learning there afforded, and looking to the future, she crossed the Continent and entered the Carlisle Indian School, from which she graduated with high honors at the age of twenty-one.

Such was Cogewea: "Chip-munk," of the Okanogans; the "breed" girl with the hypnotic eyes, who stood dreaming on the vine-clad porch of the "H-B" Ranch, the home of her oldest sister, Julia Carter. An ambitious girl, and, although having passed through the mill of social refinement, she was still—thanks to early training—whole hearted and a lover of nature. The wild appealed to her. Since her return from school her every day companions had been the cowboys of the range. With them or alone, she took many a thrilling dash on the back of a Wan-a-wish, (2) across the low swelling plains or among the buttes and coulees of the broken uplands. Fond of books, the best authors claimed her attention when she was not riding or helping with the routine work of the house.

Cogewea was liked by all the rangers. She was close to their rough natures, for had she not been nurtured by the same elements? She commanded their respect as but few women of her blood could command it. While ready to die for her, they knew the demarcation between harmless friendship and gross familiarity. She understood the "beast" in man and how to subdue it with the same daring confidence which had characterized her younger days of mountain riding.

The sun dipped lower, as Cogewea, gazing out over the undulating hills to the west, dreamed on. What had the future in store for her? What would it bring? Would it, through her, illuminate the pathway of others? Could she fill any sphere of usefulness; or would she, like the race whose hue she had inherited, be brushed aside, crushed and defeated by the cold dictates of the "superior" earth-lords? She had struggled hard to equip herself for a useful career, but seemingly there was but one trail for her—that of mediocrity and obscurity. Regarded with suspicion by the Indian; shunned by the Caucasian; where was there any place for the despised breed!

The girl's reveries were broken as the range riders burst into view over a distant swell. She saw them thrown into sharp silhouette against the sun, leaving its last crimson touch to plain and the beautiful Pend d'-Oreille, as its blue waters swept southward around the Horseshoe, from which the ranch derived its name. She thought of the canoe which ruffled its bosom no more.

The huge Clay Banks on its eastern shore loomed grey and sombre in the shadowy gloaming, never again to reflect gleam of signal or camp-fire. The buffalo no longer drank of its cooling flood, nor thundered over the echoing plain.

Cogewea turned to the east, where the great Rockies, towering and majestic, were still bathed in the ruddy glow of the sunset. For a moment the topmost pinnacle stood clothed in scarlet flame, then the dusky wing of night, sweeping from eastern realms, fell darkening over all. Cogewea imagined that the time-grizzled peak beckoned a parting farewell, and a chill of loneliness struck to her heart. The world was receding!—and she buried her face in her hands to suppress the sob which welled to her lips. Then the sound of hoof-beats broke upon her ear as the riders came cantering to the barn corrals.

There is magic in the rhythmical chime of hoof-music —inspiration—exhilaration. Instantly the girl of moods forgot her brooding and with light-hearted impulsiveness, ran down the intervening slope to where the five cowboys were unsaddling their mounts.

No prudishness marked the movements of this strange, self-reliant girl. The product of an epoch, false modesty—the subterfuge of the weak—had no part in her makeup. Before reaching the gate she was greeted with the cheery: *"Hell-o Sis"* from James LaGrinder, the ranch foreman. Cogewea returned the greeting in the same free way. Jim, as he was commonly called, was also a half-blood. He was a tall, spare built man of sinewy limb, wiry in action. His black eye was keen and restless. A scanty mustache adorned his sensitive lip, which he was wont to pull and twist when in deep thought or anger. When this danger signal was observed, the "boys" steered clear of their foreman. With strong, well-chiseled features, his bronze face was handsome for one of its type. As a rider, he had no equal on the range and was an artist with the rope. Quick-tempered and a dead shot, with his suspicious Indian nature, he was not regarded as a safe man to cross; although the handle of his six-shooter at his belt bore no notches. His schooling was limited to indifferent reading and writing. Twenty-seven years of age, with a life on the range, he was a typical Westerner—a rough nugget—but with an unconscious dignity peculiar to the Indian. All in all, Jim was hardly the social equal of the Carlisle maiden. He assumed the role of a "brother protectorate" over Cogewea, hence the "Sis" with which he addressed her. He betrayed his love for her in his own simple way, which at times appeared to the other boys as not exactly brotherly. Cogewea had not resented this attention. She was coquettishly blind and had encouraged poor Jim with her jokes which he took as reciprocal. Had she realized the true emotions in that strong impulsive bosom, she certainly would have been more careful. She was toying with fire.

Cogewea waited till Jim had his horse rubbed-down and stabled before they walked to the house side by side, under the knowing glances of the other riders. "Lucky dog," declared the white owner of the stock ranch, John Carter, who regarded Jim as a suitable match for his favorite sister-in-law. He hoped some day that his foreman would become a junior partner of the "H-B" brand.

John Carter was of Scotch descent, a well built man of middle age, good natured and amiable. Marrying his half-blood wife when she was but sixteen, he was more of a father to Cogewea than otherwise. Nor was she slow to take advantage of his fondness for her and was seldom refused any favor she might ask. Her escapades sometimes annoyed him, but she never failed to get back into his good graces with an additional link forged about his great, affectionate heart.

CHAPTER II.

THE ROUNDUP AT HORSESHOE BEND

There was a savage, sunny land
Beneath the buzzard's wing,
And there, across the thorns and sands,
Wild rovers rode like kings.
—*Badger Clark*

I T was the first of June, and the great horse round-up was under way. More than a dozen cowboys were engaged by the "H-B" for the occasion and many of the ranchers joined since among the wild bands in the hills were numerous strays belonging to the scattered homesteaders. Every day they came until a score or more riders were congregated and fed at the Carter ranch. No wonder that Cogewea had but little time to read or dream, for she helped her sister with the housework and the care of the two little boys, Denny and Percy, tots of two and four years.

Before the sun had peeped over the far towering Rockies, the string of riders was disappearing behind the sloping ridge on the southeastern shore of the Pend d'Oreille. They rode in divisions for the hard chase. Since the opening of the Flathead Reservation to settlers it was no longer possible for the stockmen to keep large numbers of either cattle or horses on the open range. Even the buffaloes, owned by private parties, were, because of a Departmental edict, disposed of to the Canadian Government; barring a few that were too wild to corral. The several bands of horses still at large, were of the untameable class, fleet-footed and wary, requiring a combination of the best riders of the Flathead —among whom LaGrinder was second to none—for their capture.

After the last horseman had passed beyond the high ground, Cogewea turned to watch the sun rise over the embattled mountains. The lofty snow peaks, first turned

crimson, then golden, as the fiery orb floated above the
rugged barrier. In transport she stood until it had
cleared the utmost pinnacle, and then turned to her
sister who had joined her in an endeavor to plan the
day's work so as to make the ever-recurring evening
meal, something from the ordinary. But this was not
easy, since the riders usually returned in groups of two
and four which rendered it difficult to arrange for any
uniformity of order. They finally agreed that the best
they could do was to "fill 'em up" on bread, beef, beans
and "spuds" and keep a boiler of hot coffee ready.
Both women were weary of the endless cooking and constant clatter of dishes, and no wonder! But perhaps
their task was hardly less arduous than that of the poor
devils who rode in the hot sun from early morning till
dark, and sometimes far into the night. LaGrinder, the
foreman, had but six hours sleep in three days and it
was wondered how he kept going.

"I'll be glad when the roundup is over," said Julia.
"LaGrinder thinks that it will last but a few more
days."

"I will not be sorry to see the windup myself," rejoined Cogewea, as she sank into the nearest chair with
something of a sigh. "Cooking and rope-throwing!"
she continued musingly. "What a combination! The
connections are manifest, but what of results? A few
somebody's wild broncs corralled; the sizzle and odor
of the branding iron amid the smother of alkali dust.
But it is all in the game! Life is a gamble, a chance, a
mere guess. Cast a line and reel in a splendid rainbow
trout or a slippery eel. Whirl a lariat and bring up a
lordly racer already branded or a scrub cayuse un-
claimed. I wonder," she concluded dramatically, "what
is on the range for me?"

"Mind that you rope a 'slick-ear'!" laughingly replied
her sister.

"Well, I am not yet riding in the matrimonial roundup," was the whimsical retort, "nor am I still-hunting
for any 'maverick'".

With this, the two sisters repaired to the kitchen and

were soon busy clearing away the breakfast table. Cogewea could not understand herself. She could find no
place in life. Her mind burned with an undefinable
restlessness. Her longings were vague and shadowy; as
something not to be attained within the narrow limits of
her prescribed sphere. If she gazed at the mountains,
she imagined that they beckoned her. Called to her as
if she were a part of them. If she gave heed, there was
disenchantment; a volatilization of a jocose dream. Like
a stream she was ever gliding on without aim or purpose.
Was it eventually to be lost in the ocean of infinity?
Even so, were not all mankind in the same channel—
only that some sweep over white sands and smooth pebbles, while others dash among jagged rocks and splinter-
edged boulders. Let hers be of the last, if only for an
object. Those of the mud-current and murky tide were
objects of commiseration.

But what is there gained by kicking? Our trail, set
and marked before our advent in life, ends with a leap
into the shadowy Unknown. Accept every thing as inevitable and with a brave heart. Smile, even though
there appears nothing for which to live. Why attempt
to lift the mask of existence? Surely, in time we will
realize and know.

Cogewea's impulse was to be going ,going, going; and
with the completion of the morning's work, she determined to take a gallop on Wanawish among the hills.
This, perhaps, would put the phantoms to flight. She
would also bring the mail, for they were expecting to
hear from her sister Mary and the Stemteema. (1)

With this resolution, the girl's despondency vanished
and she was humming a low tune as she entered her
bedroom door. Within a few moments she reappeared,
attired in a neat riding habit which portrayed her trim
form most perfectly. Swinging a quirt, her silver-
embellished spurs jingled musically, as gaining the veranda steps she turned to call to her sister cheerily:

"Good-bye! Take a few hours off and let things drift
till I return. Plenty of time! The whole universe is

chock full of time; with all eternity awaiting us just over the Border.''

''You want to watch your horse,'' admonished Julia, as she came to the door. ''John said only the other day that Wanawish bucks hard sometimes.''

''Why! you talk as if I were a tenderfoot and had not been raised among the bunch-grass cayuses. Using but one stirrup I can ride anything standing on four hoofs. You are wasting valuable time with your admonitions. Wanawish and I understand each other.''

''But Cogewea; you are too reckless in your riding.''

''Good-bye! my monitor,'' she again hailed with a merry laugh. ''Look for me to help you with the evening feed.''

With this parting flung over her shoulder, this girl of moods ran down the slope to the barn; her canine friend at her heels. Her spur fouled and she stumbled through the door, which stood ajar. Regaining her feet, she caught sight of the dog and scolded:

''Go back, Bringo! You'll get licked up town and your mistress will have a fight on her hands.''

The girl had a habit of talking to her dumb friends and they seemed to understand. But Bringo did not always mind. His super-intelligence discriminated between an actual command and one of implied simulation. Turning to her horse she continued:

''Hell-o! Wanawish! How are you, old chum? Do you feel like kickin' up dust on the cross-trail today?''

The horse whinnied and pawed restlessly.

''Why, Wanawish! Hungry again? You had your oats not more than an hour ago. Your appetite is equal to that of a bronc buster.''

Giving the horse an additional measure of grain, Cogewea proceeded to saddle him with all the ease and grace of an experienced rider. Inured to the hardships of the range, but few of the boys could surpass her in this respect. She led Wanawish from the barn, and notwithstanding he was saddle-broke, he circled and pranced as if the process were entirely new to him. Some of the cattlemen claimed that he had once been an outlaw and had at least one man to his credit. But of this fact, his mistress was in blissful ignorance.

Cogewea galloped away without a backward glance and did not see Bringo skulking at a distance. The girl was naturally light-hearted and her mood had changed. The human mask was up, as she was wont to express it. She rode at a steady pace over the flats and coulees, her spirited steed pressing steadily on the bit. She was considered a good equestrian and no one knew it better than herself; but like all riders, she was somewhat nervous at times. This "ague" comes occasionally to the masculine puncher, even though possessed of the most iron courage. But a rider should be immune to fear, should never show the least indications of white-blood. Cogewea would not for the world let the boys know that she was afraid. It just happened that she was never thrown in their presence and that was why she boasted about her good horsemanship, as all range riders do. Boasting is a recognized weakness of the range.

Cogewea's intentions were to go to the little town and get the ranch mail and return home without delay. When she reached Polson, she did not stop to visit but remounted and rode southward. She galloped till she came to the steep Polson Hill, then climbed more slowly. Reaching the crest she reined her horse to admire the scenery of the beautiful Flathead. The day was clear and cloudless. Looking northward she could see the Flathead Lake with its shimmering crystal waters. On the east shore the Rockies reared their lofty snow-covered summits, while the foot-hills blended with the tint of the trees growing among them. The western shore was fringed with huge hills and rocks with deep sloping gulches breaking through its banks. The Flathead River entered it from the north, while the Pend d'Oreille flowed out of it to the south. Steamers and launches could be seen going to and fro on its waters, carrying passengers and freight. No railroads had yet crossed the Reservation except in the extreme southern part.

The girl remained several minutes lost in reverie; then turning her steed with a quick movement, she

loped down the wagon grade. By making short cuts
she thought to reach home sooner than by the main road,
and in so doing, she came to a high ridge. On its brow
she reined in Wanawish in startled amazement. Not far
down the slope was a prostrate form—a rider—while
his faithful horse was feeding on the bunch-grass near
by. Recovering from her surprise, she approached. It
was James LaGrinder sleeping in the broiling sun. Her
first emotion was of pity, knowing the hardships he had
encountered during the past week. But the spirit of
mischief predominated, and poor, tired Jim was to suffer humiliation at the hands of one for whom he would
at any time have laid down his own life.

Catching his horse, she led it away, leaving the foreman to dream of the "one nearest his heart." Thought-
less girl! Had she known that the rider, after a long,
hard chase had dismounted to readjust his cinch, and,
thinking to give his winded mount a few moments rest,
had sat down only immediately to fall asleep from utter
exhaustion, she would not have left him afoot so far
from home. But ignorant of all this, she rode away
elated. What a joke, she thought, for Jim to be obliged
to walk six miles when he awoke.

Cogewea had proceeded about a mile, when there was
an ominous buzzing among the rocks at the side of the
trail. Before she could realize the situation, Wanawish,
wildly snorting, gave a lightening leap and began bucking at a terrific rate. Caught unawares, Cogewea landed
sprawling in the sage. Half dazed she sprang to her
feet; unhurt save for a slight bruise on the arm. Wanawish, with another defiant snort, tossed his head and
with Jim's horse in the wake, fled towards home. Her
frantic: "Whoa Wanawish!" had no effect and soon
both steeds were lost to view over a swell.

Cogewea smoothed her crumpled hair, replaced her
Stetson and brushed the dust from her skirts. Then
shifting her quirt to the left hand and drawing a six-
gun, she went in search of the cause of her mishap. She
found it—an immense rattler still coiled under the sage,
a score of feet away. She essayed to approach, when

an angry *whi-r-r-r* warned her that familiarity would
not be tolerated. She stopped, drew back a pace or two,
her black eyes sparkling with resentment. Perhaps it
was owing to her early mental training as well as to a
naturally dramatic nature, that she addressed the serpent.

"Miserble creature of a despised race! Look upon
the sun for the last time, for you are going to die. I
know all about your standing with the tribes. My uncle
has told me of your *tahmahnawis* power for doing secret
evil to the people. (2) Your 'medicine' is strong and my
grandmother would not hurt you.   But *I* am *not* my
grandmother! I am not a full-blood—only a *breed*—a
sitkum Injun and that breaks the charm of your magic
with me. I do not fear you! Besides, I happen to know
of the machinations of one of your progenitors in a
certain garden several thousand snows ago, where he
deceived and made trouble for two of my ancestors. An
ancient book contains a law wherein is said something
about a woman a bustin' your durned head; and *I* am
that *woman.* Yes, I understand about you a bruisin'
my heel. You have already done that—only it happens
to be my elbow. You have humiliated and disgraced
me. Suppose Ji—the boys knew of this? Take *that,*—
you ornery cuss!"

Her hand shot out, followed by an explosion and the
vibrating rattles flew into atoms. She continued:

"That was only to show my contempt for you; a sort
of counting *coupe.* You are a fine looking warrior without your warsong. No you don't!" as cowed, the rattler uncoiled and began to glide away. "I will not spoil
your   handsome mug,   but   just"—bang—"decapitate
you."

The monster writhed in a convulsive twist, the head
hanging by a mere shred of skin. The ball had neatly
severed the neck close to the jaws.

Cogewea replaced the empty shell with a cartridge
from her belt before restoring the pistol to its holster.
Then stepping to a big boulder where the repulsive
snake was hid from view, she sat down. She gazed along

the trail where the escaped horses had fled. Chagrined, she felt that a few tears would be a relief. But she was not going to cry. She tried to think of some excuse to offer at the ranch for being afoot. It must never be known that she had been thrown. A cold nose against her hand, interrupted further musings. It was Bringo. The dog had kept out of sight and was chasing a "jack", but came bounding at the sound of the shot. Bringo, looking into her eyes, expressed his joy by vigorous wags of his tail. Her hand dropped to his head.

"You dear dog! You are the best friend that I have."

Bringo pressed closer trying, animal fashion, to comfort his mistress. The girl was touched and her lips quivered as she brushed the dust from his head. She felt his companionship.

"Wanawish is so mean!" with a little catch in her voice. "What shall I tell the boys? They will always laugh at me. Just think of falling off a gentle cayuse like Wanawish. And I am known as the best girl-rider of this entire region. What would Jim say if he knew? He is—"

"Did you call me Sis? What you shoootin' at? I nearly run my laigs off a gettin' here."

Cogewea, startled at the voice so nearly over her, sprang up to see LaGrinder standing on a brow of the ridge. Her cheeks flushed. (3) Of all men he was the last she wished to see at that moment.

"My! you frightened me!" she gasped. "It's a wonder you don't let a feller know you're coming."

"Why! I—I thought you saw me! that's why you're talkin'." he answered with an aggravating smile.

"I didn't see you! I was only talking to the dog."

"Talkin' to the dog? Well, do you call him 'Jim' when I'm out of sight?"

Cogewea made no reply.

"Where's our cayuses? I saw you with them just before you got over the ridge."

"Gone!—I guess." There was a suspicious quiver in her tone.

"Gone where?"

"Ho—home, I guess."

"How's that Sis?"

"We—l— well! I—I!"

"What is wrong, Sis?" Jim spoke kindly and the smile had left his face. "What is it? I heard you a shootin'."

She tried to answer him, but could not. The lump in her throat prevented. She continued to smooth the hair on Bringo's head.

"Aw! don't cry over spilt coffee, little squaw."

Woman-like, the tears came. She buried her face in her hands. Jim felt that he would like to take her in his arms, but he was well aware that such action would be resented. He repressed this impulse and continued, finally drifting into his usual bragging about his good riding.

"If you got spilt from Wanawish, why you should a been more careful of the devil. Didn't you know that there cayuse was an old outlaw? Used to have him in a Wild West show, where I was 'rena boss; and when the company busted up, he was sold back in this here Injun country, 'cause no one could ride him but me. He was trained to buck from a colt and I'm a little scared of him yet; and here I'm the best rider a roun' this here range; best on the Flathead. I won the champeenship belt in Wyoming, a couple o' years ago, and I can beat any cowpuncher in the states of Texas, New Mexico, Arizona, Montana and Idaho. But I ain't stuck on scratchin' Wanawish when he's a sowin' wild oats, which he'll do when frightened or fed too darn' well. He ain't safe for any woman! Most bucked me off at the beef roundup last summer, when he got locoed at a rattler. Pitched like hell! and any one else would have landed in the sage."

Cogewea's tears were gone. Jim's "medicine" was generally consoling, but she deemed it unnecessary to tell him the particulars of her mishap. In feigned disgust she exclaimed:

"There you go again, Jim! I have often told you to

quit your lying! That is your main fault and I'm not going to hesitate telling you of it. You are certainly entitled to the championship as the best liar this side of the Halls of Congress."

"Now little squaw, you can't deny that I ain't a good rider. Nobody ever talks different to old Jim! Savey?"

"I know that you are a good cowpuncher, but you get me all out of patience when you start those stunts about your 'belts'. I know that it is not the truth! If you would cut out peddling hot air, you would be all right. And Jim," she continued warningly, "you want to quit calling me a *squaw;* especially before strangers. Do you hear? Some of these days I will murder you with a good heart! If you were not a half-breed yourself, you would never dare call me such names."

"Where do you bury your dead, little Injun?" Jim laughed derisively. "Do you smoke-cure the scalps of your victims?"

"Jim! I could learn to hate you."

The eyes of the enraged girl flashed ominously. The Westerner realized that he was on dangerous ground and hastened to retrench. His tone was most conciliatory:

"Come, Sis! I was only a teasin' you. I didn't mean anything; but only kiddin'. Let's bury the hatchet!"

"The only way that I can forgive you, is for you not to tell what you know about me getting thrown from Wanawish."

"Is that all?"

"Yes, that is all. And you had better not whisper it to a living soul; especially the 'H-B' boys. This is going to be a secret between us two." She caught the smile returning playfully to the sun-tanned face, and continued admonitively: "You better dare not any way! If John knew that his foreman was in slumberland this time of day, you know what it would mean. Fired in a jiffy! Savey?"

Her threat only amused Jim. He gazed at her firm, intelligent face a moment with admiring eyes.

"Sis! is this all the secret we ever goin' have 'tween

us? Can't we have somethin' better?"

She scrutinized his appealing features, but her eyes grew cold.

"Don't be an idot! James LaGrinder. You know what I have always said! Say no more on the subject, if you want my friendship."

"Friendship's alright far as it goes, but it ain't sometimes satisfyin'. There's a cravin' considerable different and I want to tell you how I love—"

"Don't Jim! Please don't spoil every thing by being foolish! I love you as a big brother and let it go at that. Men are such irrational beings! It seems that a girl cannot be their 'pal' but that they take it she is hat and belt in love with them. I hate men like that! I like those who know and understand."

"Ain't you a jumpin' at 'clusions?" was the cunning retort. "I was only sayin' as how I love to think maybe some time I'll 'sperience that there cravin'."

"Perhaps I did jump prematurely and without a visible landing," she replied, laughing confusedly, "but the symptoms of an immediate 'cravin' ' was so palpably manifest! However, I am sure glad that it is settled for we can now walk home with no misgivings as to a mutual understanding."

Jim made no response as they started on the weary five-mile tramp to the ranch. His heart was heavy and he thought her absolutely heartless. But he felt sure that she loved no one else, and found solace in the reflection that he might yet "have a chance"!

CHAPTER III.

A RANGE IDYL

It's like a tale from long ago,
And far across the sea—
Could that land be the land we know?
Those roving riders we?

—*Badger Clark*

THE bunk house and shed-barns of the Horseshoe Bend ranch, looked as though they had been thrown promiscuously from the sloping hillside to their present site on the lower grade. The dwelling was a large, old fashioned log building with a massive stone chimney at one end. Although constructed on allotted Indian lands, it was typical of the pioneer homes of certain parts of the West, and at one time traceable across the continent. The large airy rooms gave to the interior a pleasant homelike appearance. The living room was commodious, with leather upholstered chairs and divan. The floor was bare, save for the buffalo, bear and mountain lion skins scattered about. The great open fireplace with its tall brass andirons, was piled with rustic wood. A case of books, and a center table with lamp, composed the furniture. The walls were decorated by a few paintings portraying wild life, several antlers of deer and elk, while above the bookcase leaned the mounted head of a mighty buffalo bull. Cogewea never looked upon this trophy without a pang of regret. The fixed glassy eyes haunted her, as a ghost of the past. With her people had vanished this monarch of the plains. The warwhoop and the thunder of the herd were alike hushed in the silence of the last sleep—and only the wind sighing a parting requiem.

It was evening, and Cogewea sat at the table toying with a pencil, her writing material untouched. She was alone and her childhood days came before her like a dream-picture. How the years had flown! She drifted

31

back to the tepee home, by the banks of the far rolling Swa-nétk-qah, (1) among the mountains of the "Evergreen State." There, her aged grandmother still lived, with her younger sister Mary. She longed to see the kind old face again; to feel the touch of those worn, wasted hands of the one who had been both father and mother to her. Of this singular girl of mountain and plain, men might think that her heart was of the stony cast. But not so! Hers was mortal. Although a dusky maiden of a stern race, she had the feminine longing to be loved and cared for. The inward throb can not always be determined by the degree of visible emotions; nor the coming down-pour be gauged by the appearance of the storm cloud.

Cogewea was aroused from her reverie by the sound of approaching hoof-beats. The steed was reined in at the gate and she was greeted by Jim's cheery:

"Hell-o, Sis! Here's your letters."

She ran down the path and was handed two white envelopes. As she read the first missive, her face brightened and she hastened to impart the news to her sister:

"What do you think! Julia. Stemteemä and Mary are coming to make us a long, summer visit."

"When will they be here?" questioned Mrs. Carter, glancing up from her sewing at the table.

"In about two weeks, Mary says."

"What's that I hear?" asked the suspicious Jim, who at that moment entered with Mr. Carter. "Who's that there talk from?" as he caught playfully at the second letter with the delicate hand writing and so redolent with perfume. "Some beau feller?"

"Bah! I have no such animal. Don't believe in 'em. It's from my chum back East. How the trail lengthens. It does not seem a year since I left school to return to this God's country. Sometimes I long to go back there, but I cannot leave these splendid plains and mountains that I love so well."

"You talk like these here cactus-grown sand-sweeps and piled-up rocks was your private and individual property; and—"

"When man was created it was said to him, if I remember correctly, 'This is your soil. Till it and earn your daily food,' and I think that I have a right to claim a part of the land, even without a man-written patent to it. But if it troubles you, then in word only will I assert my just title to the scenery thereof. Savey?"

"Sure you can! By gollies! little squ—Cogewea. You'r 'bout the queerest I ever saw. Sometimes you talk nice and fine, then next time maybe yo go ramblin' just like some preacher-woman or schoolmarm. Can't always savey you."

"That's what others tell me," she answered simply, as she turned into the living room, where Carter and three of the riders were chatting about the ranch stock, range grass and homesteaders. These last they derisively dubbed: "Missourians," although they came from nearly every state in the Union. There has always been friction between the unpretentious homesteaders and the larger stockmen. Uninterested in this topic, Cogewea took a seat apart, and near the shaded lamp. She was elated that her grandparent and sister were coming. This younger sister, like Julia, had imbibed more of the primitive Indian nature, absorbed from the centuries-old legends as told them by the Stemteemä. Recognizing the new order of things, Cogewea realized that these threads in the woof of her people's philosophy, must be irretrievably lost unless speedily placed on record. She was pondering on this, when Jim, returning from his accustomed round of the barn-corrals for the evening, drew a chair near her own in an endeavor to be sociable in his own rough way. Observing her pensive mood, he asked:

"What you thinkin' 'bout, Sis?"

"Me? Oh! I was contemplating the possibilities of becoming an authoress, of writing a book. I have the theme all right and there is plenty of material yet available. What amuses you?" she suddenly asked, noticing the foreman's smile of incredulity, as he unconsciously pulled at his scant mustache.

"I was just a thinkin' what a book you would write up."

"Why? I can see no particular joke in writing a book."

"I mean if you was in bad humor; as when spilled in sage-trail by Wanawish, " he answered in a lowered tone. "You sure would 'tract readers with your tellin', if you happen to use that there same every day talk and a puttin' in Sundays."

"I may surprise you yet, James LaGrinder! even if I am a 'squaw' as you call me," was the spirited retort. "I may use the pen! The wiseheads laughed at the theories of Columbus. They insisted that the world was flat while the great explorer contended that it was round. Who was correct? Columbus is now honored by all nations for the correctness of his ideas."

"All right, Sis! You and Columy have it your own ways; but I happen to know a spot or two where the world is purty durn' flat, and other places where it is a standin' on end and mos' ready to topple over."

Cogewea laughed. For once she would not quarrel. Their conversation flowed from one channel to another, varying and ceaseless. Jim was light-hearted. What had changed the girl's mood, that she was so kind to him? he wondered. He little dreamed that it was because he had shielded her on that afternoon when two riderless horses had come home, leaving them afoot out on the sage-plains. With all the bantering of the boys, Jim had kept a closed mouth. He had kept faith with Cogewea.

The evening passed all too quickly for Jim, who lingered to have a last word or parting glance from the girl. But it was to no purpose. She gave a jovial "good-night" to all indiscriminately, as the four boys strung out from the living room for the bunkhouse. As soon as they had passed the gate, Jack Galvin, a lank, quarter-blood Texan of uncertain qualities and known as "Rodeo Jack", exclaimed:

"Jim, yo're a lucky cuss! She's a plum' fine gal, best ever walked an' spunk'er nor hell! Can sho' hold her

own! Talk 'bout roastin' th' whites! She can sho'
arg'y with any of 'em. An' s'ciety! Jus' watch her a
usin' them there han' rags at th' table! she sho' ain't for
any of us fellers an if Jim lan's her, it's cause of his more
Injun 'plection as well as blood-'finity. Some times them
there high toned 'breed' gals are fer harnisin' up with
th'r own kin', an' I don't blame 'em. Not many white
men wo'th any thin' shine up to a squaw, 'less she has
lan' an' some herds. I ain't stuck on no gal, but I
know a lady when I see one an' this here gal is sho' of
that cast. I 'low as how I'm a leavin' nex' week, it
ain't no slam to own up me 'temptin' bein' sof' with her
once. An' say! I thought a blizzard busted loos';
such a col' wave struck me. Hones'! I wished for a
overcoat on that there July day. An' it sho' took a
quart of th' hottest to quaker th' chill. She's too long
dis'ance for my rope.''
  ''I'd like to cut Jim out myself,'' spoke up Celluloid
Bill. ''But Lord! there ain't no chance! Yo' can't
mash with that there gal! One day she beat me in a
hoss race on th' upper trail, an' she bested me with th'
rope. I kinda hinted splicin' lariats. I got no furder!
She went in th' air like a wil' bronk at th' fust cinchin'.
Jim's th' main guy an' it must be 'count his shade bein'
a little darker'n mine. Any how he's there like a duck an'
th' maverick who beats him is got to be a thorybred.
But somebody'll lan' her! When them there gals begin
talkin' of not lovin' an' a dyin' ol' maids, yo' lookout!
There's a sho' sign of a wedin' in th' air. Come now,
Jim! Own up! When's th' day? We want get th'
fiddlers an' weddin' presents ready. Yo' can 'spect
silver plates an' them there cut glass thin's costin'
nearly a month's wages to buy. ''Bob,'' he continued,
turning to a companion at his side, ''yo' 'member time
we batched?'' Bob's answer was a grunt. ''Time th'
folks was gone an' yo' cooked for us? When yo' used
a little glass dish for soap after we busted t'other one;
an' how mad Mrs. Carter was when she came home an'
foun' us a usin' it? She said as it cost seven kales an'
we didn't b'lieve it. But 'twas true! Them there

thin's cost like hell, but it's th' kin' I'm goin' buy Jim
when he hitches up. But he won't tell! Maybe it's
goin' be a s'prise, ain't it Jim?''

Jim was silent. He only wished that it could be true.
Celluloid continued, turning again to his second companion:

"Bob, what's been yo' 'sperience? 'Fess up an' tell
what transmised when yo' an' her was a chasin' maver-
icks on th' big flat las' spring? What did that there
gal say when yo' went kinda easy talkin' on her? No
use sayin' yo' didn't, 'cause it was a chance what no
man'd pass up askin' what was a battin' on his min'.
Yo've been through th' fire same as them there three
Hebo Phillistiners in th' furnace, only under differ'nt
'vironments."

"Aw! come off an' quitcher rakin' up ol' trouble
what's mos' forgot," responded Bob in a dragging moan.
"I hater think of that there time once more; I hater
sleep an' dream it all over tonight."

"Celluloid Bill's" correct name was William Cam-
eron. A spare built, light complexioned half-blood
Cheyenne, he got his range sobriquet wearing a white
celluloid collar when he first came to the ranch. Of a
talkative sort and fond of mischief, he was leader in
most of the "H-B" escapades.

Robert Morgan, known as "Silent Bob", was a tall,
spare built, even-tempered man of thirty, who hailed
from the mountain regions of West Virginia. Proud of
his southern blood, he ever insisted that he was a "Virginian" proper; and that the new State was not a
legitimate child of the Union, since it was born in the
throes of war. He lamented the division of the "Old
Dominion", and refused to recognize but the one State.
His voice slow and drawling, it seemed an effort for him
to talk. But even at that he was a general favorite with
the riders throughout the range. True as steel, he would
fight for a friend.

Long after the boys were in dream-land, Jim tossed
on his hard bunk. He pondered about the future, which
had never before troubled him. He recalled that ever

since Cogewea came to the ranch, life seemed to owe him something. Sometimes he imagined that she cared for him, but the next moment his hopes would be dashed. He could not understand the girl. She was a strange medley of amiable sunshine and shadowy indifference; insusceptible alike to chiding or cajolery. Thus Jim lay pondering, till the little clock on the shelf seemed to say: "Cogewea! Cogewea! Cogewea!" He covered his head with his blankets to shut out the pleasingly wakeful sound. He tried not to think of her; to sleep, but somnolence kept persistently aloof. Amid the darkness he imagined her brilliant eyes ever before him.

The "best rider of the Flathead" was in love.

Jim did not know when he fell asleep. It must have been towards morning, for seemingly he had scarce closed his eyes, when he felt Celluloid shaking him to get up for breakfast.

CHAPTER IV.

COGEWEA HIRES THE TENDERFOOT

Thus his name became a by-word
And a jest among the people;
—*Hiawatha*

THE sun was bursting over the mountains, por-
tending a cloudless day. Cogewea stood at the
gate waiting for Silent Bob to drive up with the
bays, Prince and Jerry. They were going to Polson, to
meet the noon steamer, which was expected to bring her
aged grandmother and her sister Mary. She was holding
the reins of Wanawish. The hack would be crowded
on the return trip, so she had decided to ride the spirited steed for the first time since the encounter with the
rattler. The horse had had a long rest and no one but
Jim seemed to know why. He saw her as he was passing and there was a note of concern in his voice as he
hailed:

"Hell-o! Sis. Goin' to ride Wanawish?"

"Why shouldn't I ride my own horse?"

"Oh! I—I thought—Let me ride him first."

"You mind your own business!" she snapped

"Aw! come now, little squaw! You know that there
hoss——"

"Is too gentle for the 'best rider of the Flathead' to
trifle with," she laughed derisively.

Further remonstrance on Jim's part was prevented
by Carter, who approached from the barn and said:

"I wish, Cogewea, that while you are in town you
would see if you can find a man for me. We are short
handed and must have another rider. Rodeo is leaving
within a few days."

"So Rodeo is hittin' the breeze!" with a twinkling
eye. "Well, that is too bad! The ranch is to lose its
only blond cow-puncher. How will it do to bring you a
light haired substitute?"

38

"Now Cogewea! don't start some of your absurd stunts!" he rejoined impatiently. "I need an extra rider and he should be an expert. Do you know one when you see him?"

"Sure! They are always——"

"Then get a man who can ride without 'choking' the horn. You know the great number of horses we have to break in compliance with my sales contract, and I want a rider of experience. Look around and secure a man and show the kind of boss you will make. Maybe I will create you foreman, when Jim becomes my partner."

Cogewea caught the wink that was intended for Jim only, and the mantling blood suffused her olive cheek to a darker hue. Her eyes flashed as she retorted:

"And, understanding the basic conditions of such partnership, I agree to accept the foreman's place when proffered."

Jim's heart sank, but his bronzed face betrayed no emotion as he turned and silently walked away.

Silent Bob dashed from the barn-yard with the prancing bays champing at the bit. It taxed the skill and strength of the sturdy driver to hold them in check. Cogewea climbed to the seat at his side, bringing up Wanawish by the hackamore. They were soon spinning miles behind them, Bringo skulking forbidden in the wake. They struck the sloping wagon grade up the gulch, leading to the little town of some five hundred inhabitants, consisting of both whites and half-bloods. The outskirts of this reservation "city" was dotted with Kootenai Indian (1) camps, where the cowboys and the "breeds" played monte with the tribesmen on the quiet; where also the irrepressible bootlegger was busy selling the natives an inferior grade of firewater at from five to ten dollars the quart. The penalty for this is a fine and possible imprisonment, when caught, but the lure of excessive profit is strong and there are always unscrupulous whites who engage in this debauchery of the child-minded Indian. Despite the efforts of the usually alert officers of the U. S. Special Indian Service, whose business it is to ferret out these miserable law-defying creatures, the traffic flourishes. Ofttimes the victim of appetite will give his last pony for a single drink. When drunk, his family suffers. The wife with her little pappooses deserts the tepee for the brush, or any place where she may find protection. Well does she know his beastly nature when under the crazing effects of rum. He is more brute than human. His inherent fighting spirit seems to possess his every emotion. He will toy with any deadly weapon he may find and will use it without hesitation. Only occasionally are there exceptions to this rule. A few become maudlin and cry over fancied or actual grievances. This is the heritage of the white men's civilization, forced—like the opium traffic of China—upon a weaker people by the bayonets of commercial conquest. It overshadows all of the good resultant from the "higher" life.

The sun mounted higher in a hot, brazen sky, beating down upon the travelers with ever increasing intensity. The hack came in view of the Flathead Lake, shimmering in the distance like molten glass.

Cogewea, though happy in the expectation of meeting her near kindred, was pensive. She was thinking of the old grandmother, who, like many of her contemporaries, had until this trip, declined riding a railway train. Where there was so much clang and clatter, there must be a corresponding jarring and shaking, which she could not endure. Thus the primitive and the modern are ever at variance; neither comprehending or understanding the other. The Stemteemä knew many interesting tales of the past; legends finer than the myths of the Old World; but few of them known to the reading public and none of them understood. Whether portraying the simple deductive ideals of a primitive mind delving into the shadowy past, or constructive of the hopes of a future yet unborn, the philosophy is a sacred one. Ever suspicious of the whites and guardedly zealous in the secrecy of their ancient lore, seldom do the older tribesmen disclose ancestral erudition, and when they do, their mysteries are not comprehended. The young people, as a rule, are interested in their tribal legends only to the extent of "cramming" some ardent writer with palpable absurdities. They have progressed beyond the pristine days. The airy tepee has given place to the stuffy houses of their conquerors; their habiliments changed and the native wild foods supplanted by those of commerce.

Over these things Cogewea was meditating. The Stemteemä had adhered to some of the old-time customs—tepee and ground-couch—moccasins and ankle-wraps. But she was lingering pathetically in the sunset of a closing era. The rising generation was educating, while the half-bloods, brought up more like the white children, enjoyed some business advantages over their full-blooded relations. But then, they were just a go-between people, shut within their own diminutive world. There seemed no place for them among either race. The Indians were unduly suspicious of them, while the whites arrogantly ignored them. Their lives darkened by the mixing of the two peoples closed all avenues to social attainments.

The Silent one, his hands full with the bays, was non-communicative and Cogewea began musing half-aloud:

"Yes, we are between two fires, the Red and the White. Our Caucasian brothers criticize us as a shiftless class, while the Indians disown us as abandoning our own race. We are maligned and traduced as no one but we of the despised 'breeds' can know. If permitted, I would prefer living the white man's way to that of the reservation Indian, but he hampers me. I appreciate my meagre education, but I will *never* disown my mother's bloood. Why should I do so? Though my skin is of the tawny hue, I am not ashamed. The Great Spirit willed it so, and His ways are immutable and not to be censured. The trail has been laid for me, the rough, stony path of life. May I do my duty well in the sight of the Deity of my ancestors. There can be no......"

Further musings were cut short by her companion, who, with a supreme effort expostulated:

"Aw! come outen it! I'm a thinkin' yo' all'd make a good preacher woman. Them there kind what wants ter be made perlice wimin an' jedges an' th' main push. Wantin' to wear th' breeches an' boss th' hull shebang. I hater......"

"What do you mean?" Cogewea laughed, her mood instantly changing. "A missionary, a police matron, or what?"

"Why! them there wimmin what go out an' make speeches an' everythin' else. Yo' know what's allers in th' noospapers, 'bout their doin's. Ev'ry paper a feller parooses says somethin' 'bout people a throwin' rotten aigs at 'em. I fergit that there name they call 'em, but yo' oughter know. I hater talk so much 'bout—"

"Oh! I know what you are referring to. *Suffragettes.*"

"Y-a-s! that's 'em. People a bowlin' aigs at 'em."

"And that is why you want me to turn suffragette, so you can pelt me with stale eggs?"

"N-no! I didn't mean that there way. I was jes' a kiddin'; 'cause yo'r a dam' good win' jammer."

"Well! now! I don't know whether to regard that as a compliment, joke or a slur."

"Aw! I was only jokin'. Can't yo' take a tumble? I hater have ter 'splain so much; I hater get so tired a talkin'."

"Yes, I tumble. But you *must* be fatigued after such a prolonged jamboree. I never heard you make so continued a speech."

They both laughed.

Silent Bob had been with the Horseshoe Bend family so long that he had become as one of them. He at least liked Cogewea, and if he really loved her, it is doubtful if he ever could have brought his words to such a declaration, although the boys contended that he had done so, as previously described. But Bob understood her perhaps, better than did any of his companions. He knew that the girl meant right, despite her odd, "for-

ward'' ways. And Cogewea admired the droll Southerner, for his crude, manly qualities; but she seemed to
prefer Jim, notwithstanding she was oftimes irritated
because of his attentions. Yet, after scolding him, she
always forgave him. She never could get the Westerner out of humor with her; nor could she long hold resentment.

Arriving in Polson, Bob drove directly to the boat
landing. The steamer came gliding in, the passengers
thronging the deck. Cogewea discerned her aged grandparent and her sister Mary, standing apart from the
others; pathetic in social isolation. The old squaw
was wearing her semi-civilized garb. A brilliant colored handkerchief was bound about her head, while the
slightly stooped shoulders were wrapped in a plaid
shawl. Wampum and ear ornaments were in evidence,
and beaded moccasins encased her small, shapely foot.

Mary McDonald, known as the ''shy-girl'', was as tall
as her sister, Cogewea, lithe and slender. Her skin was
of the fairer type, inherited from her white father. Jet
was her hair as the raven's wing, while her eyes were of
the deepest blue; with long, dark sweeping lashes, which
emphasized the native beauty of her strongly featured
face. Her Indian coyness and modesty of manner, had
not been broken by her convent schooling. Her dress
was orange and becoming to her trim figure. She loved
the ambitious Cogewea, with a deep, sisterly love, although she had often been embarrassed by her indepen-
dence of action and speech.

Scarce was the gang-plank in place, when Cogewea
rushed forward to assist Mary with the baggage, leaving the none too strong grandmother unencumbered.
The little troop, as it filed ashore, attracted no attention
from the assembled loungers, but there was one passenger who observed its individuals with mingled curiosity
and disappointment. He was a medium sized, rather
handsome man of about thirty four, light complexioned,
thin lipped and with a cold, calculating grey eye. His
dress was that of a business man rather than the sport.
Fresh from a great eastern city, he had expected to see

the painted and blanketed aborigine of history and romance; but instead, he had only encountered this miniature group of half-bloods and one ancient squaw. Observing Bob with the team and attracted by his generally "range" appearance, he accosted him, expressing his vexation and disgust for the writers who had beguiled him to the "wild and woolly."

"Yo' can strike 'em back on the reservation whar they wear feathers an' scalps," answered Bob with an inward chuckle, "but yo' don't fin' th' gen-u-ine article a cavortin' in a bus'lin' concentration like this here miterpolish."

"Indeed!" exclaimed the stranger with sudden interest. "I would like to see some of them. I grew tired of the tameness of city life, and came out here hoping to secure employment on some large stock farm. I want to rough it a while among Indians and cowboys."

His allusion to a "farm" branded him as a truly *verdant* tenderfoot; and Silent Bob's eyes twinkled as he rejoined:

"If yo' don't have no 'ticular difference 'tween *farmin'* and *ranchin'*, yo' might strike a job with my boss."

"What is the difference? I supposed that farming and ranching were just the same?"

"Y-a-a-s! a farm is whar they keep hawgs, an' milk a pen full of cows an' feed calfs outen a bucket an' get milk blowed all over yo' clo'es. A ranch is whar they keep hosses an' cattle an' run 'em on th' range, an' roun' 'em up in corrals an' bran' 'em with a hot iron. On a farm they hire tame white men an' sunny school- teachers. On a ranch they have wil' Injuns an' wil'er range riders; all a wearin' big hats an' silver spurs; an' a totin' of a six-shooter or two, with maybe notches in th' han'els. It's sho' th' life all right, with mos'ly b'ar steak an' coyote dessert."

"Where is this ranch?" the "verdant" questioned delightedly. "I want to see your boss."

"Outen some ways on th' reservation. But yo' can see an' confab th' boss right here."

"Where?" and the Easterner glanced eagerly about.

"I do not see him."

"Naw!....him? Who said yo' could?"

"Why! you did!"

"Yo' have another guess a comin', stranger. I said yo' could see th' boss an' yo' can if yo' aint blin'. Aw! Hell! I hater be aller time a speelin'; I hater get so tired——Say! Cogewea!" he called as the group of three approached, "this here's a feller what wants to go out on a ranch; an' bein' as yo' is already good as fo'man, yo' better take him."

Cogewea's cheeks burned at the reference to "foreman." She had not supposed that Bob had overheard the morning conversation at the gate. Smothering her confusion, she turned and addressed the stranger, noting his general appearance.

"Are you wanting work?"

"W-h! yes!" he stammered in surprise, lifting his hat politely. " I had thought of farm employment, but since the gentleman has explained the difference existing between farm and ranch, I think that I would be pleased with the latter."

Cogewea glanced at Bob, who winked slyly. The old spirit of mischief took possession of her, as she again turned to the applicant:

"Can you ride?"

"Er-yes!" he replied with embarrassment, having in mind his childhood days when he rode the plow team to and from the field in central New York.

"All right! forty per, grub and bunk. You can 'bump' out on the 'chuck.' We are going to start now."

With this, Cogewea handed her aged kinswoman into the rear seat with Mary, and turned to mount Wanawish standing a few feet away.

"Throw yo' grip under th' seat an' climb up an' roost with me," drawled Bob, with foot on the brakebar.

The stranger did as directed and they were off. The drive home was uneventful. Wanawish seemingly had forgotten his escapade of a few weeks previous, and cantered contentedly in the wake of the hack. The Easterner, after a fruitless endeavor to draw Bob into

conversation, subsided; and save for the occasional low
monotone colloquy carried on by the Indian women in
their native tongue, the journey was made in silence.

CHAPTER V.

THE TENDERFOOT'S BRONCHO RIDING

The trail's a lane! the trail's a lane!
How comes it, pard of mine?
Within a day it. slipped away
And hardly left a sign;
—Badger Clark

THE morning repast was over before John Carter could find opportunity to speak with Cogewea about having employed Alfred Densmore, the "tenderfoot." The boys were at the barn, saddling their mounts preparatory to chasing the horses from the "wings" into the main corral. Carter still lingered at the house. The girl knew all too well what was brewing and had avoided meeting him the evening before. They met on the veranda and she was cornered. His clean shaven face appeared unusually stern as he spoke:

"Cogewea! you should have known better than to hire that tenderfoot. I wish that I had gone myself. It is just like a woman any way! When you ask them to do any thing of a business nature they always make a mess of it. Are you ever going to grow up? Will you ever be a woman.... a full fledged woman of mature judgment.... and quit these baby ways of yours? Will you ever cease your mischievous and annoying pranks?"

"Why John!" she exclaimed with well feigned surprise. "You talk just as if I were an irresponsible; a mere infant. I notice that I am as tall as my honored brother-in-law; and so far as growing up is concerned, I don't believe in becoming old. Only once are we young. Bask in the morning sun while the dew still sparkles, is my philosophy."

"Yes! that is right, too; but frivolity and business can not be ridden with the same saddle. You should have

47

procured some one who knows something about breaking broncs. Why! that fellow will commit suicide rangling those wild horses. I simply leave the entire deal in your hands. Should he happen to kill himself, you will be held responsible.''

"Oh! quit your jawin'. Let's call it square and smoke the peace pipe.''

"I am willing, but never let it happen again. I wish now that I had asked Bob. He would have done better. What will I do with a crippled man or a dead one? I'll have the expense of burying the guy.''

"I will foot the bills and give you a mortgage on my allotment. Besides,'' she continued mockingly, "I only acted within my rights as your prospective foreman.''

Carter left the veranda partly placated. He could not remain angry with his jocund sister-in-law.

Cogewea stood watching Bill and Bob drive the horses into the main corral. Jim was still at the barn door brushing his horse's legs. He lingered thinking that she would come to him as of old; but instead, she went directly to the corral, where Densmore sat on the fence absent-mindedly whittling a small stick, smooth and round. He was waiting to ride his first horse. He was hardly satisfied with his surroundings. Where were those picturesque Indians that he was promised to meet? Instead, he had been lured into a nest of half bloods, whom he had always understood to be the inferior degenerates of two races. He could not fathom the "forward" girl with the musical, though unpronounceable name. What was she? He had had much to do with women and was a reader of character, but this one was unfathomable. What would his refined mother and sisters say, could they see him in his present surroundings?

A slight rustle at his side caused him to turn. There stood the "forward" girl on the third rail from the bottom, her brown arms over the top rail.

"You look lonesome, Mr. Densmore," she said without formality, "and I thought to come and have a chat with you.''

At this freedom, the tenderfoot had nearly toppled from his seat with astonishment. He had yet to learn the ways of a plain's cowgirl. An introduction on the range might be in keeping among the more conventional whites, but at the "H-B" such formality was unknown. The Easterner's embarrassment passed instantly and tipping his hat, he answered:

"I am glad that you take an interest in the welfare of a stranger, for our former meeting was of the most casual; Miss...."

"Aw! shake that miss! Just call me every day Cogewea."

"You certainly have a very romantic name, but I'm not sure that I can speak it."

"Co-ge-wea. Cogewea. It's simple."

Densmore, after many attempts, succeeded in pronouncing the Indian cognomen, and then asked for her surname. The girl's black eyes twinkled, as she answered amusedly:

"I never mentioned any second name. All my friends call me Cogewea, and that is what you will call me if you want to be a pal of mine. It means *chipmunk* in our language."

"I think it suits you just splendidly; Miss...."

"Aw! drop that Miss! It's Cogewea or nothing. You said that you could ride, Mr. Densmore?"

"Y-e-s! Please call me just plain Alfred; for I prefer it. I will try to master that wood-land name of yours."

"Alright! But say!" was the rather anxious query. "Can you ride a genuine bronc?"

"W-hy--a--yes," was the stammered reply. The tenderfoot supposed "bronc" to be but a western phrase for donkey.

"Where did you ride?"

"I dropped down here from Canada," was the careless reply.

Cogewea's intentions were, when questioning him, to warn him against the outlaw which she knew would be saddled for him. But when he said that he could ride a

bronc and that he came from Canada, she almost laughed outright. Somehow she now wished that he could
ride. How it would surprise John and the boys if he
vied with them. She knew that some very good riders
came from Canada, but she did not dream that he was
directly from eastern Ontario. She supposed that he
was from British Columbia.

While Cogewea and the Easterner were thus conversing, the boys were planning sport at the expense of the
tenderfoot. Jim's swarthy face darkened a shade when
he saw the two perched on the fence engaged in friendly
conversation. He was unconsciously biting his scanty
mustache. Something in his breast seemed to hurt. He
thought that Cogewea was taking too much interest in
the stranger and he would humiliate him.

Ignoring the stirrup, the foreman seized the saddle
horn from the right—Indians invariably mount from
the right side—and bounded gracefully into the saddle.
Touching the heavy silver mounted spurs to his horse's
flanks, the animal trained, went into the air, bucking
for the distance of a hundred yards and then settled into a smooth lope; ascending the slope to the upper end
of the wing where the boys were cutting out some of the
wild horses to be driven into the main corral.

Densmore looked on with surprise at this exhibition.
He wondered if that was what they called a "bronc"
instead of a donkey. If so, the performance seemed
easy. Jim was a cool and graceful rider and to the
Easterner the task of remaining in the saddle did not
appear one of difficulty.

"Say boys!" Jim spoke in an undertone, "we're
goin' to have a little circus of our own. We'll saddle
Croppy for that there swell guy. White shirts and
stand-up collars don't go on this here ranch. We'll
have fun to the finish. He'll be lucky if he gets off with
a skinned nose and elbows. His high bridge will be
scratched some. We'll see some saddle chokin', eh! pardner?" turning to Silent Bob to second him in his purpose. The Virginian dragged:

"I kinder hater see the pore feller throwed; I hater dig a six-foot grave this hot weather."

"We'll help yo' dig it," volunteered Celluloid Bill.

"The feller said he could ride," interrupted Rodeo Jack. "I asked him an' he said with that there polished manner of his'n: 'Why cer-tain-ly!' An' he comes from that there King George country an' maybe he has a little s'prise up his sleeve for us bronc twisters."

"Hell! We'll chance it." rejoined Jim. "No rider ever wears a stiff caddy; and Croppy hates a plug-hat worse nor pizen. John said to give him an old skate to ride, but he aint a goin' to loco our little show. He's gone 'cross the river in the skiff to see that there geezar over there." Jim waved his arm towards the opposite side of the Pend'd'Oreille, where another stockman lived.

The horses were driven into the main corral. They were of every size and color, from common cayuse to thoroughbreds. The poor frightened animals trampled one another unmercifully; their eyes wild with fright. Two colts were killed by the mad pounding hoofs circling the enclosure. Jim rode into the center of the corral. He swung his rawhide rope and shot it over the head of Croppy, the far famed Flathead outlaw that very few riders dared mount. The horse reared, plunging and fighting hard; but the experienced cowpuncher soon had him closely "snubbed" to his saddle horn. The other boys hurrying to his aid, the frenzied animal was soon blindfolded.

Cogewea now decided to stop them from saddling the horse, but before she reached them, they were putting the last hitch to the cinch. She had hesitated too long. The stranger had touched a cord in her womanly heart and she half repented the part she had taken in the game. But it was now too late. Densmore was donning chaps and spurs proffered by Celluloid Bill. It would be better for the tenderfoot to risk death in the saddle than to face the constant taunts which he would be compelled to endure should he prove a quitter. Jim's voice was rather derisive as he called.

"Hey there! pardner. Here's your hoss. Better come scratch this here feller."

The "pardner" hesitated. He felt unusually shaky. Cogewea with her quick eye noticed it and said unconcernedly.

"What's wrong?"

The Easterner did not attempt to answer, but braced up with a wan smile. The girl wished that she had warned him in time. But now what could she do? She was well aware that the boys would make life intolerable for him did he dare back down at the last moment. Jim again called.

"Come on pardner, be a sport! Put your spurs to this here cayuse. He's tired waitin' for you."

Densmore walked across the corral and stopped near the outlaw. Jim continued to sneer.

"Are you 'fraid of this here old plug?"

"Aw! don't be a quitter!" Rodeo bantered. "Come on an' ride an' show us some of yo' Canadian stunts. I thought yo' said yo' was a broncho twister of the North country."

"I did say that I could ride," retorted Densmore with flushed temples, "but I did not say that I could ride a horse that requires four men to handle."

"He's gettin' col' feet," drawled Bob. "Aw come on. Don't pike on us, or we'll hafter get Cogewea to break yo' cayuse fer yo'.I hater see the little gal a showin' yo' how to ride; I hater see yo' a missin' so good a thin'. "

At this sally the boys all laughed. Densmore glanced at Cogewea, who was also smiling. She had climbed back on the fence out of possible danger. He now determined to ride if it took the last breath. He stepped to the horse whose flanks were quivering with excitement and whose open mouth was foaming. Croppy was backed against the corral, while the rest of the horses from the opposite side of the enclosure looked on in wonder.

Densmore placed his foot in the stirrup, but he was shaking like a leaf in a summer breeze. However he was not going to back out amid the jeers and sneers of those Westerners. He found the other stirrup. Jim pulled the handkerchief-blind from Croppy's eyes and the boys all leaped aside. The "circus" was of short duration. The maddened horse bawled and bucked as only an outlaw can. Densmore grabbed the saddle horn and held on with all his strength. The riders yelled in a chorus.

"Let 'er go there feller! Don't choke 'er!"

The rider went catapulting through the air and landed in a crumpled heap in the corral dust. Cogewea jumped from her perch and was at his side before any of the boys had made a move. She tenderly lifted his bleeding head to her knee. A long gash showed above the temple, from which the blood flowed freely. His right arm was limp. His face was colorless and the girl believed him dead. The riders rushed forward. She looked up to meet the eyes of Jim. Her own gleamed with scorn; as she faced him a moment before finding speech.

"James LaGrinder! this is all your work and you will pay dearly for it too. You knew that Croppy was a brute—an outlaw—and you knew that this man could not ride. You had no business getting him on the devil."

"Why—I—I—I thought he could ride! the d—"

"You hurry and get some water as quick as God will let you. I think this man is dead. *Hurry!*" she called after him in an anxious tone.

Jim hardly heard the last words. He was running down the sloping river bank with a tin can in his hand. He dipped it in the stream, but the water gushed out from the torn side. He threw it aside with an oath. Taking his new sombrero, he scooped the water and started up the hill on a run. Evidently perturbed, his tanned face was immobile. He felt that he was the cause of the tenderfoot's death and many things flashed through his mind as he ran. He had meant no serious harm to the man; but his jealousy had prompted him to saddle Croppy instead of an ordinary bronc. His joy was great when reaching the little group, to find that the Easterner had opened his eyes. His face was drawn with agony, but he uttered no complaint. Jim held the brimming hat to his lips. He drank deeply. Cogewea bathed his head and face and bound his temples with the silk handkerchief which the foreman tore from his own neck. She ordered him to ride for the old doctor, who was homesteading some miles away. He mounted and rode as if the injured man were his own brother.

It was Cogewea who commanded.

When the doctor arrived, he found the right arm broken, which he set and put in splints. He stitched the wide gash over the temple without a moan from the patient. The tenderfoot, though he could not ride, showed no weakness in the presence of his tormentors. Then the kind hearted doctor left him, telling Cogewea how to dress the head-wound and that he was going to depend on her to nurse the gentleman. Cogewea, feeling remorse and in a measure responsible for his condition and determining to make amends so far as in her power, accepted the charge gladly. She later came in with the riders for her share of scolding from John Carter; but she took it good naturedly.

Notwithstanding it was jealousy that prompted Jim to go to the extreme in "breaking" the tenderfoot and it pained him that Cogewea would be so constantly in the injured man's company as nurse, he did everything possible to render the invalid's lot more tolerable. Governed as much by the unwritten Indian law of justice as by that of the White man, he promptly met the doctor's fees. But the other riders insisted on sharing this expense. Rodeo observed:

"It's a durn sight more comfor'able than helpin' Bob dig that there grave th' guy don't need."

Rodeo agreed to remain on the ranch until the "bronchos" were all broken and tamed.

CHAPTER VI.

THE FOURTH OF JULY

And history a tale has gained
To please the younger ears—
A race of kings that rose and reigned
And passed in fifty years.
—*Badger Clark.*

HEY! get up there! you fellers!" yelled Jim as he yanked the blankets off Rodeo Jack and Celluloid Bill. "You ain't goin' sleep all day when Fourth of July comes but once a year?"

Rodeo stretched, and yawned sleepily as he got from his bunk, growling:

"Durn it! didn't know 'twas so late. Sun shinin' a ready an' cayuses not out for final trainin' *Wough!*"

Hurrying on his clothes, he glanced around to see Bill with head covered—evidently to shut out the sunlight—with no effort at rising. Banging him hard with a pillow, he screeched:

"Get up here, feller! Yo' can't 'spect our hosses to win in no races today if yo' don't hustle an' give 'em some little exercisin'."

"Gee whiz! Can't yo' let a feller sleep?" mumbled Bill drowsily. "To th' loco with th' hosses! They'll win anyhow in the buckaroo 'formances. Yo' may bet yo' hat on that fac'."

Jim and Rodeo were busy at the wash stand, furnished with a single tin basin, a towel of uncertain color and a broken mirror; the frame retaining but a small portion of the original glass. As Bill donned his clothing, he caught sight of Bob still in his bunk, and turned to his tomentors with the plaint:

"Say! yo' fellers! Yo' yanked me out an' yo' don't get Bob up. I see where I ain't got no friends. Get up there, Bob! I won't let no galoot snooze while I

55

have to train hosses this time o' mornin', even 'tis Fourth
of July.''

With this, Bill rose from the side of his bunk with
only one boot on. He strode across to Silent Bob and
tore the covers away. The Southerner moaned in his
slow voice:

''Aw! gwan! I hater have my mo'nin' nap spilt for
a little thin' as a Fo'th o' July cel'bration; I hater come
home ter night drunk an' sleep with my spurs on.''

''Yes;'' rejoined Jim, '' if the Kootenais don't win
'em from you at monte; or you don't loose 'em a scratchin' them there broncs' in the big doin's today. They're
goin' have some Fourth this year. Printed bills big
'nough to cover your bunk. Prizes for the best bronc
twister; the ladies and squaw races and a great Injun
war dance. Gee! boys! Let's hurry and get things
sailin'. Must win some money from them there swell city
chaps. I'm goin' to the barn and rub Diamond down.
Sis will ride him in a try this mornin'. Wants to get
'quainted with him before handlin' him in the races
this afternoon. She must win! and she ain't the one
that can't do it, either.''

Jim hurried to the barn and was surprised to find
Cogewea already there, waiting for him. He had supposed that she was not yet up. Procuring a bottle of
Indian herb-liniment, he proceeded to bathe with brisk
rubbing, the legs of Diamond; a racer widely known as
the ''Bay Devil.'' He had been bought by Carter on
a recent trip to the Bitter Root country, and at a very
fancy price. The horse was not used to ''wimin folks'',
as Jim expressed it, and at Cogewea's approach, he arched his neck, his eyes dilating with excitement. She petted
him, but it was not for the first time. She had attempted being friendly with him on several occasions and
was succeeding slowly. He was still nervous and showed impatience at the rustling of her skirt.

The mettlesome Bay trembled as Jim placed Cogewea's
saddle on his back and brought him into the open. He
held the bit while the girl lighty mounted, then sprang
to one side as the fiery steed reared and was off like

an arrow. Without the aid of stirrup, the lithe Westerner sprang to his own saddle and was away after the
flying racer. He did not come up with Cogewea, till
she reined in at the head of the gulch, ready for the
trial dash over the temporary training track. The great
Bay knew! He was pawing the ground restlessly;
champing at the restraining bit. Jim gazed at the picturesque rider admiringly. The black tresses reaching
far down her back, undulated in billowy waves as her
steed pranced and cavorted from side to side. Her cheeks
were ruddy from the morning air, her eyes brilliant
and sparkling.

"Well, when are we going to get started?" she exclaimed impatiently. "What are you looking at me for?
I'm not the boss!"

"Now Sis, don't be so mean! I'm just a wonderin'
what a looker you are with them there fine cheeks this
mornin'."

"Aw! come off your perch! Quit kiddin'! Let's
hurry! I have so much to get ready before we start for
town."

"Alright! You run the Devil for all he's got and we'll
see how far he beats the White Star. But the Star is a
plumb good cayuse and believe me, he moves like a
shootin' sky-meteor."

"You signal when we are to go. Easy! easy! there
old boy," patting a velvety shoulder. "Save your
strength for the flying course."

The Bay was reeking with perspiration; while the
White Star closely watched his mate. The grey seemed
to understand that he was being matched against a foe
worthy of his metal. Bringing the steeds abreast Jim
warned:

"All ready! *Go!*"

Cogewea scarce heard the command, as the horses
leaped away. A less expert rider would have been hurled from her saddle. Out the smooth track the racers
stretched themselves. Objects along the wayside seemed to swing by at an astonishing speed. The road was

a gliding ribbon of earth. Cogewea's Indian love for exciting sport was augmented when she felt the hot breath of the grey at her stirrup. The quirt hanging at her saddle bow was now brought into use and at the sting of the lash, the Bay Devil forged ahead. Again the nose of the Star began to lap the middle of the Bay, and again was the whip made use of. But all too late! The goal was passed without any retrievement of lost ground. Jim circled, pulling up to Cogewea as she checked her mount. The "best rider of the Flathead" laughed in glee as he accosted her:

"Well, Sis! who won? Twenty yards more and the Star would a beat that there brag thoroughbred.I told you the Star's a greased streak, though a busted up cayuse. Used to be the fastest on the range and he's won lots of dough for me. Kinda spoiled him by usin' him for a cow hoss, but he remembers old traits and he don't take dirt from many on the track. You can ride him today if you wish. He's gentler than that there hoss and you know what he can do. Better let old Jim handle the Bay Devil at the crowded track. It takes the best rider of the Flathead to—"

"In-*deed!* You think I can't ride a real race horse? Guess you have forgotten how I bested you to the tune of an even hundred at the races when I was home on vacation two years ago. But maybe that was before you was known as the 'best rider'."

"Now Sis, don't pout! I didn't mean anything. Am only anxious for you to win the ladies race today. Want to see you put it over them there high toned white gals who think they can beat the Injun gals a ridin.' If you ride White Star, I'll bet my summer's wages on you and I know durn' well he'll come out in the lead."

"Say, Jim! I'll ride the Star in the squaw race," exclaimed the girl in elation. "I'm part Injun and can participate in that as well as in the ladies race. They can't stop me from riding in both races, can they? If there's any difference between a *squaw* and a *lady*, I

want to know it. I am going to pose as both for this
day."

"That's a go, little squaw! The Devil in the ladies
race; the Star in the squaw race. Come! let's get
home."

Turning their mounts, they rode back to the corrals
on a slow trot. A curl of smoke from the kitchen flue
denoted activity in that department, while the boys
were all busy at the barn. Bill was giving his saddler
training exercise at the end of a rope; Rodeo was braid-
ing his cayuse's tail, decorating it with ribbons. Bob
was leading the two bays up from the river bank where
he had taken them to water; all harnessed and with
manes and tails gaudy with tricolored streamers. Leaving the racer with Jim at the barn, Cogewea hastened to
the house to help her sister prepare the morning meal.
She set the table, when Julia said to her:

"I wish that you would get the Stemteemä ready.
She insists on going and says that this was why she came
so far to visit us; to see the Fourth of July celebration
and the Kootenais give their war dance. I know you
will not mind going horseback. The hack is too small
for all of us and Mary should be with the grandmother."

"Sure!" was the genial response "I'd just as
soon go in the saddle; in fact prefer it. So the Stemteemä is going? Well, there is class to her."

"Oh! Cogewea! Do not speak lightly of poor grandmother."

"Why! I'm not saying any thing mean about her.
Was just admiring her grit. I know why she is going.
It is not for the firecracker celebration of the Declaration of Independence---which is not for our race---but
for the Indian *pom-pom*. She is thinking of the olden
days when she was younger than now. The joy of her
heart is participating in the war dance and the medicine
dance." (1)

These ceremonies, held sacred by the more primitive
tribesmen, are now, shame to say, commercialized and

performed for a pittance contributed by white spectators who regard all in the light of frivolity.

Breakfast over, the lunch basket was filled and the
children hurriedly dressed. Bob drove the bays to the
gate and yelled:

"Hurry! yo' fellers. I hater be late at them there
races; I hater be last at th' grub pile."

Cogewea came out and informed him that they must
first go to the tepee for the aged Stemteemä who was
waiting, as Mrs. Carter was not quite ready. She sprang
to the seat by his side and they were soon at the lodge.
The grandmother was waiting. Her luggage consisted
of several blankets, a bag of dried meat, berries and
roots. Her eyes beamed with childish delight, as they
drove back to the house for the rest of the party.

As the hack rolled away leaving a dense trail of dust,
Cogewea turned back into the house. Densmore was
lying on a couch, too badly shaken to undertake the trip
She gave him instructions in the care of his wounds. He
was not suffering, but he appeared rather depressed and
she was half tempted to stay and minister to his wants.

But the call of the races was loud in her ear. She turned to the window and watched a string of cowboys from
other ranches passing. Some were leading horses while
others had only their mounts They were several hundred yards away, when Jim came from the barn leading Diamond, the racer. She tripped back to her patient, bade him a cheery good bye and hurried from the
room.

Cogewea was at the gate when the foreman rode up
and dismounted. He held Diamond while she mounted,
the horse surging at the bit. The Westerner, leading
Croppy whom he intended riding in the "outlaw" contest, vaulted to his own saddle and they were off. Cogewea was unusually silent, Jim doing most of the talking. When they reached the big flat, she said impulsive-
ly:

"Let's gallop! I hate to ride slow through here. This
vast expanse seems in keeping with swift hoof-beats."

"Yes, but not too fast," admonished the more prudent Jim. "Remember we're ridin' our kale winners, but a little change of gait kinda routs a hoss's walkin' mussels."

Striking an easy canter, several miles were passed before rein was drawn at the foot of an ascending grade. Reaching the crest of the hill overlooking the little town they saw the people gathered in hundreds on its outskirts. The yells of the range-riders came wafted on the breeze, while the scene was enlivened by the silently stalking, gaudily blanketed Indian. Jim dismounted to tighten saddle cinches before descending; this done, they were soon mingling with the crowd. But the "H-B" boys were not to be seen. Entering their horses for the various sports, they had sought the monte games or gone in quest of the bootlegger.

Cogewea entered Diamond for the ladies race and White Star for the squaw race. She found her sisters with the children at one of the ice cream stands, enjoying the cooling luxury after their hot, sweltery drive. Stemteemä was with a large number of Indians, men and women, who were engaged in native gambling games under a long, improvised shed roofed with pine and cottonwood boughs. Beneath this shelter, the dancing would take place later, to be continued far into the night.

CHAPTER VII.

THE "LADIES'" AND THE "SQUAW" RACES

Where, in the valley fields and fruits,
Now hums the lively street,
We milled a mob of fighting brutes,
Amid the grim mesquite.

—*Badger Clark*

"HURRY, Sis!" called Jim, as Cogewea joined him where he was holding the Bay Devil. "Race is on in a few minutes and you want Diamond handled a little 'fore startin'. Ride through the crowd to the track and get him used to the yellin' and shootin'-crackers."

He helped the girl to mount, her face showing but slightly, the heart's throb of anticipation. A riding habit of blue corduroy fitted her slender form admirably. Red, white and blue ribbons fastened her hair, which streaming to the racer's back, lent a picturesque wildness to her figure. Securing the stirrups, she requested Jim to tighten her spur-straps, as they seemed a trifle loose, adding:

"We just must win this race from the whites. See! the Webster girls are among the mounted ladies and they have mighty good horses. But if any of them beat me, they will sure have to run for it."

"My 'spirit-power' tells me you're goin' come out first in this here race," replied Jim solemnly, as he gave a final tug at a refractory spur-strap. "Signs all favorable for winnin'."

Cogewea was assigned place abreast the other riders, her number placing her on the outer circle or flank of the field. Verona, the eldest Webster girl, was a noted rider and her jet mount, known as the "Black Snake", had never lost a race. This was the first match between the two famous riders, and as Cogewea fell into line,

62

Verona, who had second place, stared at her contemptu-
ously and spoke in a voice loud enough to be heard by
those standing near:
  "Why is this *squaw* permitted to ride?   This is a
ladies race!"
  Her companions were unanimous that it was a gross
outrage and that they should protest.   Stung by the
biting insult, Cogewea retorted:
  "Perhaps I am allowed because no *'ladies'* of the sil-
very-hue have entered and this race is being tolerated
only that the audience may not be wholly disappointed."
  Further colloquy was cut short by the stentorian
voice of the starter, as he raised pistol in air:
  "*A-l-l rea-d-y!*" BANG!
  The field was off! and it soon became apparent that
the actual contest was to be between the two mighty
racers.   For the first quarter, the Black led the Bay,
by a full length.   In the next quarter, the Bay crept
ahead until they were running neck and neck.   The
white rider plied the lash and the gallant Black respond-
ing retrieved in part, the lost ground.   But at a touch
of the spur, the Bay Devil forged along side, where,
despite the fierce scourging by the white rider, he hung
like a Nemesis.   Soon he was a half-neck in the lead,
when Verona, maddened at the thought of being beaten
by a presumptuous "squaw", swung her shot-loaded
quirt, evidently designed at disabling Cogewea's bridle
arm.   But the Indian girl's quick eye enabled her to
avoid the heavy swing, and as the next descended, she
caught and wrenched the whip from the frenzied rider's
hand.   Enraged at the brutality of the assault, she
struck with all her force, but the blow falling short,
landed athwart the Black Snake's head.   This slightly
checked his speed and the Bay Devil won by nearly a
full length.
  The "H-B" boys yelled and threw their sombreros in
air as the well matched leaders passed over the chalked-
line, the balance of the field thundering in the rear.
Diamond, the Bay Devil, circled far before his rider

could stop him: and when at last she brought him
about, he was reeking with perspiration and quivering
with exertion and excitement. Jim was there and helped Cogewea to dismount. He blanketed the racer and
led him to the stables, the girl walking at his side.

"By gad! Sis," he exclaimed. "I'm some glad you
won this here race. I knowed the Bay Devil would come
through if only he had a nervy rider like you; my tiny
squaw."

Her eyes sparkled at the compliment, for "squaw"
had not been intended as epithetical. She was silent
and Jim continued:

"You're sure one gritty little Injun, hittin' back at
that there high-toned white gal as you did. The "H-B"
boys are all glad! They saw what she done to you first
and know who's in fault. But the white fellers a back-
in' the Webster hoss are breezin' trouble if the judge
gives you the prize. They have the dough and that's
what talks, but the best rider of the—"

"She struck first and I had a right to defend myself," broke in Cogewea spiritedly. "It made no difference in hitting her horse, for I was ahead anyway.
I had my eyes kinda half shut on account of dust and
coudn't see very well."

The Westerner understood and laughed. Reaching
the stable, he unsaddled the Bay and giving him over
to a care-taker, threw the saddle on White Star.

"Now Sis," he spoke earnestly, "if you win this here
'squaw race, I'll buy you a swell present; cause I'm
goin' double up on bets. I raked home fifty bucks on
the Bay Devil, and it'll be a hundred on the Star. He's
sure some hummer when unwindin', and the way to get
his best, is not to whip. Just pull on reins 'nough to
give him his head, then see the White Star do some me-
teoric shootin'."

"Leave it to me while you may prepare to deliver that
present," was the self-confident reply. "I'm going
over to the Kootenais and rent a buckskin dress. I
have no native costume and this garb would be a dead

give away; for they may kick on me riding this race."
Then mounting, Cogewea cantered to the Kootenai
camp, where she had but little difficulty in securing
a complete tribal dress. Very soon she came from the
tepee in full regalia, her face artistically decorated
with varied paints. The Indian children saw and gig-
gled among themselves. Remounting, she doubled the
bright shawl over her knees, lapping it securely. When
she rode back to the track, the "H-B" boys recognized
her only by the horse.

Proceeding to the grandstand, Cogewea paid her entrance fee of two and a half dollars. Supposing that
the Indian girl did not understand English, the judge
turned to his companion with the remark:

"Some swell looker for a Kootenai squaw, eh?"
Mighty good pickin' for a young feller like you. Wish
I wasn't so badly married! I'd sure keep an eye out
for her. But the Missus would raise a hurry-Cain if
she knowed that I rather like some of the squaws around
here."

The young man's reply was of like sinister import, and
then they began conversing in lowered tones. The
girl's eyes filled with tears, as she turned away; brooding over the constantly light spoken words of the "higher" race regarding her people of the incessant insults
offered the Indian women by the "gentlemen" whites.
She regretted with a pang, the passing of an epoch,
when there were no "superiors" to "guide" her simple
race to a civilization so manifestly dearth of the primitive law of respect for womanhood; substituting in its
stead a social standard permitting the grossest insult
and indignity to the weaker, with the most brazen im-
punity.

Cogewea brought White Star in line with the seven
other cayuses, with their Kootenai, or Pend d'Oreille
women riders. These last were gaudy with silk handkerchiefs bound about their heads, bright shawls, and
with beaded mocassined feet. Cogewea alone was bare-
headed, her raven hair reaching loosely below the sad-

dle cantle. She was met with glances of hatred for
the despised "breed". Some of the Indian men were
still hanging to the restless racers, as their wives or
sisters made secure their wraps and settled more firmly
in the saddles. The audience lined either side of the
track; on the one the whites clamoring vociferously, on
the other the Indians sedately silent.

The eight horses moved prancing to the place of starting. Cogewea was assigned position near the centre
of the group, where White Star manifested unusual
spirit, causing more or less annoyance to the other riders. One of the Kootenai girls turned to her and spoke
sharply in good English:

"You have no right to be here! You are half-white!
This race is for Indians and not for *breeds*!"

Cogewea made no reply, but she was overwhelmed
with the soul-yearning for sympathy. For her class—
the maligned outcast half-blood—there seemed no welcome on the face of all God's creation. Denied social
standing with either of the parent races, she felt that
the world was crying out against her.

The signal for starting was the accustomed pistol shot,
and Cogewea, perturbed by the aspersions of the Kootenai woman, was caught unawares. For some distance,
the full-bloods running well bunched, led by a good
score yards; but soon she felt the scorching sting of innumerable sand and dust particles, thrown in her face
by the hoofs of the flying seven. Shielding her eyes
by half-closing them she bore on the reins with slightly
increased force. The White Star responded by passing
first five and then six of the contestants, and the main
dust-cloud was in the rear. Gradually the distance between the two leaders lessened and at the end of the
third quarter, the Star began to lap the pinto, whose
rider was considered the best on the Flathead. Contrary to the known custom of the Indian race rider,
this woman had, up to this point, refrained from using
the whip. She now brought it into play and for a space
was able to maintain the lead. But not for long was

this to be. Soon the steeds were running squarely abreast, but as they dashed over the line, White Star was leading by half a neck.

As usual in a close race, those of the whites who had backed their favorites most heavily, crowded to the judges' stand disputing, in language more emphatic than elegant. In marked contrast, there was no contention among the Indian track-gamblers. With them, both winnings and losses alike were accepted with stoic indifference. Jim came to Cogewea, in evident contentment, as he spoke:

"You won, Sis! The judge is in your favor. He says you beat fair and on the level and wants you to come to the stand and get your twenty five bucks. He asked me to bring you over there. He is anxious to see you."

Together they rode to the stand and to the surprise of the judge, Cogewea answered his salutation in perfect English. 'His Honour' soon found that this breed girl was not the type he had figured, and he cut the conversation short by directing his assistant to pay her the prize money. He had lost all interest in the Kootenai squaw rider of only a few moments before. He was still more surprised when Cogewea addressed him:

"Pardon me! but there is forty-five dollars more coming to me, as winner of the ladies race."

"You don't mean to tell me that *you* are the one who rode in the ladies' race—that you are claiming the first money on both the ladies and squaw races?" he exclaimed with fierce bluster.

"Yes, I rode in both races! Did all that I could to add to their interest."

"And you now have the effrontery to claim both prizes?"

"Why not? I won both of them."

"Which was irregular and will not be allowed. A protest has already been filed against you in this race, in behalf of Miss Webster, to whom the first prize money will be paid. You never would have led coming in had you not quirted her horse over the head. You will get only

the prize for the squaw race. Here Sam!'' speaking to
his assistant for the second time, ''pay this squaw the
twenty five dollars as I directed. It is the money she
won in the squaw race. Pay her that and no more.''

Cogewea again demurred, when Jim, who still sat his
horse interposed:

''Here! Sis, you take this here money as the Judge
offers it. The prizes are different and you don't want
to get the two mixed.''

Cogewea did as directed and the judge turned away
to greet some newly arrived friends: The Westerner accosted him:

''This here business should be settled fair. Every
one who saw the race know how the quirt fightin' come
'bout. If the money don't belong to the little gal, why
then she ain't goin' to ask for it. But if she won it,
then it's hers and you ought give it to her. I am willin'
you decide, as you're the proper judge.''

''I have decided it and she has been given all the money that she will get.'' was the emphatic reply.   ''No
Injun can come around here and dictate to me in regard
to judging these races. Do you savey that?''

''The white man's rulin' is law,'' rejoined Jim calm-
ly, but maybe you'll tell the little gal just why she's not
to have this here prize she won so fairly in the ladies'
race.''

''Because,'' sneered the now irate judge, ''she is a
squaw and had no right to ride in the *ladies'* race. I
would advise you,'' he added in a menacing tone, ''to
get away from here if you do not want trouble. This
thing is settled and settled for keeps!''

''That's right, pardner,'' exclaimed a heavy-faced
man who, with a group of followers edged his way
through the crowd of spectators. ''When it comes to
the pass that a *squaw* can enter a *ladies'* race and be
permitted to win over a girl like Verona Webster, and
that too, by quirting her horse over the head, then it is
time that *white* people step out and let the damned Injuns run the races! For one, I'm not goin' stand for

it and all the boys are with me! If any low born *breed* is looking for trouble, he can now find it in sight!"

The last words were directed to Jim, and the speaker's hand rested dangerously near his pistol's grip. But the half-blood, who had been brought up amid the rough elements of the range, displayed no perturbation at this tirade from the new comer, who stood to the right and apart from the disputants. The position was strategic and Jim was at a disadvantage, should there be gun-play. With stoical disregard, he again addressed the judicial dispenser of prizes:

"Only one word more, Judge, and I ain't trailin' for no disagreeableness. You paid the little gal the twenty five dollars 'cause she's a squaw?"

"Yes, and I am *not* going to pay her the forty five dollars for the same reason; that she *is* a squaw! Do you get that?"

"Stay by it, Judge! We're with you to the last cartridge!" vociferated the heavy face and his backers.

"My hearin' ain't no ways defective," came the serene reply without notice to this side clamor, "But I may be locoed as to your meanin'. I take it, that the little gal bein' a *squaw*, she can't be a *lady*! Is that it? She's a waitin' to hear you say that. Tell these here people your 'cisin regardin' the character of the little gal."

The judge was astounded. Here, contrary to all precedents, was a tribesman persistently contending against a deal—however unfair—meted out by his, in every way—"superior." Sitting sidewise his saddle and chewing at a scant moustache, he was looking into the eyes of his antagonist with exasperating calmness. The brazen effrontery of the breed was maddening. The judge, a man of tried nerve in more than one gun fight, like a storm-cloud about to pour its wrath upon a waiting world, paused; choking with livid rage. Addressing a stalky individual wearing a police badge of exaggerated dimensions, who had just stepped within the circle, he bruskly ordered:

"Here, Marshal, put the irons on this rider and lock
him up as a dangerous character! He is charged with
malicious interference with an honest distribution of
race awards, by coming here armed and attempting in-
timidation of the program officials. There will be plenty of witnesses to make the complaint stick, and he can
consider himself fortunate in spending a few months
behind bars rather than dangling at a rope's end, which
would have happened within a very few seconds had
you not so opportunely arrived."

"Slide down from that hoss, Injun, while I ornament
yo' with the bracelets," blustered the constable, advancing as he produced a pair of burnished handcuffs. "An'
don't make a mistake by thinkin' it only a joke, savey?"

Jim remained immobile, and something in his demean-
or caused the minion of the law to hesitate. It was at
this moment that Cogewea, with swift dexterity, dashed
the wadded bills which she had received, full in the face
of the fuming judge,, and vehemently broke forth:

"*Take* your tainted money! I do not want to touch
any thing polluted by having passed through your slimy
hands! And, since you are disbursing *racial* prizes re-
gardless of merit or justice, pass it on to the full-blood
Kootenai woman, who, like your white protegee, won
second place only. She is as much entitled to it as is
Miss Webster to the money which you are so chivalrous-
ly withholding from me. I am as much Caucasian, I
regret to admit, as American, and measured by your
rum-fogged ideals, a mere nobody; with no rights to be
respected."

In low tones she then spoke to Jim in their own tongue. The Westerner, slightly hesitating, readjusted himself in his saddle, turned and rode away by her side
without so much as a backward glance at his gun-bestud-
ded enemies. The spiked-heel of might had, as ever
scored, but at the cost of no inconsiderable amount of
self dignity.

Silent Bob, who had unobserved moved to a point of
vantage, sighed audibly:

"Mos' glad th' meller-dramy's over. I'd hater get all shot up an' my 'surance 'sessment unpaid; I'd hater miss a chanct of again skinnin' th' Kootenais'."

The Southerner was well aware that he was assuming an extremely unpopular attitude, and one likely to be resented, but aside from scowls and muttered imprecations, his challenge passed unnoticed.

Discomforted by the withering disdain of Cogewea, and the burning contempt for their prowess by her companion, the pugnacity of the "bunch" had suffered a most undignified backset.

CHAPTER VIII.

THE INDIAN DANCERS

To the sound of flute and singing,
To the sound of drum and voices—
—*Hiawatha*

THE bucking contest—without finals—was to take place in the big corral, where Jim and Cogewea now repaired. Expert riders of the range were there with several outlaw broncs. For an hour the sport waxed warm and furious, many a lithe horseman biting the dust. Finally Croppy was led into the arena and while held by professional snubbers, Jim lifted his silver mounted saddle to the quivering back. The maddened struggles of the horse availed nothing against mechanical contrivances in the hands of superior intelligence, and the saddle was quickly and securely clinched. Jim turned to the spectators and called banteringly:

"Twenty bones to the feller who can scratch this here gentle cayuse, and sixty bucks more if he wins first prize as a scienced rider."

Croppy was widely known and no one accepted the challenge. Jim well knew that he alone of all the "rangers" could "stick" him. He continued:

"Two dollars to one, to the limit of five hundred, that no 'twister' can stay with this here lady's saddle horse to a finish."

"He knows he's plum safe in howlin' such bluff," growled a lank cowpuncher perched on the corral fence. "No rider has ever stuck that there whirlin' devil 'cept Jim hisself."

"Yo' hatched a truth if never afore," replied his companion. "Th' only time I ever chawed gravel was from th' back of that there tornado. I must a went purty high, up where 's'ronomers say th' air is too light to breathe, 'cause I didn't find no breath for quite

72

a spell after navigatin' back to earth. No! I ain't
hankerin' for Jim's money to again tackle that there
dose of animated pizen."

The Westerner slowly tucked his beaded gauntlets
under his belt, as he concluded dramatically:

"The same money that old Jim, though not feelin' the
best, will now ride the only Croppy of the Pend d'Oreille, straight up."

This boast was passed unchallenged, and Jim turned
to mount. Placing his foot in the stirrup, the snubbers
fell back and the battle was on. Horse and rider went
into the air , but when they came down, the "best rider
of the Flathead" was firmly settled in the saddle. Croppy seemed to buck as never before. Around, and
across the corral he went; "pivoting" and "spiking",
"sunfishing" with all the intricate movements of the
confirmed "twister"; but to no purpose. He could not
dismount his tormentor. Jim, in abandon enjoyment of
"this here rockin' chair", was complacently fanning
himself with his sombrero. Rearing high, the frenzied
horse fell backwards, but the active rider saved himself
by slipping from the saddle. The baffled steed regain-
ed its feet only to find the man again on its back. Bawl-
ing with rage, Croppy renewed the fight with increased
vigor, but all in vain. In the midst of the most frightful plunging, Jim drew his watch and called the time
of day; the audience screaming its delight.

At length, that the horse might not be conquered and
its staying qualities impaired for further exploitation,
the rider with rare agility sprang to the ground, landing squarely on his feet. The spectators were wild with
enthusiasm and gave Jim an ovation as the champion
bronc twister of the Pend d'Oreille.

With the bucking contest over, many now hurried to
the big brush shed where the Indians were to dance.
Jim and Bob worked their way through the crowd to
the center space set aside for the performances. The
music, discordant and monotonous to the whites, is all
rhythm to the Indian ear. The sudden break in time

and pitch has a significance well understood by the initiated. The musicians are usually trained professionals and are held in high regard by their tribesmen. Sacred and emanating from the Great Spirit—giver of all life —no sacrilege is permissible at either the spirit or the war dance. The great drum (1), placed on an outspread blanket on the ground, is surrounded by the players, sitting in a cordon about it. These strike the instrument in perfect unison with single batons or sticks, terminating with elongated knobs of cloth or soft buckskin. The women contingent sits in an exclusive circle adjacent to the drummers, their voices blending harmoniously with those of the men.

All is ready; and "attention" bursts from the drum, to be echoed by the leader in animated song; decorously taken up by the other singers. The music swells in stirring cadence, but the dancers, enveloped in blankets crouching about the edges of the cleared arena, remain statued and immobile. They must not show haste or impatience. Suddenly a tall, grizzled old warrior stands up, and lifting high his ceremonial elkhorn club and whip combined, gives signal that the dance begin. The recumbent figures arise. Stripped of blankets, they appear dazzling and resplendent with feathers, wampum and native finery; with here and there the naked body of a bronze athlete glistening with symbolic emblems done in brilliant paint. The dancers must not lag or remain inactive after the signal to proceed. If they do, the leader is privileged to use the whip with no uncertain vigor, nor must the laggard resent such chastisement! (2)

Watch the dancers! There is that aged battle scarred warrior whose movements denote the gliding serpent—the crouching panther—the stalking cougar— the leaping mountain-cat—the on-rushing swoop of the aerial eagle. Mark that visiting, stately Nez Perce! Although facing the sunset, decadence shows not on his sinewy form. A nephew of the immortal Chief Joseph, he was young, when, in 1877, he fought and scouted

over that thousand mile trail in a mad dash for the
Canadian border, a dash unprecedented for brilliancy
of achievement, throughout the annals of American warfare. That warclub he so exultingly holds aloft, still
retains the sanguine stains of mortal combat.(3) His
step is that of the conqueror rather than that of the
vanquished and fallen.

See those young men! Their slouchy *"traipsing"*
tells of contact with the meaningless "waltz" and suggestive "hugs" and "trots" of the higher civilization
—a vulgarity—a sacrilegous burlesque on an ancient
and religiously instituted ceremony. Like other of his
tribal cultures, the Indian's dance is suffering in modi-
fications not always to be desired as morally beneficial.

There! that youth a mere lad! He has attained to
the age when he is making his debut, as it were, declaring his intention of taking up the role of man and warrior in his tribe. For this privilege his parents or
friends must give liberally in goods and horses, to be
distributed among the assemblage at a later hour.

Not the least interesting is the dropping of a solitary
feather from his regalia by an unfortunate young dan-
cer. This trophy must not be recovered by the one
losing it, but for his carelessness he will be required to
pay such fine as the chief in charge may impose. No
one touches the object until the conclusion of that particular dance, when the bravest or most noted warrior
—the Nez Perce—calling upon his secret protective
spirit-powers, proceeds to take it up. This is accomplished only after one or more seemingly futile attempts,
amid the excited *ki-yiahs* of his dancing companions.
The feather is retained by the Nez Perce, who then re-
cites some thrilling incident of personal prowess in
battle. For this honor, he donates a blanket to the general distribution fund, while the loser of the feather
atones for his disgrace by contributing a saddle-pony.

There is a lull in the wild, circling war dance, which
is ever measured by many breaks and rests. The old

warrior in charge announces a change, which an interpreter renders in English.

"*La-siah* has spoken. The men will now take women for the final dance. For the benefit of those who do not understand, we will explain the custom, which has come down to us from our ancestors of other snows.

"Every man has this privilege. He can choose any woman from the assemblage to dance with him while the drummers sing the song of good-will. But he must pay her something; any thing he may see fit, as her value. If he likes his partner, he will pay well; but less if he does not care much for her. The woman has the same privilege of choosing and paying. As you circle in this dance, the position of the hand and arm of the man will make known how his heart and mind runs out to the woman.. If he wants a maiden for wife, we will know it. If he wants to rob another man of his wife, we will know it. He must not do crazy things nor speak the lie with sign-actions. He must do the truth towards the woman. A married man may dance with a maiden for friendship, and the young man may dance with a married woman for friendship. This is a ceremony of friendly good will; where all the distant tribes may meet in harmony; a peace to be regarded well. All may dance, but it must not be mockery. It must be from the heart which should always be true. La-siah has shown you his mind."

The Chief of the Pend d'Oreille came into the dance space with Cogewea. His warbonnet of eagle feathers was the best, a great billowy mass of swaying plumes. The floating tail piece, extending down his back in long undulating waves, just brushed the ground. His moccasins were decorated with bead work done in symbol, representing many suns of labor by his patient squaw. His broad chest was emblazoned with native wampum, as well as ornaments and beads highly prized. These last, his grandfather had purchased with beaver skins from the Hudson's Bay Company nearly a hundred

snows before. In his hand he carried his *te-kee-sten,*
(4) with feathers and strips of fur attached.
The dancing was immediate, with other couples joining the ever lengthening, and widening circle. Moving
to the left, the short measured side-step was a unit,
with emphasis on the advanced foot. The music at the
drum had changed to a softer melody, suggestive of love-
passion, peace and good-will. Unlike the fierce, stirring notes of war, thrilling with the thunder's shock of
death, there was the murmur of rippling water over
pebbly mountain beds; the soughing of summer breezes
through leafy groves the glad carolling of birds at the
mating season. And over all was visioned the halo
of an ancient glory, when the protective spirits dwelt
more near the tribes.
The song died to a note like an echo from the canyon's cliffy depths The dancers stopped, holding their
places. La-siah and his *Caller* came forward to name
the presents. The Pend d'Oreille Chief spoke in a low,
dignified tone, to be interrupted by the Caller.
"To this maiden of another tribe, I give, as a token
of my good will to her and her people, one of my best
horses. It is the *pinto,* ridden by my wife and which
took second prize in today's race. My gift!"
Cogewea's heart bounded with gladness but Indian
etiquette forbade any outward demonstration of gratitude. It was for her to reciprocate in a subsequent
friendship dance.
The Nez Perce Chief, who had danced with the "shy
girl", took from his shoulder a splendid "King George"
blanket and passing it to the gift-exchanger, through
him spoke:
"Members of the different tribes meet here and are
no longer strangers. This robe, which has sheltered
me from the winter storms, carries with it the warmth of
the Nez Perce's heart for this girl and her people. It
is good to be friends!"
Jim gave to Stemteemä a blanket of rare design, which
he had purchased from another Indian for that pur-

pose, and from whom he had secured a dancing costume. At that moment he ingratiated himself in the old heart, far more than he ever realized. That gift, received in stoic silence, was bread cast in the van of a fast gathering flood destined to break, dark and turbulent on the border shores of both their lives.

The sun bending to the western horizon, Mrs. Carter and Mary, with Stemteemä, prepared for the home going. Bob could not be found, and John Carter who had been detained in Polson for the past three days on a cattle deal, was obliged to drive the hack on the return trip.

The moon was peeping over the great Rockies, before Jim and Cogewea rode out of the little town. They were both well content despite the unpleasant episode of the races but he noticed that she was in an unusual hurry; at last they were started. The girl was thinking of her patient at the ranch. While busy celebrating, she had almost forgotten Densmore, but now his face came before her. Jim would have ridden slower, but she urged a faster pace. Where the road permitted, an easy swinging lope was maintained by the mile. More to break a monotonous silence, the Westerner spoke:

"Sis! you comin' tomorrow for more of the big doin's?"

"I do not care to. One day is enough for me to celebrate; although I suppose the Indians will carry this on for the next week."

"Guess they're goin' have ten more days of it. I bet we don't get none of our boys back for a week. Bob was lost this evenin' and they all will not be satisfied till they go broke. It's time 'nough then, they figure, to come home and tame down. Last I see of Bill and Rodeo, was at the Kootenai camp a playin' monte with La-siah and them; a keepin' hid from the Government ossifers. They was a hittin' the jug heavy, too."

With a chuckle, Jim touched his horse with a blunt rowel and they galloped over the long slope homeward. His surmise proved correct. It was seven days later before any of the riders returned. Bill and Rodeo each carried a black eye, while Bob's nose was very much in evidence. There was not a dollar left among the trio.

"Well, yo' know durn well how it is; when yo' hit them there jugs how thin's go," explained Celluloid Bill. "Yo' jus' can't quit till th' money's all gone. If me an' Rodeo have a pair of bad lookers, it's 'cause we fought like men with them there long haired Kootenais. We hadter have th' darn thin' out an' out with 'em."

"I hater have my nose a feelin' so bad; I hater have th' blame thin' a pintin' North," soliloquized Silent Bob, as he tenderly caressed his swollen proboscis.

Jim made good his promise of a present to Cogewea for winning the squaw race. It was a handsome silver mounted bridle.

CHAPTER IX.

UNDER THE WHISPERING PINES

To love the softest hearts are prone,
But such can ne'er be all his own;
Too timid in his woes to share,
Too meek to meet, or brave despair;
And sterner hearts alone may feel
The wound that time can never heal.

—*The Giaour*

TWO weeks had passed since the incident of Densmore's riding; everything drifting along the usual channel. The hot July days were beginning to heat the great Clay Banks of the Pend d'Oreille, but under the dark pines lining its shore, were found spots cooled by the breeze from the stream. It was here that the injured man was spending the morning alone with a book. Cogewea, his nurse, had gone for a ride, an errand to a distant neighbor's. He had exhausted an hour in a vain attempt at becoming interested in the pages that he turned to no purpose.

At last: he would lay aside the volume and study nature. He noted the many colored flowers which perfumed the air; the squirrels and chip-munks frisking among the boughs overhead, or scurrying along the ground. The birds caroling in the thicket, and the fishes swimming lazily in the waters where the shadows fell dark.

But he grew more restless. There was a disturbing element to his meditations. The wild life interested him no more than did the book. That "breed" girl came ever before him. It was vain that he tried to blot her from memory, to banish her from vision. She peeped from every flower; those flashing black eyes reflected from the pebbles glinting in the sunshine. Her tresses streamed on the eddying current, and her voice was in the notes of bird-song and the chipmunk's chatter.

Alfred Densmore, the cold, calculating business man
out from the East for adventure and money, was half
in love wih this wild, tawny girl of the range, the romantic "Chipmunk of the Okanogans."

The idea struck him as absurd. He shook himself as
if to throw off the shackles of irresolution. It was impossible! such weakness! He was only fascinated, he
argued. Those liquid, mesmeric eyes had cast a spell
over him—a dangerous spell. With a gesture of impatience he flung his half-smoked cigarette into the
water and spoke so the squirrels could hear him:

"What a fool! I am not really falling in love with
that squaw! Ridiculous! What of my club associates?
My sisters would never tolerate it, and it would break
my mother's heart. My father would never dare call
me his son again. He would disinherit me! It is impossible that I so far forget myself, my birth and my
social standing. Besides, there is another who—"

He bit his lip, extracted a fresh cigarette from its
case, lit it and drew at it furiously.

"Never! Never! I don't dare! Pshaw! she only takes
my fancy. What if she has been good to me?" he muttered. "I have known others of her 'stripe' just as
kind. It is the way of all such women! They are alright
as objects of amusement and pleasure, but there it must
halt. Fairly educated, she can show refinement when the
mood strikes her, but she makes easy to fall into the
rough, uncouth ways of her associates—the ill mannered
rowdies of the cow-trail. None of such for you, Alfred
Densmore! A be-pistoled woman who can swear a little
on occasions may be picturesque, but she is no mate for
a gentleman of the upper society. Had she strings to a
good mine there would be an inducement, but a squaw
without compensation—a sacrifice without adequate requital—bah!"

With this soliloquy, he dismissed the "dream," and
casting himself upon the ground, was soon buried in his
book.

Cogewea returned from riding at an unusually early
hour. She seemed interested in the welfare of her pa-

tient, for she went immediately to him under the pines.
Densmore heard the jingle of spurs and glanced up to
see the girl advancing, swinging a quirt in idle abandonment. A neat riding habit set off her splendid figure to
advantage and the Easterner felt his heart bound a
trifle faster as he surveyed this "exquisite living picture." Perhaps he had been too harsh in his deductions. Could there be guile in a face of such open
frankness? What could be expected of the best with
such environments? Her forward ways were but those
of innocence. A wild flower unscathed by sun-blight or
frost—a ruby unflawed—a jewel worthy of any setting.
But after all, she was a *squaw*, while he was of an altogether higher cast. Densmore brushed aside all feelings
kindred to love, but he gazed at her with a fascination
ill becoming one of his superior breeding. Cogewea, ever
observant, grew slightly confused as she exclaimed:

"Well! have you nothing to say? Am I such a curiosity that——"

"O! pardon me. I was just thinking."

"Of what?"

"Of—of how nifty you look in your new suit."

"John bought it for me, a summer present. I guess
he savied it was time that I possessed some glad rags!
Maybe he tumbled that I had about earned them, cooking for the broncho busters and playing nurse at the
same time."

"You certainly have been a royal little nurse, and I
am afraid that I can never thank you sufficiently for
your kindness. But I hope to compensate you for it
all some day."

"Aw! come off! I am not asking pay! Guess I owe
my services for the part I had in getting you busted up.
How is your arm?"

"Seems to be getting along finely; but there is a dull
pain in my head most of the time. I trust that it is
nothing serious."

"Doubtless a mere 'aching void' and no occasion for
alarm," came the solemn reply. "If the malady is deep
seated, an abatement must not be expected in so short

a time. An absorption remedy of any nature is usually
slow of results and a persistent and potent application is
ofttimes necessary.''

Cogewea had seated herself at Densmore's side and
was listlessly flecking the grass with her riding lash.
Her patient hardly knew how to take this diagnosis of
his head trouble and its remedial prescript. He gazed
at her steadily, boldly, as an enigma to fathom; but the
mask was impenetrable.

"Yes! I know," he at length acquiesced, "but I feel
so lonely at times. No one to speak to; every body busy
but me. Only the birds and squirrels for company. Can
you blame me for growing impatient?"

"Birds and squirrels are good company. The wild
creatures are primitive and are closer the creative
Spirit than we imagine. I love them! But if they do not
interest you, why don't you talk to Stemteemä? Both
of you have time to throw away. Go visit in her tepee.''

''I am afraid that she would chase me away with her
cane as she does Bringo and Shep at times,'' he rejoined
with a short laugh.

"That only attests that you no more understand her
than you do your little companions here of the grove;
for they are similar in character. I'll tell you what we
will do some of these days. We'll call on her together.
Do not expect your afternoon tea of fashion's boredom,
but you will be regaled on jerked venison, dried roots
and berries. I will have her tell some stories that may
hold interest for you—stories of the past—of the time
that was. She will speak in Okanogan and I will interpret for you. I love my Stemteemä for her very golden
worth. She has been a parent to all of us children.
When mother died, she was the only relative we had—
after daddy left us for the glitter of gold in the Yukon;
and which——''

Cogewea caught herself as though she had betrayed
a secret; for seldom was the father's name ever mentioned. The girl tried, in charity, to believe that he had
long since followed her mother, but there was an ever
haunting uncertainty—a dreaming of that which is more

fearful than death—gnawing at her soul. With her, the present only is to concern us, is to be lived sacredly; and that somewhere out on the trail awaiting us, is the best friend that mortal ever known. *Desolution!*. who liberates us from the perishable. Nor does he watch for our coming with sinister designs and foreshadowing the gloom of an invisible night; for the door which he swings back opens into the dawn of a morn redolent with renewed life; where avenues of progression wind along shimmering streams—tree-lined and where birds are singing—coming down from wondrous mountain heights. To this girl of "heretical" philosophies, Death was but the unfolding of a long bud-bound flower; the bursting forth of a rock-hampered fountain. Imbued with such lofty ideals, it is not surprising that she preferred thinking of her parent as dead—in the general acceptance of the term—for that most dreadful of all denouncatories: *"Thou art weighed in the balances, and art found wanting.";* loomed terrifically against the back-ground of her conception of a life of profligacy.

The touch of sadness in Cogewea's voice as she spoke of her parents, was lost on the Easterner. But the mention of "gold in the Yukon" had aroused to new life his latent passion for wealth. It was the one god of his ambition to go back home a rich man. For this, he had left the city and society. He must make good; he was not so particular how, but in some way. He had struck a rough, strange people and was gaining an exuberant experience with which to regale his associates upon his return to his old haunts. There must be wealth somewhere in this new country—mines of it among the Indians—requiring only brains and strategy to possess. He had discovered that this romantic girl was a nature's religionist. He would court her ideals, but it would be for a purpose. He would amass this fortune—transfer it to his own pocket—and then—his reverie was broken by Cogewea:

"I must go now! Sister will need help with the dinner. You better be there within an hour or you might miss your fodder."

"Wait! just one moment," remonstrated Densmore as she hurried away. "I want to ask a favor."

"Spit 'er out!" she called, half turning back.

"Will you write a letter for me this afternoon?"

"Is that all? Surething! I thought you were going to strike me for a round thousand, from the way you hesitated. Come to your trough at *sitkum sun.* S'long!" with the wave of a hand.

"*Trough! system sun!* What do you mean?"

"Grub at noon. *Sitkum sun* is mid-day. *Chinook.* I learned it on the Columbia. It is hardly spoken here."

After dinner and the kitchen work disposed of, Cogewea joined her patient under the pines. She sat near him on the river bank, writing material in her lap. With his left hand Densmore was awkwardly tossing pebbles into the water.

"What do you want me to write?" she asked cheerily.

"A letter to mother," and by way of emphasis, he pitched a larger stone farther into the stream.

"All right! You rangle and I'll use the brandin' iron."

Densmore settled in an easy position and dictated as follows:

"Polson, Flathead Indian Reservation; Montana.

July 21, 19—

"Dearest Mother:

"A friend is writing this for me. I recently met with an accident to my arm which precludes the use of a pen. However, it is not serious and with the good nursing that I am receiving, I will soon be fully recovered. My nurse, while not a professional, is one of the very best; kind and affectionate. It is refreshing to meet with true friends in a strange place, and my nurse is certainly devoted to——"

Densmore paused. Cogewea looked up, a deep blush suffusing her dark face. Her startled eye caught his steady gaze, and her head dropped lower over the tablet as he finished the sentence:

"—her trust. She is writing this for me in the open and under the river pines.

"I think that I will remain here for an indeterminate time, since I have formed a strong attachment; and even love for my——"

Cogewea was not trapped a second time. She did not lift her eyes as she inquired in frigid tones: "Is that all?"

Densmore concluded without seeming to notice her question:

"—environments. The people here are all in marked contrast to our home society. Of this I will tell you when I am able to write you myself. There are both thrills and romance out here.

"Address me as above. Tell sisters to write me.

"With love to all,_

"Your son,
"Alfred Densmore."

"Shall I add a post-script and say that your nurse wrote this and that she is an Injun squaw?" asked Cogewea severely, looking her companion level in the face.

"N—no! I—I hardly think it necessary at this time," he stammered confusedly. "Mother might not understand."

"Very well. You can look the letter over while I address the envelope and if it suits you—if it is true to your dictation—it can be posted this evening. Rodeo will drive to town and return with supplies in the morning."

Densmore took the proffered sheet and glancing through it, returned it with an ill suppressed smile, expressing his satisfaction. Cogewea folded and sealed the missive without comment and tossed it into his inverted hat at his side. There was an embarrassing silence for one short moment, when she rose and said simply:

"I must go and help sister with the children and the house work."

"Why such hurry?" I thought you had the afternoon off, and that perhaps we could visit your grandmother and hear those wonderful stories you promised me."

"Not today!" she called back without stopping. "I think that Stemteemä is sleeping."

"Touchy as powder!" he chuckled as he lay back on the grass in evident delight. "I thought so! She tumbled—gave herself dead away. Now Mr. Alfred of the "circle", go your length in untrammeled pleasure with this brown beauty of the range. But no matrimonial tangle! Bah! What a match! A scion of the ancient house of Densmore, wedding a breed girl of the Okanogans. What a figure for the ball room and social functions of city life. Ye gods! My family must never know. But that possible gold of the Yukon! Who can tell what fish may be swimming my way. Surely, the catch would be worth the bait!"

CHAPTER X.

LO! THE POOR "BREED"

Estranged from sympathy and joy,
Bearing each taunt which careless tongue
On his mysterious lineage flung.
Whole nights he spent by moonlight pale,
To wood and stream his hap to wail.
—*The Lady of the Lake*

COGEWEA seated on the veranda was endeavoring to interest herself in a book. It was a hot, lazy afternoon and she was alone. The family, including the shy-girl Mary, had gone to visit an Indian relative, leaving her with the old grandmother, whose small lodge stood not far from the farm house. Stemteemä never would consent to live in a modern dwelling with a solid roof, so her tepee had been erected, permitting her to continue after the ancient manner of her fading race. She was now sleeping on her blankets, after toiling all the forenoon at basket weaving.

Cogewea had willingly stayed at home. The letter writing under the pines the previous day had had a disquieting effect. What could Densmore have meant? The world should appear more beautiful than she was finding it. She had half expected the Easterner to join her, but he had, immediately after dinner, repaired to the bunk-house and was indulging in a *siesta*. The girl, vexed and disappointed, had resorted to reading but with no concentration of thought. The theme, an unjust presentation of Indian sentiment and racial traits; *The Brand*—stigma of the blood—did not tend towards calming her perturbed mind. In sheer desperation she continued poring through the pages.

At last Cogewea became absorbed—absorbed with rage. The writer, wholly ignorant of her subject, instead of extending a helping hand, had dealt her unfortunate hero a ruthless blow. The girl's fury increased as she

read, but a step on the walk caused her heart to quicken.
She refrained from looking up. It must be——

"Sis! do you know where there is an awl? The one
at the barn is done-for and I want to mend——"

"Oh! I don't know!" she broke in with piquant resentment. "Look for it yourself and leave me alone!
I'm cross as a bear! I almost hate myself today. Every
thing is against me, even to this maligning, absurdity of
a book. The thing does nothing but slam the *breeds!*
as if they were reptiles instead of humans. *You* are no
good! along with all the rest of us. You are only an
Injun!—a miserable *breed!*—not higher than the dust
on your white brothers' feet. Go away!"

Jim turned without comment, walking towards the
bunk house. He was biting his mustache, his lips compressed with anger.

"The damn' tenderfoot!" he muttered to himself.
"I'll get square with the cuss, if there's lead throwin'
teachin' him some sense."

At the door he almost bumped into Densmore, who
was just emerging from the building. In tones ominous
with intensity, he accosted him:

"Sis is cross as hell! Gave me the devil; said I was
no good, only an Injun and all sorts of things. If I ever
find out who is a tellin' her lies—if I ever know—
there'll be somthin' doin' 'round this here ranch; savey?
There'll be hell to pay if old Jim gets wise."

For a moment he glared at the astounded Easterner,
and then strode to the barn; hatred gleaming in his eyes.
His muscular hands were clenched with such force that
the nails dug into the palms. He now hated "that
cussed tenderfoot"; hated him for usurping all of
Cogewea's time. He was willing that she nurse the
stranger, but she had treated him with coolness ever
since the accident occurred. And now the white sneak
must have been throwin' dirt or she would never have
called him a "miserable breed."

Densmore was still standing where the irate Westerner left him. He had been too surprised to offer any
reply. What had Cogewea told Jim, that he was so

angry and threatening? He could recall nothing that
he had said against him of any consequence. True, Jim
had been instrumental in the mishap, but he had tried
to forget that, since he had learned more of the western
ways. Where was the mistake? He was tempted to go
to the girl and learn the trouble, but paused upon second
thought. He did not want to quarrel and Jim had said
that she was cross-tempered. He would go fishing and
wait a more propitious time; until she was in a better
mood.

With this determination, Densmore took rod and reel
and sauntered towards the river. But he could not forget the bitter words of the foreman. Suddenly he struck
the ground impatiently with the but of his pole! The
Injun must be jealous of him!

"Why the copper colored savage!" he muttered
aloud. "He can have the squaw for all I care. I like
the girl only as any pleasing chattel. As a game, she
affords amusement, but hardly a dividend. The wild
Brownie will be forgotten when I return to civilization.
But I must not cross that hot headed fool too severely."

Cogewea had not meant to be ugly to Jim when he
interrupted her reading. She was out of humor and
tried to blame it to the book. It was not suited to her
ideals. Inwardly fuming, she had said that which she
afterwards regretted. Jim had scarce reached the barn
when she experienced remorse for her out-burst of ill
temper to the one who had always shown her naught but
kindness. She liked Jim, the great, big hearted protector that he was. She recalled his devotion and championship of her cause at the recent races and secretly
vowed that in future, hers would be more a spirit of
reciprocity.

With sudden impulse she threw the hateful volume
to the floor and springing up, slipped to the gate. She
looked to the bunk-house, which seemed deserted. She
saw Stemteemä, now awakened from repose, sitting at
her tepee doorway. For a moment she stood, then
hastened to the barn. Jim was nowhere in sight, but a
thin trail of dust led over an eminence out on the flat.

Densmore with angling rod and basket slung over his
shoulder, was disappearing among the river pines.

The girl turned back to the house in disappointment.
She had wished to placate Jim by carrying to him the
pipe of peace. With a frown, she picked up the book
and began perusing it again. The story, interesting to
the whites, was worm-wood to her Indian spleen. However, she determined to see how much of an ape the
author had made of her breed-hero.

By adroit sketching, she had, in a short time the gist
of the plot.

The scene opened on the Flathead, where a half-blood
"brave" is in love with a white girl; the heroine of the
story. He dares not make a declaration of his affection,
because of his Indian blood. He curses his own mother
for this heritage, hates his American parent for the sake
of the girl of his heart. He deems himself beneath her;
not good enough for her. But to cap the absurdity of
the story, he weds the white "princess" and slaves for
her the rest of his life.

Cogewea leaned back in her chair with a sigh.
"Bosh!" she mused half aloud. "Show me the Red
'buck' who would *slave* for the most exclusive white
'princess' that lives. Such hash may go with the whites,
but the Indian, both full bloods and the despised *breeds*
know differently. And, that a 'hero' should be depicted
as hating his own mother for the flesh and heart that
she gave his miserable frame. What a figure to be held
up for laudation by either novelist or historian! No
man, whether First American, Caucasian or of any other
race, could be so beastly inhuman in real life; so low
and ungratefully base as to want to hide his own mother.
The lower animals respond to this instinct, and can
people suppose that the Indian, who is of the heroic, has
not the manhood accredited to even the most commercialized of nations? The truth is, he has more love of the
undying type than his 'superior' brother ever possessed.''

Cogewea reflected bitterly how her race had had the
worst of every deal since the landing of the lordly Euro-

pean on their shores; how they had suffered as much from the pen as from the bayonet of conquest; wherein the annals had always been chronicled by their most deadly foes and partisan writers. In the light of unbiased facts, they had been no worse than any other race under similar conditions, and perhaps not so bad; the Caucasian not excepted. Human skins had never been nailed to *their* places of worship. In the comparison, although a *breed,* she spurned with resentment the implied inference that she was not the social equal of the most exalted of her self-constituted supermundanes. She felt a native pride in her Red forefathers who had fought so patriotically for home and country. Sterling manhood and womanhood, she was sure, carried with it, the elements of racial vanity; and as a stream cannot rise above its source, the ''slaving hero'' was doomed to a malarial death amid the brackish pools flowing from the quill of this neoteric writer.

In the meantime, Densmore had fished in vain. The fly went unsnapped. Little did he understand the habits of the finny tribe. The trout were taking their *siesta.* Disgusted, he reeled in his line and returned to the house.

Cogewea was startled from her reverie by a shadow falling across her lap. The broad shoulders of Densmore barred the rays of the low hanging sun. As she glanced up, he cast his hat at her feet with the challenge:

''If my hat is permitted, I shall regard it as propitious that I may follow.''

''Come in, Shoyahpee!'' (1) was the not altogether friendly greeting. ''I just want to quarrel with somebody and you will do as well as any one.''

''You can't quarrel with me! Cage—Cogewea. I am——''

''Yes I can, I must! But I'm not mad at you. It is this book!''

''What is wrong with the inoffensive bundle of paper in board covers?''

''Wrong? It is all wrong; absurdly foolish. It is lo-

coed; crazy! I cannot express my contempt for it; it is
so ridiculously low and shamefully shallow."

"The plot must be a terrible one," rejoined her companion with a cynical smile. "Is there an author concerned?"

"It is said that 'the Lord pities a fool', retorted the
girl without apparent notice of his flippancy. "If this
is true, then the writer of this volume is entitled to a
double share of Divine commiseration. With the Indian,
a demented person is supposed to have been deprived
of reason through the medium of a medicine man or
other occult channels. This author must have met
with the same misfortune on a grand scale. The jocose
part of the romance is that it contains a few tribal
phrases, supposedly the names of birds and animals.
These have been conferred on some of the characters,
or pet saddle horses; which, if properly translated,
would shock the public immeasureably. The 'production' would be discarded by all respectable readers."

Jim, who had returned from a jaunt of inspection
over an adjacent field, dismounted at the gate in time to
hear the reference to the Indian names. Catching the
drift of the conversation, and seemingly forgetful of the
recent unpleasantness, he asked with mock gravity:

"Is all names in them there pages un'erstan'able?"

Glad of an opportunity of amendment for her rude-
ness of a few hours before, Cogewea laughing, replied:

"You ought to know, for you helped supply some of
them. We were just having a slight argument, and to
help settle it, you better explain your part in the makeup of this book's contents."

Rejoiced at being able to aid in the discomforture of
Densmore, the foreman's eyes twinkled with suppressed
amusement, as leaning over the gate, he spoke:

"I was there when the boys was a stuffin' one poor
woman. It was at the first buffalo roundup when lots
of people come to see the sight. A bunch of us riders
was together when this here lady come up and begins
askin' questions 'bout the buffaloes; and Injun names
of flyin', walkin' and swimmin' things and a lot of

bunk. Well, you know how the boys are. They sure
locoed that there gal to a finish; and while she was
a dashin' the information down in her little tablet, we
was a thinkin' up more lies to tell her. We didn't savey
she was writin' a real book, or maybe we would a been
more careful. Yes, *maybe!* Why, them there writin'
folks is dead easy pickin' for the cowpunchers. But I
see she took more to the full-blood talk than what I tell
her.''

Jim indulged in a low laugh, as Cogewea, turning to
Densmore, took up the conversation:

''There, you have it! But that is only a glimpse of
the real situation; of what the tribesmen give would-be
writers. You now understand why I contend that the
whites can not authentically chronicle our habits and
customs. They can hardly get at the truth. A promul-
gator of the law of requital—good and bad—he is aware
of how he has ever been deceived and taken advantage
of, and he has no scruples in returning, as he thinks,
some of the coin. Of course he does not understand
the true situation; and when the ridiculous 'facts' which
he narrates are once in print, he has the worst of it. I
have heard the Indian boast of the absurdities told to
the white 'investigator'. It is practically impossible for
an alien to get at our correct legendary lore.''

Densmore, nonplussed at the unaccountable change
in the attitude of the foreman towards him, and wishing
to fraternize, thought to do so by again resuming the colloquy:

''Well, you must be a truly suspicious people. But
has it ever occurred to you that you may be standing in
your own light—casting shadows over your own road
to progress? Distrust is a fearful barrier to those who
would help you. Confidence is conducive to good fel-
lowship, facilitating both social and business interests.''

''Not bein' in the beatin' game ourselves,'' responded
Jim sullenly, ''that there 'confidence' card has been our
undoin'. I ain't a dyin' for any more shufflin' of the
bait by any hombre.''

''The world is filled with a great variety of people,''

observed the Easterner with a nervous laugh, "but your race must be doubly peculiar, judging from the slight effect that the white-blood has in the mixing."

"The Indian is a peculiarly mysterious race; differing from all others," broke in Cogewea. "We breeds are half and half—American and Caucasion—and in a separate corral. We are despised by both of our relatives. The white people call us 'Injuns' and a 'good-for-nothing' outfit; a 'shiftless', vile class of commonalty. Our Red brothers say that we are 'stuck-up'; that we have deserted our own kind and are imitating the ways of the despoilers of our nationality. But you wait and watch!" exclaimed the girl with animation. "The day will dawn when the desolate, exiled breed will come into his own; when our vaunting 'superior' will appreciate our worth. Fate cannot always be against those who strive for self-elevation. But oh! it is hard when the foot of the strong is ever on your neck. Of the hundred million composing this great Christian Nation, how few are our actual friends; working friends. Those we have are mostly in the far East and consequently cannot know of the multitudinous wrongs which we are compelled to suffer. Occasionally a local champion is found who is big enough and strong enough to defy popular sentiment and fight for us, but it is self-sacrifice. He loses social standing with his own race. We may be too sensitive about our blood, but I often don my war bonnet and go scalp hunting."

"I'm a thinkin' you must have on your war bonnet now, "interposed Jim with a low laugh. "You sure hand it to the pale faces steamin' hot. Like a four minute phonograph, when you get started you run to the end of the trail. You keep unwindin' the lariat till you fetch up at the picket-stake with a jerk. You've got to have your spiel. But I hear the boys a comin'! I hear the hoof-drums of their cayuses a comin'! I'll leave you fellers to fight it out yourselves."

The foreman turned to his horse in manifestly high spirits at the turn of events. Cogewea was evidently "soured" on the entire white race; the tenderfoot included. It was apparent that she would never forsake her Indian associates; never turn from her own blood. Densmore in evident displeasure, also rose to go. His voice was cold and unsympathetic, as he spoke:

"This is nothing of interest to me. I can not argue with a lady. I do not dare!"

"And I am only an Injun, after all!" she retorted bitterly.

The Easterner laughed derisively at her outburst of temper, and left for the bunk-house. The throb of hoofs came nearer and nearer, mingled with the silvery jingle of spurs. But for once the stiring chime failed to reach a responsive chord in the bosom of the girl; who, feeling friendless and unhappy, passed into the house. She wondered if Densmore would, in the presence of Jim, have spoken to her as he did.

Cogewea found solace in consigning the maligning volumn to the kitchen stove.

CHAPTER XI.

AT THE TEPEE FIRESIDE

Go not eastward, go not westward,
For a stranger, whom we know not!
Like a fire upon a hearth-stone
Is a neighbor's homely daughter,
Like the starlight or the moonlight
Is the handsomest of strangers!
—Hiawatha

COGEWEA sat squaw-fashion on the bearskin in Stemteemä's tepee, her daily visit with hot food for the old grandparent. She was telling her of the riders; jokes played, of the horses and dogs, nor did she forget the children. She was awaiting Densmore, who was to join them for the promised story. At last he came and called:

"May I come in?"

"Is the door-flap fastened that the pale face must beg like a Blackfeet slave prisoner for entrance? None ever knocks at the tepee door. The Indian home is also the home of the peaceful stranger; nor is an enemy, when once within its walls, to be molested."

Densmore recognized the voice, and lifting the blanket-shutter, stooped through the low entrance. Cogewea pointed to a worn buffalo robe and gravely motioned him to be seated, as she spoke:

"If you visit here in our wigwam, you must affect the role of a genuine 'buck'. Throw your veneered manners aside and be a real Injun. Command me to bring you water in a basket-cup, let me regale you on dried fish and meat; berries, camas and bitter-root. You must eat till you are completely filled and when you depart, take with you any remaining food and the robe on which you have rested. This, in recognition of the honored visit you have made us. Such was the custom among the tribes snows ago before we were ruined by an alien, rum-flavored civilization.''

"Were such the usages under all conditions of tribal life?"

"Sure! Carried away with you every robe that you may have used while visiting a neighbor, and gave likewise when receiving company. If this was olden times, I would have all of Stemteemä's robes and blankets up at the house ere this. I am here at least three times a day and seldom miss sitting down for a few moments' chat. You must excuse me,'' she continued as she shifted position, ''while I stretch my numbed limbs. I am a young squaw but I guess modern life has disqualified me for the ways of the tepee.''

Cogewea now reclined, head resting in her hand, elbow braced on the ground. The aged woman spoke scoldingly in her own tongue; the words coming quick and sharp, with impressive gesticulations. The girl's reply was also in Okanogan, as she drew her feet under her skirts. Densmore listened with manifest uneasiness. He surmised that the grandmother was averse to his presence and that he was the object of the disquieting colloquy. From the intonation, he was very sure of this. Cogewea read his thoughts and addressed him:

"I beg your pardon for thus discoursing in an unfamiliar language. We are all only mortal and at times perhaps a little conceited with ourselves. I know about how you feel and I am speaking from experience. When people converse in a tongue that I do not understand, I always conjecture that I am the subject of conversation. Doubtless this is ofttimes a mistake. I was just receiving a calling down from this dear old soul. Some more of her ancient ideas. She was chiding me for exposing my ankles in your presence.''

"If her contravention is in deference to me, she is unnecessarily perturbed. I am not at all averse to——''

"It was the custom in other snows,'' Cogewea broke in hastily, ''before that—to us—misnomer civilization came, that a young unmarried woman must sit, if occasion demanded, on her feet in her parent's tepee from morning until nightfall. Aside from her immediate relatives, no man must ever see her ankles. Should this at any time happen, the girl was given to the man for nothing. Considered of no future value, she became a reproach to her family. Conditions might exonerate the maiden from direct blame, but yet she was disgraced. Did a man take unwarranted advantage to thus embarrass a girl, dire results to himself would likely follow, unless her people could be placated by his taking her to wife. (1) This is why Stemteema was scolding me. She is fearful lest I lose my money-value, which I am afraid is not much.''

The tepee was rippling with the musical laughter of the ''forward girl'' girl, and again the chiding voice of the aged squaw gave warning of disapprobation; which caused Densmore to shake with suppressed merriment. Cogewea recovered her self composure and after conversing with her grandmother for a few moments, during which time the old woman appeared placated, she explained more fully that in tribal days the girls were bartered, going to the man who could produce the greater amount of wampum, ponies or other wordly goods; and that the daughter of a chief brought the most to her parents; because she was considered as a ''princess.'' The Stemteemä was at one time a winsome princess, trafficked to the wealthiest fighting man of the Arrow Lake tribe; a man who had reached middle life, while she loved a dashing young warrior of her own tribe, an Okanogan. The latter fell victim to the rage of the husband, when he found that the younger man held the affections of his comely wife. A husband had the right to kill any man who sought to take from him his wife, while on the other hand should a warrior desire the wife of another, they could duel for her. (2) If the husband fell in the fray, the victor took his place at the tepee fireside among the papooses and other squaws, when more than the one woman.

''If that was the manner of your people in past years'' observed Densmore, ''and since we are trying to play true Indians, I can possess you without the price of beads and horses, for which I am thankful, living as I am on the charity of your brother-in-law. But I hope to be earning my salt now soon. When my arm is out of bandages I shall ask you to teach me to ride. The accomplishment of that feat is the ambition of my life."

"Most assuredly!" was the answer, eyes twinkling, "but don't try mounting a 'bronc' until you have learned to manage a gentle cayuse."

"I certainly had my lesson that time!" was the retort with a tinge of bitterness. "I can ride an ordinary horse, but I had no idea that it was *breaking* untamed horses you were referring to when you asked me if I could ride. But after the mistake, I could not explain without your thinking me afraid and a coward. When the boys jeered me that day, to make affairs still worse, you laughed also. Then I didn't care! I grew desperate and didn't give a rap what happened. But let that go! How about that ankle usage? Can I not claim you on that score?"

"Oh! stop kidding!" was the rather piquant reply. "If we were to follow the old native idea, if you wanted me for your squaw, you would first have to humor my people, from Stemteemä down to uncles, aunts and cousins, including both parents if they were living. Then, if all were satisfied, the wedding would take place, but not after the manner of the whites, with swell dinners, wine and dancing; honey-mooning and such baubles of fashion. No minister of the gospel would tie the 'divine' knot, to be broken later in the divorce courts. The ceremony would be:

" 'Here, warrior! take your wife. Support her! but let it be with her own help. Protect her! and if any man comes between you, you have the right to kill him. '

"That is all the ceremony there would be. No book-form invocation, no sacerdotal blessing of the 'higher' order. The ritual of my progenitors must enter into any marriage of mine."

While the barbaric entered into this primitive conception of wedlock as explained by Cogewea, perhaps it was as near right in its essence—considering the educational status of the two peoples— as that of this Nation, with its double-standard of morals and its *Reno* hackle. It was in vogue the centuries; and there was no lost virtue among the tribes as now. No woman dared go wrong; (3) and her bonds of matrimony were more sacred to her than if a half-score Christian ministers had forged the mystic knot. In this day, it requires but a few dollars in some crafty lawyer's pocket to sunder the 'holy bonds' which unite as 'one' in the sight of God and the angels. The casting of stones is at best precarious.

Cogewea was neither pagan nor heretical in her philosophic deductions. She believed in the one Divine Ruler, nor did she accept any substitute. But she was at a loss about the churches. There were so many of them! all differing in creed and all claiming to be in the right. Fighting each other! mauling with the gospel-club. Her people Roman Catholics, she was alone on the trail; having no choice of denominations. Where was the difference? All were trending towards the same goal—the same plain. The Great Spirit of her race and the God of the white man were the same Deity. only under different names. However, the Indian had the greater respect for his Divinity, never reproaching nor finding fault with Him. Her conviction was: "Let every one choose their own path" and live true to their own concepts; for somewhere and somehow all trails converge to but one common channel. Life, as pertaining to this existence, is a mere chance, a potential gamble. Mingled sunshine and shadow — mostly shadow. Bird-song and wailing—mostly wailing. The finale: A leap into the dark! Impressive obsequies—provided you have left the price—and the bouquets you missed on the way.

A covetous light had come into Densmore's eyes, which escaped the notice of Cogewea. But not so with Stemteemä, who sat opposite him. A close reader of character, it was not necessary that she comprehend any

part of the conversation in determining the motives of
her pale faced visitor. Apparently unheeding, she discerned and understood, as the Easterner again took up
the topic in which he was now deeply engrossed:

"Cogewea, do you really mean what you say about
the marriage ritual of your ancestors governing your
union?"

"Why should I toy with the flames?"

Evidently puzzled by her enigmatic answer, Densmore
hesitated long before venturing to reply:

"Perhaps you're right, doubtless you are right! I
don't know. I am no student of theology, but we are
agreed on the marriage question. That ankle process.
It is great! Why not——"

"Sure!" was the coquettish interruption. "A peculiar
world, this, with its varied peoples, rites and customs.
Whether the consummation of bride-catching depends
upon the consummate skill of a plains horseman and the
superior fleetness of his mount; or the Bushman's ability to surprise and knock out the two front teeth of the
object of his affections with a club; or a tribesman's
fleeting glance at an exposed ankle; the nuptial bonds
are perhaps, as effective as those of the anthemed ceremony, law-invoked and ofttimes baptized with a Bac-
chanalian flow of wine. Whatever the mode of procedure, the primal objective is the same throughout all nature; the nesting birds of the air and the denning creatures of sea and land included. *All* must be equally guided and sanctioned by a Divine cause ruling universally.
But seemingly, married people seldom get along harmoniously. They do not respect the solemn, codified
altar vows; which, mayhap in cases are too exacting.
Selfishness is at the bottom of all such troubles. I would
prefer remaining an old maid, although the Indians do
not approve of bachelor-girls running loose about the
country."

"Neither do I," agreed Densmore with a laugh.
"They look too lonesome! I have turned Injun and am

ready to take you according to the ancient manner of your tribe. What do you say?"

"I have explained the terms," was the laughing reply. "First please my relatives. Begin with Stemteemä. She heads the list."

Before Densmore could respond, the grandmother again spoke sharply to the girl, which stopped their further conversation.

"I think that you had better 'skiddo'!" said Cog·ewea. "Stemteemä is growing uneasy of your presence. She says that she has been through smoking long ago, but we have not asked her for the story and now she will not tell it today. To humor her you must hike! Go! She wants to lecture me, I know, or she would not be so anxious for me to remain alone with her. You can feel sorry for me."

The Easterner would have demurred, but was silenced by a gesture. He left the lodge in a very ill frame of mind. Chagrined and disappointed, he had failed to fathom the girl. It was several minutes after the door-flap closed before the Stemteemä broke silence.

"My grandchild! you talk too much to that pale face. He does not mean right by you! he is having sport with you. He wants to make a fool of you, that all the young people may laugh. You think he has love because he follows you. Not so! He is blinding you with false words. He is here to cheat you; all that any white man wants of the Indian girl. It is only to put her to shame, then cast her aside for his own kind — the pale faced squaw. Do not be foolish! my Cogewea. Do not bring grief to my old age; do not wound my heart. You are too free with all men, especially this strange *Sho-yah-pee* I do not like him! His eye speaks the lie. You must not be so much with him. If his intentions were good, he would want to take you to the priest and marry you. All that the pale faces desire of Indian women, is pleasure and riches. When they get these, they marry back among their own race. I have lived many snows and I see the right way. You have heard my words."

"My grandmother," spoke Cogewea after due silence, "do not mistrust me. I have not wronged in dealings with this Sho-yah-pee. I do not forget your counseling of other suns. I will always remember and I may stumble, but I shall never fall."

"The young bird needs the protection of its mother's wing," rejoined the old woman solemnly, "for the hawk is ever near. I know that you mean right, my grandchild; my heart tells me that. But I dream of you often and my guiding spirits point me the trouble lurking along your way; that this white man is seeking your undoing. You will be wronged! His tongue is forked; his breath is poison. His eye lowers dark with evil. Child of my daughter! be warned! Have care of your actions! be afraid of this stranger! I am old, and I want to die happy. But this can not be if I see you on the desolate trail of a living death. My heart is sick! I can say no more."

Tears were welling from eyes as yet undimmed by years. The Stemteemä had always been suspicious of the Caucasian, and her long contact with the race had well justified her antipathy. A good judge of character she distrusted Densmore as a dangerous companion for the impulsive, free-speaking girl under her care. Cogewea was visibly affected when she again vouched safe to speak.

"Now Stemteemä! you misunderstand. I think Alfred is a good man. I have never heard him utter a word that could be termed ungentlemanly. We were only talking about the Okanogans of long ago, when they were married without the priests; in the snows that you once knew."

"I once heard him say that he gambles. You think that I cannot understand the white man's language, but I do some of it. A man who gambles will not be a good provider for his family."

"Please, Stemteemä!" coaxed Cogewea, taking the wrinkled hand in her own, soft and tapering. "Do not be mad at him! He wants to hear stories of long ago,

when you were a child. You will tell him some, won't
you? I will translate into his own language."

The ancient woman pondered long before answering.
There was a struggling with memory. With eyes partly
closed and gazing into space, her face betrayed no emotion. She had drifted back nearly a century— to childhood days by the rolling tide of the mighty Swa-net-
qah. She again hears the roar and rumble of the great
water-fall and the laughter of children playing. She
hears the scalp-halloo, announcing the victorious return
of the foraying war party. She sees, as the sun sinks
in the west, the hunters enterting the village, stagger-
ing under the spoils of the chase. She sees the women
toiling at the river's edge, stripping and curing the
stores of golden salmon. She visions the festive gathering and the dance; the council fire and the winter-
evening story telling. All this! then the sombre reality
of tribal decadence sweeps a dark and lowering cloud
over the silvery dream of the past. The former Princess of the Okanogans starts! passes her hand across
her brow and speaks as by inspiration:

"Yes! I will tell this Sho-yah-pee a tale of the long
ago. I will tell him of the coming of the pale face;
when the tribes were many and strong. When the warriors were brave and did not turn from the enemy.
When the women were true; and virtue, like a plumed
bird, adorned every maiden's brow. Yes! I will tell
him of the invasion by the despoiler, and of the wasting
of my people. Of the dawn of the night which burst on
the Okanogans, heavy with the vapors of death, from
over the trail of the sunrise, I will speak and you shall
interpret my words."

CHAPTER XII.

ON BUFFALO BUTTE

Love is sunshine, hate is shadow,
Life is checkered shade and sunshine,
* * * * * * *
Day is restless, night is quiet,
Man imperious, woman feeble;

—*Hiawatha*

THE riders were in the hills to capture a few stray bronchos, escaped from the general corral. They had succeeded in chasing them into a cunningly constructed "blind" in a wooded canyon where the colts were branded, and were now returning to the ranch in high spirits.

"Jim," called Celluloid Bill, as he half turned in his saddle to face his foreman, "yo' ain't goin' to let that there tenderfoot cut yo' out from yo're gal when he can't ride a cayuse an' yo' the champeen broncho twister of th' Flathead? Ain't goin' let th' feller get th' best of yo' in th' deal are yo'? He follers her aroun' like a stray maverick of th' range."

"Sho' thin'!" broke in Roedo Jack with well feigned earnestness. "That there guy is plum' good schemer. I knowed for some time now that he fell offen th' cayuse an' busted his elbow a purpose so to be with Jim's gal. No 'scuse for his twistin' his arm under his-self as he did. An' th' gal 'pears mighty 'tentive to the guy. I never hit th' love trail for any great distance, but I can see a danger signal when it flares up like sheet lightenin' an' big as half section of sage desert."

"I hater see Jim get bad lef'; I hater see that there guy win. Mos' wish we'd a dug a six-foot grave," moaned Silent Bob.

"You may have a chance to dig that there grave yet," growled the foreman, who usually stood these banterings

in guarded silence. A man of few words and deep passion, this chaffing at this time stirred his inmost soul.
His bosom was torn with conflicting emotions. What
had come over Cogewea? She no longer rode out with
him on the range as of yore, nor strolled among the
river pines in the gloaming. He had not objected to her
nursing the tenderfoot. Indeed, he was glad that she
could do so; but his heart was bitter towards him for
stealing her affections. What right had this man with
his smooth, polished ways to step between them? Could
he be sincere, or was it through revenge for the trick
played him? In either case, Jim now determined to
bring the affair to a climax at the very first opportunity.
He had never asked the girl for her hand, but he would
do so, and if she refused in preference for the stranger,
he would take his "medicine" so long as every thing
was on the square; but if the guy was false to the little
gal — Jim's face grew stern — there would be a funeral
at the Horseshoe Bend.

Jim's meditations were broken by Rodeo, who, pointing to the east where Cogewea on Wanawish could be
seen passing over a low swell, exclaimed with deliberate
exactness:

"Behold, old skate! yo' gal an' alone for a wonder!
Better hit up th' breeze afore that there blond headed
pal of yourn follers her like a calf. Any slow bird can
get the mornin' worm but it takes th' swift winged hawk
to capture any thin' worth while."

"Dam' the feller!" retorted Jim in a burst of temper.
"If I know my own name, no pretender that can't ride
is a goin' get her."

"Aw hell!' Yo' talk like yo' mean business!" flung
Rodeo with provoking sarcasm. "Talk is cheap! It
takes money to buy a bottle of bitters."

"You bet I mean it! Old Jim don't waste no time
a boastin'."

"Gwan! Yo' worked aroun' them there corrals so
long, feller, yo're startin' a peddlin' their dust."

"You'll see! If somebody is doin' me dirt, there'll be

somethin' stirrin' and don't you forget it.   I ain't kickin' if all is fair.''

With this the foreman, ignoring further jibes from his companions, swung off at right angles and headed for Buffalo Butte, where he knew the romantic girl would be admiring the sunset. He rode at a hard pace. He was mad! desperately mad to think that the fellow who could not ride should come along and splash into the affairs of the best rider of the Flathead, and take from him his girl.

But as Jim rode, his anger abated. The cool evening breeze fanning his hot brow, mellowed the hatred that rankled his brain. The world grew more pleasing. Charity, the greatest of divine attributes, swept bitterness aside. Surely Cogewea could not love the polished stranger. Had she not left him and ridden alone to the hills? Perhaps he would find her willing to listen. What girl could afford to ignore the hand of the best rider of the Flathead? And when this brown nymph did accept him, there would be fiddlers and an old fashioned dance at the big log house. No waltzes nor two-steps, 'cause he couldn't do 'em. Only the quadrilles and the ''Virginia hoe-down'' of other days; with a ''clog'' by Rodeo Jack. There would be a jug of ''tangle-foot'' to complete the festive joy. There would be no starched guys from town with white shirts, stiff collars and plug hats, with hair all parted in the middle. None but cowpunchers with gaudy shirts, and with silk handkerchiefs about their necks; and the old maid homesteaders from out on the flats. The enamored foreman imagined that he heard the caller yelling:

''S-w-i-n-g! yo' pa'-d-ner!'' and:

''Don't forget that purty little gal,
The gal yo' left b-e-h-i-n' yo'!''

And the light step to the tune of the ''Red River Jig.''

Thus the bronzed rider dreamed, his stoical features softened by that most refining of emotions— love!

Cogewea had galloped across the intervening miles

of flats to the foothills. Here she slackened pace and
climbed the steep ridge to the summit of Buffalo Butte.
Dismounting she left Wanawish, with a lariat trailing
from his neck, to feed on the bunch-grass, while she
mounted a large rock, where she had often reclined. The
glow of the setting sun lit the western sky with the
ruddy sheen of a prairie fire. The splendid Flathead
valley lay below, while the mighty Rockies, like Cyclo-
pean battlements, towered in the east. Cogewea gazed
enraptured. A vision of the dim misty past rose up
before her. The stately buffalo roved in the distance,
while the timid antelope stood sentinel on the neighboring heights. An Indian village on the move, wound its
way like a great mottled serpent over the crest of the
highest ridge. It reached the brow, where each separate
horse and rider showed in sharp silhouette against the
horizon, then vanished over the crest. The girl arose
and stood as in a trance. Slowly, with outstretched
arms she whispered.

"My beautiful Eden! I love you! My valley and
mountains! It is too bad that you be redeemed from the
wild, once the home of my vanishing race and where
the buffalo roamed at will. Where hunting was a joy
to the tribesmen, who communed with the Great Spirit.
I would that I had lived in those days,—that the blood
of the white man had not condemned me an outcast
among my own people."

Cogewea sank down, burying her face in her hands.
A half suppressed sob burst from her lips, convulsing
her slender form. In silence she remained as the evening shadows deepened about her. She had often stood
upon this butte at the close of the summer day in dreamy
sadness, but never had she felt so lonely and forsaken.
The form and face of the white man constantly intruded upon her vision. She had thought to ask Densmore to ride with her, but some impelling influence had
deterred her. Did she really love him? Did he love
her? The warning of the aged grandmother was troubling, and in sheer desperation she had fled to the solitude

of her old haunt, the wild, lonely butte. Her sobbing was broken by:

"What is it, Sis? What troubles my little squaw?"

Startled, the girl looked up. Jim was standing over her tenderness depicted in his usually stern face. She did not answer and he repeated, his hand mechanically hovering about his pistol's grip.

"Tell me! Cogewea! what is wrong. Has that there tender——"

"Nothing! nothing Jim! only you have spoiled my evening hour."

There was a piteous attempt at a smile and her eyes, tear-dimmed, turned from his and gazed out over the now shadowy valley. Jim, touched by her visible emotion, stood irresolute for a moment and then asked simply:

"How have I spoiled it, Sis?"

"By coming here when I wanted to be alone. Why did you come?"

"I came 'cause you have no time for me at home, only for that there white man. I want a chance to talk to you without some one buttin' in on me. I saw you crossin' the flat and I was lonesome for you. I most had to come. Do you really care 'cause I spoiled your evenin'?"

"Not exactly since you are here," she murmured faintly.

"Now, Sis! if you care, why, I'll go away."

These last words came more as a plea. They touched the heart of the sensitive girl. She turned to him with a smile of old.

"No Jim! I do not want you to go. Stay and ride home with me. I was just kidding you. I would not hurt my big brother's feelings for the world. I think too much of him."

"Will you ever care for me more than you would a brother?"

"That is the most that any woman could care for a man. What more do you want of me?"

Her light bantering made him desperate and he blundered:

"Cogewea! Sis! I want you! I want you to marry me and you must not say no. Tell me that you will. I cannot take no!"

The girl looked up in surprise. This was the last thing that she had expected from the man facing her and asking for her hand in his own rough way. This man she loved only as some big, kind protecting brother. She sympathized with him for the blood ties of the breed, and here he had misunderstood her.

"Well, I be doggoned Jim!" she at length exclaimed in evident embarrassment. "I hadn't the least idea that you cared for me in that light. You sure have surprised me! I always thought that it was only a brother's love you had for me. I am sorry that I have nothing more than a sister's love to offer you in return for your devotion. I love you as a big brother and no more."

"Brother hell! Then who in blazes do you love?"

"No one that I know of."

"Are you sure Sis? Do you mean it good?"

She did not answer and man-like, he took it for granted that she was not sure of her own mind. His soul was tortured with racking uncertainty. He was like an animal at bay — was going to fight for what he regarded his own. He questioned eagerly.

"Then you—you don't care for that there feller— you don't love that there tenderfoot guy?"

"Why! I— I— like him."

"You do! eh! Have you only a *sister's* love for that there guy too?"

Cogewea's mind was busy; she was fighting for time. She knew this man of the range too well to trifle with his sincere heart.

"No- no!" she said slowly, "I do not love him with—"

She hesitated in utter confusion. The steady gaze of the Westerner disconcerted her and her eyes again sought the refuge of the gloaming.

"And if that there feller asks you to marry him,"
continued Jim in a voice pathetic in its earnestness,
"what would you do about it?"

"Is it information that you are after?" she asked
with a degree of impatience.

"Sis! I just want to know if I will ever have a chance
—a show—some of these days; or some time?"

"Listen! Jim! let me tell you. He will never seek
my hand. I know this, because of my blood. He is of
a very proud family and I am a 'breed.' You understand the situation. Of course I do not consider myself
inferior to him even if I am a 'squaw.' But that is
why I say he will never ask me to be his wife, even if
I did care. It is a cinch that I will never propose to
him, and should he ever ask me, I would refuse."

"Do you think, Sis, that you would? Do you——"

"Yes, because he is a white man, and I am an Indian,
or half, rather."

"Then you think that is a good reason?   I'm glad,
but lots of Injun women marry white men."

"Yes! I do think it a good reason. You know how
sensitive we all are about our Indian blood. No difference how little we have of it, it seems to stick in our
minds. If I was to marry a white man and he would
dare call me a 'squaw'—as an epithet with the sarcasm
that we know so well—I believe that I would feel like
killing him. That is my reason. Should I marry my
own kind, he would never throw my Indian descent in
my teeth."

"Then there may yet be a show for me?"

"No! Jim! never! You must give that up. Dismiss
it from your mind. I cannot love you in the light I
should want to love a husband. Too many homes are
ruined; too many lives are blighted because of the lack
of love at the fireside. It is the only element which
will prevent husband and wife from drifting apart. Love
is essential to the perfection of every life and when
denied at home, will be sought elsewhere. I will never
marry a man unless I love him and he is of my own

kind. Money will never buy me. I'd rather die unmarried than sell myself for the glitter of gold— the
gold which is so rare among my own people."

Although Jim's heart ached in every fiber, he showed
no visible perturbation. With a forced laugh and a
wave of his brown hand which swept the valley, he said:
"And here! out on this here flat, we have old maids
by wagons full. They're lonely and maybe dyin' for
somebody."

"Yes! they are an industrious class of women and
mostly school-marms all making their own living. Why
don't you marry one of them? You would be ahead
by a broad hundred and sixty acres of land; could afford to quit punching cattle, settle down and boss your
own domain."

Jim picked up a small stone and threw it far down
the steep ridge before answering. His attitude was
melodramatic.

"I might marry one of them if they'd ask me. But
I'm afraid I'd drown her if she ever happen to call me
a 'buck'. I'd sure be spectin' 'mestic complications!
None of them there school-marms could ' preciate the
best rider of the Flathead."

.."Of-course not! It would take a real sport to do
that. If you depend on your riding ability to win a
sweetheart from among those 'Missourians;' you will
sure die of a sour crop."

"Sis! I'll never marry any one if not you!" he exclaimed with sudden impulse. "And listen to what
I'm tellin' you! If that there white man takes you 'way
from me and I find he is playin' you false— and I think
he is—I sure will leave this feller's mark on him—
Savey?"

This speech was delivered in a low even tone and as
he spoke, the Westerner's hand touched the hilt of the
six-gun at his hip. Cogewea's breast thrilled with a
sickening fear. All the warnings of the Stemteemä and
her own wavering doubts concerning the Shoyahpee,

came rushing through her mind. Her voice was tense with piteous anguish as she pleaded.

"Oh! Jim! You do not mean that he might be false? You cannot mean that you would kill him? You are only guessing at a wild improbability. It is impossible. You are taking chances!"

"You bet I mean both! Straight goods, Sis!"

"Then James LaGrinder, I will never marry. Never!"

Was she sincere? She doubted herself. Jim stood impassive, arms folded and gazing out over the darkening Flathead.

"Let's hike for home," she exclaimed. 'It will soon be dark and here we have been chewing the rag for an hour."

She jumped off the rock and began coiling her lariat. She tied it to her saddle, mounted Wanawish and started down the steep declivity. Jim rode in her wake a rejected suitor. He pondered!

"She loves no one and may yet come my way. I can afford to wait. She can't love that there eastern guy— a feller who falls off a hoss so soon."

But his newly awakened resentment for Densmore, he could not banish, nor did he try to smother it. Brooding ,he now hated him. He felt that he was false, not a true man. There was bound to be an accounting sometime; a reckoning when Cogewea would learn of his true character. Until then, he would abide his time.

Silently the two wended their way down the bluff trail. When they reached the flat, with hardly a word they spurred into a gallop homeward. Their thoughts were disturbing as they rode through the gloaming. These were of the tenderfoot, who had come into both their lives. The lonely cry of a night-bird, and the plaintive wailing of a solitary coyote in the distance, seemed fitting to perturbed mentality. They arrived home to see Densmore returning from an unsuccessful fishing trip. Mary, the timid, fair-skinned half-blood, was beating a tin pan, a belated supper call ever welcomed by the hungry riders.

CHAPTER XIII.

A VISIT TO STEMTEEMA'S TEPEE

Filled the red-stone pipe for smoking,
With tobacco from the South-land,
Mixed with bark of the red willow,
And with herbs and leaves of fragrance.
—*Hiawatha.*

THE hot, sweltry days of August were closing. The tenth of September, which marked the opening of the great fall roundup—when the riders of the "H-B" would remain in the saddle from morning till night—was drawing near. It was Sabbath, and the ranch home was almost deserted. The boys, arrayed in brilliant shirts, with flaming silk handkerchiefs knotted loosely about their necks, had departed early; some going to Polson to play monte with the Kootenais, while others headed for Sloan's Ferry, a favorite resort of the rangers some miles down the river.

The boys surmised that Silent Bob had a new girl, a homesteader out on the flat. Seemingly he did not care to go with them of late, but dragged behind, ever managing to get lost on the trail. He was beginning to wear fancy ties and to take unusual care of his Sunday-best-clothes. The boys also remarked that he stopped at a certain lonely shack, where his sorrel stood at the wooden gate till sundown every Sunday, before he ever thought of going home. They knew not her name and with all their joking they got nothing more from Bob than a slow:

"Aw! shucks! I ain't a castin' no ropes for any schoolmarm troubles. I hater think of bein' tied up for life; I hater think of bein' bossed by a Missourian."

Jim had manifested but little interest in this particular excursion. He felt "kinder knocked out" and wanted to rest. Celluloid Bill urged:

"Better come on with us to town to skin the Kootenais. We'll bring home a jug. They say that there bootlaiger has a big supply cached, an' th' Gov'ment ossifers cain't locate him. But by heck we can! Come on! don't buck! Yo' ain't got no colt to home yo' 'fraid of losin' have you'?—old sox! Yo' ain't scared somebody corralin yo' slick-ear, are yo'?''

At this sally the boys all laughed and Jim, unable to withstand their banterings, proceeded to saddle his horse and join the crowd, growling with ill concealed annoyance:

"It will take a durn' good roper to corral the colt that the best rider of the Flathead can't get his lariat on. You savey that?''

Cogewea stood on the veranda and saw the gay cavalcade as it streamed from the barnyard, the horses cavorting and the riders swinging their sombreros, yelling with exuberant abandonment. She noticed with what grace and ease Jim sat his saddle. She admired his strength and skill and could almost love him—but for the white man who had come so strangely into her life. For all of the foreman's fierce temperament, he had never shown her the least disrespect. On the other hand, he endeavored to augment her happiness by sharing her troubles. His rugged, uncultured exterior was offset with a well meaning heart and a deep loyalty to friends. The girl watched the boys until they swung onto the upper road and were lost to view behind a curve. She then started for Stemteemä's lodge, but met Densmore as he emerged from the bunk-house. His arm was no longer in splints, and he had several times ridden out on the flats, always careful, however, to have a gentle horse. Cogewea accosted him:

"Why didn't you go to town today?''

"Because I wanted to see you; and—and perhaps you can prevail on Stem—Stem-tam—your grandmother to tell the promised story.''

"Is that really why you stayed?'' she asked in doubting tones.

"Well—the boys do not appeal to me and doubtless I do not appeal to them. I am not in their class and they naturally deem it quite a joke to make it 'hot for the tenderfoot', as they are pleased to call me. There is the foreman. He does not like me and I am sure that I am not in love with him. He tried to get me killed," continued the Easterner bitterly. "He knew that I could not ride a horse that the most experienced riders here are unable to back."

"Oh! you are mistaken!" retorted Cogewea with a tinge of resentment. "While the other boys may not stick Croppy, Jim can do so easily."

"Perhaps! but I do not believe that he can, from what I have heard about that horse. But even so, that does not excuse him from trying to get me killed."

"Jim did not try to get you killed! With the deep, soft mulch of the corral spread like a great pad over its entire breadth, there was no special danger of fatality. The same joke had been played often and you were the first to meet with more than a scratch. Jim was sorry enough and did all in his power to make amends. He has the best of hearts," she concluded with a suspicion of anxiety in her voice, "but I would not unnecessarily antagonize him."

Piqued and disappointed at her attitude, Densmore replied with a degree of warmth:

"Why! you speak as if I were entirely dependent and helpless!"

"No, not that! but you do not understand a cow-puncher. They are the truest of friends when you are one of them; only you cannot be too careful. Do not incur needless enmity! Nothing is to be gained."

Not fully comprehending the situation and stung with what he regarded open partiality on the part of Cogewea for the dusky foreman, the Easterner felt a smothering rage toward Jim. Could it be that this low-bred rope thrower was barring the way to his desires? Desperate, he declared heedlessly:

"Alright! You may be correct, but we'll see. I did not start the feud, and there are different ways by which it may be ended."

A thrill of apprehension passed over the girl. Jim's
declaration on the Butte came to her with chilling vivid-
ness. It was indubitable that should Densmore blindly
cross the fiery breed, a tragedy was likely to ensue.
But nothing was to be accomplished by argument, and
glad of an excuse to dismiss an unpleasant theme, she
exclaimed with a return to her old-time gaiety:
"Oh! I forgot! You wanted to hear the story promised by Stemteemä. I will run and see if she will tell it
now."

With this, she sped down the slope and soon returned
with the information that they could go to the tepee
within a half hour; that the aged woman would then
be ready to talk and would tell of her people of an
earlier day. Cogewea went into the house to procure a
great, silk handkerchief to present to the grandmother,
while Densmore took a chair on the veranda to await
the time of going.

The Indian is a strange race. Most of the old people
do not make use of English, although the majority of
them understand many words and can speak them but
will not do so unless absolutely necessary. If alone
with the whites, they will talk if occasion demands; but
if in the presence of the younger Indians, they can hardly be induced to do so. They are afraid of being laughed
at for mistakes made. They dread ridicule from their
own kind far more than the mockery of the alien.
Recognizing the linguistic ability of the educated youth,
it is expected of them to assume the role of interpreter.

The Stemteemä was no exception to this rule. It was
when she lived on the banks of the Columbia with her
three little grandchildren, and it was mid-winter. A
fringe of ice covered the stream along the shore, leaving
an open channel in the center. The ice was very un-
sound, with many air-holes in evidence. A couple of
young men came from the town to fish. Going out on
the ice, they became fearful and returning to the shore,
came directly to the tepee. When the children saw them,
Cogewea proposed to her sisters, Julia and Mary, that

they pretend not to understand English, to which they
readily agreed. The visitors called at the doorway to
know if the ice was safe and if there were any fish.
To this, the children stared blankly and the grandmother scolded them for not informing the men that
the ice was bad and that they would get drowned
should they venture on it. Cogewea countered by asking why she did not do it herself, if she understood what
was wanted; to which she replied:

"I can speak when I have to do so. But what did you
learn the language and books of the pale face for?
They do no good unless you make use of them when
needed?"

The strangers, supposing that they were not understood, and after commenting on the dress and appearances of the tepee occupants, turned back to the river.
Cogewea had meant to warn them before reaching the
danger zone, while her two more timid sisters had fled
in hiding. The grandmother raged and threatened,
then growing more perturbed, rushed to the river bank,
calling and waving her arms in frantic signals. The
fishermen looked back, laughed and continued farther
out on the ice. Cogewea was on the verge of calling to
them, when the old woman let loose a jargon of English,
which proved effective, if not in real classic style. She
saved the lives of the venturesome boys, who often visited at the lodge after that. (1)

If anything is to be accomplished with an Indian, it
is imperious that an agreement be made good; that an
appointment be kept inviolate. Ever suspicious and
wary, a broken faith is a very difficult chasm to bridge;
and knowing this Cogewea saw to it that they were not
belated at the lodge. Entering, they found the occupant
sitting on a bedding of blankets. At the girl's prompting, Densmore shook hands with the aged woman and
then sat down on a buffalo robe which had been placed
for him. Cogewea took place at the side of her grandparent, and after an interval spoke:

"We have come to hear the Stemteemä tell of other

snows; when the tribes were strong, and of the coming
of the Shoyahpee.''

Unhurriedly and in but few words the ancient squaw
made reply. Cogewea explained that in conformity to
an epochal custom, the grandmother would, before beginning her story, take a smoke, that she might be
in the mood for talking. She must have time to gather
her mind's thoughts.

The girl then gently took the tobacco pouch from the
trembling hands and bringing the small stone pipe from
the same receptacle, filled it with the fragrant *kinnikinnick;* and lighting it, returned it to the smoker. During the ensuing ''peace pipe invocation'', Cogewea, at
Densmore's request, elucidated on the mysteries of this
rite of antiquity:

''Smoking is an exclusive characteristic of our race,''
she said. ''Its origin is scarce preserved in the dim legends of the past. The oldest pipes were straight, tapering trumpet-like tubes, made of clay or stone. Perhaps
these were closely contemporaneous with the non-angu-
lar variety, showing the funnel-like orifice for both the
stem and tobacco. Ofttimes these later pipes assumed
fantastic forms, representing animals, birds, reptiles,
human and mythical beings; many of them evidently of
a sacred nature. They are found in certain old burial
grounds and are claimed by some writers to have belonged to a different race than ours. But we were always here. I hate this latest supposition that we came
from China or Japan. Neither of those people nor any
other ever smoked until they had learned it directly
or indirectly from us. They modeled their pipes after
ours in a general way, though improved in form. The
Indian recognizing this proficiency, copied the white-
man's pattern, which is traceable from the primitive to
the present conformation.

''We had our peace pipes and our war pipes and no
important undertaking was ever attempted without a
smoke-prayer. These were usually assembly, or council smokes; the pipe being passed from one person to

another. There always have been, and are still some individual men who do not smoke; but in our tribe, as in many others, even the women indulge, but not universally. It is not uncommon to see a young woman drawing on a cigarette in just the same manner as a white society lady. But these 'coffin-nails' are of the white man's inception, along with his multitudinous diseased adjuncts of civilization: whiskey, beer, wine and opium with attending crimes and ills. And to cap the irony of it all, he brings the 'glad tidings' of an endlessly burning hell where we are roasted for emulating his 'superior' examples.

"Smoking is the only ideal of our race that the Caucasian has deemed worthy of perpetuation. This, perhaps, is because it has been considered the worst of our vices. But the Shoyahpee converted it into vice. We did not use strong, straight tobacco and virus-infected wrappers. We employed a very mild and almost, if not entirely harmless mixture of bark and leaves, and among some of the tribes, a minute amount of tobacco; such as you see Stemteemä now smoking. Southern Indians used more of this narcotic plant than did their northern cousins, and here in the far northwest, we had none of it. Often the smoking material was slightly oiled by rubbing it with buffalo, or other melted fats. This was especially true of the plains Indians. The process improved the flavor and also augmented the fire-holding qualities."

Further dissertation by Cogewea was interrupted by the Stemteemä, who, putting aside her pipe, spoke in a low guttural tone. She was ready to begin her story.

CHAPTER XIV.

THE DEAD MAN'S VISION

I beheld too, in that vision
All the secrets of the future,
Of the distant days that shall be.
I beheld the westward marches,
Of the unknown, crowded nations.
　　　　　　　　—Hiawatha.

"THIS was long ago," began Stemteemä, "many many snows. It happened in the time of my grandfather, when he was a young chief of the powerful *Schw-ayl-p^k* (1) and the *Okanogans.* This story I am telling you is true. It was given me by my father who favored me among his many children. I was his youngest child from his youngest wife, who was cherished among his twelve wives. He told me the tales that were sacred to his tribe; honored me with them, trusted me. Treasured by my forefathers, I value them. I know that they would want them kept only to their own people if they were here. But they are gone and for me the sunset of the last evening is approaching and I must not carry with me this history.

"In that time the pale face and his vices had not reached us. The country was wild and the Great Spirit was kind to the tribes. Berries grew on the fruit-bushes in abundance, while game and fish were plentiful. Buffaloes were to be killed on these plains, all ample for food, robes and lodge-sheltering. There were so many that the prairies showed black like the shadows from passing clouds.

"My ancestors were warriors and medicine men; the one brave and fearless, the other wise in the wisdom of spirits. My grandfather and father could not have become chiefs had they not been courageous from small to great things. A leader must be a good hunter. He must not know the word 'fear'. He must endure the hardships of war, waged every spring and fall against the fierce Blackfeet and Sioux. If favored by the Great Spirit, he would win in battle and return from war more beloved by his tribe. Ponies were taken from the enemy, and their best looking women brought home to become wives. Any others were killed, or some times retained as slaves. A warrior's ability and bravery was estimated by the number of captured ponies or scalps he could display in the village. These evidenced that he had met the foe, that he was not boasting the lie. This was why scalping was practiced by all the tribes.

"Always, the falling of the first snow was the sign that the Great Spirit was calling. The tribesmen then ceased hunting the buffalo, deer, elk, moose and antelope. Gathering in the village, everything was laid aside for the *Spirit's Days*, which were fourteen sundowns. They danced in worship to the Spirit, to continue His favors to the tribe; that the trees, the grass and herbs be perpetual; that the deer and all game be plentiful the coming season and that the red salmon again swarm up the Swanitkqah. I am old and I am wondering why the salmon no longer come as when I was a child. The stream then throbbed with the big fish.

"We have been told that it is wrong to pray to the Great Spirit as we were taught. But since we adopted prayers to the white man's God-spirit, we have died from pestilences which he brought. Even the buffalo are no more; gone to the shadowy Hunting Grounds of the hereafter, with the warriors of old. I shall soon follow, where the pale face can not dispossess us, for he will not be there. He will no longer lure our children from us with his smooth tongue and books, which here serves to make them bad by imitating the destroyers of our race.

"With this whitening of the first snow—this calling of the Spirit—the medicine man had built a great lodge of poles and bark, or of dressed skins. A long fire-hearth was in the center, that the dancing might be lighted at night, as well as give warmth for the people. These lodges I have myself seen before the Black Robes stopped us from such worship of the Indian Spirit.

"They danced for fourteen sundowns, thankful for the past successful season, for health and victory in war. Each hunter and warrior supplicated that he again be permitted to see the new life of spring. All that time, day and night they danced, as long as strength lasted. Some of the warriors did not sleep. This was to show their endurance, their ability to stand the rigors of the warpath and the chase. It was at one of these dances that this story I am telling you, happened.

"Berries, game and fish had been abundant and the people had plenty of dried foods for the winter moons. They danced the fourteen sundowns, when suddenly and without any illness, one medicine man died. He was perfectly well when he dropped dead. Immediately the wind came up and it stormed fiercely, shutting the dancers in.

"They used to bury the dead in tops of trees, or, if he was a chief, medicine man or a great warrior, his body was left in his own tepee and his best horse killed at its doorway. This was, that he might ride the swifter to the Spirit Land. Their finest robes and skins were also left with the dead, as a gift to the Great Spirit, that He might take pity on the family and call no more of them over the death trail. The village then moved to a new location, leaving the dead alone.

"The medicine man was really dead and cold for two sundowns. The storm was bad and they could not take the body to its own tepee for burial. On the third sunrise, to the astonishment of the people, the dead man came back from the death-sleep. Life returned and he stood up from the robes in which he was wrapped. The women, frightened, ran away, but the warriors dared not run. It would be cowardly to fly even though they could not understand. The newly alive medicine man called:

"Come all you braves and warriors! I have something to tell you, for your own benefit. I came back to warn you, to show you the right way to go. It is important and I will speak before I go again and forever.

" 'The messenger of the Great Spirit took me away. He took me high, up very high. I could see you, oh! my people, around my poor body. You were wailing over that which is but a part of the earth; only useful here but nowhere else. While I was in the clouds, I could see that which is moving towards you from the sunrise, slowly—driving—surging in big herds like the buffaloes we hunt on the plains, only more vast. Terrible it comes, and gathering force it sweeps the land like the cloud-rack of death. Listen! Oh! my people. I saw the future as you see the mountains when the sun is undimmed by vapor from the waters. I asked my guide, whom I could not see yet felt his presence, to let me return and warn you; but he refused.

" 'We ascended higher, still higher until we reached the big bright doorway of the sun, which shines that the flowers, the grass and trees may grow to gladden you hearts. Again I begged my guide to permit me to come warn you of what is to be. Then some one I could not see, heard only his loud voice like the rushing of the wind through the forest—mingled with the melody of the waterfalls—calling to me:

" 'Go! man! go back! I am not ready to take you into the Happy Hunting Grounds till you have performed a duty assigned you. Go! warn your people of what is coming over the morning trail!'

" 'Then taking my hand, my guide pointed to the future—what is in store for you, my people—what the future holds for you. Listen!

" 'I saw a pale-faced nation moving from the sunrise; as many as the trees of the forest. My guide said to me: 'They are coming to take your hunting grounds from you'. Then knowing my thoughts, he exclaimed in pity:

" 'No! You cannot fight them as you do the common enemies of your tribe. They are many! Many more than your own race; many as the stars you see. When you kill the front of them, others come from the back of them; many more, double the number. This is to be! Do not attempt war with them. You would be crushed like the pine-cone by the mountain avalanche.

" 'The first of the strangers will come to work for your good,' said my guide. 'Only a few of them will strive to help the tribes; not for this life's benefit, but for the Hereafter; where the warriors gather when they leave this earth. You will know them; with their white skins and with hair on their faces. They will show you a new trail to the Great Spirit. You must believe them! for they, too, point to the hunting grounds of the future life which cannot be taken from you. These good men will help you from becoming lost on the night trail.''

" 'Again my guide pointed and I saw the pale faces fighting among themselves for the possession of our lands. Their feet were drowned in human blood of war which thundered everywhere.

" 'See!' said my guide. 'When this takes place, your people will long be gone. The land will be no more as it was. Go! now, man! go back to your people with the message given you. Tell them what you have seen, and to listen to the first pale face who comes to them. He will not deceive them, but will show them a better trail to the Spirit Land.'

"Then it seemed that I was falling! falling! falling! Plunging through wet clouds and it was far. But when I awoke, I was back here in my old, deserted body. I saw this body from the high, and I did not care to live in it again. I had not regretted leaving it for a better life.

" 'My friends and relations! I have now done that which the Great Spirit demanded of me. I am ready to leave you again, never to return. I want to go back where all is beauty and goodness, where the hardships of the warpath are unknown.'

"With this, the medicine man fell back among his robes and died forever. (2) My grandfather heard his words. He told the strange story to my father, who in turn gave it to me. I know that it must be true, for my father never spoke the lie. He did not talk two ways. I have heard the old Indians in my childhood time, wonder at the story. This is why the Black Robes were believed when they at last did come.

"The tribe watched and waited for the coming of the pale faces, but it was many snows before they came. It was so long that the prophecy of the dead-man was almost forgotten. The younger generation began to think it untrue; only some *chip-chap-tiqul*[k] (3) of the older Indians.

"My father was then a young man, a big chief, who ruled after the death of his father. He won fame for bravery among the tribes. (4) One day a warrior came to him in haste and deep trouble. He had found a pale faced man almost dead with cold and starvation and had brought him to his tepee in the night to be fed and warmed. What should be done with the strange being?

"The Chief ordered him brought to his own lodge, where it was discovered that he had hair growing on his face. The Chief then remembered the dead man's words and that the stranger must be treated well.

"After the white-skinned man had revived, he began teaching the way of the new trail to the Spirit Land. He wore a long black robe, from which he was called 'Black Robe'. He remained all winter with the Okanogans and learned much of our language. He told them that there were many more pale faces from where he came, that it was far away in the snow country towards the sunrise. That he and another Black Robe came together, but the bad Indians of the north had killed his companion. He had escaped. Maybe the Great Spirit took pity on him.

"When he began telling the Okanogans about the good White Spirit, they must not have understood, for they prayed to the Black Robe himself. They believed that he was more than man. Had not the dead man told them that the first to come would be able to show them a better way to reach the Hereafter? He must be in communication with the Great Spirit and thus understood their petitions. He forbid them praying to the sun, moon and stars, which the Indians thought to be the lodges of spirits.

"The Black Robe stayed till the snow disappeared before the Warm-winds, when he went towards the sunset. He said he was going to teach the tribes living there how to reach the White Spirit. That was the last ever heard of him. Maybe the bad Indians killed him, but we never knew.

"The Okanogans prayed the 'new way' for many snows, when they grew tired and almost forgot the words of the Black Robe. Then they saw the pale face again, two of them. They had no black robes, but the people tried to pray to them, as they remembered the words of the Black Robe. The pale faces only laughed at them. But this is another story which I may tell you some time.

"I have told you of the first pale face to come to our village and tribal grounds. The land is now all turned to the production of the white man's food, which we must also use. But we old people prefer our natural food; that which the earth gave us without scarring its bosom. The deer and other game; the fish, the berries and the roots were always here; placed here for us.

"It was good to live in a lodge with no roof to smother you; where you could breathe fresh all the time. It was this former life that we loved; when the men were brave and the women were true. This is all that I will talk today."

CHAPTER XV.

THE SUPERIOR RACE

. . . So well
His legendary song could tell—
On ancient deeds, so long forgot!
Of feuds, whose memory was not;
Of forests, now laid waste and bare.
—*Lay of the Last Minstrel.*

COGEWEA and Densmore left the Stemteemä in her lodge, to dream of the past. Thus would she live to the close of her days. The tepee would never be deserted for the dwellings of civilization, which had only proven death-traps for her race. Strolling to the river bank, the two sat down under the pines. Densmore was the first to speak. More to court favor, he broached a subject in which he felt no particular interest.

"Cogewea! are all those supposed facts as narrated by your grandmother concerning the first coming of the white man, or only legend? They seem to be no part of the chronicles."

"Why! man!" exclaimed the girl in unfeigned surprise, "didn't you see that she was in earnest? Sincerity was manifest in the telling. There are plenty of facts that are never alluded to by the recording historian. Are oral impartations of mind-stored truths to be reckoned as naught? A fact, like the life germ of a seed, is no less a fact from having been stored for a time."

"Well—yes! I thought the grandmother was in earnest, but mistaken. Lewis and Clark were the first Caucasians to reach and explore the great Northwest. That is recognized history."

"They were the first white *explorers* of the Northwest, but *not* the first to penetrate its sylvan wilds. It is my belief that the last two 'pale faces' Stemteemä
129

Caucasians to reach and explore the great Northwest. That is recognized history.''

''They were the first white *explorers* of the Northwest, but *not* the first to penetrate its sylvan wilds. It is my belief that the last two 'pale faces' Stemteemä mentioned were the famous pathfinders sent out by the Government, and I am sure that when you hear her story of these men, you will agree with me on that score. Stemteemä was a small child at the time of this second coming, and she has certainly seen more than a hundred snows. Of this, there can be no doubt. My mother was the youngest of twelve children and if she were now living, would be in her late sixties at least. The grandmother was shrunken with age as far back as I can remember. My early ancestors were all favored with remarkable longevity—those permitted to live out their natural lives—and retentive minds; some of them filling the role of tribal historians. While I am familiar with this prospective narrative of Stemteemä's I prefer that you hear it from her directly; that you may be convinced that I am not imbued with a mere fairy tale. The legend—as you seem to term it—of the 'Black Robe' can hardly be gainsaid.''

''It is all 'bilk' to me! I cannot conceive that any man, however zealous in the cause of soul-saving, would, without any prospect of worldly compensation, consider for a moment an undertaking so fraught with hardship and deadly danger. To my mind, such course would denote a mental unbalancing.''

''Without the fervent qualities of the true missionary, I agree that it is difficult to comprehend the motives which plunged into the wilderness the Black Robes. And, while I have read of the recognized earliest adventurers to reach our regions, I am confident that the first white man to come among my primitive people, was a priest from the Hudson Bay outfit in Canada. This was years prior to the advent of Lewis and Clark on the waters of the Swah-netk-qha. Doubtless this Jesuit was killed by Indians farther west after he left our tribe. The

Schu-ayl-p^k, from the very first, were peaceful with the whites (1) and I cannot understand why investigators have never learned of this visit of the Black Robe and of his subsequent disappearance. He was followed by others who were equally fired with a zeal to serve their church. They were the forerunners; the dispensers of a new philosophy destined to supplant the simpler faith of the forest children. This is the principal reason that the Colville-Okanogans are Catholic adherents. Many of the older natives became converts and proved loyal to the creed. The word of the priest with them has ever been law and whatever that dignitary says still goes, and all my folks are of like ilk. I suppose that it is good. At least it is the only thing that has ever been taught them of this 'better life.' But as for me, I tolerate dictation from no dogmatist."

"Then you are not a professed Catholic?"

"No, hardly! Stemteemä and my sisters are, but I am not. The little grandmother thinks that I am, but the girls know and help me to keep it from her. I claim the freedom to attend or forego any and all churches just as I see fit. It would break the Stemteemä's heart if she knew the truth, and the priest would simply raise the dickens—if not something hotter."

Cogewa's low, musical laughter chimed musically with the soughing of the pine tops as she recalled whilom escapades. Amused by the pun, Densmore joined in the merriment, but the girl's mood changed instantly to one of seriousness as she shot the interrogatives:

"What are your religious views? What is your choice of churches?"

Taken wholly by surprise, the Easterner answered rather confusedly:

"Me?—Oh! mine has been a somewhat varied experience. Born a Methodist, I was immersed in a Baptist pool. By turns a Congregational deacon and chorister; a vestryman and Sunday school superintendent in the Episcopal fold; I eventually landed as an elder

among the Presbyterian elite. A sort of free prospector,
I have panned wherever the colors showed most promising; which I really have found to be the evangelistic
field. There were 'prophets' of old and there are 'prophets' of today, if only one has the powers of discern-
ment. Aside from man-made creeds, the churches in toto
are very much the same, as I may judge.''

"You should be a qualified criterion on church dog-
matics!'' was the half amused reply. "They are of
one specie but different breeds. Lap-poodle, or grey-
hound; draft-horse or track-speedster; one brandin'
iron should suffice for them all. I cannot fathom this
wrangling among the various divines. There must be
a diversity of gods to please them all. Some deal directly with Deity, bearing their own burdens to the
altar in personal supplication; while others make use
of a solicitor, an intercessor, who for a stipend, does the
sin absolving stunt. Many contend for an abundance of
water—a tank of depth—in the carrying out of a beautiful symbol, while equally conscientious devotees are
content with a mere drizzling sprinkle. Why all this
bickering discord? Snows before the Indian ever heard
of the white man's God, he firmly believed that there
was a higher order—a Great Spirit—somewhere in, or
towards the sky mystery. The sun and the moon, he
adored as the lodges of the Supreme. The stars were
gleaming rays of hope; and throughout all nature there
was a recognized governing wisdom, most reverently
and devotedly worshipped. Among the tribes there was
no quarreling about creeds. Was it right to totally up-
root tenets of such philosophy?

"Judging of what I have seen of the native American
since I came here,'' observed Densmore, with a degree
of warmth, "I do not think that the uprooting has been
entirely effective. But, admittedly possessed of redeem-
ing qualities, your philosophy did not lift your race
from the thrills of savagery. The coming of the Mayflower was as a spiritual light bursting on a darkened
New World.''

"Zealous and good Christians," rejoined Cogewea, "see in the Discovery by Columbus, a guidance of Divine Providence, in that a new faith was brought to the natives. This may be, but the mistake was with the priests and teachers who did not understand that there was no fundamental difference in the attributes of the deities of the two races. They lacked the preceptive sagacity of a certain great reformer of nearly two thousand years ago; who, when carrying the Message to the benighted Athenians, 'stood in the midst of Mars hill' and declared that it was of their 'Unknown God' to whom he had noticed an altar erected, that he spake. It was wrong! woefully wrong! to compel the untutored native in some instances with fire and sword—to forsake his ancient beliefs with all their sacred traditions. Has he, by the change been mentally, morally or physically strengthened? Too often the high sounding claim of progress emanating from missionary religionists and Indian Bureau politicians, are chimerical; and, as the Indian expresses it, mere 'blanket-blind'. They murk the stream that the piteous wrecks strewing its bottom may not be seen. Viewed in its proper light the coming of the Mayflower was, to my people, the falling of the star 'Wormwood'; tainting with death the source of our very existence." (2)

While the theme was not altogether engaging to the crafty Easterner, he was playing his cards; and he resumed with studied intent:

"I do not assume to be conversant with Scripture, but I believe that Christianity is founded on unquestioned revelation from Deity, first through the prophets and later as taught and exemplified by the Son. Has there ever been any such manifestations among your own race? The Great Spirit has never directly or indirectly communed with even the wisest of your seers. Such contentions are mere prattlings of the Satan-inspired medicine men, as I have often heard explained by theologians well versed on the subject. Evidently there can be but one *true* religion."

"All philosophies," explained Cogewea in piquant tones, "are true which trend to a betterment of earthly conditions; to a mental and moral advancement of its devotees. The term *false* religion is a misnomer. A useful life has no dread of the future. *Our* faith has never suffered from commercialism. What of yours? What of the salaried followers of Christ? Do you see any scourging of money-changers from the Temple? The ambiguity of pew-rentals should be guarded against by the 'called' of God. The offering plate was never known in our worship. As the scroll——"

"Yes! but the revelation! the revelation!" broke in Densmore impatiently. "There can be but one revealed philosophy."

"——of the future was unrolled to the primitive prophets and to the uneducated Galilean fishermen," continued Cogewea without noticing the interruption, "so were there revelations to many of our tribesmen. The vision of the dead man was that the coming of the first pale face would result beneficially to the people, spiritually; but the storm-rack of death would shriek in the wake of the myriads to follow. This prophecy has proven true. Where is our once strong and virile race? The white man's God has not saved my people from the extermination which came hand in hand with this 'spiritual light bursting on a darkened New World'. Woe! and degradation has been our heritage of the invaders' civilization; the invader who taught that *our* God was a myth. His teachings and example have failed to fit us for *his* heaven, while they have unfitted us for our own Happy Hunting Grounds. (3) I am wondering if there will be any place for us in the hereafter. As a half-blood, I suppose that I will be left entirely out in the cold."

"Why do you always say 'our' people, or 'my' people, when referring to the *red* side of your house?" asked Densmore impatiently. "You seem to forget that you are as much Caucasian as Indian. Your sympathies should be equally divided."

"It is because I prefer the Indian!" was the passionate reply. "I have no more occasion to feel debased on account of my native blood, than pride for my heritage of foreign shame."

"I do not understand!" protested Densmore irritably. "What do you mean by 'foreign shame'? Have you lost sight of the superiority of the—the—"

"*White* race!" came the ironical prompting. "Why struggle with a phase so easily spoken?"

"Perhaps," observed Densmore abashed and ill at ease, "you can explain just what you mean by terming your foreign descent a 'heritage of shame'. Such declaration might have far reaching interpretation."

"It has!" broke in the girl fiercely. "What has our race gained by contact with yours? When have you considered our rights—our ideals? When have you not flaunted your higher standards—your superiority? Under the sheep-cloak of philanthropy and benevolent intentions, you have despoiled us as a nation, dispossessed us of our country, and, dethroning our manhood and womanhood, entailed on our youth the cursed taint of an hitherto unheard of blood-pollution. What has been our compensation? Not a 'measure of wheat', but a double measure of broken promises. Not 'three measures of barley,' but thrice three measures of secularized debasement; with the stern admonition that we 'hurt not the oil and the wi—' no! the 'wine' you very considerately left without the ban. Surely! by our rivers have 'we sat down and wept'. Yea! the mountain tops have heard our lamentations. For my race, Hell has ever glared in the *vanguard* of the 'pale horse' and rider, passing interminably, and with phantom glide over the Death Trail, ending in sunset. Trouble and affliction; dependency and thraldom has been your benefaction, filled with the mutterings of Sinai, and the belchings of Kilwea. Our star has gone down in the grisly swirl of flame and blood; its ray supplanted by the hideous leer of the specter of extermination. When you show me a solitary treaty made with us by the

Government which has not wantonly been violated;
when you cite an Indian war where you have not been
the flagrant agressor; then will I admit the *moral* superiority of the Caucasian, and in beliefs and manner
become one of you."

"Cogewea," spoke Densmore after an awkward pause,
"I am not disposed to contend that point with you.
There are more pleasant themes. We cannot help what
our forebears have done. Why not relegate all racial
differences to the discard of forgetfulness? Let you
and I form a peace-pact! I want to learn more concerning that tribal marriage ceremony. Tell me about
it!"

The Easterner took the girl's shapely hand in his.
She looked up hurriedly and half frightened. Her eyes,
bespeaking bewilderment and earnest inquiry, met those
of her companion, burning with latent fervency. With
the color suffusing her olive cheek, she asked, simply:

"Why do you want to learn now?"

"Because I love you!"

"What has that to do with the Indian marriage ceremony?"

"Cogewea! You understand what I mean!" was the
passionate reply. "A union by the native mode would
be romantic and just as binding as that of—"

"Let's go home!" exclaimed Cogewea abruptly, dis-
engaging her hand and springing to her feet. "The sun
is nearly down and those hungry boys will soon be loping in. I must help sister with the supper."

"Cogewea! Stay a little longer! I have something
to say and—"

"Say it tomorrow when we ride out on the old buffalo grounds. Then," she continued with a laugh, "you
may have the full floor, since I have monopolized most
of the time today."

CHAPTER XVI.

ON THE OLD BUFFALO GROUNDS

No more shalt thou from grassy and beflowered spot,
In peaceful rest look upon the silent world;
Nor again, in thy majestic wrath, arise and hurl
Thy mighty form in fiercest fray—
(To the Last Buffalo) Sandbar

DENSMORE'S declaration under the pines had thrilled Cogewea, as no words ever had. Could he really love her and was he sincere? She questioned herself. Perhaps after all she was to come into the life she had ofttimes pictured—a home—a husband who loved books and who would appreciate her efforts at making their domicile a place of endearment and happiness. Refined, he was so particular about his dress and he never ate with his knife, where, in the free, wild range, table manners were given but slight consideration. Somehow she wished that he could throw a rope like Jim—and—swear a bit on provocation. Perhaps he would learn.

But why did he harp on the tribal marriage ritual, rather than that of the white man's law? Surely he must know that this custom was being fought by those in authority and that it would not be recognized by either court or society, as legal. If he was aware of these facts, then perhaps he was trying to trap her. The warning of the grandmother came to her with deepening force. But, she reflected, he had been in the country only a short time and naturally would be ignorant of the true situation. Any way, he had declared his love for her. When he should find the Indian rite to be obsolete—impossible in the premises—he would think differently, she argued. In the meantime, by forgetting that he was not her blood, the happiness of the hour was hers.

It was the middle of the afternoon, when the two rode
away from the ranch, Bringo skulking in the rear. Cogewea did not scold him. She was too happy. They
proceeded slowly, until they reached the crest of the
first ridge; the girl leading over the narrow trail. Here
she paused as if uncertain of her own mind. It struck
Densmore that she was unusually silent and meditative.

"Where to?" he asked.

"I hardly know," she answered dreamily. "Guess
we're on our way somewhere. S'pose we go to Buffalo
Butte, my favorite roostin' place. There is something
that always draws me there."

"You are the guide! It is mine only to follow."

For a moment Cogewea sat her horse motionless, her
eyes fastened on the distant butte. Suddenly the smoul-
dering fires of an unusually moody nature seemed to
leap into flame, as she exclaimed:

"Then come along, Mr. Shoyahpee; for we are goin'
do a little ridin'! The spirits are callin' and I dare not
lag."

As she spoke, this girl of elemental mystery, turned
Wanawish, and touching him with the spur, raced down
the slope and across the expanse of lower level with a
reckless daring born of the range. Her companion, attempting to speed, could seemingly maintain no cohes-
ion with his saddle. Mentally cursing, Densmore held
to the chase for a mile or so, thinking that she would
stop. But there was no slack to the mad dash.

Characteristic of the Indian, Cogewea did not once
glance back to see how fared her escort. The Easterner noticed with what rhythmical ease she sat her cours-
er. Her graceful form, bending slightly over the saddle
bow, appeared an integral part of the flying steed. A
great brilliant handkerchief billowed above the shapely
shoulders like a silken banner in a gale. Caught by a
sportive gust, her sombrero went sailing out into the
sage. Describing a circle and with no check to Wanawish's velocity, she swooped down like a hawk and
snatching the erratic head-gear from the ground, was

again off over the trail. On she sped, across the big flat
like a falcon loosed from bars; this free girl of the out-
doors. The wild blood of a wilder ancestry was calling,
and the wine of youth was strong.

Soon, Cogewea had passed from sight and her convoy
plodded gingerly on. Aggrieved, he was tempted to
turn back. Had she not wilfully ran away from him?
But upon reflection, he determined to continue on to
the tryst. The anticipation of an uninterrupted evening with this strangely fascinating girl of such diversity
of temperament, was predominant. Perhaps the goal
of his aspirations was within reach. Why had she selected this lonely, isolated height for their outing?

Reaching the butte, Cogewea slipping the bit, left
Wanawish to crop the sparse bunch-grass, while she
climbed to her old perch on the summit of the rock.
There she sat dreaming. Her forbears had, in other
snows, come from the now state of Washington, to contend with the dominant resident tribes for the privilege
of hunting the buffalo for meat and robes. The far
stretching prairies, the flats and coulees now decorated
by the six-by-ten shacks of homesteaders, were once this
animal's domain. Was it any wonder that the old Indians were soul-weary, preferring to go the shadowy
way, where again the buffalo may roam unmolested by
the invasion of the white man.

True, she reasoned, those poor settlers must live, the
wild places subdued; but should it be at the expense of
the helplessly weak? The unalterable edict had gone
forth: "Civilize or go under!" but where had there ever
been a primitive hunter - race, able, ultimately to
survive a sudden and violent contact with a highly developed agricultural civilization? The native American
could be no exception to this most inexorable of nature's
laws. Development along any line, like the growth of
the sturdiest tree must be methodically slow; coordinate
with an Intelligence beyond the most vivid comprehension. A few more generations at most, and the full-
blooded Indian shall have followed the Buffalo—not those

sold to the Canadians—but those of the sunset trail. The bleaching relic of the Prairie Chief, with the broken arrow point at her feet, constituted a fitting monument to the past primitive life of the Flathead. Woe! to the Governmental structure builded on the ruins of devastated homes. For how long had any such ever survived?

But bloody though the subjugation, it did not compare with the deadly effects of the *benevolent* manner in which her race had been ruled since the enactment of the various treaties. The Indian Bureau was a blighting curse; its officials, with an army of employees, when not down right thieves conniving with favor-currying politicians and grafters, were, in the main, blundering incompetents, who could not for one day make good in any well regulated and honest business channel. Habits, the building of untold centuries of wilderness life, were sought to be changed within a single generation. It had taken the Caucasian thousands of years to climb to his present state, even with the utility of the various animals suited for domestication and so very essential to the progress of any people. The Indian had had none of this great advantage. Aside from the fierce wolf-dog, the *llama* of far off South America was the only quadruped of the New World that could be utilized in this respect, even had it been known to her people and its importation possible. Charity and common sense had not marked the white man's dealings with the various tribes.

Skilled in the art of white washing, brooded the girl, the Indian Bureau was an octupus, with life extracting tentacles reaching into every Indian reservation of the Union. A vampire! whose wing cools with the breeze of never-to-be-filled promises, the wound of its deadly beak, while it drains the heart's blood of its hapless "ward." Where rested the wrong? The Bureau! a branch of the Government. The Government? the dollar-marked will of the politician. The politician? the *priest*, and the *Levite*, who "pass on the other side" from the bruised, and robbed victim of systematized plunder-lust, lying naked by the trail. Should an occasional *Samaritan* stoop to minister to the sufferer's wants, he is rebuked by the Bureaucrats, and warned that such charity is ill advised; wasted where not an exigency. Surely, had the Indian been driven to drink of the waters of Marah, nor had there risen a Moses to cast into the embittered flood, a branch from the tree of sweetening properties. (1)

Heedless of passing time, Cogewea still sat meditating. There were the Blackfeet, many of whom she knew. From a vast territory "given" them from their own lands reaching down to the banks of the Yellowstone, they were now crowded into a cramped area on the frosty confines of the National Glacier Park; their more habitable domain taken from them without their consent, and without the least of compensation. In their case, as with other tribes, a treaty with the conqueror, had proven subservient to the supercilious will of the dictator. From a once virile, self - supporting people, they had, through massacres by United States troops, and starvation because of thieving, pilfering Bureau agents—ofttimes selected from the ranks of ministers of the gospel—dwindled to a pitiful, diseased remnant of their former independent greatness. (2)

But the Blackfeet tragedy was not the only bundle of sombre facts to rise specter-like on the girl's vision. There were the few remaining warriors of the Nez Perce martyr, Chief Joseph. Heroes, patriots! Victims of plutocratic chicanery, and broken faith on the part of the "powers that be!" Justice, bound and gagged, still vept on the mountain tops of the romantic Wallowa(3). Not an Indian reservation in the land, where loot, robbery, and general malfeasance did not overshadow all the beneficence claimed for the natives through contact with an advanced civilization. Unqualified for the new conditions thrust upon him, no voice in affairs most vital to his very existence, the tribesman is obliged to accept a pottage mixed for him.

in the kitchenry of a political pap-fostered Bureau of
more than six thousand salaried guardians (?) of his
interests, paid for out of his own tribal funds. Overwhelmed by pent-up feelings, Cogewea murmured
aloud:

"And all this in the land of the free-booter, and the
home of the slave! Prate not to me of the superiority
of a philosophy which tolerates such conditions, over
that of my savage ancestors. In my agony, with uplifted hands , I cry to the stars as the torch-lights set
by the Great Spirit: 'How long! Oh! Night Watches
of the Ages, must this injustice endure! Woe is my
people! Surely, have the Four Riders of the Apocalypse
passed through the valleys, over the plains and mountain ranges of our former possessions.''

Densmore reached the summit of the butte to find
Cogewea seated on the rim of the table-like rock, swinging a shapely foot, and listlessly tapping the cliffy wall
with her quirt. She had removed her sombrero, and as
he approached from below, her form was cast in sharp
silhouette against a limpid sky-line, where it appeared as much in place as when in saddle. At sight of the
Easterner, her mood changed and she called mischiev-
ously:

"Hell-o, Sir Shoyahpee! From whence, my gallant
knight-errant of the wilderness way?"

"Why did you run away from me?" he asked with a
degree of petulance, ignoring her innocent flippancy.

"You are too slow for me," was the laughing reply.

"Too slow? In what way?"

"Why, in heeding the call of the morning to speed
the sunlit trail."

"Oh! I heard no call! Heard nothing but the hot,
dust-ladened wind rustling the desert sage. I came
nearly misunderstanding you."

"Aw, quit kidding! This is a time for sociability.
Leave that cayuse with Wana-wish, and come on my
grandstand. Help take care of this scenery. It is a
bit more than one pair of optics can do with justice."

Densmore mounted the rock and settled himself at her side. He manifested but slight interest in the great panorama unrolled to the eastward. His unpoetic nature was not visibly impressed by the picture so soul-inspiring to the girl.

"Isn't it grand?" she questioned. "These are my prairies, my mountains, my Eden. I could live here always! I shall hate to leave them when the final summons comes. Wherever I go, I recall every outline of those embattled ranges, nor can the vision close at the grave. When away, I grow lonesome, as a child for its mother. I become heart-sick for a sight of those snow-shrouded peaks, so rich in legendary lore."

"Would you not leave these sandy wastes, those piled up stones of chilly bleakness for a life of social elegance and untrammeled gayety?"

"Leave this"—she exclaimed with outstretched hand — "where our forefathers fought, where they hunted the buffalo? Leave the land where our braves rest in their last sleep? Never! I could not be content elsewhere. Do you see that?" indicating a half concealed object at the base of their perch, "It is the skull of a former mighty buffalo bull; horns time-roughened, and all bleached and grey with age. It is the last piteous wreck of a once 'Monarch of the Plains.' Colleague of my race, with him went our hopes, our ambition, and our life. A gift from the source of all existence, the buffalo was valued by the tribes above all animals. My nation was ruined when this, its larder, was destroyed by the invader. I can not forgive the wrong."

This lofty sentiment received scant consideration in the calculating reply of the covetous Densmore.

"It may appear harsh, but the day has come when the Indian must desist from his wild, savage life. The Government is working hard for his betterment, and he should respond with a willingness to advance by adjusting himself to the new order of things. The opening of this reservation to settlement, tends to mingle him with his white brother, leading to an inter marriage of the two races. The tribesman will learn wisdom from his new neighbors, who will teach him how best to wrest his food supplies from the soil. The change was inevitable, and why should you go on the warpath? You are too broad minded for such antiquated ideas. Educated, you should put improbable concepts aside."

"I believe you mean well," was the impatient reply, "and a few whites do try to uplift my race. They purpose right, but they do not understand the Indian mind; never will, it would seem. Had a tribesman gone to your European homes with the ultimatum: 'Desert your heavy houses; come into the open and adopt our mode of life,' I am sure you Caucasians would have regarded him as an unreasonably brainless arrogant. Preposterous as such analogy may be, it adequately expresses the native conception of foreign intolerance. But I suppose that what is, was to be, and we must accept the inevitable."

"Obviously the transition from savagery to the civilized state has been a stormy one for the Red man, but the voyage having been accomplished, he will, under the benificent guidance of a liberal and just Government, steadily advance to the highest plane of mental, and physical development. Doubtless he endured some hardships during the days of warfare, but all that is compensated by his present day treatment."

"Compensated by present day treatment!" repeated Cogewea scornfully. "Such density is excusable, since your sojourn has been in the North-country, for not one in twenty thousand of true citizenry are informed on the 'Indian Problem', past and present. Partisan writers have chronicled the story of conquest, and political stranglers see to it that the public is kept blinded to actual conditions. And the Indian's 'mental and physical development!' What a joke, if it were not so pathetically tragic."

"But, my little war-maid," expostulated the obdurate Easterner, "are you not a bit over zealous, and therefore mistaken in your contentions in this respect?

While I came from Canada directly, I was raised in the Atlantic states, and have seen reports from the Indian Commissioner covering the administrations on all the reservations. From the statements therein contained, the Indian Bureau is...."

"A nasty smear the Government escutcheon," broke in the girl fiercely. "A stagnant cesspool swarming with political hatched vermin! Stenchful with the fumes of avarice and greed; selfishly indifferent to the Macedonian cry of its victims writhing under the lash wielded by the hand of Mammon! Pitch is a fastidious cosmetic, compared with the Bureau slime."

"Now, you are surveying the situation through colored lenses," persisted Densmore. "It can not be that the tribes in general are grossly mishandled. Doubtless there are occasional mistakes in the appointment of Indian agents, as in any other branch of business, but these are removed. In the North-country you would hardly dare criticise the administrative government so severely."

"I know! I have been in the North-country, in fact have lived across the border. But I am not there now, nor am I criticising our Government. It is of the Indian Bureau that I am speaking. A child of unnatural parentage, fostered by undemocratic principals, it has no legitimate place under a flag claimed to stand for all that is embodied in the word 'Liberty.' If you think that I am prejudiced, that I am unfair in statements, look up the facts for yourself, but do not depend too strongly on information emanating from the Bureau. Its reek can be found on any of the reservations. It is here with the Flatheads, with the Crows, with the Nez Perces, the Colvills, the Yakimas, and the Chipewas of the White Earth. The Pueblos have their troubles, their Crandall's, but the California tribes should not be cursed with agents. They have no reservations, *all* their lands having been stolen from them." (4)

"Cogewea, I can not agree with you on that score. The public would not tolerate such conditions."

"Easy there! for the ice is thin. The great mass of people who have to struggle for existence, have not the time nor ability to investigate or fight other than their own battles. The wealthy, church-going Christians, have irons in the fire and are too busy with their prayer bribes—ofttimes coming up on the collection plate, whereby they are to squeeze through the celestial gate—to bother casting a crust to the under dog of an 'inferior' race. This leaves the business man and politician a free hand with the 'Indian Problem.' Although brought up in the tenets of Christianity, do you wonder that at times I revert to the more simple beliefs of my ancient people?"

"Perhaps not, but does not the Indian's taciturn and solitary nature stand in the way of his assimilating the highest standards of life?"

"If you refer to the white man's highest standards, I do not know. There has never been an adequate test of his ability along that line, never having come in general contact with them. He has been kept too busy absorbing the lower standards so bounteously thrust upon him, to ponder on the possibility that perhaps his white brother was not treating him to his best in stock. The tendency to measure your neighbor by your own code of morals, holds good with the Red man, and, since his gifts are always the best that he possesses, he judges the pale face accordingly; by the goods which he delivers."

"Well, the native excelled in the art of refined hair-lifting if nothing more," interjected Densmore with a forced laugh. "Nor was he altogether a failure at kindling torture fires, though averse to supplying the ember-fuel for his own tepee hearthstone."

"Scalping was not an exclusive American fashion," parried Cogewea. "The ancient Scythians, at least were addicted to this pastime, who also used enemy skulls for drinking cups. The *stake* roasting, however cruel and revolting, was never mixed with religious creeds and the worship of a God whose chief attributes,

we are taught, are love, justice and mercy. A born
fighter, the Indian preferred death to ignominious ser-
vitude; and these qualities, instead of being detrimental
may yet prove his redemption, if only he can survive
the imbecilities and harsh supervision of an obsolete
Department. Once secure in his battle for a square
deal, he will go forward, and his racial affinities—the
product of climatic and celestial influences—will stamp
themselves on the entire Nation. This characteristic
at times urges me on. I like to contend for that which
I deem to be my rights. I must go on the war path and
have my say or I'll *bust!* Savey?"

The Easterner regarded his companion with open
amusement, as he rejoined:

"Yes! you are evidently right in that. Are you in
the scalping mood to-day, my little Joan of Arc?"

"If I were, the subject material immediately available would hardly suffice for the appeasement of my
warlike proclivities." was the spirited retort. "But it
seems that every time I come to this butte of hidden
mysteries, sympathy for my trampled race — the once
dignified native American—throbs my very being. When
I remain here till nightfall, I can hear the death chant
and wailing of the spirit-Indians whose bones are being disturbed by the homesteader's plow. I can see the
tepeed villages melting before the blaze of conquest and
the shattered nations sweeping desolately towards the
ocean-laved portals of the sunset."

"Where did you get that old buffalo skull and the
fragmentary arrow point?" queried Densmore, abruptly changing the subject.

"I found the skull in a small canyon away out on the
big flat to our right. I was riding at the time, sort of
sight-seeing in the last buffalo roundup; corralling of the
bunch taken to Canada. The herd was owned by Mes-
chell Pablo, the 'Buffalo King of the Flathead.' He has
a well regulated home on the creek some miles from
here, where he lives in state. Almost a full-blood Indian, his ancestors hunted buffalo on these same grounds,

as did mine of the Swa-netк-qha, who made annual trips
here.

"The broken jasper arrow head I picked up on the
main Indian trail, now unused, where it winds over the
ridge you see yonder; where the cloud-shadows are so
thick. Both are relics of an era gone with the sunset
of other snows. I brought them here where my Indian
nature loves the solitude; where there is yet a lingering
semblance of the wild."

"It must have been exciting, the corralling of the buffaloes," said Densmore. "I wish that I could have
witnessed the sport."

"It was a grand and never to be forgotten sight," replied Cogewea sadly. "But it was pitiful to see the animals fight so desperately for freedom. Although I
participated in a way, it brought a dimness to my eyes.
They seemed to realize that they were leaving their native haunts for all time. To the Indian, they were the
last link connecting him with the past, and when one of
the animals burst through the car, falling to the tracks
and breaking its neck, I saw some of the older people
shedding silent tears. But what else could the owner
do than sell them? The reservation had been thrown
open to settlement and the range all taken by homesteaders. Pablo had to make some kind of disposition,
so he sold his herd to the Canadian Government. The
few too wild to corral, were killed. They were considered too dangerous for the white settlers, but we never
found them dangerous when we were here alone."

"I suppose that the animals were regarded as unpro-
fitable, compared with other possibilities; and as standing in the way of the progressive development of the
country."

"Yes, they were killed for the benefit of the 'Missourians'. The United States Government has a few corralled at Mission Hill, where there is a reserve for them.
Some have been there for many years and the final
stragglers were brought in last spring shortly before
you came. People were here from all over the country

to see the first general chasing. It took the best horses
and riders of the range to do the work."

Cogewea then told of an amusing incident in that
connection. The irrepressible camera man was there
and he thought to obtain a rare picture of a band of
stampeding buffaloes, bearing directly down upon him.
He secured his negative alright, but with lowered horns
the animals charged and he had scant time to spring
into the branches of a nearby tree, where he hung, thus
narrowly escaping with his life. A noted "Cowboy
Artist" was in close proximity and he drew a sketch
of the discomfited man swinging to the tree with the
rushing buffaloes passing under him. It was, perhaps,
a more interesting picture than the camera could have
secured.

Thus the hours glided and the sun was bending to
the western horizon, when Densmore, murmuring an endearment attempted to place an arm about the girl.
Cogewea avoiding the embrace, exclaimed with a start:
"It is growing late! See how the shadows are lengthening eastward and here I have not made medicine
over my old grey companion that I love so well."

"Why don't you love someone human, instead of
that grizzled buffalo skull? A man, I should think,
would be far more interesting."

"I have yet to find him!" was the evasive answer, in
pathos tones. "My field of conquest is a limited one."

"In what way is it limited?"

"To my own kind: the breed."

"You do not mean that! Would you not marry outside your own kind?"

"No! Never! I do not dare"

There was a perceptible quiver in the voice and the
girl felt Densmore's grip tighten on her arm. His eyes
were burning into her own and to hide her confusion,
she turned her gaze to the distant peaks of the Rockies,
now glowing in the sunset. The Easterner spoke warm-
ly:

"Cogewea! I do not believe you! Is not the pure-white race just as good? Why erect an imaginary barrier about your life? A true mate is one who has sympathy for your ideals; who understands and is willing to adapt himself to your ways. Don't you think that I would make a good half-breed? I like the customs for which you have declared, and — and I am anxious to learn more about that marriage ceremony."

"If I thought you were in earnest— that you really wanted to know?"

Cogewea had turned on her companion, wondering questioning eyes. The breed girl was reaching where there were thorns.

"Cogewea! little darling!" Densmore whispered as his arm stole about her. "I love you! and yesterday you promised...."

"It is late!" she exclaimed slipping from the rock. "We had better go!"

"But listen! my very own! I want to say many things to you; that of which I wished to speak yesterday. Stay just a little longer! It is not late! Suppose it does grow dark? We can follow the trail. I must hear the ghosts!"

"I don't believe they would be abroad where there is a Shoyahpee. They would frighten you if they did come. Let's vamoose!"

"Cogewea! Tell me that you care for me! that you.."

"Aw! let up! This love makin' is hell! Let's ride!"

CHAPTER XVII.

FRENCHY—TOY OF THE COWBOYS

The sunburnt demigods who ranged
And laughed and lived so free,
Have topped the last divide, or changed
To men like you and me.

—*Badger Clark*

EVERYBODY was busy at the Horseshoe Bend. The annual beef roundup of nearly a month's duration was just three days distant. While the number of stock was less than in former years, the range was wide and it still required many skilled riders with relay of horses to accomplish the work with celerity. That was why John Carter and his foreman were anxiously engaging help to fill out their quota of men. The boys were overhauling chaps, bridles and saddles, oiling rawhide ropes and grooming horses. Each vied in going into the field with the best conditioned equipment; nor must theirs be second to any of the other outfits with which they were to come in contact. All silver mountings were burnished to glittering splendor. "War bags" were carefully made up, consisting of one change of underwear, socks, a top shirt and plenty of "tobaccy." Bedding, tents, and many necessaries used on the range were being methodically collected. A cook for the chuck-wagon and a rangler for the saddle-string were yet to be secured.

As Cogewea came from the tepee where she had taken food for the Stemteemä, a stranger approached on horseback. The dogs ran at him, barking furiously and his spirited cayuse whirled, snorting; the rider saving himself by clutching the saddle-horn. The girl noticed that he bounced in the saddle like a rubber ball, also that he wore a green flannel shirt and that when he dismounted, his buckskin breeches bagged at the knee. They were of a style seen only in the early days of the West, and appeared out of place even on the Flathead. He wore high-heeled boots, a broad sombrero, and a scarlet kerchief was about his neck. Cogewea had nearly laughed at the comical figure. She divined at a glance that he was a tenderfoot trying to play the role of a real westerner, even to the formidable looking six-gun at his belt. He doffed his hat with a sweeping bow and a polite: "Bonjour!" to which she returned a cheery: "Hell-o!" He then spoke:

"I wassasoom blee-ad!"

"Some what?"

"Blee-ad! I wassa soom le-tal blee-ad."

"Aw! shake yourself. Speak English!"

"*Mon-dieu!* I wassa soom blee-ad! soom le-tal bis-a-cat!"

"Oh! you want a cat, a little kitten?" Cogewea laughed amusedly. "Well, we have none to spare. We are short of cats just now; stock all run down. Can book your order."

"*Sac-ré!*" he almost screamed, throwing up his hands in despair. "I wassa blee-ad! soom bis-a-cat. You let-a me star-ruv; go hun-gar-reé?"

Mary, hearing the "stampede" from the veranda, called to her sister that it was bread, or biscuit that the stranger was asking for. He was liberally supplied and as he passed the gate, Jim accosted him and after a few moments conversation the stranger proceeded on his way. But within an hour he returned with a companion and one packhorse. Both were employed to help on the roundup and were soon known as "Frenchy" and "Jake". The latter, Jaquis De Mont, a cook, was assigned to the chuck-wagon. Frenchy, whose name was Eugene La Fleur, was elected rangler of the saddle-string. The scion of a wealthy Parisian family, he had been struck by the American craze, eventually drifting to the Flathead in quest of adventure. It afterwards developed that he had only recently dined at a Chinese restaurant and asking the waiter the name for

bread, had been answered: "Blee-ad." This, the
Frenchman had repeated over and over to himself that
he might not forget. Meeting with Jaquis, who had
long been connected with the range, he became infatu-
ated with the picturesque life of the riders so graphic-
ally depicted, and determined to become a "real" cowboy. Talkative and of a verdant nature, he was destined to become the brunt of many a rude joke. Confiding, he believed implicitly all that was told him, never
seeming to comprehend that he was being victimized.

"That there Frenchy is too easy pickin' for a rec-'
eation," commented Rodeo Jack that evening, as he sat
smoking with Silent Bob near the bunkhouse door.
"Ya-a-s!" drolled the Silent One. "He's like them
there P'ilisters, what Paul tol' 'bout. Swat him on one
jaw an' he turns 'tothern for yo'.' I hater take candy
from er scrapless kid; I hater scratch er bronc what has
no buck."

"I bet he's a moosical cuss an' can sing," broke in
Celluloid Bill, as he joined the smokers. "He's got
laighs jus' like a canary."

The boys soon learned to like Frenchy, for his game
qualities. Carter congratulated him on being a sport to
the backbone; explained that the boys meant no harm
but were a lot of fine fellows and that it was a part of
the range diversion which all new comers must endure
before they could become good cowpunchers. The Parisian had really accepted work on the ranch merely to
ride and in time he succeeded, but not until after many
falls and truly hard bumps. Like a child learning to
walk; when thrown he got up, brushed the dust from his
buckskins and was ready for another try. If he was
to become a rider, he thought, the bruises and scratches
were the price. The victim of Croppy, he was hurled
half across the corral, but he came back smiling. He took
it all as a course of necessity, it never dawning on him
that he was being duped and affording amusement for
others.

"It beats hell how that French guy eats dirt and keeps

a goin'," commented Jim as he left the corral on the
evening of Frenchy's first day. "He ain't none like that
there dood tenderfoot, who can't get off a hoss without
hurtin his-self."

Frenchy had been at the ranch two days, and noting
that all the riders had clean clothes for the roundup,
decided that he, too, must do some washing. So after
nightfall he repaired to the river, disrobed and gave his
ancient buckskins a thorough scrubbing. He then carefully hung them on the corral fence, where the boys
assured him the warm wind would dry them before
morning. He had scarce repaired to his bunk when the
riders were busy at his breeches. With low laughter,
Bill caught the waistband, while Jim and Bob took each
a leg. They pulled until the leather would stretch no
more. Wet buckskin is very elastic, and when returned
to the fence, the garb had no semblance to its former
self. The trio then went to their bunks with uncon-
cerned gravity.

Next morning the unsuspecting Frenchy was up before day break to get his breeches. What was his dismay
to find them almost dry and twice their usual length,
while the legs were no more than the width of a shirt-
sleeve. He hurried to the bunk house greatly excited.
Wildly gesticulating, he talked so fast that no one could
understand him. He was in despair. He had no other
change except his French dress suit, nor could he get
into his newly laundered buckskins. The boys were all
ignorant as to what could possibly have happened to
them.

"I bet it's the wrong time of moon to scrub buckskin," volunteered Jim. "I forgot to think 'bout it last
night. I always heard my grandmother say not to wash
buckskin till the moon changed."

"Aw! come off!" exclaimed Celluloid Bill. "Them
there breeches was hung up too wrong. Yo' oughter
hang 'em north side up, same as th' pole on a map."

"Naw! yo' fellers is 'way off!" broke in Rodeo Jack.
"I betcher a Wahbegosh has been a stretchin' uv them

breecherloons. I see th' tracks uv a big 'un yesterday as I come over the upper trail. It was a headin' in this directions, but I didn't s'pose it would cross th' river, 'cause they don't like no water 'ceptin' is it ocean deep. Wahbegoshes are hell at pullin' breecher laigs."

"It's a *strather* in th' air, what done th' work," drolled Silent Bob. "When it strikes 'em on t'other side fust, it 'spans 'em; but if it hits 'em t'other side las', it shrunks 'em up an' 'longates 'em. I hater see them there fine breeches in such onfashion'ble shape; I hater see Frenchy a ridin' th' roun'up with naiked laigs."

At length, Jake, feeling sorry for his pardner, took the buckskins to the river and moistening his hands, rubbed the garb damp and worked it back to its original shape. Frenchy got into his clothing just as the tin pan sounded for breakfast—the last meal at the ranch table for the next three weeks.

The outfit was soon under way, moving across the great flats to the range hills reaching far up into the higher mountains. Densmore, now fully recovered, was left with a helper in charge of the ranch. He was not at all averse to this arrangement. With Jim eliminated for so long a time, he felt confident of his ability to win Cogewea to his deep set plans. He was sure that the aged grandmother was against him, which was of no small moment, since the girl was devoted to her and often sought her counsel. But he determined to bend all energies to winning the old squaw's favor, and to this end he employed commendable zeal, had it been more honorably directed.

But the Easterner had not reckoned with the Indian character!

CHAPTER XVIII.

SWA-LAH-KIN: The FROG WOMAN

With her moods of shade and sunshine
Eyes that smiled and frowned alternate,
Feet as rapid as the river,
Tresses flowing like the water,
And as musical a laughter;

—Hiawatha

A WEEK had passed since the roundup outfit left the ranch. The lengthening days brought with them the indubitable evidence of an early and short lived autumn. The deep green leaves were transforming to mellow golden and the blaze of crimson glory. The grass was sere, with no indications of the usually short, velvety after-crop so peculiar to the arid range. The song birds no longer trilled among the pines of the Pend d'Oreille. Flown to the South land, their notes were supplanted by the discordant honk and scream of the migratory water-fowl, echoing along the winding shore.

Densmore often went shooting on the big flats where numerous small lakes were in evidence. To the surprise of all, he proved a successful hunter and bagged a goodly number of both ducks and prairie chickens along with an occasional goose. Badger, a noted wolf-hound and Bringo, were his constant companions on these excursions, ofttimes chasing down the wily coyote and the fleet footed jack rabbit. Densmore had also become handy with the rod, bringing home fine strings of fish. Stemteemä was kept bountifully supplied with these delicacies, nor did the sportsman forego an opportunity of ingratiating himself in her favor. But the ancient woman received the gifts with stoic indifference and with doubtful gratitude. Perhaps it was more to please Cogewea, that she accepted the offerings, regard-

156

ing them as a part of her daily food supply. The girl
sometimes accompanied the donor in these presentation
visits, acting as interpreter. The keen witted grandmother discerned that her grand child was growing more
fond of the hated Shoyahpee; and that she was also
endeavoring to win her to regard him with greater favor. These symptoms she noticed with increased perturbation and had spoken to Julia on the subject. But
the older sister, who had given the situation but scant
or no thought during the press of summer work, was
inclined to regard the possible alliance in a different
light. She, herself, had married a white man who was
good and kind to her, and consequently her racial prejudices were not so strongly pronounced.

Cogewea, in walking habit, stood gazing pensively
from the window. She saw Julia, leading little Denny,
enter the low doorway of the smoke-browned tepee
just as the well proportioned form of Densmore emerged from the bunk house. He carried two fishing rods
and had a trap slung over his shoulder. Coming up
the path, he stopped at the gate, turning towards the
house. Mary, the shy girl, sitting on the blanketed
floor of the veranda beading a pair of moccasins, paused
in her work to glance at her sister as she passed down
the steps to join him. Mary could not like this Shoyahpee, with his smooth tongue and beguiling smile. She
and the Stemteemä had many times counselled concerning him and Cogewea, but she had never revealed to the
old grandmother how much the two were together. Resuming her task, the girl frowned with evident vexation
as the couple strolled towards the river.

Densmore was discoursing on the charms of city life
as they passed the tepee door. Inside, Stemteemä was
crooning an Indian lullaby, which intoned musically
with the sleepy baby prattle of Denny. The song was
hushed suddenly. No bird carols greeted them as they
approached the stream, and the squirrels and chipmunks
appeared too busy storing their winter hoards to notice the intrusion. Following the bank for a mile or so,

they came to a promising pool, deep and clear, at the base of an overhanging cliff. Here they prepared to cast.

"The kale that I land the first one," challenged Cogewea as the two flies struck the water simultaneously. "Taken!" was the quick acceptance.

Scarcely had Densmore spoken when his line cut the water in a straight drive, the reel spinning yard after yard of singing cord. Far out in the stream a silvery form leaped, scintillating in a radiant curve, sending up a shower of sparkling spray as the fish clove the water. The played out line slacked and the fisherman reeled in, minus hook and fly.

"King of the Pend d'Oreille!" exclaimed Cogewea. "How gamy! You...."

Her own line spun with a musical purr, and deftly handling the reel, she slowly brought the stampeding salmonoid too, in a wide, sweeping circle. The battle was on, but with a skill attained only through experience she finally landed a shimmering beauty of rare size.

"Lost! Shoyahpee!" she taunted. "Lost two ways; your trout and your wager."

"I will lay an even five thousand against your hand that the next is mine," bantered the Easterner as he adjusted a new fly.

"I fade you!" was the prompt acceptance.

Again they cast and again she won.

"Please ante!" laughed the girl, as with a dextrous movement of thumb and fingers, the catch was rendered unconscious before removed from the hook.

"Would you have been as prompt in delivering, had I won?"

"An *honest* gambler is supposed to meet all obligations unequivocally," was the evasive answer.

"Nor will the *true* sport deny to an unfortunate loser the opportunity of retrieving," came the ready counter.

"Certainly! My digits and winnings against an even ten thousand."

"You are mine!" was the confident response as the
fly was twirled over the water for "luck". "Now listen for the wedding chimes."

The game was growing wild and fascinating. This
time the Easterner lost only by the fraction of a minute.
"Betting is off!" declared Cogewea when Densmore
proposed a still higher wager. "Those chimes are remote, for I don't believe that you could redeem even
now."

"There is where your reckoning is faulty," a crafty
light in his eyes. "I am nothing near my limit. I can
make good several such doubles."

"Well, I make no more wagers today," in a tone of
finality. "My *tahmahnawis* tells me that the signs are
bad. Besides, we have enough fish already. There are
still a few left of your yesterday's catch and it is wrong
and wasteful to hook them just for misconceived sport.
Indians take only enough for food and no more."

"Wait a moment! I think there is a big shiner by
that rock and I want him."

"Aw! come on and don't be selfish. Leave a few for
the next fellow who may really need them. Let's rest
on this mossy log and watch the river as it glides on its
way to the ocean. You can tell me something of interest."

No further urging was required, and Densmore, reel-
ing his line, joined her on the fallen forest giant. Spy-
ing a small land-toad, with the end of his pole he mis-
chievously turned it over and over towards her. Noting the action, the girl exclaimed in agitation:

"Oh! Alfred! Don't do that to the poor little helpless thing. Besides, it will bring a storm sure. Indians
claim that if you place a frog on its back, it will cause
a storm without doubt. There is an old legend which
tells the story of *Swa-lah-kin* the 'frog woman.' (1) It
is in connection with the sun; that if you turn the frog
thus, she will look up at the sun and flirt with him as
in the beginning. He hates her so badly that he
will wrinkle his brow and a tempest gathers which wets

the earth. This forces her odious flippancy to find shelter out of his sight."

Densmore picked up a fragment of bark and getting the Batrachian on it, threw both into the stream with the observation:

"I guess with that cold bath the little miss will do no more flirting for a while. Anyhow it is too clear for rain today."

Cogewea glanced upward. The sky was blue and limpid with the exception of a single diminutive cloud which appeared to draw nearer to the hot, blazing orb of day. Pointing to it, she admonished:

"I told you that she would bring rain. See that little cloud? It will unfold and spread until the heavens are covered in no time. It is her! the Swah-lah-kin of the myth. She has flirted with the Sun and we will get soaked. There will be a downpour swift and without warning. You have done the mischief and spoiled our afternoon."

"I supposed that you were enough educated to know better than to believe all those ridiculous signs of your people," chided the Easterner.

"What if I am slightly educated!" came the retort with a tinge of resentment. "The true American courses my veins and *never* will I cast aside my ancestral traditions. I was born to them!"

"And the Pend d'Oreille has its birth far up in the mountains, but it does not remain there; slumbering within the gorges and fastnesses of wooded slopes. Bursting from its gloomy confines, it grows into a thing of magnificent grandeur, averting stagnation by constant action."

"But it is no less water than when it issues from its rocky defiles, only less pure. And is it really so enigmatic that the fluid should run down hill? You white people will never understand us. I think it quite easy for us to turn to the Shoyahpee's ways, compared to his qualifications to become Injun—honest Injun. I refer especially to his word of promise. He seldom keeps an agreement, while the word of a tribesman is law—or was until he became contaminated with the touch of your civilization.''

Densmore made no reply. He drew a handkerchief from his pocket when a loosely folded letter fluttered to the ground. He picked it up, glanced at the heading, then tore it into fragments, scattering them to the wind.

"From your sweetheart?" queried Cogewea, with a mischievous smile.

"My mother," he answered carelessly, but with a degree of embarrassment.

"Tell me of your mother. You have spoken but little about your family."

"Why!—I—I thought that I had told you."

"No, you never have. But you have learned all about my people, from Stemteemä to my very cousins. I have never realized what it is to have a mother's love. I was too young when she died."

"I have one of the best mothers in the world! You would like her! Cogewea!" he exclaimed with sudden impulse, as he placed his arm about her. "I love you and some day I want to take you to her. Will you go?"

She did not resist his advances, but asked pleadingly:

"*Do* you think that your mother would like me? *Would* she really be glad; do you think?"

"Sure! little one! Why do you doubt?"

The plotter felt the girl tremble as he drew her closer. Was realization within his grasp? He had lied broadly, but what of that. There was pathos in her voice as she made reply:

"Because I am a *breed!*—only part white. But few recognize my kind socially. We are often made to suffer from the ungenerous remarks and actions of those who feel themselves above us."

"To the truly high minded there are no racial barriers. Why should you care to remain exclusively Indian? What is the incentive?"

"I have my Stemteemä and my sisters, besides other

kindred ties. Then, there are the traditions of my ancient race.''

''But you can not exist on sentiment alone. With no vested or property interests to demand your continued presence, you should feel at freedom to see something of the world. I take it that there are no such bonds.''

''Sure! Not only my allotment of eighty acres of the finest of land, but I have—Why do you ask?'' she broke off suddenly, lifting inquiring eyes.

He stood the scrutiny with calculating coolness. She had very unexpectedly increased in value. Taking her shapely hand in his, he answered with apparent sincerity:

''I meant nothing. I am only anxious to make you happy. Listen! my little Injun sweetheart! I have plenty, all that you could wish for. I want to share my wealth with you. You won the wagers at fishing. Suppose we form a partnership and call it settled by me doubling your winnings?''

''I would not sell myself!'' was the scornful reply. ''Money cannot bring happiness. Too often its heritage is one of unfathomed misery.''

Densmore realizing his mistake, retrenched hastily.

''You misunderstood me. I am but endeavoring to show you that I care deeply and am anxious to be to you all that a husband should. If I could only hear you say that you care for me—that you love me ever so little.''

He was straining her to his breast and he felt her responsive form quiver. He attempted to lift her warm lips to his own, but she held aloof.

''Cogewea!'' he whispered, smoothing her raven tresses. ''I love you to distraction! I am willing to meet you in every way that you desire. I will be Indian. Tell me more about your tribal customs. That marriage ceremony——''

The girl, struggling free, started up in sudden fright. With arm outflung, she exclaimed in terror:

''Look! See how the frown of the Sun-god darkens

the earth! He bends his shaggy brow over the portals of the West-wind and hurls his anger along the sky! He breathes! and the air is thick with anguish! It is the *Swa-lah-kin!* *You* did this!'' she cried angrily. "You should not have turned the frog! Come! let us hurry home! We will be fortunate if we escape with only a drenching.''

Densmore's eyes followed her outstretched arm and he leaped to his feet in amazement. The western heavens were overcast with a mighty canopy of black, billowing clouds, hurtling upward towards the zenith with appalling rapidity. The onslaught was swift and terrible in its silence. Only the faintest hum, like the smothered cords of an Aeolian harp struck by the softest zephyr, was audible. Never had the Easterner witnessed an elemental conflict of such awe-inspiring grandeur. Seizing their effects, they hurriedly started for home.

Gathering momentum, the storm came sweeping onward with lowering front; the chaotic cloud-rack, a sable wall blotting out the universe. The low, indistinct murmur increased in volume until the cadence became a mournful dirge' in the pine tops. This was but a prelude. Murky with misty shadows, the wind, in one fell swoop enveloped the fugitives, nearly carrying them off their feet. Clasping hands, they struggled in the face of the gale now shrieking like a thousand Harpies about their bursting ears. Densmore's hat went sailing out over the river, while Cogewea's broad-brim fluttering, was held secure by feminine anchorage. Bracing hard, they made but slow progress and were still a considerable distance from home when the first spattering raindrops, like the skirmish shots of a hostile army, struck them. When within a hundred paces of Stemteemä's lodge, the anguished heavens were rent by a lurid tongue of lightning, followed by a crash which seemed to rock the very earth's foundations. The dreaded *Thunder-bird* (2) was abroad on the storm and at the gleaming flash of his eye and the booming crash of his ponderous wing, the rain descended in torrents.

"The tepee! the tepee!" screamed Cogewea above the roar of the tempest.

Densmore tore back the door-flap and completely soaked they stumbled through the opening. The interposition of the canvas walls against the sudden gale was most grateful. It was solace to hear the deluge beating against the swaying roof. The wings of the smoke-flue had been closed and the seemingly frail structure made entirely proof against the onslaughts of Thor. Not only Julia, but Mary was there and, what, with the two children sleeping among the blankets, the wigwam was well crowded.

Stemteemä spoke to Cogewea, her tone sharp and emphatic. The girl answered at length in Okanogan and without her accustomed blithesomeness. The little audience gave rapt attention as she narrated the frog incident on the river bank. The grandmother and Mary cast looks of displeasure at the Shoyahpee, but Julia appeared less impressed. The conversation was necessarily loud, because of the howling of the warring elements without, which seemed to increase in momentary violence. However, the storm ceased as suddenly as it began and the sun shone upon a drenched world.

After a futile attempt at gayety, Densmore departed for the bunk house; and the aged woman requested Cogewea to go change her clothing and then return to the tepee. She had a story of the past which she desired to tell her three grandchildren.

CHAPTER XIX.

THE STORY OF GREEN-BLANKET FEET

And he wooed her with caresses,
Wooed her with his smile of sunshine,
With his flattering words he wooed her,
With his sighing and his singing.

—*Hiawatha*

COGEWEA soon returned to the tepee in dry habiliments and with a show of her old gaiety. Seating herself on the vacant buffalo robe, she spoke: "Well! my little Stemteemä, what is it to be—praises or a scolding? The Shoyahpee did not know that turning the *Swa-lah-kin* would bring a storm and when I told him what he had done, he pitched the thing into the river hoping to stay the Sun's anger."

The aged woman made no reply, but drew assiduously at the little stone pipe which Mary had filled for her. She continued in silence until the *kinnikinnick* was exhausted and then stowing the pipe away, she began impressively:

"My grandchildren! I am now old and cannot stay with you many more snows. The story I am telling is true and I want you to keep it after I am gone.

"*Green-blanket Feet* was my best friend and she told me this tale after she came back to our tribe from the Blackfeet. I remember her as a girl. How comely! how graceful. Eyes clear as the mountain stream; reflecting innocence and the dreamer. Cheeks blooming as the dusky wild flower of spring, with hair in two braids, reaching to her knees. Her feet were small and shapely. The pride of every Indian woman is the gift of a small foot. Her's was a generous heart and a confiding nature. But wayward, of adventures in the deep forest she had many. Her father and mother had died, leaving her no other protector but an old aunt, with

165

whom she lived. This aunt could not compel her to
stay in the tepee and sit on her feet like the other
maidens of her tribe. She was trouble-free until she
met her fate in the false Shoyahpee.

"My friend was at the spring in the woods, when she
first saw the pale face. He carried a gun and had killed
a deer. He spoke with a soft voice, but the tongue was
strange. His words she could not understand, but the
signs he made were pleasing. His eyes were afire with
greed, but the young is ever blind. The buttons on his
capo, blazed as the sun. She brought him to the lodge
of the aunt, where he left the deer as a gift and then
went away.

"The following sun the white man came to visit at
the lodge near the spring, and many more sundowns was
he there. He planned until the girl gave her heart to
him. She soon deserted her aunt, her people for the
Shoyahpee, who lived at the fort.

"Yes, my friend left her own kind to dwell with her
white husband among the pale faces. After many
moons, a papoose came, a girl. She was glad to see the
little Shoyahpee, nearly as white as its father. A snow
passed and another papoose came; this time a boy. The
mother was now wearing the white man's manner of
clothing and was eating his food. She often longed for
her people. She sometimes visited them in their lodges
and her children kept warm her heart.

"The blow fell when her youngest child was two
snows old. The white husband came to her while she
was making moccasins for her little girl and said:

"Woman! listen well my words. I am called away;
far towards the rising sun. It is from my Chief, whom
I can not refuse. It is at his bidding that I go. If you
want to care for our children, you can travel with me,
but you may never see your own people again. You
can stay here, but I will take the papooses and go. I
am not coming back.'

"My friend's head drooped and tears visited her eyes,
the first since childhood. She now realized the true

gravity of taking a man not of her own kind, what it really meant to her life. She must make choice between him and her own race, desert or cling to her own children. He was not good to her, but her little papooses! She could not let him take them from her. She would go with him as far as he would permit.

"It was only a few more sundowns when the Shoyahpee with his wife and papooses rode away accompanied by another pale face with a cayuse pack train. The woman had promised her people that she would never forget them, that some day she would return. Her voice trembled as she said good bye, then she rode swiftly away. The youngest papoose Robert, was laced on his cradle-board and hung to the horn of the saddle. Kitty, the oldest, sat behind her mother, secure in the binding folds of a shawl. The names were those given the children by their white father. I saw this mother ride away without once looking back. It was many moons before I beheld her again and this is what she told me:

" 'When I went with my white man, I felt as if I were dying. Leaving my people was harder than had I let him go back alone to his kind. Only for my children did I go. I was heart-sick! Every tree, every little bush spoke to me; every stone called to me as I passed the nooks where I had first met the Shoyahpee. The birds sang in tones of sadness and the water's fret was wailing. But I clung to my little ones and followed my hated husband from sundown to sundown; camping on the trail. I watched closely and learned the country as we passed. I might come back to my people.

" 'We traveled till the big mountains were crossed and we reached the wide, flat lands where there are no trees and but little water. We were among strange tribes, enemies of the Okanogans. We saw buffalo roaming in great herds. There was other wild life which reminded me of the land of the Okanogans. Every sun, my mind grew heavier until I could hardly endure to

go farther. But when I looked at my papooses, I could
not leave them alone with their white father.

" 'The Shoyahpee grew meaner to me as we trailed.
He beat me! kicked me out from the night camps. One
sun I made my mind brave to turn back and I lingered behind the pack train. When he saw this, he
called me to hurry! I thought: 'What shall I do?'
I whirled and rode hard back over the trail. I was
flying to my people with my little ones. But not for
long was the race. The pale face followed, shooting.
My cayuse fell, shot through the body and killed. I
pitched to the ground, stunned by the shock and unable
to rise. The pale face came up and beat me with his
quirt. He kicked me where I lay and called me vile
names. This made me hate him as a reptile of the dust.

" 'I now had to walk, carrying my baby on my back.
Kitty rode behind her father and sometimes slept,
bedded and tied on one of the horse-packs. I was
watched in every movement. I was made to walk ahead
on the trail and at night do all the work about camp.
A few sundowns more of this, when I determined to
run away in the dark with my baby. I grieved to leave
my little girl, but what else could I do! I had noticed
the eye of the Shoyahpee and he meant thus to treat me
after bringing me from my distant home. He intended
killing me when near the journey's end. Better to live
with one of my children than die and leave them both.
I could carry my baby.

" 'I remember the time! It was clear and hot, as we
resumed our travel. Over the plain which seemed to
have no end, we hurried. I was tired when the evening
came. I was glad for the chance to rest.

" 'I have wondered if other than the squaw mother
can know the heart ache and yearning for her young.
I knew that this was to be my last sundown with my
oldest child. I talked to my papooses, talked in our
native tongue. Although Kitty, the oldest, had seen
but three snows, she seemed to understand me. In her
baby way, she cooed, nestling on my bosom. I tried to

impress her that whatever might come in the snows ahead while with her white father, she should ever remember her Indian mother. I knew that it was not for me to attempt stealing her from the pale face. I never could carry both children back across those wide, desolate plains. I feared for him to keep me and the papooses. Bad tempered, he carried a gun and he slept but little at night. He forever watched until he thought I was asleep.

"'I recall the night! The evening was starlight, no moon in the sky. I lingered long at the campfire, playing with my oldest child as a farewell. Kitty appeared to comprehend and clung to me as never before. I had settled my mind to take my youngest papoose no difference what might come. At last Kitty fell asleep from exhaustion and I sat holding her in my arms. Her father called to me angrily to bring her to bed which I did. I hugged her and kissed her brow, although this is not the custom of our race as with the whites. I whispered in her sleeping ear: 'Oh! my little child! Life from my own being! do not forget your Indian mother.' Kitty murmured in her sleep; I could not catch the words. Was it a spirit's voice? I gazed at her longingly for a moment, then went out from the tent; dropping the door-flap behind me.

"'I walked to the fire where lay my youngest papoose, ready wrapped on his cradle-board. He was sleeping! Once more I turned hungrily to the white man's tent—not for him—but for the child I loved as my life. But my people! They were calling! as I stood by the dying embers out there on the boundless plain. I could hear their voices coming to me from the Westland. I would go! for I was not wanted by the white man, who would sometime kill me if I stayed.

"'I had some food tied in a handkerchief, a very small amount. I took up my papoose and walked slowly out from the dim fire light. When hidden by the shadows, I placed him on my back and threw my green blanket over him. Then I ran swiftly away. Halish, a wolf breed dog that we had with us, came to me from hunting on the prairie. I glanced back to see the two pale faces bounding from the tent, each with a gun. They made after me and the fright, I think, caused me to drop into a badger hole large enough to shield me from sight. (1) The dog stopped over me and I pulled him down close to me. I was glad that he was the color of brown. Though half wild, he appeared to know, for he lay perfectly still. The two men passed by, cursing loudly. I could have reached out and touched my white husband, nor did he suspect my place of hiding. The Great Spirit must have favored me, for my papoose did not move nor make a sound. I think, too, that he was awake.

" 'The pursuing pale faces fired their guns into the night darkness and threatened me, but to no effect. Then they coaxed for me to come out from the shadows, but I was so afraid that I hardly breathed. Twice the wolf-dog showed his gleaming fangs, but he did not growl. I did not tremble, but I knew what it meant should my Shoyahpee husband find me. I had long known that he was keeping me only to care for our children and not that he had love for me. I was told by the other pale face, that he had a white squaw far away, who bore him no papooses. I had been lured from my own kind by this stranger with the voice of the wood-bird, but whose tongue, like that of the serpent, was forked and false.

" 'The two men kept stirring all night and it was nearly coming day before I dared move. The great dog still lay guarding me. My little papoose awoke at times, but I hushed him by taking him to breast and covering his head. I partly raised from my crouched position and looked towards the tent. The Shoyahpee father was sitting by the fire, rocking Kitty in his arms. Just then she put her little hand to her eyes and I knew that she was crying. I lifted myself and thought to go back to the camp. But as I drew near, I heard the mean words of the man, concerning me, what he meant to do should he ever catch me. I had lived with him long enough to understand his language in part, and to know what he was saying. I was afraid to go nearer.

" 'I gazed yearningly at the group, then turned to the sunset. I did not dare look back. I would fail, my heart would grow weak in the resolution to leave if I again saw my child crying. The grave, faithful Halish was with me as I tramped. The sun rose high and gleaming before I stopped to rest and watch back over the trail. The white men might follow me, I thought; but I never saw them more.

" 'I walked and camped for many sundowns, till I came to a small bush, where we had stopped before and where I knew to find water. I drank! as did the dog. It was so cooling from the hot sun. I determined to stay and rest for a while. I spread my blanket and stretched in the shade. I bathed my papoose and self in the water. I thanked the Great Spirit that He had protected me so far.

" 'But my food was gone. Ofttimes I was hungry and would have starved, had not Halish caught rabbits and brought them to me. I made sage brush fires by striking flints which I had found on the plain. At this bush camp, I was roasting a rabbit on a stick stuck in the ground by the fire, when suddenly the wolf dog jumped up and looked keenly in the direction that I was to go. That made me look also and I saw a thick cloud of dust coming towards me; a big cloud. As it drew near, I heard a deep rumbling roar like a storm and at once I knew my danger. Halish barked, then lifted his head and howled mournfully. I snatched up my papoose and ran out from the way of the stampeding buffaloes. My breath was almost gone before I cleared their way. With lowered heads they passed so close that I could have struck them with my hand. Halish, leaping ham-stung a young bull and soon had it killed. Amid the turmoil and dust, I saw the half naked Blackfeet riding hard upon the flanks of the herd; shooting and thrusting with the spear. I threw myself down quickly, but

Halish, who stood snarling with the front feet on his
kill, was seen. I prayed to the Great Spirit but He
seemingly had forgotten me, for the Blackfeet came
riding towards me. Halish sprang in front of me, his
back bristling and teeth bared. The leader of the
Blackfeet raised his gun but before he could fire, I was
shielding the dog with my own body. The gun was
lowered, when I had quieted my protector, and I was
made prisoner. When my captors saw the young bull
killed by the wolf-dog, they were pleased and this, I
think, caused them to spare his life. I was surprised
to see so many hunters. It was an annual hunt and
their camp was not far away. They took me! and I
rode one of the ponies. I could not understand their
language. Their tongue was different from that of the
Okanogans.

" 'I was brought to the Chief's lodge, which was
made of tanned buffalo skins, painted and decorated
with *tul-le-men*. (2) The Chief, an old man, had seven
wives, the youngest a mere child of fourteen snows.
He called his warriors and they had a council over me.
This lasted for some time, but at last through signs,
they made me to comprehend my fate. A prisoner for
life, I was consigned to the Chief's lodge to wait on
all his wives and relations. I was a slave.

" 'I stayed with the Blackfeet one snow, till the sun
shone warm again and the prairie grass was green. My
papoose was now walking, running about the doorway
of the lodge. He resembled his sister and I loved him
the more for it. But I hated the memory of his white
father, who had lured me from my people; who had
brought me all this trouble. To think of him was bitter.

" 'I was treated badly by the women of the Blackfeet. A slave for all of them, ofttimes I had not enough
to eat. I used to steal *pemmican* for my papoose, when
he would be crying with hunger. Much of this hardship, I think, was because I had chosen a Shoyahpee
husband instead of one of my own kind; that my child

was half white. The Great Spirit must have been displeased with me.

" 'One sundown when my child was playing in the
tepee, he fell into the fire. His clothing, which I had
brought from the Okanogan country, was of the white
man's make and burned more quickly than buckskin.
He fell! I ran to him but it was too late. His hair
was blazing and his little moccasined feet were roasted
as meat. For only one moment he clung to me, and
then was gone forever.

" 'My heart was broken. I could have borne to live
with the Blackfeet the rest of my life, if only my baby
had been spared to cheer my days. For, were they not
of the same race as myself? Though enemies of the
Okanogans, they were Indians and far different from
the hated Shoyahpee, whose very touch was taint to our
blood. Then I reasoned that it was better that my child
go, than to grow up a despised breed and a slave to an
enemy tribe.

" 'Only a few sundowns passed after I had buried
my papoose—buried him alone under a clustering
thorn—when I determined to leave the Blackfeet. All
the young warriors were out hunting the buffalo and
only a few old men and women left in the village.
There was one aged woman, the mother to the Chief's
favorite wife, who was very cross to me. She usually
sat on the opposite side of the doorway from me. I saw
my chance. The sun had passed the center of the sky,
was on the downward trail and it was hot. All the
women but this one were outside the lodge shading
themselves while I worked. I noticed my old enemy sitting across the way. She was nodding in her sleep, a
laquhia (3) in her hand. She had been eating dried
meat soup. I glanced to the doorway before stepping
around the fireplace in the center of the lodge. I slowly
took the *la-quhia* as she held it. I picked up her pot of
soup and ate as fast as I could. I was hungry! almost
starving. Finally I left the *la-quhia* and drank from
the pot. When it was empty, I replaced it at her side,

leaving the *la-quhia* as if she had dropped it. I then went back to my own place.

" 'The old woman awoke to find her soup all gone. She looked at the pot, then at me; but she seemed not to understand what had become of the broth. Soon she was again nodding. I reached to the back of the lodge where was kept the Chief's bow and arrows. His *te-kee-sten* (4) hung by the side of the war pipe. I threw the *tokee-sten* to the ground. I stepped on it! Then I drew one big breath through the sacred pipe, but left it hanging where it was. I took the bow and arrows for future use. Slinging the quiver over my back, I placed an arrow to the bowstring and came out of the tepee painted with the Chief's own *tul-le-men*. I ran for the river, then deep, swift and muddy from heavy rains. I was a good swimmer and did not fear the water.

" 'The distance was not far and I heard the war whoops of the old warriors in pursuit and the women calling as they followed after. Even the dogs joined in the chase. Turning, I let fly an arrow at the foremost man, striking him in the shoulder. This checked the hunt and being a fleet runner, I kept well ahead of the enemy. I flew down the slope as light footed as the deer in our Okanogan forests. Gaining the river, I dashed into the flood. I was not afraid! Brush was over-hanging the current under a low bluff and I made a hurried dive for it. My Spirit protector remembered me. I caught a limb and held there with the grip of renewed hope. I brought my head out of the water under the bushes for breath. Three Blackfeet were standing on the bank above me talking. I was now able to understand most of their language and I could hear them well. One said that I must be drowned, while an-other one thought that I was hiding under the bushes. He walked onto the bush, almost over me, but it bent to the water and he drew back. I do not know! Maybe he did not want to get his moccasins wet or was afraid of being drowned. He backed up the bluff where they all sat down and watched for me till the sun was hidden in darkness.

" 'I was glad when nightfall came to my rescue. My hands were numb and my limbs stiff from the chill of the water. My strength almost gave way but I called on my secret powers to aid me. I must reach my people, —calling to me from the land of the Okanogans. I drew myself from the flood by the bushes, but I lost the bow and arrows. I was defenceless as I started for home, guided by the stars. I was off the trail that I had followed with the Shoyahpee a snow before. I walked all night and all the next sun, before stopping to camp and rest. I traveled suns and suns over the great plain and was often very hungry. Losing the bow in the river, I could shoot no game.

" 'I wished for Halish, but the mighty wolf dog was dead. Some of the Blackfeet had gone far to hunt the woods-deer and took him with them. A mountain lion attacked a young hunter and the dog fought for him. Both dog and lion were killed, but the Blackfoot escaped, disabled for life. I missed my old companion's help and watchful guard.

" 'It was too late for the eggs of the prairie birds, but I dug roots and sometimes found a few berries. Once I saw a great eagle swoop down and kill a young antelope not far from me, but could not fly with it. I fought the savage bird and took the fawn of goodly size. It furnished me with food for some days. My moccasins were worn out and I made new ones from the skin, cutting it with a sharpened stone. My awl was a pointed bone and the sinew was thread. But the hide was tender and the jagged rocks often passed over, cut them to pieces. I was now glad that I did not leave my green blanket behind when I escaped from the Blackfeet. I tore strips from it with which to wrap my feet. I passed the tribes of the Pend d'Oreilles, Kootenais and the Flatheads. All were good to me. They supplied me with dried berries and meat and I traveled on. I was going home!

" 'I was glad when I came in sight of the big river we love so well. I like the salmon better than I do the meat of the buffalo. (5) I love the wooded mountains more than I do the treeless plains so endless. The land of the Blackfeet is not so fair as that of the Okanogans.

" 'But my heart is buried with my little papoose in the wakeless sleep; and I long for the child who went with her white father. But I am to blame! I preferred him to my own people and he drove me away. I pray to my Great Spirit to favor me in seeing my child again. I now have children of my own kind, but they do not take the place of my first born with its unknown fate.

" 'When I reached my people, they were all glad to see me. My feet were bare except for the worn strips of my once fine four-point (6) Hudson Bay blanket. This is why I am called by my tribe, '*Green-blanket Feet*'. The name connects me with the false tongued Shoyahpee of other snows. It is the strong, clinging memory—hated thing—which recalls the face of the one I once loved; whose words I believed. The blanket was his gift when I first went to him. Let the maidens of my tribe shun the Shoyahpee. His words are poison! his touch is death.' " (7)

The Stemteema's story was finished; her audience had listened in rapt silence to the end. Several moments passed before she again spoke:

"Cogewea; you must be more careful of that Shoyahpee. I do not like to have you with him so much. You must quit going with him alone. It is against the rules of our race for a maiden to do so. You must stop it! He only seeks to harm you. The fate of *Green-blanket Feet* is for you; my grandchild unless you turn from him. (8) Wisdom ever visions well."

Cogewea's ivory teeth closed firm and her tapering fingers dug into the shaggy buffalo robe before she ventured self defense:

"The wisdom of the Stemteema is of the past. She does not understand the waning of ancient ideas. The

young bird flies more sprightly than do the old. The
Shoyahpee girls go out with their men friends and nobody cares.''

The grandmother was silent for long, before making
solemn reply:

"Wisdom comes with the passing of the snows. My
head has been frosted by the breath of time. The nestling knows not the wide trails of the air. Winged danger abounds where the hawk is abroad. The Shoyahpee
women may cling to their ways. The Nation they bear
speaks loudly of wrong.''

Then, after another interval of silence, she concluded
gravely:

"The grandchild is not full Shoyahpee. She is only
half! She must forget her white blood and follow after
her Okanogan ancestors. To their women there came
no shame.''

While Cogewea felt she should respect the words of
her venerable monitor, she rebelled at the thought that
she must not love the fair skinned Easterner too well.

CHAPTER XX.

A TRAGEDY OF THE RANGE

Miles and miles from the living dead
And the tracks that the city men beat.
For I shall ride on the nape of the wind
And shine in the rainbow's arc.

—Herbert E. Palmer

IN the meantime, the "H-B" outfit was bending all energies to a completion of the roundup, looking forward to a return to the "flesh pots" of Mrs. Carter's kitchen, as Rodeo expressed it, who was blessed with splendid gastronomical appurtenances.

Among the last riders to be picked up by Jim, was a handsome, active man in his early thirties. Superbly mounted on a fine black gelding of remarkable swiftness, an expert with the rope, this tall, lithe stranger proved a valuable asset to the force. Because of his proneness to sing and trill Southern plantation melodies, he was soon dubbed the "Dixie Canary". Educated beyond his associates and possessing an exquisite voice, he rendered the evening campfire gatherings more cheery and it was not long before the singer was a general favorite with all. Devoted to his horse, he rode without whip or spur; and he invariably made his couch alongside of *Twilight*, as the great black was known. The boys declared that the Canary even shared his blanket with his dumb companion, when the nights were chilly.

Of his past life, the Canary was never known to speak; a prerogative courteously recognized in range etiquette. Ofttimes he appeared distraught, to live over again some pathetic episode of other days. On these occasions, oblivious of his surroundings and gazing southwards, he ever sang a low, sad, child-like refrain:

"You may holler down my apple tree;
I don't like you any more!"

Then gathering himself with a start, the Canary would hasten about his duties with alacrity, as if to down some hauntings of troubled memory.

In a remote and wild section of the range, the riders were gathering in the last herd-stragglers, working in organized order. In the final rangle, Rodeo and the Dixie Canary, had, in a dice contest, drawn a particularly rough mountain belt, gutted by deep gulches and yawning precipitous canyons. It was still early morning, when the two reached their assigned field of operations; and separating, they climbed parallel ridges, to be followed to a conjunction at the head of the gorge. This route would lead them miles into the fastness of the upper timbered range, where comforts of the "Last Rest" awaited them. This camp consisted of a corral and a crudely built log cabin, with wall-bunks constructed of poles and covered with pine boughs.

The sun was tipping the crest of the lower hills, when Rodeo, reining in his horse, gazed intently across the canyon, where the Canary had appeared on the skyline. The mighty black was skimming along the summit, to suddenly disappear as if swallowed up by the earth. After a few moments Rodeo continued his way, evidently satisfied as to how fared his companion, whom he knew to be an experienced and dexterous horseman. He knew, too, that Twilight was the most sure-footed equine of the outfit.

The evening brought a cold wind from the north, which, by nightfall, was fraught with a bone-chilling, drizzling rain. Rodeo was the last to reach the rendezvous; and long after the fog-thickened darkness had settled down over the gorge and mountain peak. Caring for his mount, Rodeo entered the cabin, made cheery by a pile of logs blazing in the open fireplace, where Jake was baking bannocks, frying slab-bacon and boiling coffee. As the wet, chilled rider broke into the circle, he was accosted with a chorus of inquiry as to the Canary.

"His moosic is absent an' th' home-gatherin' is lonely," observed Celluloid Bill. "Life ain't none too sweet at th' bitterest."

"Why! ain't the Canary here?" Rodeo's voice attested his deep concern. "I s'pose he got in long ago."

"Whar' yo' leave him?" questioned the Silent One. "I hater think of th' Canary bein' out such a night; I hater not hear his singin' befo' goin' to bed."

"We rode different trails a comin'," answered Rodeo.

"When did you see the Canary last?" asked the foreman.

"Airly mornin' on Badger Ridge. He was ranglin' to beat hell, a bunch of stampeders a headin' for Standin' Boulder Gulch. Hiss hoss kinder snuffed out; seemed to go down an' not git up. It was at some big rocks an' I thought maybe he passed behin' them. Say! yo' fellers!" he continued in agitation, "do yo' s'pose anythin' happened to th' Canary? Do yo' think—"

Rodeo's voice broke. His mind had been ill at ease ever since he had witnessed the mystifying episode on the remote and isolated heights, and now the sudden realization that it might prove a tragedy, upset his usually passive nerves. Silent Bob was on his feet.

"Boys, I'm a goin' to fin' th' Canary who sings of Dixie. Do yo'-all want to go? I hater—"

The Silent one turned aside, blinking hard. The firelight evidently hurt his eyes. During the brief interim of their acquaintance, an attachment had sprung up between the two Southerners, undemonstrative, yet warm and reciprocal. The response to his appeal was an immediate donning of caps and buckling on of spurs by all the riders. The even voice of the foreman interrupted the proceedings:

"Boys, this here is a ser'ous undertakin'; a ridin' that hell-busted country this black night. *But we're a goin!* Listen: Our hosses, all tired out, ain't yet had much rent and but little feed. Let 'em eat while we swaller some grub and hot coffee. We'll make better time for it after gittin' started. Them lanterns better have more oil. Fill your canteens with fresh water."

The logic of this was apparent to all, notwithstanding
the impatience to be off. It was agreed that Carter, who
was suffering from a sprained ankle, French and one
or two others unfamiliar with the region, were to remain with Jake in Camp, as being of no actual assistance in the undertaking. Within an hour the cavalcade was wending its precarious way over a weirdly
wild and dismal country, storm-swept and mist-shroud-
ed. The feeble rays of the camp-lanterns penetrated
but a few feet, the wall of dense blackness that ever
loomed just ahead of the leader. For an interminable
time the horses toiled, their riders growing numb in the
saddle from wet and cold. Even at that time of year,
a "northerner" in the mountains was a grim reality for
the summer-clad men. Compelled to make wide de-
tours in surmounting some cliffy height, or in avoiding
some abyssmal canyon—rock-ribbed and yawning—it
was long after midnight, when, because of an inade-
quate knowledge of their bearings and because of the
exhaustion of their horses, the rescuers were constrained
to dismount and await the coming of day. Accordingly saddles were removed and the animals staked to
graze on the sparse vegetation, while the slicker-encased
riders crouched together for mutual warmth and comfort. Fire was not to be thought of.

Well towards morning, the rain ceased, but lowering
clouds and mists barred all safety of movement. Not
until the fog had been dispersed by the sun's rays, did
the searchers find that they were still several miles from
where Rodeo had last seen Canary. Despite all possible haste, it was a long hour before the scene of a
ghastly accident was reached.

Dixie Canary, one side badly crushed, was semi-con-
scious, delirious. He was huddled against Twilight,
whose velvety muzzle was pressed against the injured
man's cheek. Later investigation disclosed that the
horse had gone into a concealed badger hole breaking a
front leg at the knee. Turning a somersault, he landed

full on his rider. That the Canary escaped death outright seemed hardly short of miraculous. The riders gathered close, feeling that the end could not be far. Rodeo bent over his companion, speaking gently. There was an indistinct murmur, "boy" alone being distinguishable.

"Yes, th' boys are all here," said Rodeo, lifting the bruised head. "We're going to carry yo' out an' git a doctor. Yo'll be alright soon."

A canteen was held to the parched lips, and the Canary drank greedily. With the draining of the contents, his head sank back, pillowed against the shoulder of the horse. Twice he tried to speak. Silent Bob kneeling, took his "Chum's" hand:

"What is it, Canary? This is Bob. Tell what it is!"

The eyes of Dixie Canary opened. A wan smile lit his face as he recognized his "Pard". A moment later he spoke, the words broken and faltering:

"Twi-light! Give—him—wa—wa—"

"Yes! yes!" hastened Bob. "Bill is a goin' give Twilight water now."

The nose of the intelligent animal was elevated and the contents of two canteens poured down its throat. There was no struggling, and when the drink was exhausted, the soft muzzle again gently caressed the cheek now rapidly growing cold. For several moments there was silence, Bob still kneeling, chafed the fast chilling brow. The passing shadow of a great buzzard, sailing low and in ever narrowing circles, swept the dying Southerner's upturned face. He started, as he glimpsed the bird of ill-omen, and faltered appealingly:

"Bob—you won't—let—that—damned—thing—"

Eyes expressive of indefinable tenderness turned to Twilight. The Silent one understood:

"No! Canary. That there feathered hoodoo ain't a goin' dese'rate yo' hoss. We'll lay Twilight 'longside—"

Bob struggled to hide an emotion that was choking. A wave of comprehension suffused the dimming eyes, as the sufferer fought for speech:

"Twilight—was all—I had. Bury us—together. Up
here where—sunshine—clouds—remind me of — of—
But no difference! Maybe—somewhere—we will be—
together again—with no—cussed—badger holes — to
bother."
There was a long pause, and then:
"Bob—I'm going. I wanted—to end — Twilight's—
suffering. But—I—couldn't do it. You will—make it
—easy for—him—won't you?"
"Twilight won't never know. He'll be with yo'! But
I hater—"
A suppressed sob shook the kneeling form. The dying singer of Dixie melodies, seemed, through sheer force
of an indomitable will, to hold an ebbing strength, for
imparting, a soul troubling secret.While the mind struggled with the gathering mists of a fast approaching sunset, the voice was less husky as he continued:
"Bob, you and—the boys have—been good friends—
to me. But you seemed—the closest! Maybe it was—
the Dixie tie. I never told—you about the—little—little
— But no use now. It's alright! Last night— she
came. Little gal— of long ago. When children—we
played in—old orchard—back home. We'd sing— 'hollerin' down—my apple tree'. Last night I was—oh! so
cold. Wet, freezing! Twilight—shivered. She came—
little gal. Spread blanket— over me and —Twilight
Sang again—that song. Placed hand on—my head.
Pain—all left. I slept warm. Twilight—seemed not
—cold. Dreamed of—the appletree,—old,—crooked.
Heard song as—we used to—"
The range waif reared himself on an elbow. An inef-
fable light suffused the pallid countenance, as the gaze
went out and beyond the circle of awed watchers. Were
those glazing orbs visioning that which is withheld from
mortal kind? The voice of the Dixie Canary was clear;
the cadence that of the campfire trill, as he sang:

I'm a comin'! I'm a comin'!
Sho' my haid's a bendin' low;
I heah tha'r gentle voices callin',

And then:
'You may holler down my apple tree;
I don't like you any—"

The poor, broken body fell back against the breast of the only Twilight.

The Dixie Canary was dead.

The sun, at his zenith, blazed down on an imposing mound of rough stone, marking the final resting place of the mysterious ''Canary'' and his inseparable ''Twilight.'' The pile was surmounted with a once fine, but now battered saddle, a silver mounted bridle with an easy bit, and fancy chapajeros. A tin tobacco box, placed in a crevice of the wall, contained a leaf torn from the foreman's time-book, bearing, in labored pencil scrawl, this legend

TO MEMERY UV
THE
DIXEY CANERY
&
TWILITE
ARECTED BY THEY BOYS

———

Angils Drempt A Singin Voise.
God Gived That Voise To The
DIXEY CANERY

A Cattle King Offered All His
Range For a Hoss Woth While.
God Knowed His Bisnis.
He Saived That Hoss For The
DIXEY CANERY

Bob

CHAPTER XXI.

A "GEEZAR" IN CAMP

Dream back beyond the cramping lanes
To glories that have been—
To camp smoke on the sunset plains
The riders loping in;
Loose rein and rowelled heel to spare,
The wind our only guide,
For youth was in the saddle there
With half a world to ride.

—*Badger Clark.*

AT last the beef roundup was over, with the fatigued riders and horses all gathered in camp. The "H-B" contingent was far from being sorry, since it is the hardest work connected with the range. A man must possess a good physical constitution with the nerve to bear up under the hardships incumbent on such a life. The cowboy is up at dawn to care for his horses, and ofttimes he rides from early morning till sunset. In some instances he does not return to camp until far in the night. He never considers appeasing his own hunger without first feeding, and sometimes rubbing down his tired mount. No difference what the weather, he works just the same, cutting out and branding the "slick-ears", as the outfit goes from one grazing locality to another. This is kept up until the entire Reservation's open range has been covered. During such *rodeo,* each stockman has his share of well mounted riders in the field.

Carter's boys were now returning to the ranch for a well earned rest; and, but for the one tragedy, all would have been as happy as a bunch of school children out on a summer vacation. That memorial stone-heap back on the sky-line of Badger Ridge, loomed a darkened shadow across an otherwise sunlit sky. But men leading the life of the range, are philosopchically inclined to accept its vicissitudes along with its measurements of joy. The yesterdays, with whatever of grief and pleasure, as a trail never again to be traversed, is well forgotten. Present duty, and the lure of the future, is Nature's balm for the wounded spirit. The boys were going home!

"Frenchy is game!" commented Carter, as they broke camp." "He stuck to his job through the roundup, and will make a real 'puncher' in time. But he'll have to learn not to bounce so like rubber in the saddle."

Jim had devoted his idle moments victimizing the verdant Parisian. As Foreman, qualified to give instructions, he insisted that, to become a good horseman, a beginner should at least ride one entire day without making any use of his stirrups. Frenchie heroically followed the suggestion, and the next morning when the camp moved, he mounted the chuck wagon instead of his horse. Perched on the blanket rolls, he doffed his hat in courteous acknowledgment to the lusty cheering of his companions as they cantered by. All this past, the Toy was now proudly riding in the midst of the merry-making cavalcade. The boys were returning home.

The last camp was pitched on the banks of the Pend d'Oreille. Celluloid Bill pushed Frenchy from the shore in an old skiff, his only means of combating the swift current, a solitary broken oar. The riders watching the sport, thought that the victim would go insane. To all appearances, he knew nothing about rowing, and the deep muffled churning of the rapids was heard but a short distance below. (1) When he saw that he was beyond immediate help from his associates, the Parisian began removing his cumbersome riding boots. This accomplished, he stood up, foot-gear in one hand. He gazed longingly at the surrounding mountains and the immediate woods; as though in a last farewell. The skiff, now in midstream was steadily gaining momentum. For one brief moment he hesitated, and then sprang overboard, to be directly overwhelmed by the turbulent tide.

Instantly the camp was a scene of animation. Celluloid, startled at the serious turn of his joke, did not falter. With cat-like action he leaped to his saddle and drove into the stream. He saw the Toy come to the surface, to instantly sink again from sight. The rescuer wisely giving rein, the powerful horse cut the water like a racing canoe. Submerged to his hips, his new "chaps" were soaked. But what of that? He was going to rescue his "amoosement-man"—his "Toy." The tanned cheek of the rider was a trifle pale. Just as he thought Frenchy gone for all time, he glimpsed his head appearing on the surge like a tossing pine canoe, only to immediately disappear. Believing that he had seen the last of his companion, Bill, who stammered when under anger or great excitement, now turned in his saddle and yelled to those on shore:

"Th-there's t-th' la-last uv th' po-pore d-de-devil! Wh-why in h-hell do-don't s-so-some of yo' pray?"

In a chorus the watchers urged him on. There was Frenchy's head again. Bill continued the pursuit.

"I hater see the po' cuss drown; I hater wade in the col' water an' fish him out," lamented Silent Bob, as seated on a rock, he complacently observed proceedings.

The "drowning" man's head was again visible, and notwithstanding the great distance, was caught in the loop of Celluloid's out-flying lariat. Turning his horse shoreward, the "rescuer" called:

"Ca-catch ho-hold wi-with yo' ha-han's! I'll pu-pull yo' o-out!"

A hearty laugh went up from the bank as Bill, trailing his rope, approached the shore. He understood its significance when the "drowning" man passed him. swimming with the steady, powerful stroke of the professional. He turned beamingly to his "rescuer" and urged:

"Com-et on! you dam-et fool! Mabee you shovet again ze boat. No?"

Bill reached shore disgusted and in very ill humor; the unrestrained chaffing by the boys but adding to his discomfiture. Passing the chuck-wagon, he unsaddled his dripping mount, taking unusual time in rubbing him dry. He felt beaten! tricked by the French Toy. His horse cared for, he sauntered to the camp fire, where the riders were complimenting Frenchy on his skill as a swimmer and his ability in coping with the most persistent of his tormentors. The Parisian was the first to mark the approach of the tall figure and challenged:

"I betcha I sweem ze re-var, coom back. I go ze bad ra-pads too! You no go? Yis?"

"Don't care to swim any river tonight," replied Celluloid with an effort at unconcern. "Too durn' col'. All I'm sorry for is yo' didn't drown. The skiff is lost which was a heap more valerable than a lot of fellers I know roun' here. It belonged to that there "Geezar" over there and he's stingy as hell. I'm a thinkin' there'll be th' devil to pay. Say! Frenchy!" he exclaimed with sudden interest. "Yo' got a lot of money an' yo' have to make good that there old tub. 'Sides, yo' let it go a purpose an' yo' had all th' fun. I have a pair boots I'll give yo', 'cause yo' lost yo' own."

Frenchy was in high glee and readily agreed to settle for the missing craft. Bill was still more surprised at the aquatic skill of the "French water-frog" as he termed him, when he learned that the swimmer had saved his boots. Nonplussed, he inquired:

"Where did yo' learn th' water so like a duck?"

"I go ze swell col-lage. Profass-ar, I teach ze dook swim. I row ze boat good plen-ta."

The boys had not dreamed that their Toy was a graduate from one of the highest educational institutions of France, and an instructor in boating and swimming; and that he commanded wealth sufficient to buy, many times over, the ranch and outfit for which he was working.

While Bill was drying his wet clothing at the fire, there came a hearty: "Hell-o! boys!" and the "Geezar" a tall, lank stockman and owner of the lost skiff, rode within the camp-light. Dismounting and dropping his bridle reins to the ground, he entered into conversation with Carter on general topics of the range and prospective beef prices. Noticing Bill, the "Geezar", who stammered slightly, asked:

"Wh-what yo' d-doin', th-there, f-foller? B-bin s-sw-swimmin'?"

Bill's anger immediately arose. He surmised that the boys had already acquainted the visitor with the river joke and that he was being made the center of all amusement for the camp; and that the "Geezar" was mimicking his weakness of speech. He answered belligerently:

"N-n-none of yo' d-durn' b-bi-bisnes! fe-feller!"

The "Geezar," laboring under the same impression as was his opponent, retorted in no uncertain tones:

"I-I'll m-ma-make it m-my b-bisness!"

Dropping his wet clothing, Bill sprang to his feet.

"Y-yo' w-wh-white l-li-livered c-cur! I'm n-not go-goin' to l-let a-any s-son of a gu-gun m-mo-mock m-my t-ta-talk!"

"I'm n-not mo-mockin' you! Y-yo're th' o-one w-who's m-ma-makin' a d-dam' fool of yo' s-sel—"

Bill struck madly, but the "Geezar", ducking, the blow went wild. He came back viciously, but Bill parried successfully and they clinched. Down they went in a heap, each struggling for the ascendancy. While Bill was the more active, the "Geezar" had the advantage in strength. He secured a grip on the cowpuncher's throat, who, finding himself losing, jerked his six-shooter. But as the gun came free, a firm hand grasped his wrist and Carter spoke:

"Hold on! Bill! You're going too far."

Jim had, at the same time, caught the "Geezar" in an iron grapple and the men were snapped apart. Bill dropped his gun into its holster, while both men were stammering and swearing furiously. Some of the boys discerning the joke, began laughing at the two unfortunates. Rodeo Jack and Leather Slim, the latter from a distant part of the range and a late recruit to the "H-B" outfit, were rolling on the ground, yelling with delight. Frenchy was doubled with merriment. Celluloid Bill glared at the crowd, while the "Geezar" sulked in rage.

"What are you fellows fighting about?" questioned Carter.

"Th-that t-there c-cuss m-mo-mocked my t-ta-talk."

The real truth struck the "Geezar" who broke in:

"W-hy I th-thought yo' w-was a m-mockin' m-me in my t-talk."

The pines rang with the roar of laughter that went up from a score of throats. Carter, holding his aching sides, managed to explain to Bill that the "Geezar" stammered slightly, and that it was not assumed as he had supposed. Even Silent Bob was constrained to smile, as he lolled by the fire. Turning to Bill, he moaned audibly:

"I'd hater see yo' kill that there po' feller; I'd hater help hang yo' for bustin uv of his haid."

The two late belligerents looked at each other sheepishly. Bill, with the second joke of the evening on him, extended his palm:

"Put 'er there! ol' pard! an' shake on it. We'll call it square."

The "Geezar" took the proffered hand and shook it heartily, as he said:

"Wh-why! at f-first, p-pard, I t-thought yo' was m-mockin' me."

"An' I thought yo' was a mockin' me in my talk. That's why I got mad."

The two again shook hands, joining in the hilarity at their expense. Later, the "Geezar" rode away and the camp quieted down, the boys smoking or playing cards by the fire light.

"Well, I'll be darned!" mused Bill after remaining in deep thought for some time. "Now if I'd a hit that there pore feller's skull an' a busted it, I'd a been hung to a tree an' two good men, best in th' country, a been gone for nothin'. Guess I'll have to jug my temper. Don't pay havin' it get 'way with a feller."

At length, each rider sought the comfort of his blankets and soon all—save one—was in slumber-land. Jim could not sleep. The three weeks from Cogewea had seemed interminable and he was glad that only a few more hours intervened until he would be with her again. Long he lay, pondering. Had she drifted farther from him during their separation? Had the hated tenderfoot, taking advantage of the situation, pressed his suit to a successful termination? If so, and he proved worthy—was true and kind to her—then Jim would say no more. He would accept his disappointment without complaint. But if, as he suspected, the Easterner was playing a false hand, then he would do well to "pull his freight" before complications set in; for should the little gal suffer wrong because of him, he would surely kill him. He would then go away and try forget all about the wild beauty with the bewitching eyes. Finally he fell asleep and it seemed that the next moment Bill kicked him with the admonition:

"Hey! ol' skate! Oats is a waitin.' Get on yo' nose bag while th' coffee's hot. Nice way for a foreman to be sleepin' when so clos' home an' his gal a wearyin' her eyes lookin' for him. Not s'prised if that there tenderfoot jaybird ain't cap'tred her; even if he can't ride a cayuse without breakin' his arm. Don't allers 'quire th' best rider of th' Flathead to carry off a prize."

Celluloid Bill turned away, chuckling, as Jim got up without a word. The sun, a glowing orb, was bursting over the distant Rockies, flooding the land with warmth and gladness. But to the foreman, over it all there seemed to loom an ominous shadow.

CHAPTER XXII.

BACK TO THE RANCH

It looks a far and fearful way—
The trail from Now to Then—
But time is telescoped today,
A hundred years in ten.

—Badger Clark

COGEWEA stood on the veranda watching the dust-column approaching from the southeast. She was glad, in some ways, that the boys were coming home. The story of Green-blanket Feet had impressed her deeply. The tribal marriage! Why had Densmore insisted so strongly on this old rite; he a man of education and wealth with all the advantages of refined society? Jim, the rough, rugged *breed* of the range, had never intimated this form of wedlock. While it was true that she had spoken in defense of this ancient custom, it was in comparison with the manifest abuses of the nuptial relations as governed by the laws of the white man. She had not supposed that he would take her so seriously and with self-application. But perhaps things would adjust themselves. In the meantime the inevitable must be met—Jim—and the coming crisis.

But, if Cogewea was restless, Densmore was doubly so. He was disappointed and half angry. The three weeks had passed during which time he had had a clear field. Retrospectively, what had he accomplished in the heart-conquest of this wildly fascinating girl of the range? Inscrutable as the Sphinx, he had failed to fathom her. At times he was led to believe that she cared for him and was willing to concede the Indian marriage; but when pressed for a decision, she invariably "shied" and seemed frightened. All his patient tolerance of her heathen philosophy and her bitter arraignment of a potent Government Bureau,

had been for naught. His gifts of game and fish had
also failed to win the friendship of the old grandmother. Baffled, he now saw the final overthrow of his
cherished plans in the return of the dashing young
foreman. However, he would change tactics. Perhaps
the game was worth a greater risk. She had hinted
at lands; and she would not *sell herself for money!*
Well, *he* was not so squeamish! A silver lining should
make a difference. For the present, he must content
himself and investigate.

As the dust-cloud rolled nearer, the individual riders
became distinguishable. Cogewea ran down the yard
path, calling to Densmore:

"See! the conquering heroes come!"

She rushed on to open the corral gate; greeted with
a chorus of cheery salutations as the outfit filed into
the enclosure. These she returned with a graceful
wave of the hand. Jim, springing from his horse, was
soon at her side. This demonstration of devotion, Densmore remarked from a distance and mentally cursed
the "coppery" breed.

"How is Sis, my little squ—? How has she behaved
while I was gone? How's that there busted tenderfoot?"

The girl's eyes blazed, but she made no reply. A wan
smile came over the bronze face of the foreman; as turning to Silent Bob he observed sadly:

"See Sis' 'glintin' optics? She's mad already 'cause
we're back home."

"I hater see them there fine lookers ablazin' like
coals; I hater see po' Jim all freezed in th' sunshine,"
lamented the Silent One as he passed into the barn. The
Westerner again addressed the object of his solicitude:

"What're you war-pathin' me for, little — ah —
squaw?"

Cogewea laughed. Seemingly she could not be angry
at Jim for long, no difference what he said to her. Turning to him, she said saucily:

"I came to tell you the news, but you ruffled me and now I'm not going to do it. You can be sorry enough!"

"Aw! come on, Sis," he coaxed with mock gravity. "Tell me, and I'll buy you some candy and ribbons next time I go to town for a spree."

"Huh! You talk as if I were some kid with 'pig-tails' down my back. I no longer wear streamers in my hair. I left dolls and toys several snows back on the trail. Your bribe hardly goes this time."

"What is them there news, little Injun?"

"But I might take some chocolates!"

"Tell me what you know!"

"Come to think, you may bring me a yard of sateen lace for a belt. Don't get it more than two inches in width."

"Is some fellers a gettin' married? Goin' be a weddin' dance somewhere?"

"You must be afflicted with that mismatic brain disorder, since it is about the first topic that enters your dome after running loose so long."

"Well, what is it? Has that there city dood croaked? If he has, then a whole pound of candy and a lot of belt runnin' gear will be sure comin'. I'd be plum' tickled for such chance to celebrate."

"No! There has been no demising about here, nor is there any altar splicing brewing that I know of. But there is to be a basket social in the town opera hall tomorrow night for the benefit of the new church building. We're all going, Julia, Mary and myself; taking baskets, including one for the Stemteemä, who will not go. Loads of chicken and goodies with every thing that a cowpuncher likes. Everybody will buy his girl's basket, if he knows which one it is."

"When yo' say it's a comin' off?" interrupted Celluloid Bill, who at that moment happened to be passing.

"Tomorrow night; and the baskets are to be auctioned and a prize given for the one bringing the most money. A dance is scheduled."

"Yo' can count me twice," volunteered the rider as he sauntered towards the bunk house.

"Next to a grave diggin', a church dance'll be tonic for the trail-wearies," sighed Jim. "I'll go my month's wages on your basket, Sis, if only I knowed your brand."

"Now don't start throwing me that hot air stuff," came the counter. "I was born farther west than Montana, and you can't make anything like that stick with this squaw. Savey?"

"I mean it, Chipmunk! Am goin' ask for my September kale tonight, so to have it ready for the big doin's. Put me wise to your feed basket, won't you? I want to sample that there grub-stake."

Cogewea spoke something close to Jim's ear in their own tongue. He laughed softly and made reply in like manner. Drawing suddenly away, she exclaimed:

"If you do, James La'Grinder, I'll get even with you and don't you forget it! You never could keep a secret, unless—" she glanced cautiously around— "you were deeply concerned."

"Aint scalp-huntin', are you? I've been lonesome! And you know I _can_ keep some secret worth while."

The girl gave him a smile as she walked away, but under that smile was planned revenge. The foreman joyed in these wordy tilts. While ever true to a pledge, about the only time that he had ever failed to make capital of a joke at her expense, was when he found her stranded afoot out on the range that afternoon, when their mutual misfortunes demanded silence.

That evening the riders and their foreman assembled in the center of the main corral in secret conclave. The topic was important; one in which honor of the "H-B" ranch was at stake. With lowered voice lest hostile ears be listening, Jim opened the meeting.

"Boys," he began, "basket social in town tomorrow night. Big doin's and dance! We're all goin' take it in, and we want to hold up the good standin' of this here outfit. There'll be city guys with hair parted in middle, all dressed in shiny shoes, white shirts, and a wearin' stiff standin' collars and choke rags. Out here from Noo York, Chicago and Omyhaw, they're huntin' lonely school marms with payin' homesteads. Them there 'venturers go in for grabbin' baskets at four bits; maybe as much as a dollar. The Hoss-shoe boys is a goin' all togged in best silk shirts and handkerchiefs; and none cinch a feed box for less than five bones. We'll dig into them there city birds and spur 'em up with dollar bids. Got to show what kind of stuff a cowpuncher is made. Money is for the new church, an' a durn' good cause, and maybe we'll be credited in the last general round-up; where every brand gets honest 'spection.

"Now here's Bob," continued the instructor. "I hear his schoolmarm has spent a week preparin' her basket. Got Boston beans; chicken done brown and built pies and cookees and things made with nuts and spices. Goin' have them there paper hand-rags, all flowered and folded to a p'int at one end and a spreadin' out at t'other end like a struttin' turkey's tail. You want to show your 'preciation and make a killin' hit by payin' ten dollars for her feed, and lettin' on you feel skunk-mean 'cause you got it so cheap."

"Aw! come off!" expostulated the Silent one. "I'm willin' to help make this here 'fair a roarin scream, but I sho' never can't foller such dev'ous 'structions. I hater get stampeded in thick woods; I hater be los' on a blin' trail."

"Never mind, Bob!" broke in Celluloid Bill. "Yo' go 'head an' nab that there schoolmarm's feed, an' as I'm some 'sperienced in s'ciety frun'tions, I'll jus' keep lamps on yo' an' if yo' lattigo slips or yo' get in quicksan', I'll rope and yank yo' to sollid groun'. Be no 'casion for failin' with my 'fishus guidance."

As if Bob's fate was settled, Jim resumed his dissertation.

"Slim," he said, addressing this late recruit, "you want to show your colors. Lots old maids from the flats goin' be there. Your pockets is full of dough, and if you capture a big feed with the cook thrown in, maybe you can begin startin' a ranch of your own."

"Chillin' breezes of Sayharry!" exclaimed that worthy, who was to remain on the ranch for a time. "Yo' sho' talk as though 'ployed to spiel for any f'aternizin' gatherin'. But yo'll see a whirlin' rope in th' game, nor does 'Leather Slim o' th' Foot-hills' ever throw for no tame maverick. Yo' gotter hus'el for th' bes', even to th' six-gun chor's echo.

"That's sho' a howlin'!" chimed Rodeo Jack. "All "H-B" boys don't vacate th' corral for no galoots; shoot scrappin' nor buck dancin'."

"You're spoutin' true, Rodeo," was the enconium of the prideful foreman. "You and Bill don't need no urgin' and Slim 'pears of the same bran'. You fellers never pull leather in no kind of contest and you can scratch the best. But there ain't to be no gun-barkin. No 'casion! This here outfit is a goin' to bust all social and law 'bidin' records of the Flathead. No gun-muzzle tooth rattlin' where religion is mixed. Savey?" (1)

"S'pose that there eastern masher'll captur' th' fine feed yo' gal goin' put up, won't he Jim?" gibed Bill. "He's had the run of th' range so long that—"

"There's where you tangle your rawhide, old boss;" and to the surprise of all the foreman laughed good naturedly. "I got that there part of program cinched. Watch an Injun patterned cano-basket, made by the Stemteemä for th' 'casion, bring the banner price of the evenin'. You just keep this here short secret safe corraled and see the brandin' iron put to a tenderfoot pertender. No guy who can't fall off a standin, still cayuse without hurtin' his-self is goin' have any show in a relay with the champeen rider of the Flathead. The race wouldn't be even amusin'."

"Frenchy," Jim addressed the camp "toy", "you buy a dozen baskets that don't look too promisin, and donate 'em to the city ginks who ain't got the dough. 'Twill be a good 'vestment for the church cause."

"*Sacre!* I geetz a plan-tee blee-ed zor zalf. Zen ze ozer—"

"*Bah!*" broke in Celluloid Bill. "Why don't yo' say what yo're talkin' 'bout? yo'—from-cross-th'-sea, toad-eatin'-son-of-Gaul? Yo' speak like a Chink with hot mush in th' crater of his map."

Frenchy stood up, threw his breast out with pride, as he continued:

"I speik ze zord vare splan-deed. At ze zosi-bla, I geet plan-tee zor ze ten-dorzoot. I maik zone zee big baz-ze-ket—"

Then growing excited, the "toy" began beating the air in the way of emphasis, when the clang of the big tin pan vibrating on the evening breeze, summoned the hungry crew to the supper table. That the bounteous repast was appreciated by the rollicking riders, was amply attested by the inroads on the tempting viands.

The meal over, the boys under cover of darkness, repaired to the river for a splash in the cooling waters. Refreshed, by the dip, Rodeo Jack and Silent Bob sprawled under the pines for a smoke and discussion of the coming social. Rodeo was in high spirits and went over every detail of dress and minor arrangements, with all the glee of a child. But the Silent one was not so sure of his premises. He had never participated in any of "them there mixin's."

"Jim's all thar' as fo'man an' boss on th' roun'up," he drawled in disgust, "but I ain't knowin' 'bout this here church bisence; whar' th' range is all differen'. I like to know th' corral fencin' ain't down an' my cin-chin' is a holdin' when I saddle on to a strange bronc. I hater get spilled in a crowd; I hater be th'—"

"Aw! what's a eatin' yo'?" interrupted Rodeo impatiently. "Yo're on a dead easy trail, an' with Bill a champerronin' yo', yo' needn't take no feller's dust. None of them there city guys 'll put anythin' over on Bill when it comes to shinin' in s'ciety circuses. He's been clean to Omyhaw with cattle onst, where he 'tended three dances in a big corral they said was a

garden. But Bill, he looked all roun' an' didn't fine'
nary a durn 'tater patch nor nothin' growin' 'cept
some kin' greas' wood in a nail-keg, an' a lit'le bush
in a half whiskey bar'l, what they tol' him was a roder-
john or somethin'. But hell! th' 'tractions! Some fiddlers, a pianer an' a sliver horn all a playin' at same
time. Bill said as it kinder took his breath when he
stepped into that there dancin' place, a kind of stam-
pedin' wing to th' main corral, with swingin' gates.

"Th' gals was all done up in jul'ry an' ribbons from
armpits to nearly th'r knees; an' paint on face somethin' like Injuns, only more permiskus. They wore
flamin' stockin's made outen 'skeeter nettin' that yo'
could see both sides at the same time an' shoes reachin'
nearly to their ankles.

"Th' men had white shiny shirts all standin' out
flat and roun' in front, an' coats with long tails a
'hind like an Injun breech-clout. But th' tailor mus'
a bin short on goods, 'cause th' coats had no flaps on
at front an' side, but cut off square at belt clean back
to hips, as if to be outen way of th' six-gun none of 'em
had. These here fellers all had on standin' collars like
one Bill brought home with him. He paid a dollar for
it, just to show what they had back there.

"One of them there gals, all dressed in th' middle,
come an' danced with Bill an' he liked it some, 'cause
no danger gettin' spurs tangled in no skirts; an' when
they get through a steppin' to th' moosic, she kicks his
hat offen his haid an' takes th' silk handkerchief from
his naik, to make a dancin' custom out of it. Bill said
as the gals seemed to like him better than they did
them there half-clouted slick-shirted guys; an' he went
back twice jus' to get onto s'ciety ways. An' yo' bet he
got there! Bill's wide awake an' yo' goter stop this
here 'durn kickin' like a range steer afore yo' feel th'
bran'in' iron. Yo'll bring disgrace on the 'H-B' outfit, an' all them there cowpunchers from t'other ranges,
will have th' laugh on us. Savey?"

The Virginian agreed that he would try "foller-th'

trail" as instructed, and if the "H-B" failed in its high aim, it should not be accredited to any wanton dereliction on his part, although the "proceedin's" was most funereal, as he viewed them.

Jim and the other boys had long left the river, the one to seek Cogewea, the others to engage in a card-game at the Bunk house. The foreman met the girl returning from the tepee, and walking together to the veranda, they sat down on the steps. He was first to open conversation:

"Ain't you glad to see me, Sis? Wasn't you lonesome when I was gone?"

"Lonesome for you?" was the laughing reply. "Bah! You torment me so! I should have been glad had you remained away forever."

"Now you don't mean that!" and there was real solicitude in the tone. 'You ain't gone and fell in love with that there white feller while I was away, have you?"

The evident anxiety of the foreman was hardly allayed by the exasperating response:

" 'Well do I know, but dare not tell!' lest I become a tattler. Does the love-lorn warrior spend his suns in dreaming-sleep that he must come to the squaw to learn of his rival's trail?"

"By gollies, little gal! I'll find out! Don't you think that ol' Jim is a goin' to be caught with his lariat a trailin! The best rider of the Flathead never—"

"Aw come off! Let that 'best rider' stuff have a rest. If you rode as well as you talk, you certainly would be great and have all the girls dead in love with you, myself included."

"Then there's hope for me!" he exclaimed eagerly. "How about last Fourth of July? Didn't I stick Croppy to a finish, when some of them there brag riders from everywhere got landed good?"

"Pshaw! Croppy was dead easy that day. I really believe you had him 'doped' for the occasion."

"Well, I'll ride any hoss that breathes, for you, Sis.

I think a deal lot of you, and I only ask that you give me a show, an even chance with that there blasted tenderfoot. I don't like his eyes and I don't think he's meanin' right by you. Let *me* love you!"

"Go to it, old boy! Guess it will not hurt me and maybe the practice will aid you in catching a real *good* girl. One who can return your affections; one capable of ' 'preciatin the best rider of the Flathead.' "

"Cogewea! I don't want a gal too *blamed* good. *You* are my kind! There ain't no more like you. Don't let any white feller steal your heart."

"I don't think that he is any *ipsoot kapswallie*," (2) she laughed amusedly. "But I will be on my guard, for I prefer *giving* my heart away rather than have some one sneak in and take it simply because he happens to find the latch string on the outside."

"Give it to me, Sis! Don't you love me just a little?"

"Can't do it, pard! I love you, but it is as a brother only."

"Brother hell!" growled Jim. "Take that there tenderfoot, who can't ride a cayuse, for a brother. He needs a sister to look after him while away from his mother."

"I don't want a *Shoyahpee* brother," was the counter. "I like the Injun breed best."

"You have an awful' poor way of expressin' your likin's. If I thought you really loved that—"

"H-hu-hush!" and Cogewea laid a hand on her companion's arm. "There comes the Shoyahpee now!"

Densmore came around the veranda. He paused as if to speak and then passed on to the bunk house. A sigh of relief escaped the girl. The foreman muttered an oath as he asked:

"Why didn't you let me finish what I was sayin'?"

"Because I don't want to see any trouble between you two on my account. And Jim," she continued earnestly, "if you really care for me, please do not kick up any dust with him. It won't pay. Won't you promise?"

The breed's soul was rent with the contending passions, love and hate. As if weighing his answer, he hesitated long before breaking silence:

"Sis, it's hard to refuse any thing you request, but if I catch that there guy who can't ride a gentle hoss without hurtin' hisself, a goin' round here with your heart, I'll be very likely to treat him as any sneakin' cattle rustler. I guess you know how that is."

"Jim," Cogewea whispered as her hand slipped to the hilt of his weapon, "I'm scared! when I see you near this Shoyahpee with gun so handy. I wish you would let me have it. Let me keep it for you, won't you?"

Jim's own strong hand closed about the tapering, brown fingers clasping his pistol's grip, as he answered feelingly:

"Little Injun chum, I love you and I'll try always to please you, but I can't give this here request. I couldn't walk level without no side ballast. No, Sis! I'm holdin' on to my old pardner, and it may all rest with you whether there'll be some funeral-trouble, 'stead of a weddin'-dance. You're a breed, same as myself. You know the callin' of the blood! A man will sometimes fight for what he wants."

"Oh! Jim!" and the girl's voice was tremulous with agitation. "*Promise* me not to make trouble with this white man."

The Westerner's words were low, measured, and deadly even:

"The best rider of the Flathead hunts no trouble. Neither does he run should it hunt him. A brother is sometimes more dangerous than a lover. As a brother, I'd be a howlin' bad actor if feelin' called on to protect my dependent sister from a low crawlin' *puch-qeeh..* (3) Ol' Jim would sure be locoed."

Cogewea laughed nervously. While the half-blood was all kindness to her, she well knew his fierce temperament and how best to placate it. It was with something of her old-time banter and spirit of coquetry, that she spoke; falling into the easy range vernacular:

"I b'lieve yo' would! Some time, if yo' don't look out, maybe I'll disown yo' as a brother. Do yo' savey? Now run 'long an' hit th' hay! I'm a goin' tumble in an' harvest a good crop of sleep. Goin' give yo' th' first dance tomorrow night!"

With this, the girl of moods sprang up and dashed into the house, leaving her dusky lover pondering in doubt.

CHAPTER XXIII.

THE BASKET SOCIAL

Yet, pardner, we are dull and old,
With paltry hopes and fears,
Beside those rangers gay and bold,
Far riding down the years!
—*Badger Clark.*

"WHY, Cogewea!" exclaimed Mary, as they hurriedly prepared for the longed-for social the following evening. "Are you taking two baskets—the canoe and that other fancy—"

Cogewea spoke in an undertone to her sister, who laughed musically, but said nothing. Soon everything was packed and the girls were helping Julia with the children. Cogewea, understanding the nature of man, that he should not, under any circumstances, be kept waiting, lest he become grouchy, was hurrying her sisters, that they might meet Silent Bob as soon as he drove to the gate. They heard the rattle of the heavy hack and the driver's unnecessarily loud:

"*Who! thar' Prince! Whoa, Jerry!* I hater have yo' a stan'in' here so long! I hater hav yo' a eatin' stake-oats all th' time."

Snatching up the children and the baskets, they hastened out. Cogewea helped the fledglings to the rear seat with their mother and Mary, then clambered to her place at Bob's side. That worthy had held the "ribbons of four" over a stage route in the Rockies, and to display his proud skill, flourished his long lash—which he ever carried—with a report like the shot of a pistol. The fiery bays leaping forward, went spinning around the road-curve at a speed to frighten an inexperienced out of his wits. The mad pace was kept until the upper grade through the coulee was reached. As the team quieted down, Cogewea spoke:

"Now Bob, own up that a man does not like to wait
for a woman!"

The Jehu turned his head to eject a quid of tobacco
before answering:

"Ev'ry man hates ter wait for anybody."

"Yes, I know! But it's *women* they hate most to wait
for; and yet they seem to think that woman was *made*
to wait for them. They do not consider the daily heart-
aches of a waiting woman, most of whom spend their
best days loitering on the trail—waiting on the slow
movements of *some* man—not all of them married women either. A few are out here on this flat."

The pun was entirely lost on Silent Bob, who manifested great interest in his bays. Cogewea was light-
hearted and did most of the talking. She joked Mary
about Frenchy, whom she had observed silently admiring the shy girl as she came out on the veranda, dressed
for the trip. Her light suit brought out the beauty of a
rich complexion to the best adantage; while her clear
blue eyes shaded by long dark lashes, were brilliant with
the joy of anticipation. Her stately form and graceful
movements would have been as much in keeping at a
court of fashion, as with the picturesque surroundings of
a western cattle ranch. Cogewea had covertly designated Mary's basket to the Parisian, with the hope that he
would be a successful bidder for it at the coming auc-
tion. Jim, too, had remarked this courtly scion of
France gazing enraptured after the girl as the hack
dashed through the gate; and smiling, muttered under
his breath:

"The poor frog-eatin' fool! Makin' eyes at that
there breed-gal who ain't got no more heart than her
witch-sister!"

The instant the hack had disappeared at the bend,
Slim of the Foot Hills, approaching Frenchy very con-
fidentially, inquired:

"Yo' goin' with me to th' big doin's, ain' yo'?"

Displaying a roll of bills, which Slim afterwards declared to be " 'nough to stumble a bronc,'' the Parisian exclaimed:

"I go zee zonzibél! I pay ze baz-ze-keét; zee Frenchee genzemon. Zee lee-teel von, zee zeneder voot. Zee biget loff!''

"Then come on quick!'' urged Slim, as he led the way to the corral. "Le's saddle up! It's gittin' late an' th' baskets'll be all sold a fore we git there. Throw yo' saddle on yo' buckskin an' le's ride! Th' sun's mos' down an' we a slackin' time with fifteen miles to unreel. Don't draw th' cinch too tight! It'll bust yo' hoss's wind.''

By this time, he of the Foot Hills had his horse saddled and all ready to start. Frenchy was somewhat slower, but soon his mount was also in complete trim for the road. He surveyed his soiled apparel dubiously, then pointing to Slim's equally reprehensible "duds,'' questioned:

"Likee zat! zee gran' veste-vál?''

"Sho' thin'! Real cowboys never dress for s'ciety like yo' city chaps. If yo' go all dood-toggl'd up, th' gals won't dance with yo'. They'd only laugh an' make sport of yo.' Jus' cinch that there belt o' yourn a bit tighter. Too durn' loose for dancin'. After buyin' go' gal's basket, yo' can loosen it up for th' big feed.''

Poor Frenchy! He had understood but little of the foreman's instructions relative to dress the evening before, and now drew his worn leather belt considerably tighter, which gave him a most comical appearance. His ancient buckskin breeches, wrinkled and bagged at the knee, were dust-stormed and discolored after the prolonged roundup. His blue flannel shirt, minus buttons, was open at the throat, while a worn silk handkerchief was knotted about his neck. High heeled boots and a slouchy sombrero, tilted jauntily to one side, only added to the wild grotesqueness of his figure.

"There, now!'' exclaimed the hero of the Foot Hills, as he surveyed his "pard'' of the evening admiringly.

"Yo'll sho' be th' 'vent of th' 'casion. Not many buck-skin garbs in this here country an' th' gals'll all fall over theirselfs to git the fust dance wit yo'. Yo're to be 'gratulated! Yo' couldn't a struck no gen'elman more 'sperienced in s'ciety ways than who's a talkin'. Yo' bet! It's scripter to take a stranger in, and yo' inter'sts is a goin' be well looked af'er. France'll be proud when she hears of th' high 'tainment of her son in Ameriky's most 'lete s'ciety. It's sho' fortunat' for th' world that th' main Smoke of the Foot Hills is with yo' to night."

The two rode away, French in blissful ignorance that the night previous, in a "pitch" card game, it fell to Slim to see that the "toy" was properly apparelled for the party. Hardly were they in the saddle when the boys at the bunk house were all busy with shaving materials, jostling each other for places before the one broken wall-mirror.

They had soon donned their best clothes, flashy silk shirts and handkerchiefs. The inevitable high-riding boot and broad hat were retained as an inseparable ad-jonct to the cowpuncher's regalia, under all circum-stances.

Amid joking and untrammeled merriment, the gay cavalcade filed from the corral, following the two de-parted riders. Densmore was with them. For a time he rode in the rear and alone, but Celluloid Bill drop-ping back, fell in with him, engaging in conversation. The topic drifted, but finally Bill settled down to a de-scriptive detail of the recent roundup, telling in general the number of hoofs each stockman owned. Carter's wealth was mostly in horses, but he boasted a goodly number of cattle, while Cogewea could lay claim to more than two thousand bovines on the one range. Thir-teen hundred and seventy-five of these had recently been sold as beef at the banner price of the season; with de-livery six weeks later. Her band of fifteen hundred horses in the June roundup were considered the best on the Flathead. Seven hundred and fifty of these were then contracted, but were yet to be "cut" from the herd. The money was then in bank, subject to her order as soon as the stock could be delivered.

The Easterner gasped! He had never dreamed that Cogewea possessed property other than the land of which she had spoken. He kept his meditations to himself, but cautiously asked about her acres, if any. Bill was not sure on this point, other than that he knew of one fine allotment and a few range sections in a body. However, Rodeo Jack knew all about this part of her possessions.

"That there breed-gal," Bill confided, "is sho' still 'bout her wealth. Don't say nothin'! 'Pears to think if it gets known she has dough, she'll get trapped by some fortun' hunter 'long th' hitchin' lines. Denies ownin' any horses an' cattle. But know! 'cause I was in both roun'ups. Rodeo got it 'bout her land from Carter, who wants her to marry Jim. Somebody'll get a fine lay-out, who can rope her in. But he'll hafter go some! Injun blood an' skittisher nor a wild bronc'."

The opera hall was all ablaze and the crowd gathering, when Slim and his "pard" reached Polson. But to hold the joke for the other boys, he proposed to Frenchy that they go to the pool room for a few games before repairing to the gathering. It was, he contended, too early for the social to open anyhow. The "toy" readily consented, never dreaming of what was in store for him. They played until Slim thought it time for the riders to be there, when he suddenly said:

"Whatcher say, Frenchy! Let's go to th' big doin's now."

"O'ritz! I ess redée!"

They gained the street and strains of music was wafted from the place of gathering. This hushed as they reached the jammed door-way. Drifting in with the crowd, Slim very adroitly guided his "pard" out onto the vacant floor. The Parisian gazed around, surprised. He was startled to see everybody dressed in their best. He instantly comprehended the meanness of the joke played him, and attempted to leave the hall. But, to the great amusement of the spectators, the boys would not permit him to pass the door, A tenderfoot was being "broken in."

Baffled, the victim shrank into the shadows away from his tormenters. He was humiliated and ashamed of his absurd and fantastic attire. He loathed the buckskins which he had imagined made him so much a real westerner. Aside from the "sporty" riders who flashed in gaudy, silken make-ups he saw the men of this remote reservation hamlet in actual cuffs and collars which he had supposed to be wholly unknown. The many bunk house and roundup jokes he did not mind, but this was the most brutal thrust of them all. Yet, while it was almost beyond endurance, he determined to bear his misfortune with apparent good grace and lay to be avenged—at least on Slim of the Foot Hills.

Thus nursing his wounded pride, the Parisian sat in his shadowy corner, and saw the shy-girl dancing with some of the rangers. He noted the small feet, how lightly they touched the floor and the glide was that of the woods-nymph. This privilege, he had hoped for, as well as the joy of bidding for her basket. Never, since leaving old France, had he felt so homesick and desolate. A collegian and from an aristocratic family, he had moved in the most exclusive circles of the Old World, but here, in Democratic America, he felt to be a social outcast. Not a woman there but would refuse him a dance.

Near midnight, the floor manager announced the sale of the baskets. The auctioneer mounted a table and began crying bids. Slim approached Frenchy, smiling broadly as if he had never in all his career perpetrated an unsavory joke. The rider was resplendent in the gala clothes which had been smuggled to him by his associates His manner was one of supreme innocence as he addressed the "toy."

"Now partner, it's time yo' show yo' 'preciation. Come an' bid on yo' gal's basket"

"Aw come on!" he urged, as Frenchy silently shook his head. "If yo' too bashful, I'll bid for yo'."

The victim's face softened. Fondling his roll, he replied in the most confidential undertone:

"Eff mak' pay fortee dollar! Zee Frenchee genzeemon no pay leetl' monee. I spiek zee bazakeét!"

"Sho' thin'!" exulted the Smoke of the Foot Hills, slapping the "toy" familiarly on the shoulder. "Yo' gota right idee an' leave it to ol' Slim to manage for yo'. Yo' cause is in han's of yo' best frien'!"

The plotter then hunted up Rodeo Jack and that confederate nearly doubled at what was whispered in his ear. He immediately took his place on the opposite side of the auctioneer, while Slim went back to the victim in the corner. He nudged Frenchy when an exceedingly pretty basket was offered. There was a negative shake of the head. Presently when a plain, though tasty basket was displayed, Slim received a poke in the ribs with:

"*Geet* 'im!"

The accommodating rider stepping forward, bid a dollar and was promptly raised by Rodeo. The bidding grew steady and at times fierce. The audience became hushed in expectancy. Slim, who had only recently drifted in from the ranges of Wyoming, was a practical stranger, but it was known that the rivals were both of the "H-B" outfit.

"Whose basket can it be?"

This question was bandied throughout the hall, as the auctioneer's stentorian voice called:

"*Fifteen dollars!*" The banner bid of the evening but now—Eighteen!—twenty!—twenty two!—twenty four! —twenty five!—twenty six!—twenty eight—twenty nine!—twenty nine!—Do I hear thirty? *Wough!* Thirty one!—thirty three!—thirty thr—five! Thirty five. Who will make it—There you are! Thirty six! thirty si—seven! Thirty seven! Do I get a raise? Nothing near its worth! Come one! Last call without a bid! Thirty sev—thirty eight! thirty eight! All in at thirty eight? Hit 'er up! A good cause! a Church

cause. A heavy feed well cooked with the cookee thrown
in! Hit the grit there, you sun-beam from the cactus
plains of Texas! Jingle the kale for the object of
your—''

But Rodeo, throwing up his hands, turned aside. The
crier barked:

"And *sold!* at thirty-eight dollars to the unidentified
gentleman partner of the buckskin negligee. Here,
take your property and pay the Deacon afterwards. We
trust you because we do not know you.''

At this good natured thrust, the spectators roared and
gave the victorious contestant a hearty "three and a
tiger''. But too generous to reap renown which right-
fully belonged to another, he of the Foot Hills sprang
upon a chair and holding aloft the modest looking basket, bellowed:

"La-dees an' gen'lmen! I ain't no speecher, nor I
ain't no s'ciety dood to sail under no false colored bunt-
in'. This here two-people grub has been bargained for
by proxa; an' th' 'praised val'er of same is a going be
likerdated by the fust an' only 'ristocat of Paris;
where range th' toad-eatin' pervi'ers of fashun. As his
'steemed pard, I ropes this occasion to in'duce to yo'
the only Buckskin Frenchy of th' noted "H-B" ranch.
Ho! there Ol' hoss in the co'ner! Come on with yo dough
an' take yo' belt fillin'; which I bets don't 'clude no
fried water-chicken. Yo' is a lucky coyote, an' yo' gal
ain't got nothin' on yo' in this here soc'al tran'fixion.''

The Smoke of the Foot Hills was again greeted with
a storm of applause, ending in a regular stampede for
the now suddenly popular Parisian. But the "only
'risto-cat,'' taking adantage of the excitement during
the rival bidding, had, unobserved, slipped through the
door and ran like a hunted deer for the livery where his
horse was sheltered. With nervous haste he saddled the
buckskin, and leaping to its back, left on a mad gallop
for the ranch. The night was pitchy dark and he had
been over the unfenced trail-road only twice. Out on
the big flat he lost his way, and circled for an hour,

when he recalled having heard the rangers say that in such case, if a horse is given the rein, it will always come safely through. This he did and in due time, reached the bunk house, bordering on exhaustion. He was enjoying the warmth of his blankets and sound asleep when the other boys arrived an hour later.

In the meantime, when it was discovered that the buckskinned " 'ristocat" had departed, there was a murmur of disappointment; but when the full import of the retaliatory ruse played on the lanky cowpuncher, by the absconded Frenchman, became known, there was a prolonged outburst of unrestrained hilarity.

"Yo' was caught with yo' rope a trailin' that time ol' skate!"

"Set 'em up to th' frog eater'!"

"Draw yo' cinch an' try for th' finals! yo' wanderin' son of benighted Wyomin'!"

"Yo' trained th' over-seas duck too well!" yelled a voice at the door. "He ain't no longer no tenderfoot!"

These, and similar cries greeted the discomfited Smoke of the Foot Hills, as he "dug up" for the basket. He accepted the jibes with good grace, contending that he knew the owner of "this here feed" and that it was worth the price.

As basket after basket was proferred, the "H-B" contingent made it lively for the city visitants; but Silent Bob held aloof. Noting this, Jim accosted him:

"Why don't you get a move on? You'll get left without a feed if you don't rustle 'round and do some biddin'. Schoolmarm's baskets is a bein' sold now. Don't forget you're from the Hoss-shoe Bend."

"Waitin' for the feed box showin' th' right bran'," was the drawling reply. "When it 'pears, I'll chip in a plenty. At presen', I'm a restin' from my laborin'. I hater be a hollerin' so durn much; I hater tire myself a talkin'."

As all things come to those who wait, the Silent one finally got his "feed" at fifteen dollars.

The canoe was the last offered. Jim, true to his declaration was a loyal bidder; Rodeo and Celluloid his principal opponents. The city guys manifested but little interest above the three dollar mark. The canoe, tastily decorated with tri-colored ribbons and sprigs of evergreen, was held aloft by the auctioneer, who expatiated on the evident merits of its builder and the superqualities of its cargo. There was at last a lull in the mad riot of contending bids, punctuated with:

"And *sold!* to the foreman of the 'H-B' Ranch, for forty-one dollars a truly silver weighted, deep water sounding line."

Again the audience was wild with applause. The Horse-shoe "Benders" were tendered an ovation. They had carried off the three banner baskets of the evening.

With his canoe under his arm, Jim talked and joked with friends and acquaintances. Everybody was hunting for partners, some to a realization of joy, others to disappointment. But all was harmony and good will. The foreman made his way to where he had last observed Cogewea. He suddenly stopped, dumbfounded. There sat the object of his search by the side of the tenderfoot. She was unfolding a napkin, disclosing the dainties of a tidy basket. The contents were most appetizing. Approaching, Jim touched her arm. Tapping the side of the canoe, he spoke evenly:

"Sis, I thought this here was your feed."

"You *did?*" in mock surprise. "Has it my name? Is Cogewea on the card?"

"Why!—I—I—haven't looked!" was the stammered reply.

"Well, you better search for the brand. There may be some mistake."

The Westerner lifted the corner of the cover and took up an embossed card. "Blank!" was written across its face. For a brief moment he stood silently, and then in an undertone addressed her:

"You think you've played one hell of a trick, now don't you! I didn't think—"

"Aw! now Jim, come off! What's hurting you? That

canoe is not the first craft to sail under false colors. Besides,'' continued Cogewea with twinkling eyes, ''you
should be generous enough to recognize that all is fair
in—in certain phases of life. It may be piratical, but
you had a gallant crew to help you plan and effect its
capture, had you not?''

Jim saw the cunning trap in which he had been caught
and despite his bitter disappointment, he felt an increasing admiration for the girl. Perhaps he had been
served right. Intuitively, his mind flashed back to that
secret council of war in the main corral, the previous
evening. He chilled! Vacancies as well as walls could
sometimes have ears.

''By gollies, little squ-Sis!'' he exclaimed with sudden impulse. ''You're a trump! But you'r nawtical
reckonin' was all wrong this time. You turned this here
boat driftin' with a mine in the hold, expectin' somebody to get blowed to kingdom come when they boarded
it. You didn't count on the secret treasure it carried,
—a code number calling for a fine pearl-set solid gold
brooch—a sure glitterin' prize for rescuin' so splendid
a craft from gettin' wrecked and all busted up on rocks
and hidden snags. It takes the best rider of the Flathead to do so improbable a stunt like that.''

''Sure! But the best of riders are sometimes caught
sleeping—not always in the sage—but when they should
be looking to their cinching. Now own up that you were
mad when—''

''Who the dickens wouldn't feel all broke up, when
a hungry feller spends nearly a month's wages for a
feed only to find it all mixed with wormwood and gall?
But you'll savey you have stung yourself when you see
that there elegant brooch bein' worn by my best gal.''

''James La'Grinder,'' and there was music in the
laughter which set the Westerner's heart thumping,
''I'll wear that prize brooch and don't you forget it!
Stemteemä donated that canoe, and the brooch goes to
her, but since she is not here and you look so lonesome
you better go share your banquet with Mary. She is mad

about Frenchy and will not eat with that Foot Hills
orator from Wyoming. You fellows ought to be ashamed
for the low trick you perpetrated. You and Slim have
been treated to a dose of your own mixing and it may
do your systems good. Now! 'Go and sin no more!' "

Jim laughed with ill affected grace, hunted Mary and
shared the contents of his canoe with her. But he failed
in all attempts at engaging the girl in conversation.
Beyond a monotone answer to his question, she was
silent.

Slim divided his high priced "spread" with a cowpuncher from a distant range, who failed in securing a
basket.

Silent Bob spent the feast hour with the schoolmarm;
while Celluloid broke bread with a winsome widow of
the flats.

Rodeo Jack feasted with a pretty miss, whose basket
he captured over the bids of one of "them there city
mashers."

Mrs. Carter's basket was claimed by a bald-headed
Chicagoan, and it was many days before she heard the
last of her "marble-domed" partner.

On the return trip, Bill saw to it that Rodeo rode
with Densmore, and that Jim, with himself in the lead,
kept well beyond earshot.

CHAPTER XXIV.

THE SECOND COMING OF THE SHOYAHPEE

Let us welcome, then, the strangers,
Hail them as our friends and brothers.
—*Hiawatha*

THE noon following the social, the shy-girl summoned Jim to the tepee. The Stemteemä wished to speak to him. Wondering what she could want, he complied, following Mary through the low curtained doorway. His greeting was an inscrutable look from the aged woman, as he seated himself on the buffalo robe. Glancing about the airy abode, he regretted that he had never thought of visiting there. The canvas lodge seemed home-like and the occupant reminded him of his own grand-parent from whom he learned the tribal language which he still retained. She meditated before speaking. At length she addressed him:

"You are an Indian," she said, gazing full into his face. "You will understand me, what I am to tell you I am distressed and need your help. There is no one else for me to go to."

Here the Stemteemä paused, as if in doubt about confiding to this strong, determined man—a stranger. But the blood-tie was there, strengthened by a mutual knowledge of language and her need was sore. Seeming to weigh all, she continued:

"I do not like this Shoyahpee, who tries to steal my Cogewea from me and my people. I want her to marry some one of her own kind and class. I do not want the white man with his marked tongue He will only cast her aside for one of his own race after he tires of her. She must take a man that we can all trust. I have no confidence in the pale faces. Always, they have made light of our women. Ever since the two white men came to us, has this trouble continued. It is a wrong many times repeated and the maidens should learn to distrust the cunning despoilers.

"My aunt fell victim to the first Shoyahpee who came to our tribe. The daughter of a Chief, she died of heart-grief. That is why I hate the pale faced race!

"You will help me to guard and watch over Cogewea. I have spoken to her older sister but Julia seems not to care. She wants her to marry a Shoyhapee, as she did herself. But not many white men are true and good like John. The eye of this other man tells me that he is bad. I have spoken all."

The whitened head bent lower in grief. The foreman's eyes glinted as he promised to try to protect Cogewea. They formulated and abandoned different plots for separating the lovers, but finally agreed that events should drift for the present. Considering his mishap with Croppy, it was hardly possible that Carter, with his conception of justice, would consent to Densmore's dismissal from the ranch, so long as he proved worthy of hire and help was needed. However, under the changed conditions brought about by the closing of the roundup season, the two would not be thrown together so much, and it was hoped that the girl would detect his true character and drop him of her own accord.

Jim rose to go, but as an after thought, asked her to hear the story of the two white men of whom the grandmother had spoken. Stemteemä exhausted the little stone pipe which Mary had filled for her, before answering:

"If you were not of my own kind, I would not talk. Although the white blood has made fairer your skin, I like you and I trust you. I will tell you this story of other snows. Troubles of the long past should be buried, but I will speak."

Then in an even tone, but at times with a cadence of sorrow, the Stemteemä disclosed how the innocence of her people was betrayed in the second coming of the Shoyahpee.

"I was only a small child, it happened so long ago," she began. "I am now an old woman! It is so long since I was born that I have lost my correct age. I did keep the snows by knotting a hemp string which I had for that purpose, a knot for each winter. But I lost it on the trail and now I only know that I have seen more than a hundred snows. I must have been very young, but the men with hair on their pale faces impressed me. I have not forgotten the incident all my life. Not with the many snows, could I forget.

"I remember well both the Shoyahpees. I was afraid! I clung to my mother for protection. With pleading and coaxing, she made me to understand that I was not to be afraid of them; that they were not common mortals as we were the warriors and medicine men, but were gods—a higher people than the Indians— which all my tribe believed to be true.

"But they were only the ordinary white men and thousands of them have I seen since. I did not then dream that in time I would have grandchildren with their blood. In after snows, when I could understand things better, my father, who was a great war Chief, repeated the story to me often. He told me just as I will now tell it to you.

" 'One snow,' said my father, 'my tribe, the Okanogans and some of the Schu-ayl-p^k, had their village on the banks of the Swa-netk-qha. The snow was just covering the earth, the first calling of the Great Spirit. We had plenty of food for the winter moons. The seasons had been abundant in roots, berries and game; and the red salmon which comes up the streams, had been as the wild geese that flock to their nesting in the north-land after the Chinook has melted the snow. The Giver of Life had been kind and we thought to thank him with a bigger dance than usual. He had favored us on the war path, had made us strong in battle. We had defeated the Blackfeet who came against us and driven them back across the great mountains. For all this, we would prayer-dance a longer time. We were building our big festive lodge, when some of my warriors came running to me in excitement and said:

" 'We have again seen the pale faces, the strangers! The Great Spirit has sent them to show us the right way to reach Him.'

" 'We were all frightened! We thought of the prayers that the Black Robes had taught us and we tried to repeat the little which we remembered. We thought that the Great Spirit was angry with us, because we had neglected worshiping Him in the way of the pale faces. It might be that He had sent the strangers to punish us in some fearful way. I was scared! But I was a big Chief, and it is not for the chief to show fear, not even in death. A chief must not flinch at pain or fright.

" 'The two pale faces camped close to our village. They did not live in a tepee. They built a lodge of logs and covered it with moss and dirt. The moss they gathered on the banks of the Swa-netk-qha, where it grew of the green shade and was plentiful.

" 'They also made a fireplace of rocks and clay, and a way for the smoke to escape as in our tepees. In one side of the lodge they put rawhide so the light would come through. It covered only a small space, but it lighted the room well.

" 'We were perplexed, astonished! We prayed to them and worshiped them from a distance. It was some time before I had the courage to go to their lodge. But finally I went with some of my bravest warriors, fearless warriors. I took a medicine man with us for protection. (1) I had made up my mind to see them and if they killed me, I would die brave. My name would not be lost! My children and grandchildren would think of my great name with honor. I believed the strangers to be men who had in them the Great Spirit, who might be angry. For this, I hesitated before taking the rash step, as I then thought it to be.

" 'With my warriors, I reached the lodge which they
had completed and were occupying. I did not knock at
the door. According to our own custom we walked in.
When we entered, the pale faces were both holding
weapons against us. Even the strange Indian woman
who was with them, held a gun in aim. She was a
brave squaw! We found afterwards that she came to
show them the trail to the big water, towards the sunset.

" 'When I saw that they wanted to fight or defend
themselves, I held out the peace pipe, but the woman
alone understood. We all got on our knees and prayed,
of the little we remembered of the Black Robe's teaching. I felt ashamed when they laughed instead of pointing us the right way to reach the Great Spirit. When
they laughed before our faces, I knew not what to do.

" 'But we smoked the pipe with them, to show that
we would be friends while they remained in our country.

" 'They had several ponies, and since they had come
from the direction of the big mountains, I knew what
those horses meant for us. If our fierce enemies, the
Blackfeet, knew we had them at our village, they would
never stop until they possessed them. We could expect an attack in the night, a battle for a small band
of ponies. That the ponies belong to the white-gods,
would make no difference to those on the war path.

" 'This troubled me and one day I decided to speak
to the strangers even if they were higher beings. My
people were uneasy! They knew what attending evil
awaited them and their children, should the Blackfeet
come. Only after many signs in talking did I make
the pale faces understand why we did not want the
horses with us. But they laughed at our fears. Then
I thought that they, being greater than the Indians,
knew everything, so made my mind easy concerning the
enemy.

" 'One of the pale faces had the Indian woman who
came with them as a wife. Of another tribe and beyond the big mountains, we could not understand her
tongue. The other pale face had no wife, and to honor

him I gave him my only sister, *Wan-na-ke,* the handsome Okanogan princess. Chiefs and warriors of our own, as well as of distant tribes, had sought her, but she was valued above any gifts offered. It was to show my friendship and worship for the pale faced god that I gave him my sister to be his wife. It was to please him and the Great Spirit.

" 'Wan-na-ke went to her white god and soon loved him. She prayed hard to please him and the Great Spirit. My people took them food, dried roots and berries, fresh game and fish.

" 'The strangers had been with us one moon, when what we had dreaded took place. The Blackfeet came on the war path for those ponies, traveled days for them. They stole on our village at night, killing some of my people, while we killed some of them. They got the horses which left the pale gods afoot; flying with them back across the mountains.

" 'The pale faces stayed with us the rest of the winter. Perhaps this was because they now had no horses to carry them away. They spent their time hunting and trapping. The beaver fur they dried in the sun, lacing them to pole hoops. We cured our skins the same way, fastening the edges with strong buckskin or hemp lashings.

" 'One day some of the Okanogans were watching the strangers from a thicket. They saw one of them go to the rack and strike the skin with his hand which threw it a distance from the frame. The Indians were frightened at his unusual strength. They were now convinced that their visitors were not mere men like themselves, but were beings from the spirit world. No human could possess such force without aid from the Great Spirit. (2) Seeing them so powerful, we prayed all the more to them from our hiding. We no longer worshiped them as at first, in the fear that they would laugh at us. But we thanked the Great Spirit for sending them to us. We had looked for them long. We knew that they had come to show us the *right way,* for had not the *dead man* foretold it?

" 'In the spring when the birds had come back from the spirit world, (3) and the red salmon were coming up the big river, my sister came to me in trouble. Her heart was poor and heavy. She sat down in my lodge and for a time was silent. She then told me that the pale faces wanted to go where the sun sinks down, where the Black Robe had gone. I wandered while she spoke. I thought:

" 'Why do they all want to go to the sunset? Is there anything wrong with the sun? Maybe the spirits have sent them to see about the sun? Maybe they have no more suns where they came from and they are going to change its trail? Maybe the sun will travel the other way, after they have reached there and attended to it?

" 'He wants to go where the sun quits the earth, where it becomes lost in the big water,' said Wan-na-ka. He wants some of your young men to take them in canoes down the Swa-netk-pha; and my brother; he wants me to go with him and leave my own people. I do not want to do this, and still I love him, my white god. He said that if I want him, I must go and leave my own blood forever. If I do not do this, then I must give him up for all time. He is leaving, he told me, maybe never to return among us. I am not to see him again. My brother, I have no other one to go to and you must tell me what to do. I am also to become a mother.

" 'I told her that she must give me time to think; that I must consult my medicine man; to have my sleep and dream among the spirits. Then I could give her advice. Wan-na-ka then spoke again:

" 'My child is to be a boy. I want him to grow up among the Schu-ayl-p^k, a wise counselor, a warrior chief. I want to stay near the graves of my ancestors, I do not want to die away from my people. I love them! I love you, my brother, and I love my pale faced husband. I have told you all, and you will guide me right in the steps I am to take. You are wise and will not show me the wrong trail.

" 'Wan-na-ka was troubled, but she did not weep. I said to her:

" 'Speak no more! Go home to your white husband. After I call the spirits and dream, I can give you a strong answer. My heart is now sick and poor in words.

" 'I consulted my medicine man and then went alone to the mountain woods. I slept! And the spirits showed me a broad trail yet unmade; creeping to us from the land of the morning sun. It is not for me to unblanket all that came to me in that vision. It is enough that I learned all about the pale faced gods.

" 'After five sundowns, I came back to my sister, Wan-na-ka. She gave me food, after the ancient custom. I was in troubled thought and I ate in silence. I made my heart strong, for I knew what I would say and the task was not easy. I spoke:

" 'My sister, we have been deceived in the strangers. Better had I not smoked the pipe with them; better had you never seen him whom you call a god-husband. Go with him! without my consent and learn what is to come to you; what the meaning of it is. He can not love you as one of his kind. Have you thought that maybe there are pale faced squaws where he came from, in the land of the morning lodge? In my dream I saw them! Their eyes are not of the night like those of the women of the Schu-ayl-p^k. They are as the summer sky when the clouds are melted and gone. Their hair is as the leaves when touched by the first call of autumn. For these strange women, I saw your pale face forsake you when far from the Swa-netk-qha. Wan-na-ka, the choice belongs to you. Go and be forgotten by both your husband and people alike! For your own good, will I advise you. Stay with the Okanogans and the Schu-ayl-p^{k}s! Where you are loved and will not be cast aside. Good bye, my sister. This is all that I will say, but before going I will answer your husband.

" 'Tell him that I must keep all of my young men. He may take the canoes, but my warriors he cannot have. I will need them for the trouble which I saw in my dream. Evil and death will come to my people

in the wake of these two pale faces. My warriors
must be strong! I saw on this great new trail a mighty
nation sweeping over our hunting grounds, armed with
dread weapons of war. I saw our villages made desolate with fire and the graves of our fathers profaned.
I saw the death-trail worn smooth by the moccasined
feet of the dead and the death wail grew loud on the
storm-rack of night. It passed! the lament grew fainter
and ceased. There were none to mourn for the last of
the Schu-ayl-p^k.

"'I turned away, and as I passed through the doorway, I heard my sister moaning:

"'Good bye, my brother! My own blood! But I
love him, my pale faced god!'

"'Not to hear more, I hurried to my own lodge. My
heart was heavy with grief. I reached my tepee, where
you were then a very small child; favorite of the youngest of my twelve wives. I sat gloomy with sorrow, my
robe over my head.

"'I never saw my pale faced brother-in-law again.
I did not want to see him. I might kill him for the
wrong he had done my sister. But it was my fault for
giving her to him in the belief that he was superior to
common man. I was ashamed for my folly! I sent
my young men to help him get ready the canoes, but I
would not go myself. I remained in my lodge, hidden
from view.

"'It was fourteen sundowns later, when I saw them
carrying their goods to the river. I knew that they were
leaving never to return among us and I was glad. But
I saw Wan-na-ka, following her pale man—deserting
her own people—as I then thought. As strong and
brave as I was, death would have been easier than to
watch her leaving forever.

"'With a poor heart, I remained in my lodge. Wan-
na-ka, my only sister, had not come to speak a last
farewell. Maybe she hated me! Why had I given my
flower to the blighter? Some one entered the doorway. I did not look up! I did not want to see anybody when my sorrow was heavy. My visitor stopped

not at the vacancy kept near the entrance for those
who might come, but stepped directly to my private
robe where only the invited might sit.

" 'A touch was on my shoulder. I did not turn!
But soon, a sob, low and smothered, caused me to lift
my eyes. Wan-na-ka was standing at my side, weeping as Indians seldom weep. I took her hand, feeling
happy as though she had returned from the dead. She
would now remain with her own people. I asked her
what was wrong, and she answered:

" 'Let me cry! I must feel better before I can talk.'

" 'All the rest of that day, Wan-na-ka sat mourning. In time, she talked and said that at the river,
her pale husband had told her not to follow him. He
did not want her in the canoe. I tried to show her
that it was best to stay with her own kind, where all
understood each other. When night fell, she went to
her aunt's lodge to sleep.

" 'It was again winter snow when Wan-na-ka brought
to my lodge a little papoose, all wrapped in furs. She
stood the cradle-board near me and bared the face of
the baby, a boy. It was handsome, but light of skin as
was its father. Wan-na-ka told me how the tribe's
greatest medicine man had foretold that if the boy lived,
he would become a mighty chief, a great leader among
the Schu-ayl-p^k. But evil spirits, sent by the medicine
men of the Blackfeet, were threatening the child with
a strange sickness, which if it came, would prove fatal,
for none could combat it. (4)

" 'The papoose grew for a time and my sister was
less unhappy. She was glad to be the mother of the
future benefactor of her tribe and race. Then when
the nights grew longest, when the sun had wandered
farthest from his summer trail, the trouble came. A
gleaming star appeared within the lodge of the moon,
and a raven flew circling above the tepee of Wan-na-ka.
(5)

" 'The papoose of the whitened skin became sick. A
great worship dance was held by our wisest medicine
men, to try to kill or drive back the evil spirits. But the

power of the Blackfeet was too strong. The life of Wan-na-ka's child went out and there was wailing for a spirit flown.

" 'The baby was buried and my sister grew weakened with grief. It was many moons before she was strong, but she was never seen to smile or laugh. Ofttimes she went into the woods and there wailed for her papoose and for the one who had deserted her. (6)

" 'After two snows, warriors and chiefs from the wide neighboring tribes came and sought Wan-na-ka's hand. She refused them all. *Kee-lau-naw*, (7) a brave young chief rich in furs and shells, was one. I favored him among the many but I would not follow the old custom and give my sister against her will. I asked her why she would not again marry; why she refused so great a chief as Kee-lau-naw, who had taken many scalps of the Blackfeet. He was the best hunter among the Okanogans and would always supply her with plenty of meat and skins for clothing. Pointing to where the sun was sinking into the earth, she replied:

" 'My brother, my heart is there, gone with him! I can not call it back. Do not ask me to marry another. What warrior would care for Wan-na-ka, who prays only for the coming of the night we call death.'

" 'I understood! I spoke to her no more on the subject. One snow later, the Great Spirit called and Wan-na-ka was buried by the side of her child.' "

The Stemteemä ceased speaking. Lost in reverie, she remained silent for a time and then concluded:

"This is the end of the story told by my father of the second Shoyahpee, and of the shame of my aunt and her people. I could tell you of like wrongs of the white man, but they are separate stories. My heart is sick with the telling! You now know why I do not want Cogewea to marry this Shoyahpee. They are all false to our race! I want you to save my grandchild."

Jim stood erect, his face set and stern. His measured words were impassioned as he spoke:

"I have heard the Stemteemä and I am not proud

of my white blood. Now listen! I love Cogewea, but she has cast me aside for this strange Shoyahpee. The white man's law permits her to choose between us, nor can tribal rules interfere. I can not fight him according to the old Indian custom, nor would I do secret injury to the meanest that live. But listen!'' and the voice was lowered to an even, deadly tone. ''If he so much as harms a tress of the little gal's head, the best rider of the Flathead will kill him!''

CHAPTER XXV.

VOICE OF THE AUTUMN LEAVES

Wooed her with his words of sweetness,
Wooed her with his soft caresses.
—*Hiawatha*

AS Jim returned to leave the tepee, Mary, the shy girl, handed him a sheet of paper on which was fastened a number of minute fragments of a letter, discolored and dingy, but neatly joined together. He read the following written in a feminine hand:

"Dear Alfred:
    "—not state—coming home. I hope—back with—fortune—went to find. —horrible Indians—that savage squaw girl—get your scalp. —careful of—half-blood lover who—gun-fight would— I am waiting—trousseau all ready—anxious for the time—Do come soon as—and do not—trouble. —game is worth—if—can get her money. —be caref—uneasy about—
                            "—love forever;
    "—gust 24—   "Livina."

"Where did you get this?" asked Jim, his eyes kindling.

"On the river bank among the pines, near the old log where the fishing is good. I was there as the morning broke."

"Did you get all the pieces?"

"Because of the Swa-lah-kin, the wind had been strong. I picked up all that I could find, for they were scattered wide. I saw the Shoyahpee's name and—"

"Did you show this to Cogewea?" Jim interrupted.

"No! only to you. Cogewea has not seen."

"Have you told the Stemteemä?"

"The Stemteemä's ears have heard, for I have translated it to her. She sent me to bring you."

"Julia and John, do they know?"

"It was not for them! They might not understand."

"Tell no one! Leave it to the best rider of the Flathead to take care of Sis and this dam' snake in the grass. Where is the little gal?"

"I saw her leave with the Shoyahpee in the direction of the river pines soon after dinner."

Jim swore under his breath and chewed furiously at his moustache. Folding and pocketing the paper, he left the lodge, walking rapidly toward the river. His impulse had been to follow the lovers and confront Densmore with the tell-tale letter, but upon cooler reflection he thought better of it. Retracing his steps, he went to the corral, roped and saddled his horse and rode to a distant field to look after some stock recently brought in. Cogewea was amply able to care for herself for the present, and it would be some pleasure to keep out of the way for a day or two and "let that there poor fool tenderfoot think the herd is a comin' his way over a greased train."

In the meantime Cogewea and Densmore had strolled along the river until they came to the friendly old log, where the anger of the sun-god had been so unwittingly provoked. He had been more persistent in pressing his suit, but she was still exasperatingly coquettish. He proposed sitting on the log.

"All right!" she answered, "but you have first to agree that you will not again bring trouble by bothering a frog. I do not fancy another such drenching. Besides, the next time a tree might fall on us, or maybe lightning strike us."

Densmore laughed and declared that he had no further desire to pose as a rain-maker, as there was a far more fascinating subject than frogs and possible storms to engage his attention.

"Cogewea!" he said, seating himself at her side, "how much longer are you going to put me off? I have offered you a home and all that wealth can bring you; and I am willing to have a minister or priest officiate at our nuptials, if you prefer, although I think the Indian mode far more romantic. I like it better.''

"Should I say 'yes,' would you dare take me East among your people? Would you take me on a honeymoon trip as do the white people?''

Her eyes were looking inquiringly into his own. Densmore's restless gaze turned to the river as he answered:

"Why sure! little—ah—sweetheart. But don't you believe that it would be more pleasant to wait till spring for such a tour?''

"Hardly! A visit to the cities is far preferable during the winter months. When spring comes with its bird-carols and renewed life, I want to be in the open where God and the sunshine are in evidence. If there is ever a season for the smothered stuffy city, it is winter; when the reek and slime is hidden by a charitable blanket of snow. Do you know, when I was back there in school I often thought, when watching the powdery flakes floating downward in such darkening masses that perhaps it was down from angel wings, mercifully scattered to blot out for a period the unsightly wreck of nature's grand old forests, converted into whiskey barrels, miserable board-walks and sewage drains.''

"Listen, Cogewea! Don't go off on one of your dream flights. Let's get married and then plan our outing as you wish. Only I think it would be best to—''

"Postpone any city visits indefinitely,'' she added as he hesitated. "Why don't you speak your mind and say that it would be 'awfully embarrassing' to take me among your relatives and friends?''

"Cogewea,'' exclaimed Densmore in an injured tone, "I am sorry that you entertain such thoughts of me. At the end of two months we could start on a grand tour of all eastern cities.''

"And why not wait till then to be married? Why this hurry?''

"Why do you wish to delay?'' he asked, taking her

hand. "Are you afraid of me? Do you doubt the sincerity of my word?"

Pausing a moment, Cogewea stopped and picked a handful of the first fallen autumn leaves from the ground. She let them slip through her fingers as she spoke:

"See, Alfred! the leaves have fallen and are returning to dust. The beauty of their present life has passed forever. Youth gone, seared and lifeless, they lay at our feet—lopped and cast down—as a love discarded for another of fairer hue. Having for a time served as a pleasurable bower for the loiterer by the wayside, they are now to be trampled underfoot! like the Indian woman of long ago—when the white man came with his luring voice and weaned her from her people—only to be disdained for a mate of his own kind; abandoned with her little half-blood papooses, outcasts and nameless to the world. Yet, still we never seem to understand the Shoyahpee enough to be cautious of him."

Densmore's lips grew compressed and a gleam of scorn came into his eyes. He felt bitter resentment, but with an effort he suppressed the sarcastic retort already framed. This girl of moods was to be humored, if won to his schemes.

"Cogewea, why do you so seriously and constantly remind me of a possible few questionable deals suffered by your people at the hands of the white man? There are bad individuals among all races, but the things of the past should be forgotten. People change and advance! They are different now and far more cultured than in the days to which you allude. The Indian is civilized and almost on a social and business level with his Caucasian neighbor. Why should I be ashamed to take a girl of pure American blood, a half-blood girl of refined taste and education?"

Cogewea remained silent and abstracted, her gaze fixed on the stream glinting in the sunbeams. Densmore took the other small, brown hand from the log where it was digging into the moss and continued:

"I love you, Cogewea! Why don't you say something? Do not look so startled! Tell me what is wrong; what is in the way?"

He placed his arm about her and attempted to draw her to him. Repelling this advance, the girl lifted her head proudly and although eyes were brimming with tears, her voice was vibrant with sublimity:

"The wrongs of centuries stand between us! The arrogance of a strong race in its questionable conquest of a weaker, though a heroically patriotic nation, has been all too manifest. This spirit of self-superiority is still with you in your every dealing with us. Go into any reservation or bordering towns, into the so-called courts of justice, and there note the contrast in the treatment accorded individuals of the two peoples. The insult to the 'white lady' becomes a joke when applied to the 'red squaw.' The 'white gentleman' goes free in the commission of an offense for which the 'red buck' is sent to the penitentiary. (1) Can you show me *why* an Indian should have faith in the Shoyahpee?"

"You are as much of one race as the other! How can you consistently choose the one over the other?"

"Of the two, I prefer the one of the highest honor, the Indian! But why not stay in my own class, the mixed-blood?"

"I surmised as much!" rejoined the Easterner bitterly. "I can not understand why you hang out with that rough-neck Jim, whose only accomplishments are rope-throwing, riding and pistol-shooting. Ill-bred and uneducated he is as far beneath—"

"I would not permit my jealousy to lead me to say ignoble things!" interrupted the girl reproachfully. "It might not be safe!"

"I did not mean to be harsh," was the cautious retrenchment. "But oh! Cogewea! I love you and why should I not be jealous?"

"Jealousy is not born of love!" was the passionate reply. "It is a child of selfishness and distrust; a reflection on the character of the object of your presumed

affections, a declaration on your part that you do not
have faith, that you do not trust. Love is confiding,
divine and elevating; but like a sensitive plant, it must
be cherished. Jealousy is poison! a serpent monster,
destructive alike to love, happiness and home. Love
can no more survive the blighting breath of jealousy
than could Pliny the sulphurous fumes of Vesuvius.
You want to get that venom out of your system."

"It is all very well for you to moralize," was the
half-sullen response, "but you do not know the fires
which consume my very soul! If you did, you would
be more charitable. Leave off pedantry and tell me
that you love me, that you will be mine! I have plenty
to keep you in—"

"Do not mention wealth! It weighs naught in the
balances of actual love. If I thought you were really
sincere—that you would never tire of me, never discard
me because of my Indian blood—then I might talk to
you differently. I hardly understand why you want
to postpone any honeymoon trip."

"I see that your Indian suspicions must be allayed,"
he rejoined with a nervous laugh, "and I will tell you,
although I had hoped to keep it from you for a time.
I have not the ready cash at present, but expect to be
possessed of more than we will need within a very short
time. We could then, I thought, take our leisure at
sight seeing through the East, and possibly cross the
waters."

"Suppose that I could overcome this temporary obstacle of money?" she questioned, as if to test his
honesty of purpose.

It was with difficulty that Densmore suppressed his
eager anticipation. Nearing the goal of his sordid aspirations, an incautious word might overthrow all. It
was with apparent musing that he answered:

"Such a possibility had not entered my mind, and,
while I do not relish the idea of you putting up the
cash for our bridal tour, it would only be in the nature
of a loan; and if such arrangement could add to your

happiness, I hardly believe that it should be my part to reject it. How soon could you have the money?"

"Within two weeks, if I decide to do it. I will think it over! If only I knew that it was right, the proper thing to do."

Again did the wily schemer pause before making reply:

"Of course it is utterly impossible for me to eliminate self-interest, but first is my consideration for your well being. Because of this, and for the reason that I believe that it will be better if I get away from Jim, I trust that you can without serious difficulty, effect the proposed arrangement. *Will* you not do it?"

"Alfred!" she implored, lifting her eyes beseechingly to his. "*Are* you really sincere?"

"I only wish that I could do or say more to convince you of my sincerity," was the bland response. "What special reason have you for doubting me?"

"Oh! I don't know. I am doing things that I never dreamed! things that I had never expected to do."

"Then, may I take advantage and ask you to be mine?"

The girl nodded blushingly, with eyes showing confusion.

"Indian ceremony?"

"White, since it is the recognized law."

"Now may I claim a kiss?"

"Yes, at the altar. Let's hit the trail! It's getting late!"

With this, Cogewea gently pushed his hand from her and turned away. Densmore caught her arm:

"Wait a moment! There's plenty of time! Let's plan—"

"No, let's go! Stemteemä will give me the twice over if I stay longer."

"Oh! do not hurry. We are betrothed and whose business is it how late we are out?"

"That may be all right with white people, but my race is different. Indian parents do not permit their

girls to stay out even with their proposed future hus-
bands. If you are to play Injun, you must fall in line!
There are no side trails.''

Before the Easterner could protest further, she was
gone. Concealing his disappointment, he moved to follow, when a startled look came over his face. In the
dust and sand there appeared the innumerable imprints
of a small, moccasined foot. They were about the spot
where he had cast the torn letter, of which not a visage
now remained. The fragments had disappeared since
the previous evening, when he had noticed them when
fishing. For a moment, he stood, mentally cursing his
stupidity in not effectively destroying the sheet instead
of leaving it exposed to possible detection. But, he reflected, the one terrific storm to which it had been subjected, must evidently have carried away or effaced
sufficient of the message to render it unintelligible. He
smiled at the memory of the *swa-lah-kin*. With this
rather hazardous assurance, he hurriedly rejoined Cogewea, who was now some distance on the path.

The two walked homeward, the countenance of the
one, now feeling secure of his prey, glowing with subtle
selfish satisfaction. The other incapable of guile, radiant
in the unbounded happiness of devoted fidelity.

Avoiding the tepee, they approached the veranda.
Seated on the steps, Jim and the shy girl were intently
scrutinizing an apparent letter, which the foreman unconcernedly folded and pocketed.

Cogewea failed to note Densmore's perceptible start
and Jim's cynical smile as the eyes of the two rivals met.

CHAPTER XXVI.

STEMTEEMA CONSULTS THE SWEAT HOUSE

> It is blessed and enchanted,
> It has magic virtues in it.
>
> .   .   .   .   .   .
>
> Nor forgotten was the Love-song,
> The most subtle of all medicines,
> The most potent spell of magic,
> Dangerous more than war or hunting!
>
> *—Hiawatha*

JIM saw the shy-girl disappear among the willows near the river, a big knife in one hand and bearing an axe in the other. Wondering what it could mean, he sat down on a boulder to watch proceedings or await her return. He fell into a deep reverie, as he carved a stock into a grotesque human-headed sand-lizard. He was unconsciously droning a weird, improvised melody which he had heard among the riders:

> There's a wailin' of the spirits
> In the desert winds that blow;
> There's a plaintive trill of sorrow
> In the friendless coyote's howl.
>
> There's a sadness in the moanin'
> Of the pine tree in the gale;
> There's a melancholia callin'
> From the darkness of the plain.

Jim continued shaping his lizard. Into the eye-orifices he fitted two bits of agate, one red, the other green.

The foreman was in trouble of late. Twice had he essayed to convince Cogewea of Densmore's double personality, and twice had he gone down in ignominious defeat. And now, in some mysterious way the accusing fragmentary letter had disappeared from his pocket the first night after its reception. A week had passed since his council with the Stemteemä, with no apparent progress toward severing the relations of the two. His every effort looking to this had only served to estrange the girl the more from himself, weakening the ties of a former warm and close friendship.

The nondescript carving was nearing completion, requiring only a few chips from about the half opened mouth, disclosing an array of formidable looking fangs.

Cogewea often took long horseback rides with the tenderfoot. Of these jaunts Jim well knew that the grandmother was not cognizant. He had thought to warn her, but could see no good in such course. It would place him in the role of a spy—at which his better manhood revolted—and could serve no other purpose than to add to the growing burden of the aged woman's grief! It was Fate! against which no mortal had ever successfully coped.

The lizard-body began to take form, as the artisan plied his blade without conscious endeavor.

He loved the girl madly! but she preferred another. Only bitterness and remorse, it seemed, could result from a further pressing of his claim. The wild appealed to his nature, and he half wished that he might leave the region now so rapidly being settled; leave and never know or hear of her living with the hated Easterner. Arizona flashed through his mind! His droning ceased, and the now completed gargoyle-lizard dropped from his hand. He wiped the cold perspiration from his forehead, as he muttered under his breath:

"I'm a goin'! I'm a goin' never to show up ag'in in this dam' country! For the best rider of the Flathead to be made a laughin' brunt of by a feller who falls off a gentle cayuse! I'm a goin' soon as I see he gets her for good."

The Westerner rose unsteadily from his seat. He started, as he caught sight of the fantastic object at his feet. Its baleful eyes, its gaping, tusk-studded jaws and its reptile-like extremities, for a moment held his gaze. Recovering himself with a near-shudder, he ground the thing under his heel, with the single ejaculation:

"Shoyahpee!"

The dull thud of an axe broke on Jim's ear. Turning, he discerned a commotion in the clump of willows at the river's edge. He made his way through the thick brush and found Mary busy cutting the long, pliant stocks, some ten feet in length and not over an inch in diameter. She had several of them ready bundled, all neatly trimmed of branches. As he approached, he accosted her:

"Well, what you doin'? What you slashin' the brush for? Clearin' land a ready for you and Frenchy to homestead?"

A blush suffused the shy girl's cheek. After a moment of embarrassment, she looked up:

"The poles are to build Stemteemä a sweat house. She wants to take a sweat today. It is trouble! and nothing will so ease her mind as to consult her sweat house, where she communes with the Great Spirit."

"Some new trouble?"

"No! Cogewea. She is afraid—"

"Yes, I understand!" he interposed as the girl hesitated. "Let me have that knife! The axe is too heavy to cut this here small brush. Your han's are too fine to be a clearin' woods. They're made for some of them there music things that the Sisters play in Church."

Surrendering the knife, Mary watched the foreman sever with a single stroke the slender growths. After a few moments, without a word she picked up some of the poles and started up the bank. Jim gathered the remaining armful and followed to a level plat only a few rods away, where the construction of the edifice was immediately begun. Everything must be according to the first guidance of the spirits in the long ago, otherwise something of a terrible nature might happen the votary.

Jim, assuming the more arduous part, deftly shaped

a round, smooth pit about six inches in depth at a point in the ground floor where it would be just within and at the side of the low, arched entrance-way. This he did while Mary gathered wood with which to heat the score of carefully selected stones to be later placed in the pit. With alternate layers of wood and stone, she soon had a roaring fire permeating the entire mass.

In the meantime, Jim had been busily engaged wattling the pliant poles into a cone-shaped net work, some four feet across and about three feet in height, with an arched opening of eighteen inches next the stone pit. The frame work was securely tied at the intersections with bark stripped from some of the poles. He covered the structure with bark from a fallen cottonwood among the river drift, exercising care that this roofing be entirely free of vents and crevices. Then procuring a shovel, he overspread the whole with four inches of dirt, packed firm by beating with his shovel blade.

The building was now complete even to the curtained doorway. Mary summoned the Stemteemä, whose eyes beamed, as she admiringly surveyed the shapely structure. Seating herself at the entrance, she sings a mystic spirit lay. Her snowy head sways in rhythm, as she waves towards the sun, now dipping low in the west. The dash of red paint across her forehead is in token of regard and high honor to the Spirit of the sweat house, which she is about to enter.

"Don't you think them there rocks hot 'nough?" asked Jim of Mary.

"Maybe they are, although I have seen them hotter. The more hot they are the better Stemteemä likes it. She says that the sweat house favors the occupant with the good spirit, when its body is almost scorching—that is the body of the sweat house. Let her judge of the proper heat."

Jim sat musing for some moments and then spoke:

"There are strange things 'bout this here sweat house business, and I have seen some of it when I was a little chap. My grandmother used to tell me the old tradition

which says that the twelve sticks bent in the frame of
the sweat house are the twelve ribs of the Spirit God,
and that these here ribs can understand what you speak
or sing to the gods. He's a lover of songs—or of his
own song—which some Injuns know and can sing. If
you sweat and he is pleased with your visit, as a rule,
he will bestow on you some favor. Should your petition
fail the first time, then try again and if he's still not
humored and pleased, continue your appeal. I have
known Injuns who would 'sweat house' for ten or more
days in succession before accomplishin' their wish.
Whatever it might be, they always got it. This is why
the older people believe so thoroughly in the sweat
house. They hold the structure, whether new or in
ruins, sacred and a thing of reverence. Guess they have
more devoted regard for their worship places than has
the Shoyahpee for his, 'less it's money somewhere.''

"Yes," observed Mary, "the mystic pervaded all that
was connected with the sweat house worship. A warrior
would not permit a woman to enter his sweat house;
and if she did, he would never use it again. Neither
would the man enter that of the woman, and each had
to build their own. And, if several were taking the
sweat at the same time, a medicine man or medicine
woman, as the case might be, generally led in the songs
to the Spirit-god. If the Indian believed that the sweat
house spirit became displeased with him, something of
a fearful nature would happen to him or his family.
Should they escape, the death of his dog or pony might
be resultant from the frown of the god. The successful
hunter must consult the sweat house often.''

"Seems too hurtin' bad that so much of the old beliefs is a dyin' out," remarked the foreman ruefully.
"Many things connectin' with the sweat house the
younger Injuns of today don't understand. The white
headed tribesmen still hold sacred that which their race
has practiced for centuries of snows. I've seen 'em
who wouldn't dare step on a broken stick once used in

buildin' a sweat house. The dam' Shoyahpee has ruined the Injun life!''

The voice of the aged woman broke in on further colloquy. She desired to enter the lodge of the Spirit-god. With a suitable stick, Mary began rolling the hot stones into the pit of the sweat house. They were landed safely but the third one, when drawn from the fire and come in contact with the air, shattered into fragments. Now there is an ancient belief that such mishap is a precursor of misfortune, loss in a gambling game or other adventure. But, on the other score, if you succeed in getting the stone placed intact, and at the same time make a wish for that which most concerns you, the omen may be regarded as propitious that you are favored by the Spirit-god, and that you will surely gain your wish. Sooner or later it will come true. Observing the breaking stone, Jim volunteered:

''Bein' as the old time rules was busted in the buildin' of this here cookin' oven, makin' it a sort of man and woman 'fair, the best rider of the Flathead is a goin' to help with them there ash-biscuits and see what comes of wishin' a good thing. If you had any wish on that there rock,'' he continued, turning to the shy girl, ''it sure went up in smoke.''

Mary laughed and denied having placed any prayer-wish whatever. She watched Jim, as with a short pole he selected the largest stone among the glowing embers. He slowly rolled the scorching boulder as it sizzled the damp earth and seemed to consume the brown leaves in anger. He muttered his ''wish'' in an undertone! The shy girl smiled, guessing well what it was. As the rock slid into place with those already in the pit, the foreman's eyes expressed contentment and a smile disclosed two rows of well formed teeth. Mary turned to him in childish glee! For the first time since their acquaintance, he seemed near to her. She now regarded him as one of her own kind. He had not scorned the sweat house! He had not thrown aside the beliefs of his Indian forefathers, as had so many of the educated half-bloods. The books of the white man had not destroyed the earlier training of his mind. She exclaimed:

"Oh! Jim! You are favored by the Spirit-god! The sweat house knows that you are the one who made his body and warmed it, bringing life back into the form when only the bones of it were left; (1) returning life to him who was once Chief of the Animal World; he who knows everything under the Sun-god. He was left here in the form of a sweat house, for the benefit of the Indian who might warm those ribs of willow. Thus, when the Red man goes to council him in his lodge, he comes to life and grants the worshipper a sought for favor. We understand such things and believe them as only Indians can. Your wish will come true!"

"Gollies, Mary!" was the rejoinder. "This comes near bein' one on me! Hadn't thought of no sweat house for years till today. Maybe been tryin' too hard to be Shoyahpee, dam' 'em!"

The face of the shy-girl glowed with strange animation, as with fire-pole poised, she answered:

"I do not wonder! This is the trouble, the *fate* of the average breed of today. They are encouraged to *try* forget their Indian ancestry, after they once learn the white man's books and ways. They banish the idea of old tribal customs and laugh to scorn that which was sacred to the generations past. Some of the Indian system is bad, much of it is good; but it must *all* give place to that of the Shoyahpee, who arrogantly proclaims that of philosophies, his alone is worthy of emulation. Ignorant Bureau officials are helping in this! They know nothing of the good medicine of the sweat house Spirit, its power to cleanse both the mind and the body. I sometimes wish that they would take a good sweat themselves; for then they might do a cleaner business."

Jim was surprised to find this girl, whom he had thought so averse to conversation, thus speak readily and eloquently on a subject of rarest interest. In reality, the discourser had been moved intuitively, an unconscious imbibing of the sweat house spirit. The teaching of the devoted Stemteemä alone had made this possible.

Jim now brought a pail of water from the river, to be used in steaming the hot stones. He then returned to the corrals, leaving Mary and the Stemteemä alone. After his departure, the shy girl looked cautiously around, before starting one of the two remaining stones towards the sweat house, to be added to its fellows in a rounded, cone-like heap within the pit. Carefully she turned the stone over and over, as though something she wished was of grave importance. As the rock reached the entrance without mishap, a low, musical laugh escaped the grandmother, who spoke to her in their native tongue. Mary looked abashed, dropped her pole and joined in the laughter.

Stemteemä disrobed and slowly stepped into the cold river for a bath before entering the lodge of the Spirit. When consulting Him, the body must be clean. There was a special favor to be asked today.

With this preliminary dip, the grandmother crawled into the mind and body-cleaning sanctuary. Mary closed the door-curtain and sat undecided whether to enter also, when a song pealed from within. Sung in the Okanogan, it vibrates—now high, now low—swelling a mournful dirge on the passing breeze. The listening girl understands!

It is the Song of the Mountain Herb!

It is the Song of the Love Herb.

It is the Chant of mystic creation!

Growing on the highest mountain peaks,

It embodies the soul of the Love Goddess!

It is the Song to soften the warrior's heart

When sung by his dusky love at the sun's setting.

It is the Spirit Chant! locked in the Red bosom

To burst anew on the morning trail of a future life.

It is Enchantment!—to the Shoyahpee unfathomable—

But Magic sacred to the comprehending Indian mind.

An Herb, or of this element likewise, the sweat house

can understand the love-plea of either maiden or warrior; that the heart may become as the melting snow.

Mary sat gazing out over the stream in abstraction. A face of the "silvery hue" seemed to be forming in vision, when she was disturbed by the under-rustling of twigs. She saw her sister part the willows and come silently to the embered fire. Cogewea stood listening to the plaintive, dirge-like invocation of the venerable petitioner, from within the now steaming sweat house. It was a plea to the Great Spirit—through the Mountain Herb—to change the heart of the Indian maiden, then being lured to a shadowy trail of sorrow by the deceiving Shoyahpee. The voice quavered to a sobbing sigh and then rose in a wailing cadence of wilder supplication.

The girl of the range was visibly affected. Reaching for the same pole that Jim had used in moving his boulder so successfully, she drew the last remaining stone from the coals. Very slowly and carefully she rolled it towards the blanketed doorway of the mystic sanctuary. Whatever her emotions, her face was imperturbable. One more turn and the entrance would be reached, when, with an audible detonation, the boulder flew in many directions leaving a visible vapor-puff. The eyes of the sisters met. With no word from either, Cogewea turned towards the house, haunted by the ill-omened sign. A spirit voice the while seemed to whisper just at her side:

"Beware! beware!"

"*Can* it be true!" she murmured. "It can *not* be true this old Indian belief in the sweat house."

The weird chant of the Stemteemä again pierced the girl's ear as she made her fearful way to escape the agonizing plaint. She half regretted having tempted the fire-rock sign. Why had it burst at the very last? If it only had reached the goal! But surely! there could be nothing in such an age-old superstition? *He* could not be false!

Cogewea entered the living room where she found

Densmore awaiting her. Julia remained in the kitchen that the lovers might have more privacy. She favored the Shoyahpee, despite the innumerable warnings of the grandmother. To these she had been indifferent, attributing the opposition to extreme old age prejudices, and an unswerving tribal custom of formerly housing the maidens and watching over their every movement until married off—always young—in conformity with ancient racial pride. It was considered a reflection on the parents, should a daughter remain single for any length of time after reaching maturity.

Stoically hiding her agitation, Cogewea returned Densmore's greeting and the two were engaged in low, earnest conversation. It was briefly arranged that on the following evening they would jointly visit the Stemteemä, and endeavor to gain her consent to their marriage; since the girl would not agree to a clandestine union, so vehemently urged by her companion.

CHAPTER XXVII.

THE FORKED TONGUE OF THE SHOYAHPEE

Listen not to what he tells you;
Lie not down upon the meadow.
—*Hiawatha*

THE last rays of the sun had faded on the western horizon when the two supplicants drew near the firelit tepee. Cogewea raised a finger to her lips for silence. For a moment they stood before she stooped to the low curtained entrance. The aged occupant welcomed her grandchild in Indian silence, but when her gaze met the grey one of the hated Shoyahpee, her own kindled and a frown knit her brow. This did not escape Cogewea, who, pointing across the fire to the familiar buffalo robe, addressed Densmore:

"Signs are unfavorable. Be seated and have patience. It means a lot of humoring to accomplish our object."

She smiled in an attempt at cheerfulness, despite the manifest displeasure of the Stemteemä. Her heart was too full of confiding love to note the latent gleam of contempt which lit the face of her companion. Seating herself by the side of the grandmother, Cogewea took the wrinkled hand in her own warm clasp and remained in silence for a time. When she spoke, it was in their native tongue, and there was a slight tremor in her voice.

"Many snows have left with the Stemteemä their wisdom, and her mind, like the mountain water is clear. Once young, she will understand, for my thoughts are those of youth. I have come to tell you the news—to ask your permission. The Shoyahpee here has asked me to be his in marriage by the priest. I am telling you that you may bless me with the Great Indian Spirit."

The grandmother did not answer. A strange light came into the piercing eyes as she gazed unperturbed at the fire, sending its sparks up the open smoke-flue. The frail hand slipped from the stronger grasp; the furrowed face was set and stern, as she slowly turned to the despised pale face. Covertly she re-read the sordid character which others seemed not to understand. And as she remained in seeming stoic indifference, Cogewea made another appeal:

"Oh! my Stemteemä! I love him so! Can you not tell me that it is well? I know that you do not like the Shoyahpee, but it is your own Cogewea who pleads!"

The voice of the aged woman was vibrant with maternal solicitude as she spoke:

"My Cogewea thinks too well of the pale faced man to know her own mind. Her judgment is sick. I am afraid to say that it is good."

"Strong love brings happiness in marriage, filling all the home with joy," urged the girl. "We would not yet go to the priest's for some time; for several sundowns. I have studied my own mind. Why should you be afraid?"

"There are voices in the night and I have heard! Your white father went away; he cared not for his children. It is a debt to your dead mother that I guard you while life remains in me. It is for your own benefit that I do not want you to marry this Shoyahpee. I can feel—I know he means wrong by you. He has blinded your eyes and you can not see that his heart is bad. I can not bear that in time he will grow tired of you and cast you aside for some pale faced squaw as the many have done in the past. Your fate would be that of my princess aunt! A spirit weeps when a budding flower is crushed."

Save for the scarce audible purr of the low blazing fire, the ensuing stillness was overburdening. When Cogewea again pressed her suit, it was but half-heartedly:

"I know that the Stemteemä's judgment is always

good, but I cannot think the Shoyahpee bad. If I only
knew! Oh! why is there evil in the world?''

The reply of the Stemteemä was earnest and pathetically appealing:

"Remember the sorrow of my poor friend, Green-
blanket Feet! No! my child! Anything else. I would
willingly give my remaining snows, if it would add to
your happiness; but to consent to this marriage which
will bring heart aches and ruin to you, I can not! I
am afraid to see a bright star within the lodge of the
night-sun.'' (1)

The girl shrank back into the shadows to hide her
tears of disappointment. The ancient woman rose to
her feet, the light of prophesy on her brow. With arms
uplifted as if to ward off an impending blow, she continued:

"I have consulted the spirits and I have seen in a
dream that the morning of the sun-lit trail my Cogewea
would choose, is short and shadowy. But its evening
reaches far into the wintry night of desolation, where
the vision is vague. I behold the flowers withered by
a mid-summer frost and the grasses scorched as by fire.
The song of the wood-bird trills on my ear with sadness
and the murmur of the waters are fraught with grief.
The young doe, torn by the blood appeased cougar, flees
helpless and forlorn. O my grandchild! Heed the warning of the Stemteemä and avoid the Shoyahpee as you
would the coiled rattlesnake.''

The venerable squaw sank to her robes, showing no
visible perturbation. Cogewea sat rigid, seemingly oblivious of her surroundings. Several moments elapsed
before the stillness was broken. It was Densmore who
spoke:

"Well! what did he say?''

"Just as I thought,'' answered the girl listlessly.
"The Stemteemä has had a vision which troubles her.
She has refused.''

"*Refused!*'' he exclaimed in a tone of marked sur-

prise and ill-concealed chagrin. "In-*deed!* And *why*
has she refused?"

"You are a Shoyahpee! She has no confidence in
the white man. Her 'no' is final. It is useless to—"

"Cogewea!" broke in the suitor abruptly. "If I
could only convince you that I mean right by you. Why
listen to the idle prattle of a childish and ignorant old
squaw?"

"*Go!* forked tongued Shoyahpee! A trapper of women! *Go! go! go!*"

The arm of the old grandmother was outstretched,
pointing sternly to the blanketed doorway. A wave of
anger and fierce resentment came to the baffled man
as he gained his feet. For an instant he glared at the
determined woman, so scornfully indicating the exit.
Silently he left the tepee, humiliated; but more determined than ever in his designs.

"The accursed she-savage!" he muttered as he gained
the outer air, grinding his teeth in impotent rage. "To
order me from her beggar's hovel, as if I were a dog!
The root eating old squaw! Looking down on the
white man who has ever made a plaything of her race!
Bear witness! ye everlasting hills! I will get even
with this proud nest of mixed vipers, if it takes half
a life time! Beware! Mother Buzzard!" he hissed,
shaking a clenched hand at the shadowy lodge. "I
will yet pluck your dear fledgling and return it to you
so soiled that your own foul wing will refuse it shelter! You have yet to learn that the master courts not
favor of his slaves!"

Snarling, and coyote-like, he slunk into the blackness
of the night.

"Stemteemä!" pleaded Cogewea. "You have crushed
my heart. Can you not change your mind? Can you
not like him just a little bit for my sake?"

"The wind changes its course and the hunter must
regulate his steps accordingly. The star which guides
the night traveler over a strange trail must ever remain
unmoved. The mind of the Stemteemä is formed!"

"Oh! you cannot think the Shoyahpee so bad!"

"I hate him as a snake! He crawls in the grass with poison fangs! He lurks by the bubbling spring to strike with blight the heart of the confiding Indian maiden! He hides in the darkness to catch her unaware! He is a trapper of women! The eagle loves the fawn because its flesh is tender! His plumage may be beautiful, but beware of the rending talons and beak! If you marry in your own class, the mixed blood, I will gladly bless you with the Great Indian Spirit. I will divide with you my money which I am to receive from the Big White Chief for the forests belonging to my ancestors. I will give you horses and cattle. But if you take this Shoyahpee, I will forget that I ever had a grandchild."

Stemteemä smoothed the little brown hand, but it lay limp and lifeless within her own. During the rest of her stay, Cogewea showed none of her old-time spirit of gaiety. Tears filled her eyes and suppressed sobs heaved her breast. The truly tender hearted grandmother was grieved and tried to comfort her, but she was firm in her determination to oppose the hated Shoyahpee of the "luring voice." Her devoted love for her favorite grandchild forbade any compromise. Death would be preferable to a marriage with such a man.

With hardly a word of parting to the Stemteemä, Cogewea lifted the door flap and went out into the cool night air. Her heart seemed lead. She knew that the grandmother meant right in her opposition, but she could not overcome the dreadful thought of parting with the pleasing Easterner. She halted outside the tepee and lifted her face to the eastern sky, as though in prayer, or appeal. The moon was just peeping over the Rockies.

"Oh! the same old moon that has shone over my happiness now seems to laugh at my sorrow! It must ever light different trails for the Indian and the Shoyahpee! Fate has dealt me a blow, such as I never thought could come!"

Her reverie was interrupted by Densmore coming from the shadows. They turned toward the house and went out of ear shot of the tepee.

"Cogewea! you are not going to let a little thing like that interfere with our marriage, are you?"

"Oh! I do not know!" she answered dazedly. "Don't you think it best that we try forget the past and start a new life of other interests? I believe it would be better for both of us."

"Now look here! You make things just miserable by thinking it wrong for the whites and Indians to intermarry. You must remember that you are only part Indian, and what is the difference so long as we love each other what the third party thinks?"

"Yes! that may be true but I have family ties to consider. The word of my Stemteemä has been *law* to me all my life. I have coaxed her into letting me do things against her wishes, but I never deliberately disobeyed her; and now I have not the heart to do this without her full consent."

"Do not be foolish! Do not get that into your little head, poor child!" He attempted to embrace her but she held him off. "I am sure that everything will come out all right, if only we get married. What can your people do else than compromise and permit things to go just as all others have done? A daughter elopes, comes home in tears and asks forgiveness. The old man usually goes into a rage, while the dear mamma comes to the rescue with the Bible, reads the admonitory verse of 'go and sin no more,' and the commandatory about 'forgiving thy neighbor,' and lo! everything is smoothed over like icing on a cake. Your grandmother will forget her objections and maybe make you a handsome wedding present when she sees how happy you are with me. She means right, the good old soul; and I will have her loving me fit to kill before many days, after once I am really in the family."

Cogewea remained silent, evidently debating within

herself the proper course to pursue. Noting this indication of progress, the arch conspirator continued:

"The Stemteemä is naturally solicitous about your future welfare and I admire her for the stand she takes. But her deep anxiety prevents her from seeing the true conditions. You should remember, too, that your grandmother is very old and incapable of understanding modern ideas and the changing conditions as can a younger person whose mind is not burdened with a century of snows. After all, is it not the inalienable right, as recognized in all reason, for every one to choose their own path in life? In pursuing this prerogative, you are not reflecting on the wisdom of the well meaning grandmother, nor are you wholly casting her aside. Even the profoundest of philosophers are sometimes mistaken, and why may she not be, especially when swayed by such strong racial antipathy, even though admitting that such may be well founded? What do you say? Let's elope! Go tomorrow—or tonight—if we can effect arrangements. What is your answer?"

Swayed by a surge of conflicting emotions, this girl of a "branded" sphere, exclaimed pathetically:

"Could it—*will* everything come out all right—do you think? *Will* Stemteemä forgive me—take me back again—do you think?"

"Why of course! little sweetheart! You are only nervous tonight. Our grandmother will forgive both of us and will be glad to do so when she hears that you are Mrs. Alfred Densmore instead of—"

"Oh! *will* she? Will she really do that? Do you honestly think it right to elope—to sneak away and be married?"

"Sure it is right, and we have Scriptures as well as examples throughout all nature for such course. Do not hesitate! I love you and I want to protect you from the cold, uncharitable criticisms of this ungenerous world. I can not do this as we now are. Let's go get married in any way that you wish."

Cogewea's words came hot and fervid, as she spoke

without her old self-confidence and balance of mind:

"Perhaps there are times when one should possess the courage of self-assertion, but should it be to the exclusions of all admonitions? If so, then the quicker it is over the better! But I can ill endure the suspense—this haunting dread of my Stemteemä's lasting disapproval. Oh! if I only knew! My Indian Spirit tells me that I am stepping wrong; that I am leaving the trail marked for me by inevitable decree! But my white blood calls to see the world—to do—to live—I—I—Oh; God of my ancestors!" she cried, with face lifted to the star-emblazoned Heaven. "Keep and comfort my dear Stemteemä should I linger away!"

Then turning to the anxious Easterner, she said simply:

"When shall we go?"

The wily plotter could have shouted his triumph. But suppressing his emotion, he affected to ponder on the problem involved in her interrogation. His reply was abstractedly:

"I must again tell you that I have only a few dollars immediately available and nothing adequate to our probable needs in view of any prolonged stay abroad. Under the circumstances, would you consider using your money as talked of the other day? I will return it with double the amount. You will," he added in a low, ingratiating laugh, "have me under the domestic whip, in that you advanced the first family loan."

He drew her to him and essayed to implant a kiss on the enticing lips, but she shrank away. Cogewea was again wavering. Perhaps she should resist this man? There still broke on her ear the snapping of the ill-omened rock at the sweat house; and the Stemteemä's vision of the young doe was ever passing before her eyes. But not for long was she undecided. The blood of youth is warm and *love* is blindly confiding. Her answer came low and cautious, as if fearful of lurking danger.

"Yes! I have the money but it is in the bank. We can not go tonight! We will wait till tomorrow."

Densmore secretly rejoiced that the friendly shadows were conducive to concealment of his exultation. His sordid dream of wealth was materializing. Of all the innumerable schemes which he had "put over"—this had been the "easiest." A light marriage ceremony—acquirement of property title—accidental drowning while pleasure boating—fatal shooting accident while hunting—sudden heart failure—or safer still—the divorce court. In mad ecstacy he again unsuccessfully attempted to kiss. Oh! the ways of the Shoyahpee!

Glancing upward, Cogewea started visibly. The moon appeared to frown his disapproval. At the gate Densmore turned back while the girl hurried into the house. She felt amazement at her own action.

Down at the bunk house Jim, with his ever quick eye, marked the gleam of satisfaction which suffused the face of the tenderfoot as he came into the light of the solitary lamp which always burned until the last of the boys had turned in. Densmore was whistling a lively air, and the foreman, perhaps glad of the excuse, called sharply:

"Hey! there feller! stop that dam' noise! Prowlin' aroun' half the night and comin' home a whistlin' ain't no joke for tired boys who want their needed sleep. You savey them there words?"

Although in the midst of a stanza, the Easterner very discreetly ceased his warbling. He vouchsafed no reply, but disrobing, blew out the lamp and slid into bunk. Gloatingly he lay, planning the trip for the next day with the breed girl. With supreme elation he contemplated the discomfiture of his haughty, copper - skinned rival; when he should learn of the success of the hated tenderfoot.

CHAPTER XXVIII.

THE SENTINEL AT THE ROCK

But she heeded not the warning,
Heeded not those words of wisdom,
—*Hiawatha*

THE streets of Polson bore an air of desertion, as Cogewea wended her way down the board walk in the early morn, nodding to an occasional chance acquaintance. Indecision and anxiety suffused her usually serene face. The girl felt at a loss and the question had come to her often:

"Why did you weaken to the importunities of the Shoyahpee against your better judgment?"

She seemed to accede to his overtures however ridiculous. The shame of the past evening when she agreed to loan him money for the proposed elopement trip, haunted her; but now it appeared too late to recede. She half wished that she had pointedly refused even though it broke her heart.

Thus meditating, Cogewea came opposite the bank as it opened its doors for the day. Crossing the street, she entered and stepping to the side desk, produced from an Indian beaded hand-bag a cheque book and wrote feverishly. Glancing cautiously around, she handed the slip of paper to the cashier at the cage window. The official scanned it, then read it the second time, before looking up in surprise to ask:

"A thousand dollars? Do you mean to draw all this —all this amount at one time?"

"Yes, that was my intention," was the courteous reply. "Haven't I enough on deposit to cover that cheque made payable to myself?"

"Oh, certainly, Miss McDonald; but it was my understanding that since you became of age and this money was placed to your credit by the Indian Agent, you were to draw only small amounts as you might need for immediate wants; and if you contemplated an investment, to advise with the bank. I know that I had such instructions from the Agent. There is that preferred stock of which I told you, still available at a slightly under-par value. Why not take a block and get in on the ground floor? We are only placing these shares among our known friends."

"The dough is my own and I think that I have the right to do with it as I please!" was the spirited retort. 'I happen to know something about your preferred stock' and—"

"But your own Agent recommended this investment to you in this very office as you doubtless will recall."

"Yes, I do recall but who recommends the Agent? I know what a time I had getting this money pried loose from the grasp of the Bureau, and I now intend handling it without any assistance from that bunch. I am no longer an 'incompetent' and in the present instance I believe that I can determine my own affairs, even to the withdrawal of my entire three thousand from your bank. While I am given control of my money, I shall be glad to consult with your firm should I contemplate any material investment—but not for any 'preferred stock.' "

Without further controversy the cashier counted out the amount of the cheque and handed it to her. With an acknowledgment, Cogewea left the bank with a heavier mind than she dared admit. She hurried to her companionable, though at times erratic cayuse, where left standing unhitched. Wanawish whinnied as she approached, and Bringo came forward to greet her. But for once the girl gave slight notice to her dumb friends.

Cogewea mounted and scaled the steep Polson Hill. There she paused and gazed longingly back at the little town nestling by the shimmering lake. She wondered when she would be permitted to see it again. Her feelings were altogether different from those supposedly of the happy bride-to-be. As if to smother a rising sensibility of her present questionable course, she abruptly turned Wanawish and raced down the sharp slope with reckless speed. She galloped over the smooth prairie until in sight of the Pablo Buffalo Ranch. The pasture and the high coral were alike empty. These recalled to her days passed, when she rode the range a care-free girl, with no "sweet love" weighing her down; when her heart leaped at the sensation of thundering on the flank of the stampeding herd. But now, the vision of the dust-cloud rolling up from the vast expanse, brought only a pang of regret.

Reaching Mud Creek—a misnomer of a truly clear stream—Wanawish showed thirst and Cogewea gave him the rein as he turned from the wooden bridge. While watching the horse take in the cool, mountain water, the girl realized that she, too, was thirsty. Dismounting, she knelt and drank. As she rose, she spied two riders on the lofty ridge overlooking the Buffalo Ranch. Mechanically she felt for her glass, only to find that in her haste it had been left at home. Although the atmosphere was clear, the distance was too great to make out with the naked eye who the horsemen were. They sat their mounts motionless, and facing towards her. As she turned to Wanawish, the thought of the money in her handbag at the saddle-bow came to her. Removing her gauntlets and gazing cautiously around that no one was observing, she made a rent in her padded saddle-blanket. Into the opening she shoved the crisp bills and then deftly closed it with a hair pin. Remounting, she swung into a steady lope for Ronan. Before passing from view, she glanced at the ridge where the two riders had been observed. Only one, sentinel like, was to be seen. Both the horse and the rider appeared as immobile as though cast in bronze. Apprehensive of the missing horseman, the girl gave rein to Wanawish and sped furiously over the smooth-packed road.

Ronan was still some distance away when Cogewea came in sight of the tall elevator of the flour mill, with its gray roof and the smoke belching up in a dark col-

umn through the clear air. As she drew near, the twelve
o'clock whistle, deep and sonorous, bellowed a re-
spite to the toilers, both white and Indian. Some hurried to homes in the little village for their noon-time
meals, while others sat by the creek with well filled lunch
boxes. A few with more extravagant tastes, repaired
to the one hotel, conducted by the same party who con-
trolled the store, post office and livery barn,—the
"Father of Ronan", as he was commonly called.

Wanawish sped across the bridge, pressing hard on
the bit as he was reined in at the hostelry. Cogewea
sprang to the ground and was met by Densmore. Or-
dering her horse stalled next to his own, he accompanied her to the dining hall. He selected an isolated
table and sat so as to command the door. His nervous
movements and unusual self-interest, drew the attention of diners and there were low whisperings of:

"Somethin' doin' with them there couple!"

The meal over, Cogewea thought that Densmore ex-
hibited unusual haste in mounting and being again off.
They galloped through the "Lane"; nor did they slack-
en pace until near Crow Creek, where they met a train
of "freighters" from Ravalli. The high seated wagons
were piled with merchandise, and were strung along
the road for a considerable distance. Some had
"trailers" and were drawn by six and eight horses.
Passing these, the elopers again quickened pace, coming to the big flat. Small lakes, where wild geese and
ducks disported, enlivened the scene. The long necks
of the birds would momentarily disappear under the
surface, as they grouped for food along the shallows.
"Shacks," the initial domicile of the energetic homesteaders, dotted the landscape. Herds of cattle and
bands of horses grazed about the plain; the latter sometimes disturbed by the flying pair. One magnificent
stallion, with ears erect, gazed at them and then snorting wildly, kicked heels in the air and chased his prote-
gees in a stampede across the far reaches of the prairie.
The proud monarch ever hung in the rear, urging the

laggards with stinging teeth-nips, until all were lost to view.

Down the lower road to Post Creek, the two rode at a slower pace. Densmore was far from being a perfect rider, although greatly improved over the stranger who had come to the ranch some months previous. As the wind blew aside his coat, Cogewea noticed for the first time the heavy six-gun holstered at his hip. A sun glint on the polished grip had first caught her eye.

"Why! Alfred!" she exclaimed in surprise. "I did not know that you carried a gun. I thought you were a man who never sported a weapon of any kind."

"I—I thought we might need it," he answered in embarrassment, drawing his coat in place. "Can never tell what might happen."

"That is true! I had never thought of that! I came away so hurriedly that I brought only my little thirty-two in my handbag."

"Let me see your gun!"

Cogewea handed Densmore her pistol. He examined it minutely and then put it in his own pocket. Cogewea laughed uneasily as she remonstrated:

"What do you mean? You are not a two-gun man, are you?"

"Now little girl," he returned lightly, "you do not want to carry this thing! It might get you hurt."

"I will bet that I can handle a gun far better than you can!"

"Don't be too sure of that, my conceited young lady! I hope that I have not practiced target shooting all summer to no avail."

"But Alfred! Please give me back my gun! I do not like to be without it, especially at this time. It is hard telling what may happen—and me with all the kale."

"I will protect you!" he volunteered with a laugh. "And as head of the family, I am really supposed to handle the purse, am I not?"

Seemingly to meet his banter, Cogewea spoke non-

chalantly, as the memory of the vanished horseman at
the rock, flashed through her mind:

"Let me have both guns! I believe that I will be
willing to trade you my handbag for the brace, even
though they do not balance properly."

"That would depend! How much did you bring?"

"Oh! I can buy several such toys and still be a long
ways from bankruptcy. Is it a go?"

"Why do you so want both guns?"

"Jim—he might follow us! You can never tell!"

"No danger! He and the boys had gone out for
stray horses when I left the ranch. My excuse was that
I was going to Ronan and would not be back until late.
They think that you are in Polson visiting friends. No
body will dream that we have eloped and after we are
married, what's the difference who cries?"

"Well, I do hope that they may not know until it is
too late. I'm afraid there would be hell to pay if Jim
gets wise before we find a priest."

"But why should you want both guns in case he did
follow?" he questioned suspiciously. "You seem to
think more of that savage than you do of me."

"I want your gun simply to prevent likely trouble,
should Jim trail us. He is too manly to ever shoot an
unarmed man in any personal altercation. He may be
a savage," she continued spiritedly, "but he has a
great big heart and that is a whole lot more than a goodly part of this highly civilized nation can boast. Too
many of the so-called *white* men are afflicted with the
worst of *black-heart*."

Densmore flushed deeply at this thrust, but he rejoined with an attempt at pleasantry:

"You may still maintain your torture stake if you
will, but I prefer holding on to my gun so long as
there is such manifest danger of Injuns going on the
warpath."

Though ill at ease, Cogewea accepted the situation
without further protest. So deeply engrossed had they
been in discussion, that their mounts took advantage

and stopped at the creek to allay their thirst. After crossing the stream, Densmore dismounted and drank. Leading his horse, he walked along the road for a short distance, to a stock trail breaking into the brush. Here he paused, proposing that they stop among the trees and let their horses rest for a time. Cogewea, still visioning the horsemen at the rock, demurred; but when her companion pointed out that the west bound train through Ravalli was not due until near seven o'clock and that it would be far better for them to remain in semi-seclusion until near that time than chance detection and possible detention at the station, she reluctantly acquiesced. Accordingly a grassy plot was sought just within the woods, where they drew the saddles and leaving the horses to graze at the end of the trailing ropes, sat down in the shade.

No definite plans had been agreed upon as to their future course, further than boarding the evening train west at Ravalli. Densmore was for going to San Francisco, while Cogewea named a nearer coast city as their immediate destination. Their ideas also differed as to time of return to the ranch. Cogewea was most anxious about the Stemteemä; to get back and make an early peace with her ancient parent was her deepest concern. Densmore, scoffing at this, interposed:

"The Stemteemä should be the least of our worries. Old age, like childhood, is susceptible of petting. I am afraid," he added with a short laugh, "of being shot up by a disappointed foreman."

"You have nothing to dread from Jim, once we are united," assured the girl. "I know him to be a man and he will never place a stumble in our way."

From this, the conversation drifted again to the topic of destination; disclosing the amount of money which Cogewea had brought. The Easterner expressed surprise that she had ventured to openly draw that amount and carry it alone from Polson. Cogewea assured him that all the cowpunchers were her friends and that there had been nothing to fear.

"Look!" she exclaimed, procuring her saddle blanket and removing the hairpin. "No body would have thought to look there for money, even had they staged a holdup."

Densmore agreed that the hiding place would most likely have proven effective had he attempted the role of bandit. He soon learned of her balance in the bank, which opened the subject of his deepest interest. He casually asked about her live stock on both ranch and range, and was astounded when informed that aside from the two cayuses they were riding, she had none. Not fully grasping the import of this appalling declaration, he fairly gasped:

"Why! don't you own most of the stock at the ranch, and all the horses and cattle of the roundup, and those sold? Were they not yours? Are not the boys working for you?"

"Those hoofs all mine—boys working for me? Who has been stuffing you! man?"

"Celluloid Bill and Rodeo Jack told me that you were a rich woman; that you owned practically all the stock on the range and had vast tracts of land."

"Bill and Rodeo? It was some of their wild pranks! They have lied to you! I am far from being a rich woman. All the stock you saw at the ranch, belongs to my brother-in-law, John Carter. The 'H-B' brand is also his property. The three thousand dollars I recently came in possession of, was inherited. Aside from my eighty acre allotment, which hardly counts for much, this three thousand is all that I have."

For several moments the Easterner remained speechless, scarce able to realize the full force of this astounding revelation. After all, was his dream of golden wealth to be disenchanted as a mere halo of the rainbow of myth? Surely! the Indian girl was joking, merely testing his fidelity of purpose. His voice was husky when he again spoke:

"Cogewea, you can not mean that I believe all this, can you? This is hardly a time for jesting."

It was Cogewea's turn to be puzzled. What was the riddle? Was this polite and polished Shoyahpee, after all, a mere adventurer, a gross money hunter? This passed through her mind before she answered rather tersely:

"I am not jesting! You would not want me to deceive you, would you? I do not understand!"

"Then, if you are telling the truth, I have already been woefully deceived and that through you," was the savage retort. "Those boys never hatched such fabrications of themselves. They were made at your instance and the only puzzle is just why you are now blocking your own game by thus prematurely disclosing facts. Your obtuse intellect, being able to contain but the one idea, has been your undoing. But what else could be expected from a nest of coppery vipers? Brazen blackmail, and I am tempted to turn you over to the proper authorities to be dealt with according to the just laws of our land! You may be thankful that I am letting you off so easy."

He had risen to his feet and before the astounded girl could divine his action, he had seized her saddle blanket and ripping out the folded bank bills, pocketed them. With stunning effect the truth dawned upon her that she had not only been betrayed, but was also being openly robbed by her professed lover and supposed protector. Enraged and smarting with humiliation at such duplicity, she sprang up, laying a detaining hand on his arm. With an oath he freed himself, dealing her a blinding blow in the face. Grasping her by the shoulders, he shook her viciously as he warned in a low, menacing tone:

"You had as well understand at once that I am standing no foolishness from you? The more quiet you are the better it is going to be for you. I am giving you unwarranted consideration. Many a man would deal with you differently and my ultimate actions are going to be governed by your own. You can always depend on a desperate man doing desperate things and perhaps if the truth was known you would find that I have not been too squeamish on other occasions."

"But you do not dare take my money like this! liar! thief! robber! blackguard that you are! The law—"

"Is absolutely helpless to help you!" he scoffed. "The law is of the white man's make, interpreted by the white man, made to talk by the white man's money. With a comparatively small amount of this which you have so generously bestowed upon me, I can make the law talk! You have no witnesses! It would be my word against yours; a white gentleman's against an Injun squaw's. What would you do? Don't think that I am not going to take advantage of the situation."

"I will have you arrested at Ravalli!"

"No, I hardly think so! If your horse should happen to have his leg broke—"

"Oh! please Alfred! Take the money and go but do not hurt my Wanawish! I will promise not to attempt following you. I will be only too glad to see you go! Oh! the ways of the Shoyahpee!"

"Your word would be great guarantee!" he snarled mockingly. "I am taking no chance nor am I going to waste further time in any palaver with you. Come on! and see how cleverly I can disable that fine steed of yours."

With this, he jerked her rudely about and started towards the two horses, still grazing. Cogewea apparently resigned, moved unresistingly. Unaccustomed to the approach of man, Wanawish lifted his head in air, and with forward-pricked ears, emitted a shrill snort of alarm. Cogewea, alert, snatched Densmore's hat with her one free hand and hurled it at the animal, emitting at the same time a shrill scream. The startled horse horse whirled and darted into a near-by thicket where he was lost to view. Cogewea laughed aloud.

"You damned ed—!"

Choking with rage, Densmore supplemented the vile epithet with another brutal blow in the face. Dragging the now dazed girl, he secured his own horse, returning with it and his captive to where the saddles were lying. His eyes were those of the murderer, as he again addressed her:

"Now, my fine lady! another screech out of you and I do not promise what might not happen. Your little trick has saved that horse of yours, but there is another way of playing safe. Maybe by the time you rest here a few hours, perhaps a few days, in seclusion, you will have had time to ponder on the absurdity of contending against your betters. You are in my power and I am certainly going to use it effectively."

"Yes, you have me in your power, but how have you accomplished that boast? Give me back my gun! You may keep your big one but I will not fear you, though I am a woman."

Craven as he was, Densmore winced at this challenge. All the venom of his perverted nature found vent in his retort:

"Bosh! you squaw! And to think that I was ordered from a smoke-dinged lair of your 'breed'! I am but half squaring accounts; and when you get back to that dear old grandmother of yours, you can tell her how nice the white man was in his dealings with you. You may then feel like talking, for that tongue of yours is now going to have a rest, if I meet my guess."

Cogewea loftily disdained reply to this tirade of abuse. Knowing the futility of resistance, she submitted without a word of protest as he securely bound her to a cottonwood, twining the rope about her from neck to foot. An effective gag was made from her own scarf. Completing his task to his own satisfaction, Densmore again adressed her, assuming a mock air of apologetic politeness:

"Good bye! little sweetheart! O statuette in bronze with a wild-wood setting! How superb! and the sun fast sinking to rest. A merry time and pleasant dreams as you hear the coyotes squalling tonight. I tried to give you a good time the past summer, and I feel that I am really entitled to this small pittance which you

have so kindly permitted me to appropriate.   I hope
that you are generous spirited enough to concede that
you have had value received.   I am placing your toy-
gun here in your own pocket, the cartridges considerately extracted of course.   Give my regards to that coppery hided lover of yours—should you ever see him—
and know that with your opportunity to convey this
last message for me, I will be far out of the state and
among really civilized folks.   After all, Densmore the
'tenderfoot' has not fared so badly financially, considering the few months that he has sojourned in the
wilds, do you think?   Good bye! good bye!''

Then hastily saddling his horse, he mounted and turned towards the highway, calling back over his shoulder:

''That you may retain your deep respect for my integrity, you will find this horse, which you have so
graciously loaned me, at the livery in Ravalli.   Of
course this is considerate of me and I know that you
will appreciate the courtesy.   So long!''

Cogewea, her limbs already aching from the cut of
the overdrawn lariat, heard the clatter of pounding
hoofs, as the false Shoyahpee fled from the scene of his
most hellish duplicity.

CHAPTER XXIX.

STEMTEEMA'S DREAM OF THE SOMA-ASH-HEE

For his heart was hot within him,
Like a living coal his heart was.
—*Hiawatha*

CELLULOID BILL and Silent Bob lounged lazily
at the big rock on the high ridge overlooking the
Buffalo Ranch. Their "blown horses" were feeding on the bunch-grass, after a hard and futile chase for
outlawed cayuses. They had stopped for a rest. The
wild herd could be seen as it fled across the wide stretch
of range to the west. It disappeared, circling Buffalo
Butte, to flash into view again on the opposite side.
There the band halted and with high flung heads, watched the enemy at the corral.

As the riders again swung to their saddles, Bill's quick
eye descried a woman riding at an unusual swiftness
over the flat to the south and on the road leading to
Ronan. Something familiar about the figure held his
attention and he drew his binoculars for a more critical
inspection. A moment later he returned them to their
case and turned to Bob whose horse stood abreast of his
own:

"There goes Jim's gal a racin' 'cross th' flat an' I bet
she's goin' to meet that there tenderfoot in Ronan;
'cause he said airly this mo'nin' he was a breezin' to
the little town today not to be back till af'er dark. Ha!
ha! Can't fool ol' Bill! He's wise to that there soapy
guy, who thinks the gal has dough. He's a fallin' in love
with th' cash 'stead of the little gal."

Bill chuckled at what he evidently regarded as a
huge joke. Bob was silent for a moment, his face serious
as he gazed after the receding horsewoman. There was
a touch of concern in his voice as he spoke:

"How'd yo' happen to know so much 'bout th' love
'fairs of that there tenderfoot guy?"

" 'Cause his eyes went wide like sascers when I tol'
him how th' gal had th' kale an' a plenty, too; an' all
th' cattle an' hosses she wanted. Made him believe
nearly all the hoofs on th' reservation was her'n, an' he
was dead easy. Fell like a log to it all! an' I tol' Rodeo
to stuff him more, some 'bout her lan' which he did an'
the fool went belt an' buckle in love with all that there
wealth she ain't got; an' th' mavricks he thinks he's a
goin' start brandin' when the roun'up opens nex'
spring.''

Celluloid indulged in another low laugh, but receiving no response from his companion, he continued:

"An' I bet they run 'way purty durned quick, 'cause
they're awful mashed! More'n Jim knows! There'd
be hellerpopin' if he foun' out 'bout this.''

When Bill again glanced at Bob, instead of the expected smile on the sun-tanned face, he saw a knit
brow and a firm set mouth. Without a word the Silent
one turned his horse and started at a steady gallop for
the ranch. He would warn Jim! he determined,It was
not wholly that he cared for his foreman's feelings, but
for the girl, whom he had learned to love as a close
friend. For her and her family ties, was he now dashing across the wastes, reckless of lurking badger holes.
He could not, somehow, recall that he had ever trusted
the smooth-voiced stranger who had come to the ranch
only as an indifferent rider, and who was now playing
a role in the lives of so many of his best friends. As
for himself, the word "home" was almost unknown
until, as a wanderer, he came among the breeds at the
"H-B." There he had been taken in the family circle as one of them. He had but a dim recollection of
a broken home in the far away Trans-Alleghany, where
his mother had been but a dream-parent, and where an
only sister had been laid away on the sunny hill-side.
Was it any wonder that visions of the obscure little
cabin among the hills of the romantic Monongahela, now
recurred to him and in his rough, though sympathetic
bosom, memories tender had sprung? In his slow

speech he had never shown appreciation for the half-
blood family, but deep within that manly nature, there
burned a latent fire of amity which even the Valley of
the Shadow might not dim. This was why Silent Bob's
face appeared stern when Bill spoke of his surmises, and
this was why he had determined, if possible, to save the
girl.

As Bob scaled an intervening ridge and came in sight
of the ranch house, the smoke from the chimney rose in
the air like an Indian signal. The far-stretching Pend
d'Oreille was deeply tinted with blue. He saw a rider
dismount at the corral, but before he reached there, the
foreman was on his way to the bunk house. He turned
his horse and followed the tall Westerner, who paused
at the door with one foot on the step as hoof beats drew
near. He was surprised to see the Southerner, his horse
reeking, pass the barn and ride directly to him.

"Why, hell-o! there feller!" he accosted sharply.
"What's wrong? Ain't you goin' to feed your cayuse
'fore you take your own grub? You'd better care for
him after the hard chase. It ain't no way to ride the
hell out of a hoss and then turn him loose hungry."

"Wrong! You'll darn' soon know what's wrong!"
was the short response. "Look here, Jim! I ain't a
buttin' in on no family 'fairs 'cause its non my biz'.
It's th' little gal! what I'm thinkin' 'bout! I hater—"

"What you mean, Bob! What do you know of any
'fair?"

"I'm dam' sho' on one thin'! This here tenderfoot
guy ain't a fallin' in love with th' gal on 'count her
beauty an' goodness nor any thin' like. It's her *dough!*
He thinks she has th' hard ol' kale! that's what he does!
Bill was jus' tellin' me on th' high ridge as she pass' a
ridin' like hell to'ards Ronan, where Bill's 'lowin' they'll
meet. I hater see this here—"

"How does Bill happen to know so much 'bout all
this?" broke in the foreman impatiently. "Is he a
keepin' record?"

" 'Cause him an' Rodeo has 'bin a stuffin' th' feller

to th' little gal's money, cattle, hosses an' lan'; an' he
went an' fell in love to all her wealth what she ain't got.
Yo're blin', feller! Ain't yo' got no lamps? That's
what th' guy's af'er and yo' a sleepin' on yo' job! I
hater think what'll hap'en when he fin's thar' ain't no
dough; I hater think what'll come to th' little gal 'way
from frien's.''

Regarding his mission finished, the Silent one turned
his horse and rode to the barn. The foreman stood as if
dazed, gazing off among the hills, muttering.

"And this is the endin' of it all! After I givin' the
field to the guy, thinkin' he really loved her and she
loved him! Sacrificin' myself rather than hurt the little
gal's feelin's, I've stood like a dam' fool a swallerin'
my 'medicine' and imaginin' as how I was a *man!* But
now! by—''

A sinewy arm was flung aloft and a hand dropped to
the hilt of his six-shooter. He whirled and strode to the
tepee under the hill, where the aged woman was singing
her "Song of the Love Herb". Jim dashed aside the
door-flap and sprang through the entrance. The chanting ceased, but the Stemteemä evinced no surprise at his
hard set features and sharp voice, in such marked contrast to his usual address to her:

"My grandmother, I have something alarming to tell
you! The Shoyahpee has played with the heart of the
little grandchild! He thinks she has money and he only
wants her for her supposed wealth and not that he
loves her. They are gone! What shall I do? I might
overtake them on the road.''

The Stemteemä stood to her full height, her hands
upreached and clasped in mute agony. Twice she essayed to speak before her voice found utterance; as she
discoursed in her own tongue:

"My son, you have brought me no news! Last night
I saw in vision the grandchild and I knew that something fearful was to happen. To me the spirits revealed
Cogewea, child of my daughter, suspended over the dark
swirl of wild rushing waters. She was struggling in the

grasp of a frightful monster—a human serpent whose
eyes were the glitter of gold—whose voice was the clink-
ing of silver. His face gleamed with delight at her
torture; at her cries for the help that did not come. I
was powerless to reach her, and my screams were as but
the summer breeze in the moaning pines. At last I recognized the Shoyahpee—he of the luring voice—a vul-
ture whose talons were rending my Cogewea, whose beak
was buried in her weakening heart.

"The waters receded and a lonely wood appeared. The
body of the grandchild was bruised, her hair torn and
tangled with the fallen autumn leaves. Then a mist
passed, and I saw no more.

"I awoke singing the spirit-song, for the great *Soma-
ash-hee* (1) had spoken to me in the darkness. I was
singing his song, and the song of the Mountain Herb
which is strength for the Indian's heart. Go now, my
son! Follow swift on the trail for my Cogewea is in
distress. You may not understand the dreams and visions of the old Soma-ash-hee woman who communes
with that which is unseen, for the snows of such wisdom
you have not yet reached. But go! And if the Shoyahpee has harmed the grandchild, destroy him as you
would the poison-snake. Be quick! and the strength of
the Soma-ash-hee will be with you!"

Jim made no reply, but darting from the lodge, he
ran to the barn and threw the saddle on Diamond, who
impatient of his daily exercise, was restlessly pawing in
his box stall. Leading the prancing racer out he caught
the saddle horn and vaulted lightly to his seat as the
Bay Devil leaped away in an easy, measured glide. He
was held in check by the experienced rider, for the steed's
endurance must be conserved for an indeterminate race.
Silent Bob, watching his foreman ascend the slope and
disappear over a ridge, soliloquized:

"Well I be dam'! He'll sho'ly get his needin's this
time—that there tenderfoot—'cause ol' Jim means biz'.
Guess I'll hit th' grub pile! I hater be so hongry as a
wolf; I hater be a cinchn' of my belt so of'en.''

With this, the Monongahelian sought the kitchen where
he was doing ample justice to the substantials set before
him by Mrs. Carter, when Celluloid, Slim and Frenchy,
all from the fruitless chase, entered.   As Celluloid
seated himself opposite Bob, he accosted that worthy:

"What made yo' leave me all flared up 'bout what I
said? A feller'd think yo' was in love with th' gal
'stead of 'spectable people. Wher's Jim?"

"Guess it'll be all off with that there tenderfoot guy,"
answered Bob, ignoring Bill's rather doubtfully meant
sarcasm. "Ol' Jim's madder'n blazes when he lef' while
'go. Thar's pizen in the air! I hater know—"

"What's Jim mad at th' guy for? Didn't know he
seen' him since mornin'. Yo' mus' be all loco'd!"

"I tol' him what yo' said on th' ridge 'bout th' guy,
an' th' gal. Tol' him—"

"Bob, yo're a durn' fool!"   interrupted Bill, anger
in his voice. "What made yo' go do a trick like that—
buttin' in on love 'fairs like that? Yo' should a kep'
yo' mug clamped! It ain't none of our put in."

It was a long moment before the Southerner attempted
reply. He seemed on the verge of choking, as he swallowed hard.   Drawing a sleeve across his eyes, he
muttered complaint about "that there pepper bein' so
durn strong."   There was a suspicious tremor in his
tones when he did speak:

"Bill, it ain I am wantin' to butt in on no body's
biz'! It's 'cause I like th' little gal an' I want Jim to
win in this here race. He's her kin'; is truer'n hell
an' a plum' good rider! No blood a mixin' with that
there money-hunter who can't stick a cayuse. I hater
see him get 'way with so good a gal; I hater see her
get th' wo'st of th' deal."

Celluloid was silent. He was suddenly made to realize the significance of the unintentional part that he had
played in an unfortunate affair, the termination of
which was as yet unforseen.

"Do yo' think there'll be some shootin' doin' when

Jim comes to them there pair?'' asked Slim of the Foot
Hills, who was fond of excitement. ''Think th' show
wo'th travelin' to see?''

''Sho thin'!'' answered the Silent one. ''I see blood
in ol' Jim's eye an' that means biz! No joke 'bout it;
nuther! t's sho' goin' be biz'! But what's a use talkin'!
I hater—''

''Say yo' fellers!'' broke in Celluloid, turning to Slim
and Frenchy. ''Hurry an' swaller yo' grub! We'll foller
our foreman who's gone to take his gal from that there
cayuse-busted tenderfoot. There'll be some little circus
an' maybe a grave-diggin' social.''

''Jim don't need no 'sistance a shoot-scrapin' any
guy, else I'd a gone with him,'' volunteered Bob. ''But
if yo'-all is goin', I'll go 'long an' see th' 'formance.''

Hastily disposing of the meal, the riders ran to the
barn where their horses were feeding. Leaping to the
saddles, they were off up the long grade. Just over the
swell, they met the belated Rodeo, who eagerly joined
them, unmindful of his tired mount as well as the lank
ness under his own belt. It was no time to spare a cayuse
nor consider a foregone dinner when a ''shootin'-dance''
or a ''lariat-stretchin' '' was in prospect.

Julia and Mary, the shy-girl, were standing on the
veranda where they hurried when the boys left in such
haste. They had watched them sweep over the ridge
and pass from sight in a rolling cloud of dust, and were
speculating on the probabilities of a tragedy, when, to
their surprise, the Stemteemä appeared coming up the
river incline. Only on important occasions did she
venture so far from her lodge. She made her way slowly,
leaning on a thorn-wood cane, and as she drew near, the
low chant of the Soma-ash-hee was bourne on the breeze.
She spoke directly to Julia:

''Your ears were closed to my words of warning,'' she
began, in low earnest tones. ''That the snows have left
my hair withered, does not bespeak a tottering mind or
that the vision is less clear. The white man's books I
know not, but the wisdom of the spirits has been given

me. Walking where there is light, I stumble not in the dark. I understand the good and the bad as traced on the face of every man. Words are written on the brow, in the eye and the heart speaks in actions. Mistakes are of youth; judgment comes with the snows.

"I warned you of this Shoyahpee, but you laughed at my words. You left them by the trail as things to be forgotten and lost. But they can not die! That which is true lives forever, but that which is false has no foundation. The pale face has at last been found out. He has never meant right by my grandchild! He only seeks the money which she has not. I have sent Jim on the trail to save her and if the Shoyahpee has harmed her as I saw in a dream, he will kill him! like the forked tongue snake that he is. The power of the Soma-ash-hee will not fail!"

To this sorrowful lament, Julia made no reply, when the venerable woman retraced her steps to the lone tepee, where she was soon joined by the shy-girl. With a troubled mind Julia turned back into the house to spend many an anxious hour awaiting tidings of the sister she loved so well. With deep regret she recalled how, unknown to the devoted grandmother, she had planned many an outing for the lovers, and how she had favored Cogewea's marriage to the fair stranger, rather than with her own mixed or Indian blood. This was not that she was ashamed of the Red race, but since civilization was the only hope for the Indian, it would, she reasoned be better to draw from the more favored and stronger, rather than to fall back to the unfortunate class so dependent on their conquerors for their very existence.

CHAPTER XXX.

THE COST OF KNOWING

You have stolen the maiden from me,
You have laid your hand upon her,
—*Hiawatha*

DUST-FLECKED and foaming, the Bay Devil thundered across the bridge at Ronan, to be checked at the livery barn. Dropping the reins, Jim rushed into the office to emerge a few momonets later with features more set than ever. Without a word or answer to the inquiries of the surprised bystanders, he remounted and hurried away through the "Lane", where Cogewea and Densmore had ridden a few hours previously. He did not notice the mocking twitter of the magpie as he crossed Crow Creek nor the sporting water-fowl on the various small lakes. The Bay Devil was becoming "winded", and to the impatient rider, the road to Ravalli seemed to lengthen out interminably. It was there that he expected to come up with the runaways.

Jim at last covered the long stretch of prairie road and ascended the sloping ridge overlooking Post Creek, with its fringe of thick brush and cottonwoods. Here he paused. His gaze swept the intervening miles to the steepled church and convent of St. Ignatius, for both Indian and white alike. He scanned most anxiously the serpent like road winding up the steep Ravalli Hill; a climb of three weary miles, overlooking the railway station of the same name, two miles beyond. Could the Bay make it before the west-bound passenger pulled in? Jim swore as he stroked the reeking neck of the iron-nerved steed and wondered why he had not thought to procure a fresh mount at Ronan.

Turning from the discouraging contemplation of the distant pass he dashed down the slope to the creek crossing. His horse showed thirst by following the trail into the stream instead of taking the bridge. Noticing fresh

hoof prints at the water's edge, Jim dismounted and
with but a brief examination was satisfied that they
had been made by the mounts of the fugitives. He was
later convinced of this when he discovered the imprint
of a boot in the dust. By a peculiarity of the heel, he
recognized this to be that of the hated Shoyahpee. He
followed the tracks for a short distance off the main
road, where they disappeared, trampled out by a recent
band of cattle.

Jim returned to the stream and again took up the
trail, but with no better success. He circled wide, satisfied that the riders had not passed on towards Ravalli. He was on the edge of despair, when there was a
rustling of leaves and Bringo came bounding toward
him, wagging a bushy tail. Jim called to him but whether
it was appreciation or an appeal, the ranch pet stretching out, rolled over, a trick which Cogewea had taught
him. Leaping to his feet the dog dashed off over a
stock trail penetrating the deeper woods. At a short
distance he turned back to Jim, who stood watching in
puzzled wonderment. He came leaping back, executed
his former antic and again took the trail whining. Now
fully aroused, the foreman mounted and followed. Suddenly Bringo forgetful of his mission—if any —darted
into the brush in pursuit of a rabbit, which disturbed,
broke cover. Jim proceeded only a few rods farther
when the trail diverged into three or four minor passages, none of them showing hoof prints of horses. One
after the other of these he explored, the tangled under-
brush precluding horseback riding. He was losing pre-
cious time and cursed the fates that sent ''that there
dam' rabbit'' across the trail at so critical a moment.
In sheer desperation he forced his way through the
brambles choking the last remaining trail and unexpectedly found himself in more open ground among the
larger cottonwoods. He listened but heard no other
than the usual noises attributable to the wild woods-
life. His impulse was to haloo, but upon second thought
he refrained from doing so.

Baffled, the searcher again returned to the place of first starting but was able to follow the clues no farther than on former occasions. Suddenly the Bay, whom he was then leading, pricked up his ears and whinnied. There was an answer, just back of the fringe of thicket. Jim's heart leaped and then stood still. It was Wanawish!

Leaving his horse, Jim burst through the thorny barrier six gun in hand.   Two rods away Wanawish was standing in front of a cottonwood, saddle lying on the ground.   For a moment he stood, half expecting an attack from ambush, but nothing materializing, he cautiously advanced.   Not until he reached the horse did he discover the inert and bound figure at the tree. With hardly a change of facial expression, he tore away the smothering gag and with knife severed the tight-binding lariat, easing the unconscious girl to the ground. Bringing water in his sombrero, he bathed the bruised and swollen face, and when the dazed eyes opened he held the flood to the dry and parched lips.   Cogewea drank deeply and then dropped back with a suppressed sigh.   Jim was the first to speak.

"What happened, Sis? Where is that there dam' Shoyahpee dog?"

Half averting her face in shame, Cogewea told of every transaction with Densmore, from the scene at the tepee the previous evening up to the time of losing consciousness soon after the miscreant had left her.   She had not known of Bringo's folowing her, but she had a vague conception of Wanawish coming and standing near her.

Jim brought his mount and removing the saddle, laved the sweaty back at the creek and then left him to roll and graze on the shrivelled grass.   He then returned to Cogewea, who, now that reaction had set in, was lying on an outspread saddle blanket sobbing.   Jim sat down near her, but it was a long half hour before he spoke; his voice low and softly modulated with suppressed emotion:

"Sis," he began, "it ain't no use tryin' to get back your dough 'lessen I could overtake that there Shoyahpee snake 'fore he reaches Ravalli which I can't. No laws of recovery like this here case is for our kind!" he continued with a tinge of bitterness, "ceptin' this," tapping his six-shooter. "I'm a goin' take you back to the ranch and 'range my 'fairs and then go a trailin! When I run a white-skinned coyote to hole, they can hang old Jim, 'cause all 'counts is then a goin' be settled. There ain't no place here now for the best rider of the Flathead."

"No Jim," answered Cogewea, who had ceased crying. "Let the Shoyahpee go! He is not worth your hunting. He got my money, but it was cheap to find him out in time. I saved my Wanawish! I was blind not to listen to Stemteemä's warnings from the Indian spirits. I do not want you to go away. It is for me to go back to the Okanogan and forget."

"The sun is fallin' low," observed Jim, rising to his feet. "We better be goin', 'cause the mountain air'll be cold for you."

While Cogewea dipped her aching head in the cooling water and rearranged her disheveled hair, Jim saddled the horses and they were soon on their way. Scarce had they struck the main road when the clatter of hoofs drew their attention, as amid a smother of dust, Celluloid Bill and Silent Bob came sweeping down the slope, followed closely by Rodeo Jack, Frenchy and Slim of the Foot Hills.

"Where is that there tenderfoot guy!" demanded Celluloid as they came to a halt.

Jim briefly explained the situation, not even withholding the money loss, and declared that it was then too late to think of overhauling the miscreant before he should have arrived at Ravalli and boarded the train; that he was well mounted and had had several hours the lead with every possible advantage in his favor.

At this moment Cogewea's bruised face was sighted by Frenchy who immediately went into wild gesticulation. When the boys saw her pitiable condition, they became frenzied. Celluloid and Rodeo felt that they were in a measure responsible for the deplorable affair and were ready to go any limit in righting, in their own way, the deadly wrong suffered by the companionable girl. Blind with fury, they insisted on following in pursuit, even with their then winded mounts.

"What's meanin' of all this here hesitatin'!!" stormed Rodeo. "Yo' goin' let th' dam' robbin', gal-beatin' son-of-a-cuss go like this? He's worse as any bloomin' cattle -rustlin' coyote an' yo' know yo'd foller one of them there sneaks plum' to hell, what yo'd stop his sinnin' again his feller man. Com'on boys! No dam' dirt like this is a goin' with the 'H-B' riders."

This declaration of purpose was greeted with a chorus of approval by the boys, but Cogewea overruled the violent measure, by pointing out the fallacy of any attempt at reprisal.

Not only was Densmore out of their reach, but they being mere "breed Injuns", any extreme measures on their part would not be countenanced, and for the same reason an appeal to the courts looking to justice, would be of little or no avail. She showed them that because of the relative social standing of the two races, there were devious ways by which the Shoyahpee would be able to escape merited punishment. She finally persuaded them to forego all thoughts of pursuit, but there was a scowl on each dark face as they turned homeward. They worshipped this free, wild girl of the range, whose word with them was law.

Brooding and dejected, Cogewea rode with Jim in the midst of the cavalcade on its return. Her heart was numb! She had lived and died in this one day. The sunset, glorious in its fiery splendors reflected from the snow-capped Rockies, held not its accustomed interest for her.

To Cogewea, the world was dead!

CHAPTER XXXI.

A VOICE FROM THE BUFFALO SKULL

As unto the bow the cord is,
So unto the man is woman,
Though she bends him, she obeys him,
Though she draws him, yet she follows,
Useless each without the other!
—Hiawatha

TWO snows had passed and the birds, again returned from the warm-land filled the river pines with
their old time melody; while the buttercups flowered in radiance. The wild rose peeped coquettishly from
its bud, and the tender grass clothed plain and upland
with shimmering green. The ermine cloak of winter,
pursued by the melting breeze, retreated still farther
into the higher altitudes of the majestic Rockies. Earth
was taking on new life and the joy of living seemed with
all—save one whose heart was emptiness— whose face
was but a reflection of her former self.

Jim stood at the door of the bunk-house and watched
the familiar figure of Wanawish, ride over the ridge to
her favorite haunt. He muttered an oath as the cause
of the blighted life came into his mind. He glanced at
the sun now past the meridian and going to the barn,
threw the saddle on the Bay Devil. He had determined
to go to the village for the week's mail in the hope of
hearing from his mother, whom he had not seen for three
years.

The foreman did not loiter on the way. Reaching
the little town, he went directly to the post office where
he received a heavy ranch mail, but no missive from his
mother. There was one however, addressed to Cogewea,
from the Indian Agent of her old home in the Okanogan
country. Some of the "boys" endeavored to prevail on
Jim to engage in a game of pool, or try monte at the
Kootenai camp; but to all entreaties he turned a deaf

ear. He thought of the lonely, unhappy girl out on the solitary butte and the letter was an excuse for going to her. He had never intruded on her sorrow, as much as he loved her. Aside from a tribal custom, he had felt that her grief was sacred and that time was the only balm. But now! well, he would carry the letter to her and if opportunity afforded perhaps!—

Cogewea lingered on Buffalo Butte, thinking of the days when all was happiness; of the many pleasant hours she had spent on this isolated height. At her feet lay the old grey buffalo skull and broken arrow point. The towering mountains greeted her vision, but not with the soul awakening emotions of the past. Life seemed to hold but little for her. Friends were not so familiar as of yore, and Jim held strangely aloof. Somehow she yearned for his old-time companionship. She realized now that it was something more than a "sister's love" which she had borne for him. This new awakening was gnawing her very life away. He surely did not understand the true cause of her despondency. After the first pangs of humiliating disappointment, her only feelings for the false Shoyahpee, were of remorse and bitter regret that their paths had ever crossed. In her generous heart, she pitied Densmore's weakness but detested his duplicity; and above all she devoutly thanked the Great Spirit for her timely deliverance.

She recalled Jim's many considerate attentions, his unselfish protective care for her, his fearless interferance in her behalf at the races, his graceful and manly acceptance of humiliating defeat at the social, the refusal of his hand on this same spot, and the chivalry of his coming to her rescue among the cottonwoods, all came crowding in upon her memory. She could not help wishing that he would—

The fall of an unshod hoof on the stony ground and the jingle of spurs broke upon Cogewea's ears. She did not look up, but intuitively knew who the horseman was. Her eyes dropped to the old skull. She started visibly! *Could* she be deceived? A voice seemed to issue from its cavernous depths in the Indian tongue; a laudation of—

"The Man! The Man! The Man!"

Then it was accusing; a plea of pity that such deep and honorable love should be requited with nothing more than insipid friendship.

The voice ceased as suddenly and as mysteriously as it came. (1)

Jim was at Cogewea's side silently holding the out-stretched letter. She missed the cheery old-time: "Hell-o Sis!" With no word of greeting, she took the missive and broke the seal. Jim stood, arms folded and leaning against the rock, gazing at the splendid pano-rama of the Rockies. She read the letter and he heard her murmur:

"The lust of gold and the mockery of money! The toil amid glaciers and the ghastly snow-fields of the North! the daddy we scarcely knew! The Shoyahpee barters his life! his very soul! for a heritage of death!"

Jim turned to see the old-time dream in the girl's eyes, otherwise he face showed no emotion save that of the sorrow to which he had grown accustomed.

"What is it! Sis?" he asked kindly.

"Nothing!" was the reply, "except that I have es-caped a lot of trouble.

"Some settlement of reservation of 'lotment 'fairs?"

"Not exactly! You know that we had not heard from daddy for over fourteen years. He was in Alaska and we thought long ago that he was dead. This letter in-forms me that he only recently died, leaving money and mining property worth several millions of dollars."

"But you don't call that missin' a lot of trouble do you?" asked Jim, his eyes showing slight astonishment.

"Daddy had remarried, made a will bequeathing his three daughters twenty dollars each, and the remainder of his fortune to his widow, a young white woman from New York!"

"Well! I bedam'! Your daddy, Sis! but a Shoyahpee to the last. My own father the same, only we don't know where he is or what became of him. He left my Indian mother many years ago, coverin' his tracks completely. Too bad that you and your sisters couldn't a had some of that there dough."

"It was all right!" Cogewea rejoined smiling, although her eyes were swimming in tears. "I don't know that I care! The curse of the Shoyahpee seems to go with every thing that he touches. We despised *breeds* are in a zone of our own and when we break from the corral erected about us, we meet up with trouble. I only wish that the fence could not be scaled by the soulless creatures who have ever preyed upon us."

"I wish I had a killed that there da—"

"Don't Jim! Do not refer to the past! It never was! It's only an impossible fearfulness! a dreadful hallucination! a nightmare of lies! It is dead! buried and forgotten!"

Cogewea's countenance had changed to something of her former self. Jim thought that she never had appeared quite so beautiful and captivating. For a time he was silent and then exclaimed earnestly:

"Sis! I always did love you some, and now I like you like hell! S'pose we remain together in that there corral you spoke of as bein' built 'round us by the Shoyahpee? I ain't never had no ropes on no gal but you."

"Aw! Jim, quit yo' kiddin'!" she answered, dropping into the easy vocabulary of the range. "I've tol' yo' that I would be yo' sister; but if yo' don't behave I'll quit likin' yo' as—as a *brother!* Savey?"

There was a banter in her tone which Jim could not mistake.

"Yes! I think I savey all right!" and he slipped an arm about the yielding form. "By gollies! little squ— Sis! Oh! hell! That there don't sound right to me no more. I—"

"Call me Cogewea! your own little Cogewea!" she exclaimed, nestling her head on his deep chest like a weary child.

For a long minute the transported Westerner held the

girl closely and in silence. Then releasing her, he said simply:

"Guess we better be hittin' the trail! It's late and night's goin' be chilly for you without no shawl."

"Do not hurry! See how magnificent those grand old mountains are in the moonlight. *Isn't* this a splendid world?"

"Yes! it is jus' 'bout right—when not too cold nor to hot—nor nothin' wrong with the corral fencin'. But the best rider of the Flathead ain't a worryin' 'bout this durn' old world no more! And I sure do b'lieve in them there hot rock signs of the sweat-house!"

"So do I!" laughed Cogewea, feeling the blood suffuse her cheeks. "But do let up on that 'best rider' stunt. Maybe you will not want to ride any more, only for fun. I forgot to tell you all that is in this letter. It transpired that owing to a technical flaw in daddy's will, we girls come in for a share in some of his fortune, amounting to a quarter million dollars each. And say! Jim! Stemteemä will now let me have that brooch, I told you I would wear."

"Well! I bedam'!" ejaculated Jim, as they turned to go.

Cogewea paused, gazing intensely at the grey skull— listening! She heard the Voice as it comes only to the Indian:

"The Man! The Man! The Man!"

The moon, sailing over the embattled Rockies, appeared to smile down on the dusky lovers, despite the ugly Swah-lah-kin clinging to his face.

In a cheap boarding house in an eastern city a few weeks later, a young man with a selfish mouth, suddenly turned pale as he read in a western paper an account of the settling of the great McDonnald mining estate in Alaska, and the marriage of his two half-blood daughters. One of them a graduate of Carlisle, to the "Best Rider of the Flathead", also a half-blood. The younger daughter known as the "Shy girl", had departed with her husband, Eugene LaFleur, a polished and wealthy Parisian scholar, on a honeymoon tour of Europe.

THE END

> The trail's a lane! the trail's a lane!
> Dead is the branding fire.
> The Prairies wild are tame and mild,
> All close-corraled with wire.
> —*Badger Clark*

CHAPTER I.

(1) *Sne-nah*: "owl-woman" of the Okanogans and *Tah-tah-kléah* of the Yakimas are in the same category. Of the many people devouring monsters, this old woman with her great shoulder basket in which she carries off victims — preferably children—to be cooked or broiled alive and eaten in her remote cavernous den, is the most to be dreaded. I have seen the most refractory Indian child subdued by the mere allusion to her name. This tradition, along with others mentioned in the course of this volume, will be given in full in works now under way by the author of *Cogewea* and the writer of this note.

(2) *Wana-wis'h*: denoting "water-rapids." While this name is properly Yakima, it is not inappropriate, for in the first part of it is found the appellation for "river" as spoken by many of the kindred Columbia River tribes.

CHAPTER II.

(1) *Stem-tee-mă*: Okanogan for "grandmother."

(2) Okanogan for rattlesnake is: *Hwă̱hwă̱-ulăh;* or *Hăh-ăh-lăwh.* The rendition varies, such as: "evil" or "wicked-crawler"; "evil of the earth"; "evil spirit of the earth"; with perhaps others forms of interpretation. The reptile is held in reverential dread by all the Columbia River tribes. It is only in the direst straits that the tribesmen will molest or injure any of them. They are averse to speaking traversely about them; but on the other hand are prone to condone and make excuse for their dangerous nature. When the Indians are in the hills digging roots in the spring time, it is not uncommon for the rattler to crawl into the tepees and seek the warmth of the bedding. Ofttimes one will ensconce itself at the head of the sleeper. When this occurs, the Indian will carefully gather the intruder on a stick and carry it away, speaking to it something like this:

"Grandmother! do not come here. I might not see you and step on you. This would hurt you. I do not want to hurt you, my grandmother. Stay out here among the rocks where the sun will soon make you warm. Do not come where I am living, where I am sleeping. I will not stay here long and we must be friends; my grandmother."

I have yet to see an Indian kill a rattlesnake, and seldom will they tell of any disagreeable experiences with them. The rattler is wise, and despite intervening distances, he understands and knows that he is being talked about. It is folly and unsafe to thus tempt his anger. Strange instances of this character have come under my own personal observation.

(3) The claim has been made that none other than the

Caucasian is susceptible of blushing. From personal observation this is an error. I have noted this characteristic not only among the half-bloods, but the full-blood Indians as well. Especially is this true of girls and young women. Naturally, the lighter the complexion, the more discernible the effusion. The blushing quality in the Indian as indicant of modesty, is, I believe, far more in evidence than pallor, resultant of apprehension in the face of unlooked for or sudden danger.

CHAPTER III.

(1) *Okanogan* for "Big river water falls," or "Big water falls." Applied not only to the *Les Chaudière* or *Kettle Falls* of the Columbia, but to the entire stream as well.

CHAPTER IV.

(1) *Kootenai,* or *Kutenai.* The name is spelled in many and various ways; but the author has adhered to the generally accepted form. A distinct linguistic stock, the *Kitunahan* family extended from the lakes about the source of the Columbia in British Columbia, to the northern part of Montana, and to the Pend d'Oreille Lake in Idaho. It is supposed that they at one time resided east of the Rocky Mountains and were driven west of this barrier by the *Siksika*, their deadly enemy.

Although brave and courageous warriors, it is noteworthy that there never has been any serious trouble between the Kootenais and the whites. They are great gamblers and still possess many of their primitive customs. In some respects the women excelled in basketry and bead work. See *DeSmet* and other early western writers. Consult *Handbook of American Indians*, pp. 740 to 742.

CHAPTER VI.

(1) The privilege of the war dance was earned by the women Among the northwestern tribes, at least some of them, it was not uncommon for women to accompany war parties on distant forays. Usually not more than two or three, always volunteers, would attach themselves to a war-band of ordinary size. An elderly woman well versed in the tribal history of her people, informed me that only the bravest of her kind would ever dare face the dangers incumbent on such trips. It devolved on them to prepare the food and do other camp work. She said: "When successful in returning, they were ever afterwards entitled to sit in council, and participate in the war dance with the most distinguished warriors." The medicine dance has always been open to both men and women alike.

CHAPTER VIII.

(1) The war-drum never figures in the *spirit*, or strictly religious dances. In these, the *pom-pom* or "tom-tom" is in evidence; and, with the Yakimas and kindred tribes, only the

skins of deer or the horse are used in the construction of the instrument. It must not be desecrated by amusement usages.

(2) Seldom is it deemed necessary for the whip to be brought into play, but I have seen a few instances where it was so used. One of these batons, given me by *Yellow Wolf*, a Nez Perce warrior, is a great spike of elk horn studded with brass nails and with a heavy lash of leather. Not only a scourge, it would be a formidable weapon, especially if wielded from horseback as primarily intended.

(3) This stone-headed club is now in my possession, a present from the Nez Perce warrior of the dance. A thrilling personal war narrative, dictated by its owner, is still in manuscript form.

(4) Refer to Note 4, Chapter XIX.

CHAPTER X.

(1) *Sho-yah'-pee*: denoting "white-man." The etymology is of foreign coinage, and in usage with but slight variation among all the northwestern tribes. The form here given and used throughout this volume is of the *Spokanes* as being slightly more phonetic than the Okanogan *so-yah'-pen*. It is the *sho-yah'-poo* of the Nez Perce, and Yakimas; and the *whe-nee-tum* of the Victorians, B. C. An intelligent Yakima told me of its introduction among his people. It was brought by the first Jesuistic missionary from some tribe not recalled, where it was applied to the white man, comparing him to the hog because of his greedy nature and proneness to "eat up everything he sights."

CHAPTER XI.

(1) An illustrative example of this strange custom is the following romantic, though well authenticated incident.

An Okanogan village was moving. One of the girls was loved by a poor young man who was unable to pay in presents the high value placed upon her by her parents. This difficulty precluded a marriage. For some cause—possibly clandestinely—this maiden loitered at the deserted camp until her companions had preceded her some distance. She then followed them, carrying a bundle of her personal effects. While ascending a steep hill, she laid aside her burden to indulge in a short rest. In so doing, she observed her lover, who had secretly appeared, standing below her. She sat down, covering her feet but said nothing. After some moments of silence, he spoke.

"You have nice clean ankles. No wonder you do not want any man to see them"

There was another long silence before she made reply.

"You had better carry my pack."

This was equivalent to a marriage. She had accepted him

as a husband. The next morning they went openly into the newly pitched village, the man bearing the woman's pack, and nothing was said by the parents. The young warrior had won his bride by a well recognized tribal law and all was well in the sight of her people. But had the girl refused his suit and made complaint to her family, serious trouble would have befallen him. The scene of this poetic occurrence is still known to the Indians as: "Where they look for ankles," or "Looking for ankles." It is on the Colville Reservation, some six or eight miles from the Columbia River.

Even now among the more primitive class of the northwestern tribes, the young girls wear abnormally long skirts reaching well down over the ankles. I have often observed them when entering a tepee or house, to seat themselves upon the floor without effecting the least exposure of ankles.

(2),This law of force held with the Columbia River tribes. *Harmelt*, the hunter, was a fine looking Indian of the Yakimas, tall, well built and active. A terrible fighter, the tribesmen all feared him. His arms and upper portion of body bore scores of knife wounds. He courted the wife of another member of the tribe, who told him that she was afraid of her husband, that he had a bad temper and might kill her. Harmelt said that he would come on a certain day with a horse and take her away.

On the evening designated, Harmelt rode into the village, left his horse in front of the lodge where the woman was living with her husband and his parents, and entered the doorway. The husband was reclining on some blankets, his wife sitting at his side engaged with work. Without preliminaries, Harmelt took the woman by the arm and said: "Come with me! I am going to take you for my wife."

The woman rose without comment. The husband, a lithe. active fellow, leaped to his feet with knife drawn and prottested: "No! You can not take this woman from me. She is my wife."

Harmelt made no reply, but led the woman from the lodge, followed by the husband. As he drew near his horse, the enraged husband struck him in the back of the shoulder with his knife—struck twice—three times. It was then that Harmelt whirled and drove his own knife into the breast of his assailant, who crumpled to the ground. He died within a few hours.

Harmelt was not seriously wounded. His buckskin shirt and heavy blanket, doubled, had saved him. He was not punished for the crime. The transaction was all within the tribal laws, where force was the recognized right to rule. In after years, Harmelt regretted his crime.

(3) Inconstancy in the woman was severely dealt with

among the Okanogans. Such disgrace was punishable with death at the hands of a relative or any member of her family. In 1915 there was still living an aged man who had shot and killed his own sister while she was sitting in her tepee, for the sole reason that she had in a single instance strayed from the path of virtue. Seemingly no such penalty was attached to a like offence by the man.

CHAPTER XIII.

(1) An actual incident in the child-life of the author. This "no-talk" trait of the Indian is characteristic of the race, permeating alike both old and young. "No savey" is a time worn expression of the tribesmen who conceives it not to his interest to understand. Sometimes this becomes jocund. I have observed even the school graduates, when going back to the blanket during festive occasions, gaze with blank stolidity into the face of a white interrogator, with perhaps only a negative grunt. This is considered a huge pleasantry to be laughed about afterwards.

CHAPTER XIV.

(1) The name applied to some of the Columbia River tribes; but in this particular, to the village and bands residing about *Les Chaudiére*, or *Kettle Falls*. See: *To the Reader.*

(2) A tradition of this prophecy is current among all the Columbia River tribes. The most noted, perhaps, was that of *Kööms-kooms*, who, in a vision, foretold the coming of a strange and powerful nation which would over-run and usurp their country. He described the superior implements of war and domestic utensils of their conquerors, along with some of the domestic animals. To this revelation can be traced the source of the present *Pom-pom*, or *Dreamer* religion of the Yakimas and others, which is undoubtedly of comparatively recent origin. The dawn of the worship which constitutes the *spirit dance* of these tribes is lost in antiquity. The text gives a true version of this Okanogan oracle. In all cases where an Indian loses consciousness, even momentarily, he is regarded as dead. "Killed" or "was dead and came back to life" is an expression they often use when narrating some serious accident to themselves or other members of the tribe.

(3) *Chip-chap-tiquⁱᴷ*: Okanogan for myth, or improbable story.

(4) See *To the Reader*, this volume.

CHAPTER XV.

(1) An historic fact. See *To The Reader.*

(2) *Revelation*, VIII. 10-11.

(3) To a direct inquiry, an intelligent, primitive-minded Yakima in explaining to me their tribal belief relative to the Happy Hunting Ground said:

"There is no hunting there as in this life. There is no

killing; no death. Suffering and hardships enter not in that place. If you wish for any kind of meat, the deer or other animal instantly appears before you. With a spirit knife you sever what you want but there is no wound; no pain with the cutting. The scar is healed as quickly as the knife passes. The spirit-animal does not suffer. It is the same way with every thing; roots, berries; all are there just as in this life. There is no war, no wrong in the Happy Hunting Grounds."

CHAPTER XVI.

(1) *Exodus*, XV, 23-25.

(2) *Mourning Dove* had much of her information first hand, but for a concise exposure of the ghastly Blackfeet scandal, see James Willard Schultz, in *Sunset* Magazine, for November, 1922; published after *Cogewea* had been written. Mr. Schultz, an old-time Indian trader, and adopted member of the Blackfeet tribe, is most scathing in his open charge of duplicity on the part of Indian Bureau officials. The hideous details of how three thousand virile, self-supporting tribesmen had been reduced to a thousand starving, disease-infected wretches, extends over two-score years, or since the extermination of the buffalo. Seven hundred Blackfeet actually died of starvation during one winter, while their "preacher"-Agent held stored corn for his hens that his own well loaded table might be supplied with eggs. Even at this day, as Mr. Schultz clearly proves, this calloused indifference to the sufferings of the "wards" is too manifest. Appeals for public aid for the half-nourished Blackfeet, were systematically forestalled by a broadcast canard that the Blackfeet were in no respect needy or objects of charity. This, too, when coffins were not even being furnished for the victims of Bureau "frightfulness."

But, sepulchral as the Blackfeet tragedy may appear, it has its counterpart on practically every reservation in the United States. Refer to the speeches of Hon. Clyde M. Kelly, House of Representatives, Sixty-seventh Congress First-Fourth Sessions, 1921-22 See Bureau airings by Mr. John Collier, in *Sunset* series, 1923; and other contemporary writers—various publications—for unearthing of the departmental plot to dispossess the Pueblos of their ancient landed holdings and their very homes. The "Fall-Burke & Bursum" regime will go down in history as one of the blackest pages in the murky annals of the Indian Bureau "system."

(3) *Chief Joseph* was averse to talking of his misfortune in war and His *Own Story* published first in the *North American Review*, 1879, was practically the only interview that he ever granted. Throughout this meager narrative there is a modest dearth of self erudition; and his surviving warriors have assured me that their Chief had an antipathy for dis-

cussing with the white man his personal history, or that of his followers in the field. Keenly alive to the bitter wrongs which he had suffered, he brooded in melancholy, dying an exile; to the last bemoaning his lost Wallowa. The personal narratives of a few of his surviving warriors now in preparation for publication, attest the shame of the Government's policy which drove its former steadfast friends to the warpath.

(4) The story of the landless Indians of California is well known, and has had recent airings through various press channels. The Oklahoma scandals are open history, while the White Earth robbery—oozing with the slime of official connivance—stands naked through the fearless exposure by Prof. Warren K. Moorehead, a then newly appointed member of the Board of Indian Commissioners. Ignorant of the mundane functioning of this august body, the Professor was duly disciplined as to his duty and part in the Bureau "machine". An avowed and scrupulous friend of the tribesmen, he has ever been a minority in subsequent proceedings. For contemporaneous treatment of "wards" on the Yakima Reservation, see *The Crime Against the Yakimas; The Continued Crime Against.—and The Discards;* by the writer of this note.

CHAPTER XVIII.

(1) See Note 1, Chapter I, for reference to unpublished legends mentioned in this volume.

(2) The Thunder-bird figures in the philosophy of all the Columbia River tribes. Refer to Note 1, Chapter I.

CHAPTER XIX.

(1) Not at all an improbable story. Such cavities are often met with in the loose desert soil; usually formed by the caving of the earth where two or more burrows are in close proximity or actually joined.

(2) Okanogan for *war paint.* Used not only for personal decoration, but in inscribing history and symbolic signs on tepees, implements of war, and other objects of certain character.

(3) Okanogan for *ladle* or *spoon;* usually made of wood or horn.

(4) The *te-kee-sten* or "medicine-cane," along with the war pipe—and perhaps the peace pipe—were sacred and not to be touched by woman. To do so was to destroy their magic and bring possible disaster to the individual owner or tribe, as the case might be. There were, however, exceptions to this rule. (See Note 1, Chapter VI, this Volume.) Green-blanket Feet actually desecrated the objects as depicted in the text. In breathing through the pipe, she invoked evil spirits and

defeat upon the hereditary enemies of her own tribe. Casting the "medicine" cane of the Chief to the ground and using his war paint on her own person, was to humiliate and disgrace him in the eyes of his own people. Had she been captured, death, if not torture, would have been her portion.

The private "medicine" is invariably buried with the Indian's body. In December, 1915, Isaw two *păh'-tash* or "medicine" canes interred with the body of *We-yallup Wa-ya-cika*—noted Chief and medicine man of the Yakimas. One was made from the slender sprout of the hard wood, *lo-tsa-ni*, whereon a grotesque and twisted growth of the larger end had been cunningly carved into a clever representation of an antlered deer. Barring three brass-headed nails used in delineation of the muzzle and front feet of the animal, the *păh'-tash* was without superficial ornamentation. The other stick was a light penant staff with a crooked hand-hold; such as is used by school and class-fraternities. It still retained some of the gaudy paper covering, and aside from the solitary eagle feather and a bit of white ermine skin with which it was surmounted, it was wholly of white man origin.

(5)   As a food commodity, the salmon was, to the *Salishan* and *Shahaptian* linguistic families of the great Columbia River basin what the buffalo was to the *Siouan* or plain Indians. Both enter largely into the legends and religious cult of the respective tribes.

(6)   *Four-point*: refering to the short stripes, or bars woven into the corner of the blanket, designated as "points." The highest number is five, which, perhaps owing to its conjunc-' tion with the *Five Rules of Speel-yi*, is greatly prized. The "points," however, pertain solely to the dimensions or weight of the blanket, the lowest being three, while four represents the intermediate size. The pattern was introduced by the Hudson Bay Company, nor have I ever seen one that was woven in the States. The favorite color is a white field with black border and stripes.

The Arrow Lake Indians, as well as kindred tribes, manufactured robes or blankets from the fur of the rabbit and the soft fleecy hair of the wild mountain goat. The material was laboriously twisted into long, heavy strings or cords and woven in square mesh, making a very complete and warm wrap or covering. Of those examined—goat-hair—only two, comparatively modern and coming from British Columbia, showed any trace of artificial coloring. Commercially dyed wool yarn had been used, the designs knitted into the original fabric. One showed a wreath done in pale red, the other a center-field of blue.

(7)   With but few exceptions the early traders, individual and incorporate, were not only inordinately immoral—marry-

ing after the tribal custom native women only to abandon
them at pleasure but they were, to all intents, scarce short
of legalized banditti. When the Hudson Bay trading post at
Old Fort Okanogan was at its height, the Indians came with
loads of priceless furs which were piled equal in bulk to the
object of their fancy, and it was called an "even swap!" Thus
for a cheap, smooth-bored flintlock gun of the musket type—
ofttimes six or seven feet in length—the Company received a
pack of the finest variety of skins stacked solidly the standing height of the worthless firearm. Into the hands of the
simple minded natives came fabulously priced beads, cheap
ornaments and gaudy cloth; blankets, weapons, ammunition
and other articles of fancied or passing needs, including foods
of doubtful quality, and into the coffers of the shrewd and
unscrupulous traders poured the wealth of a nation. Nor has
the looting ceased! The methods have only changed to suit the
ever shifting conditions of the years.

(8)   In the Stemteemä's narrative of *Green-blanket Feet*,
the author has purposely incorporated incidents connected
with two or three different occurrences. The story as preserved by the immediate descendants of the unfortunate woman
and as given me by her granddaughter, Mrs. Susan Winegarden, nee Hunter, follows:

One of the traders sent to the Okanogan from St. Louis,
was Robert Pelkey. To the Post came Sophie Antwine, a comely maiden of the Arrow Lake band. These Indians have always been noted for their light complexions and pleasing
manners. Young Pelkey and Sophia became fast friends and
later married in accordance to the tribal rite. This was nothing unusual. Adventurers, traders, and army men—especially officers—often took "wives" from among the natives.
The women entered such unions in good faith, but with the
men the "contracts" were to be ignored upon personal con-
venience. Military men who afterwards won international
fame during the Civil War left progeny of mixed blood among
some of the Columbia River tribes.

To the Pelkeys, two children were born: Robert and Kitty.
On these pledges the Indian mother lavished all the love inherent with motherhood. But her happiness proved fleeting!
The husband soon tired of his dusky wife, and planned secretly to desert her. Not wishing his children to grow up as Indians, he determined to steal them away and take them back
to his old home to be educated. They were then about two
and three years of age.

One day Sophia first missed her babies, and then her husband. She learned that he had left with the children by pack-
train for Fort Benton, on the Missouri River. This frontier
post was the nearest river embarkation for the East.   The

recreant spouse made the journey in safety and without encountering hardships other than usual to a trip of its kind in those days.

When the wife and mother realized the full extent of the blow, she became possessed with the sole thought of recovering her little ones. With no preparation and without any goodbyes, she immediately set out on foot; following the trail where, ever "just ahead" was being borne all that was dear and sacred of earth to her.   Feeding on berries and roots, sometimes stopping with friendly tribesmen or at a settler's cabin—but more often sleeping in the open—starving! she resolutely held to the long, lonely way.

But the wanderer fared well through this first part of her travels, as compared to what she was destined to endure. An enemy country must be crossed.   The *Blackfeet, Sioux,* and other plains tribes were warring, killing or taking captive any who came their way.   Having been warned by the friendlies, Sophia was ever alert to possible dangers; but at the cost of valuable time.   On one occasion she found herself between two opposing war parties, and for three days was compelled to hide in nothing more than an abandoned badger-den. Often she sought refuge in the brush and timber along streams and "washouts"; but through it all she undauntedly pressed onward.   Her moccasins worn to shreds, she tore strips from her blanket—green in color—with which to encase her feet. From this, she was subsequently sobriqueted by her tribe, "*Green-blanket Feet.*"

Weary and famished, the woman at last arrived at Fort Benton.   Directed to the boat landing, she hurried there only to see the steamer just loosed from its moorings, backing into mid-stream.   Standing on the deck with others, was her unfaithful husband with their two children.   With outstretched arms, the wailing mother stood on the shore and watched her babies until they had faded in the distance.   The relentless Missouri had aided in the consummation of another tragedy.

Sophia was now alone and friendless and far from home. She had fought a fearful fight and lost; and now, penniless and without a single backward glance, she faced the sunset on her long, dreary return tramp.   Her lagging footsteps were no longer buoyed by the incentive of loved ones "just ahead." The same fierce struggles were encountered, as empty-handed she plodded back to a broken home and her waiting people. As the journey neared the end, so did the green blanket. Strip after strip had been torn away to furnish protection for her feet.   When she at least reached the Okanogan, the Hudson bay blanket was but a memory, but "*Green-blanket Feet*" had become a reality.   The annals do not reveal a more pathetic incident of mother devotion.

In time, Sophia Pelkey was married again in accordance to the Indian mode and had five children. Her last husband, a white renegade, in a drunken rage one day stabbed her to death. When the older children entered the cabin, they found their mother and her baby lying side by side; both in sleep, from which the one would never awaken. She had always kept her children with her, save only when they attended the mission school.

In St. Louis with their paternal grandmother, Robert and Kitty Pelkey found home and schooling. The father eventually drifted West and settled in Walla Walla, Washington; and when his children had reached early maturity, he sent for them.

Kitty married Alonzo Hunter, sergeant in the U. S. Army and stationed at the military post near Walla Walla. It is averred that at the time of her marriage, the girl was not aware of her Indian descent By accident, she and her brother met Mr. Charles Brown, a later son of *Green-blanket Feet*, who acquainted them with the history of their Indian blood.

The Hunters moved to Missoula, Montana; and to them three children were born; John, Charles and Susan. The mother died when Susan was but three years old. The boys were placed in a Government school and later given allotments on the Flathead Reservation, where they were still recently residing. Susan was taken into the family of a Montana pioneer and at the age of seventeen married Mr. Rolla Winegarden. They settled in the land of her Indian ancestry, in northern Washington.

Robert Pelkey, Sr. died in Missoula, about 1898-1900. Robert Pelkey, Jr. died a few years later. He was a printer by trade and worked for various newspaper firms of Montana. He had achieved some prominence as a writer, when his career was cut short by drink. His three children now reside about Iron Mountain, Montana.

As a sample of Indian Bureau administration, it is interesting to note that while the two brothers and other relatives of Susan Winegarden, nee Hunter, have been granted land allotments as recognized tribesmen, she has been denied this right, notwithstanding the Flathead Indian Council voted her a member of the tribe. But as absurdly unjust as such "ruling" may seem, even though she had resided with a white family, it has its counterpart in scores of similar cases on the different reservations.

Kathryn Maud Wilcox, born September 13, 1910, was refused allotment on the Yakima Reservation, although her older sister, Ruby, as well as Georgia, a younger sister, were both alloted as Indians. The father is a mixed-blood, and an allottee.

CHAPTER XXI.

(1) The Upper Falls of the Pend d'Oreille are about eleven or twelve miles above the Horseshoe Bend, with intervening rapids to the Lower Falls. For two miles the river roars through an impressive canyon from four hundred to six hundred feet in depth. For three fourths of the way the walls of the gorge are sloping hills broken at intervals by imposing cliff formations. For the remaining distance, the foam-crested waters tumble between sheer, slate colored embattlements of the greater height. This stream, outlet of the Flathead Lake, is shown on old Government maps as "Flathead River"; but it has always been known by the old timers as the "Pend d'Oreille," according to Mr. W. F. Millar of Polson, County Surveyor

CHAPTER XXII

(1) One such incident as here hinted was witnessed on the Flathead, during the period covered by this story.

(2) *Chinook* for "secret thief."

(3) *Puch-queeh'*: "grass snake." Belonging more properly to the Yakima, the phrase is expressive of distrust, a reflection on the declared intentions of a supposed friend. In every way it is the world wide "snake in the grass."

CHAPTER XXIV

(1) In tribal life, the power of the *medicine man* is to be reckoned with. In all gatherings where two or more tribes are represented, it is the business of the accompanying medicine man to protect his people against the possible machinations of the medicine man of the rival band. This is done in various ways, but the most spectacular coming under my personal observation, was during a festive period, where the medicine man in native garb, mounted on a white horse—a favorite color of the warrior class—rode circling back and forth in front of his own village, the while chanting a low weird *tah*, or medicine song in unison with the measured tread of his mount.

(2) While history records no account of Lewis and Clark having wintered among the Okanogans, this tradition of the second coming of the *Shoyah'pee* as narrated by the *Stemteemâ*, is, in its essence, true as handed down by this tribe. Perhaps time has confused it with accounts of the later expedition brought to them by their more southern neighbors.

After the departure of the explorers, or *voyageurs*, and the return of the Chief's sister to her people, she explained that the skin had been lacd to the drying-frame with the bark of young willows—perhaps with the willow itself—and had been struck from its fastenings after the lashing had become dry and brittle. The Indians watching from a distance supposed the lacing to be buckskin, and knowing the tenacity of such they attributed to the strange white beings a supernatural power.

In this relation another incident is preserved. At the abandoned cabin of their visitors the Indians found a fragment of what they believed had been a foot covering. The material was unlike anything they had ever seen, and they "danced" over it for several suns, endeavoring to fathom its magic. It was described as possessing a strong and very peculiar odor, now supposed to have been some kind of water-proof goods.

(3) The *Okanogans*, unacquainted with the destination of the migratory birds, believed that they flew to the *spirit land*, at the approach of winter, whence they returned with the coming of spring.

(4) This attributive power of the *medicine man* to accomplish fatal injury from great distances, is not at all unusual. *Yoqm'-tee-bee;* "bitten by a grizzly bear," a prominent Chief of the Yakimas, was suddenly and mortally stricken in 1910, by a Columbia River medicine man, sixty miles away. One of his followers in describing the death of this chieftain said to me:

"I saw him kill Yoom'-tee-bee, just the same as if you stick a knife in his breast."

Yoom'-tee-bee was a physically strong man and from all outward appearances in the prime of health. His demise was attended by some strange and rather startling occurrences.

(5) Among some, if not all, the Columbia River tribes, to see a star within the halo, or "lodge" of the moon, denotes a death not far delayed. If a bright star, it will be a young person; if a dim star, an old person. A shooting star is also a precursor of death and should never be watched. If ending in an explosion of sparks, the victim is to be one of wealth and prominence. See Note 1, Chapter XXVII, this volume.

The *raven* is a bird of ill omen, ever flying in the vanguard of disease and scourges. See *Legends of the Yakimas;* by the writer of this note.

(6) The partisan historian has ever loyally refrained from touching on the moral shortcomings of our border heroes. The Indian wives of two United States army officers who rose to national and international distinction, were well known in this far northwest; both of them leaving mixed-blood offspring. The grandson of one of them told me that his grandmother never spoke of her white husband without weeping, always declaring to kill him, should she ever meet him.

(7) *Kee-lau-naw*: Okanogan for "grizzly-bear."

CHAPTER XXV.

(1) The general reader does not realize the gross and petty wrongs to which the individual Indian is subjected, even

in the courts of justice. The following are but a few coming under my own personal observation.

A young Yakima, of good repute when sober, tanked on the white man's "fire-water," attempted to ride his horse upon the veranda of a suburban home. Failing in this, he rolled from his saddle and was soon in á drunken stupor. The Sheriff was notified and an officer brought the unconscious redskin to the lockup. In the Police Court the next morning, he was fined "Ninety Dollars for Drunkenness and Disorderly Conduct."

Just nineteen days from this occurrence, a degenerate though sober white renegade, rode to the tepee of some Indian hop pickers not far from the city, where he found an aged squaw and her young granddaughter alone. Dismounting he assaulted the girl, who, with the venerable grandmother, fought her assailant. Becoming enraged, he beat the young woman with a heavy quirt with which he was armed, bruising her about the neck and shoulders in a frightful manner. He rode away when the girl fell insensible to the ground. These Indians were of the "better class," and although the same Sheriff who was so prompt in the other case was notified, and the miscreant was well known, *no arrest was made.*

I saw a policeman take two free drinks at different bars and within ten minutes go out and arrest a perfectly sober Yakima minor, whose pockets when searched yielded up a solitary fish hook and line and a ten penny nail. This lad, clean and well dressed, spent a night in a vermin-infested cell overcrowded with drunks, and next morning, despite a presentation of facts, the boy was fined by a booze-fighting police judge for "Drunkenness and Disorderly Conduct." It is solace to know that within a few days this same "Judge" was beaten up by carousing white companions in a drunken saloon brawl.

A young Yakima was convicted in the Superior Court for a minor offence and sent to the penitentiary. The evidence was largely circumstantial and one of the acting jurors confided to me that, had the boy been a white man, he would have been acquitted, but as an Indian he was convicted. The victim was guilty of no greater crime than that of wearing a bronzed skin, the bestowment of nature's God.

A Yakima was arrested on a stabbing affray; had his hearing and was entitled to freedom. He was ill, it was winter time, and his family was suffering; yet still he was held in durance vile. I went to the Prosecutor, a deacon in a prominent church, and was blandly informed that "through professional courtesy" the Injun was being retained until his counsel could collect the residue of an exorbitant fee—*actual imprisonment for debt.*

CHAPTER XXVI.

(1) The bent poles forming the skeleton frame of the *sweat house* were regarded as the bones, especially the *ribs* of the once living "Chief of the Animal World."

CHAPTER XXVII.

(1) "Lodge of the night-sun." Alluding to the halo, or circle observed about the moon under certain atmospherical conditions. (Refer to Note 5, Chapter XXIV, this volume.) A very similar belief in this celestial death omen prevailed among the hill-people of the Trans-Allegheny; and it is also found in northern Scotland, if not of still more universal range. As forecasting weather conditions, a tribesman of the Columbia River will say in connection with the halo and the stars: "The moon is throwing aside his children! A change is coming in the weather."

CHAPTER XXIX.

(1) The *Soma-ash'-hee* always appears in a dream or vision, in the nature of a communication or revelation from the major deity, or *Great Spirit*. The mediumistic channel of this enigmatical impartation may be an animal, bird, reptile, or some inanimate object; the elements or celestial bodies, and not infrequently the departed human dead. Events of the future are revealed and certain rules are laid down by which the devotee must be guided if she or he would profit by the occult power conferred. Not every Indian attains to this favor. It comes only to those who have found "medicine" during the fasting time of life, which is childhood. Children are sent into dreary and solitary places at night where, alone, they commune with the mysteries of nature, and where often there appears to them some apparitional tutelary, which instructs them in the "medicine" of hunting, of war, of occult healing and the wisdom of prophecy; in short, covering practically every avocation in Indian tribal life. Ofttimes children of very tender age are "staked" or tied out in desolate and terrifying spots—some of which I have seen,—for the purpose of obtaining this strange and mystifying "power." Youths of more years are placed under the care of some man renowned for his occult and skill along certain lines, who guides and trains his proteges for their coming sphere in life. He sees to it that his charges are given ample experiences calculated to foster and develop the primitive attribute of self preservation in meeting and combating all exigencies of danger under whatever form, and above all, respect and reverence for the spiritual. A boy may be sent alone into the awesome woods, there to listen the whole night long to the "song" of the "dancing" grizzly; into the barren desert hills where the impressive silence is fraught with communicative wisdom; to weird and

ghostly bodies of water inhabited by monsters and indescribable terrors; to the proximity of old burial grounds where passing flames and other unearthly demonstrations are in evidence—the entire system trending to a development of the heroic and the religious in the primitive mind—the mind closest to nature and to nature's God. This training was extended to both sexes.

CHAPTER XXXI.

(1)   (Refer to Note 1, Chapter XXIX, this volume.)

To hear voices from inanimate objects as intermediary to the Great Spirit or Great Maker, is not uncommon in Indian philosophy, but more frequently the revelations come through some member of the animal world. However, the celestial bodies, thunder and lightning, the wind and other elemental forces, are often channels of Divine communication. The Indian as an integral is profoundly psychical.